THE
UNFOLDING

BOOK 1 IN THE BRAIN STORM SERIES

LESLIE EDGEWATER

outskirts
press

Chapter 1

Who was pounding on her door at 8 a.m. on Saturday? "This better be an emergency," she grumbled as she got up. She peeked out and saw a man wearing a brown uniform.

"May I help you?" Bella shouted through the locked door.

"UPS, Ma'am. I need a signature, please." Bella walked over to the window and saw the UPS truck. She unlocked the door and reached for the signature pad. She looked curiously at the return address on the envelope. UPS Overnight from Phoenix.

To: Bella Sanders, Executor, Neusa Estate

Please contact the law office of Attabury & Murdock for a copy of Anna M. Neusa's last will and testament. As executor and sole benefi-ciary, you must settle any unresolved claims against the estate and all debts immediately. Any remaining assets are yours.

Bella walked over to the stairs and sat down. How could she inherit the estate of someone she didn't even know? Since Mom died she hadn't heard from her. Because Mom and Grandmother were estranged, Bella didn't even know how to reach her. How did the law firm find Bella? After recovering from the shock, Bella went to the kitchen, put on a pot of coffee, and thought about what would need to be done in order to get to Phoenix in time for the funeral.

Bella owned Sanders Publishing. She informed her staff that she would be taking bereavement leave. While traveling, she would Skype daily to stay in the loop, and handle what she must from Arizona.

Next, she called the company managing Grandmother's property.

Linda, her agency contact, would make sure that everything was in order for her arrival. All too soon it was time to pack.

Bella checked to make sure she had her airline e-ticket, the law firm contact information, and the phone number for the management company in her purse. Next, she picked up her tablet and a few files for her backpack. A week's worth of clothes and shoes went into her suitcase along with her incidentals. She put everything else into boxes for her assistant to ship to Phoenix by the end of the week. That would give her time to get to Arizona, bury Grandma, and decide whether or not to stay in the house. Everything was set.

Bella heard the airport limo honk its horn. She grabbed her carry-on and purse, wheeled her luggage out the door, and was on her way.

The ride to Lambert Airport was quiet. Bella thought about how fortunate she was to be able to rearrange her plans so quickly. Not everyone had the flexibility she enjoyed. It had taken her agency a while to get to this point, but it was paying off today. Publishing was a career you could manage from anywhere with a good computer and a capable, highly motivated staff. She had both.

Contemplating Grandmother's state of affairs, Bella pictured a small cottage with a white picket fence. She imagined the house filled with antique furniture, fine linen table cloths, lace doilies and old photos. Since she'd never seen the house, inside or out, it was fun to think about what the residence of a 96 year old widow looked like. Daydreaming, the time passed quickly.

The airport was crowded. There were long lines for security. Bella checked in and printed her boarding pass at the kiosk near the door to avoid waiting in line at the gate. The extra $10 to get a seat assignment early was well worth it. She was among the first to board. Stowing her bag in the overhead compartment, she moved into the window seat near the exit door. She stuffed her backpack underneath the seat and got comfortable. In three hours she would be touching down in Phoenix.

Shortly after shutting the door, the pilot announced a slight delay. About five minutes later the flight attendant re-opened the airplane door. Boarding late was a limping soldier in full uniform. He walked with a cane. Immediately, the passengers rose and began to shake hands with him. It was awkward for the passengers, because the soldier had to shake left-handed in order to keep his right hand on the cane. As he made his way toward her, Bella rose, stepped into the aisle, and offered the man her window seat with extra leg room.

"Thank you, ma'am, but that won't be necessary," he politely declined.

"Nonsense," Bella insisted, "take a seat. I'll swap with you. Now, what's your seat number?"

"It's right next to yours." He smiled kindly at Bella, who was blushing. "You're very kind, ma'am." He sat in the seat next to her, put his cane down on the floor, and buckled up.

"Are you flying to your next duty station?" Bella couldn't wait to change the subject.

"No, ma'am. I'm going home."

Bella looked at him carefully, wondering if she should continue this topic of conversation. She decided to change the subject.

"This is my first time in Phoenix. Any places you recommend?"

"As far as what, ma'am?"

"Please, call me Bella."

"Nice to meet you Bella. I'm Allen." He extended his hand for a shake.

"Well, I might need a place to stay, but I'm not sure where I'll be exactly…what part of town." Bella realized she was going to a completely strange place. All she had was an address.

"What brings you to Phoenix?"

"My grandmother's funeral."

"I'm so sorry for your loss, ma'am."

"Thanks." Bella looked over at the man. She could see that he was no stranger to loss. Her freedom had cost him a great deal. Feeling like the conversation might be going in a direction that could be awkward for them both, she decided to end the small talk.

"Thank you for your service, Allen."

"You're welcome, Bella."

Bella shifted in her seat. She leaned back, covered with her long cotton scarf, and closed her eyes. Things that seemed so important two days ago seemed pretty minor right now. She was healthy, free, and alive, fully alive.

"Please make sure your seat belts are fastened and your tray tables are stowed." The flight attendant was making announcements to prepare for landing when Bella woke up. She reached below her seat for a brush and lipstick.

"You don't need that. You're perfect just the way you are." The soldier was charming!

"Thank you, Allen!"

"You're welcome. If you like, I can show you to the car rental kiosk when we land."

"No need. I'll just get a cab to Grandma's and figure things out from there. She might have a car sitting in her garage, if she has a garage."

"You don't know?"

"Sadly, no. She and Mom were estranged."

"I hate family skeletons." The soldier lowered his eyes.

"Me, too."

Bella felt flutters as the plane touched down. She was motion sick. Sitting quietly, she closed her eyes. The plane came to a halt on the tarmac. In a few minutes she'd be inside the terminal. Since she carried everything on, she could head right for the taxi. Then she heard Allen's voice.

"What if your grandma didn't drive?" He smiled at her, raising an eyebrow.

Bella pondered his question. She had no idea what to expect.

"I'll take you up on the offer to point me to the car rental kiosk!" If she didn't need the car, she could simply return it.

They walked slowly into the airport. Allen escorted Bella to the Avis kiosk, then politely went his own way. This was Phoenix.

Chapter 2

Thankfully, Bella's rental had a GPS. The Phoenix population was 1.5 million. Being from Freeburg, Illinois, population 3,000, Bella couldn't have imagined how big it was. It was probably better that way. It might have scared her off. She smiled as she thought back to her conversation with Allen. Suddenly she knew why it was so hard for him to recommend good places to eat. There were cafes on every corner, and there were thousands of corners. It was an ethnic smorgasbord!

"The destination is on your right. You have arrived at your destination." The GPS had brought her right to the door of Sandler Property Management. Parking was difficult, but Bella found a spot in back.

"May I help you?"

Bella looked up to see a cheerful woman about her age sitting behind a desk. She felt her body relax as she approached.

"I'm looking for Linda."

"I'm Linda." She motioned Bella to sit down. "You must be Bella."

"That's me."

Linda opened the file and pulled out a checklist. All the boxes were checked.

"It's great to have good help," Linda began as she started laying forms out in front of Bella.

"I know exactly what you mean," she shook her head in agreement.

It took a few minutes to get through the paperwork before Linda gave her the keys to the property. She looked forward to a cozy retreat after an overwhelming baptism of traffic and big city energy.

"In case we get separated, here is the address for your GPS." Linda handed Bella her copies of the paperwork. She tucked all but the address in her purse.

"Thanks."

Bella was glad she had help navigating because, being a tourist, she was doing some sightseeing. According to Linda, they were heading into the Alvarado Historic District, which Bella pictured as close old houses with windows that neighbors could look right into. But, much to her surprise, she was in an affluent area. These stately Spanish and Mission style homes with wrought iron second-story balconies had meticulously manicured lawns. Bella saw the sign for Heard Museum, and made a mental note to visit if time permitted.

"The destination is on the left. You have arrived at your destination."

Bella stared at the estate open mouthed. Was this Granny's house? When Linda knocked on the window Bella jumped and nearly bumped her head on the roof of the small car. She opened the door and stepped out. Stunned, she stood motionless and speechless.

"Tell me about this place, Linda."

"Better yet, come inside. Let me help you with your stuff."

"No need. I just have one rolling suitcase and my back pack."

"I hope you'll find everything satisfactory," Linda talked as she led her into the front foyer. "There are five bedrooms and six baths, so you can sleep in a different bed every night, if you want to," she teased as she smiled. "Close your mouth. You might swallow a bug." They both started laughing.

"I had pictured a small stucco cottage with a white picket fence. This is about as far from that as you can get. Wow!"

"Yeah, Ms. Anna had a way with folks. She was unique, gifted. People came from far and near to see her." Bella didn't understand what Linda was talking about.

"Tell me about her."

"What would you like to know?" Linda's face registered shock.

"Everything. I met her when I was three, but don't remember it. I only saw her one other time before my mother's funeral. I didn't even know her full name until the law firm gave it to me."

"Honey, today's not long enough to get into all that. Get settled in. I scheduled cable and internet connection for tomorrow morning between eight and noon. Call me if you need anything else. Come over to my house around seven for dinner tomorrow evening. I'll give you the details of the memorial service and luncheon then. Your grandmother made all her own arrangements. My home address is on the back of my card, on the kitchen counter."

"You've been most helpful, Linda, thank you! What can I bring tomorrow night?"

"Just you. Welcome to Phoenix."

"Thanks."

Bella wandered through the house in amazement. If she had to guess, she'd say it was about 5,000 square feet of remarkable living space. The cozy widow's cottage she'd imagined turned out to be a Spanish style mansion with a red tile roof, romantic balcony, courtyard, and out buildings. It was a lot to take in. Bella's curiosity was peaked. She had a lot to learn about her grandmother.

Sitting dreamily on the edge of a bed, she questioned what actually happened to separate Mom from Grandma. There were things she wanted to know. What would she discover about her family when the skeletons were released from the closet?

All the rooms were grand, but this one overlooked the pool and courtyard. The walk-out balcony had a small, white, wrought-iron table with two chairs. It was a perfect place for Bella's morning ritual, coffee and creative writing. This was her room.

Barreling down the stairs after her things felt good. The movement energized her. She decided to put on her sneakers and go for a power walk. The fresh air would do her good.

Bella was not prepared for the fiery hot air that filled her lungs as she breathed deeply. She endured one lap around the long block before deciding to call it quits. Walking around to the back gate, she entered the yard. She wanted to take off her shoes and walk barefoot to the pool, but figured the concrete would be hot. A mental list of things she'd need began to form: flip flops, swim suit, sunscreen, cover-up, and hat.

Making her way back inside, she looked through the kitchen cabinets and refrigerator to find them empty, except for bottled water. She'd need everything. Grabbing her purse off of the counter, she decided to exit through the garage and see what was out there. To her delight, Bella found a red Corolla and a Toyota truck. So Granny liked Toyotas…it was a start. Tomorrow she would call the agency and make arrangements to return the rental car.

Bella used her GPS to find Grocery stores. Safeway and Sunshine Market were close by. She decided to visit both to get a feel for the flavor of the neighborhood. Tomorrow she would ask Linda where she could buy a swim suit and essentials. Then it dawned on her, the pool house probably had everything. She would check later.

Bella stocked up on the staples at Safeway. She'd be staying a while. There were legal matters to attend to, and realtors and bankers to visit to settle Grandma's debts. But those would come after the funeral, which was in two days.

Bella liked some of the specialty items at Sunshine Market. She bought some fat ripe strawberries, hazelnut coffee and French vanilla ice cream, then headed home. She couldn't wait to check the pool house for swimwear. A sunset dip called her name. Afterwards, berries and ice cream by the pool. Grandma lived a life of privilege. Bella hoped she was happy.

As she turned the corner, she saw a car parked out in front of the house. She heard music in the back yard. After putting the groceries away, she ran up to her room to look outside. There was a young man vacuuming out the pool. By the looks of things, he had hosed down the concrete and cleaned the pool filters. They were still sitting on the sidewalk next to the chemicals.

"Do I have to wait a certain amount of time before getting in?"

"No ma'am. But it'll take me a little while to finish. I'll be done before sunset, though."

Bella bounded down the stairs and out to the pool.

"That'll be fine. Do you come here often?"

"No ma'am, you?"

"No. This is my first time here."

"Are you related to the owner?"

"I *am* the owner."

"WOW! You look fantastic for 96! You don't look old at all!" The teen's mouth fell open and his eyes nearly popped out in utter amazement.

Bella laughed from the belly. Then the boy joined her.

"I'm the *new* owner. This was my grandmother's house."

"I'm so sorry for your loss, ma'am."

"Please, call me Bella."

"Jacob… Jake." He extended his hand. Bella shook it.

"How often do you come, Jake, and who pays for the pool cleaning?"

"Sandler Property Management pays me. My mom, Linda, owns it. You met her."

"Yes I did. I guess I'll be seeing you tomorrow night for dinner."

"Okay then. I'll just get back to work." Jake laid the net beside the pool and walked toward the pool house shed.

"Great."

Bella strolled over to the pool house. It was locked. She walked back to the main house, and to her delight, there was a key caddy just inside the back door. There were two sets of door keys. Bella grabbed them both and headed back outside.

The pool house was completely furnished with hats, flip flops, and at least six different sizes of swimwear in the bedrooms. There were one-piece suits and mix-and-match bikini tops and bottoms in lots of attractive styles. Did Grandmother do a lot of entertaining? Bella had questions for Linda.

The refrigerator had all kinds of soft drinks, beer, wine, and mixers for other kinds of cocktails. The liquor was stacked on top. The cabinet had all kinds, colors and sizes of glasses in it. Bella chose a plastic glass and a cold bottle of lemonade. On an end table next to a wicker chair were a couple of old books and some magazines. Bella chose Southwest Living and headed out to the poolside. Jake was gone. She had the place all to herself.

It was quiet in the courtyard, and Bella relaxed in a shaded lounger near the pool steps. She tried to read an article in the magazine, but couldn't concentrate. She was in a relaxed, almost meditative state. Her head was heavy. She leaned back, put the magazine down, and glanced around.

From the corner of her eye, she noticed an older woman with long, flowing, grey hair and a white hat standing nearby. Bella came up from the chair hastily, but when she turned around, nobody was there. Walking around the immediate area, she found no one. She went back into the pool house and checked the bottle she'd poured into her glass. There was no alcohol in it. Had she imagined it?

Bella decided to get wet and snap out of her dream state. She dove in the deep end and swam laps, alternating between the crawl, side stroke, and the butterfly. It was refreshing. She climbed the pool steps and reached for the towel. Glancing up at the house, she noticed that same woman again. This time, she was standing on the balcony looking down at Bella.

"Hi. Can I help you?" Bella felt strange being so casual. But up to this point, she didn't know if the woman belonged here. Perhaps her grandmother had a live-in housekeeper. Bella went into the house and up the stairs to her new bedroom. She walked out onto the balcony, looked around, and again found no one.

"Hello? Hello? Anybody here?" Bella wandered through the entire house. The front door and garage were locked. The gates were locked. She was secure. Just for safety sake, Bella decided to call the police.

"Police department," the operator answered.

"This isn't an emergency, but I'd like to speak to an officer, please."

"One moment, please." The line was silent as Bella's call was transferred.

"Detective Sanchez."

Bella explained what she'd just seen. She asked the officer if he could stop by. She googled the alarm company and asked them to come by and familiarize her with the alarm system. Twenty minutes later there was a policemen at her door. Shortly after, the technician from the alarm company arrived. Bella made a note to tell Linda about changing the alarm system code tomorrow night. Her list was growing. It had been an eventful day.

Bella took a quick shower. It was already getting dark. She grabbed her bag and headed into the bathroom. There was no soap or shampoo in the shower. Toiletries were added to her growing list. Inside the top drawer of the vanity was a brush and comb. The second drawer had a hair dryer.

After wolfing down a turkey sandwich on whole wheat with some juicy berries, she finished her meal with a bowl of French vanilla ice cream. She was ready to tuck in with a good book. She walked into the library and sat for a moment in the leather high-backed chair. Bella loved everything about this room. Someday she would have *her* books in libraries like this one everywhere. That was her dream. Now that she had her own publishing agency, it would surely happen.

Granny had a big cherry desk, a comfortable leather chair, and some pretty picture frames sitting on the desktop. She walked over, sat down, and nearly fell over backwards in the chair when she saw the pictures. It was her mother in ballet slippers and her in a tutu. Right beside them was a toe dancer. It was the lady she'd seen by the pool. Was this her grandmother? Could she have seen a ghost? Sitting motionless, mouth hanging open, Bella examined her beliefs about disembodied spirits. Today, in the presence of this woman, or apparition, she felt no sense of threat.

"Grandmother? Grandmother, are you here? Can you hear me? Can you see me? I'm not afraid of you. I'd love to see you again." It felt odd talking to a ghost.

But Bella wasn't afraid at all. She was simply curious. There was no response. Could people on the *other side* choose between being seen or unseen? Could she be present right here without Bella knowing? Bella's heart was racing. She was excited. This is the stuff that scary sci-fi novels were made of. But this wasn't fiction. She *did* see the lady in the picture, not once, but twice! Of course, no one would believe her. Who knows what the cop must've thought.

"Oh well…" Bella said out loud. She felt foolish, but then realized that there was nobody there to hear or judge her, except of course, Grandma.

"Grandma, if you can hear me, I have questions. I'm going to be spending time here with you, if your finances permit it. If you're unable to speak to me in a voice, why don't you leave me some kind of clue about what you are trying to tell me?" Bella's mind was racing. She was trying to communicate with a ghost! How crazy was that? Was it even possible? Then she got an idea.

"Okay, Grandma…I will take a picture of this desk top, and if I wake up and something is rearranged, I'll know you can hear me. Then, if I don't wet myself, we can go from there."

Bella turned off the light in the library and walked down the hall to her room. She was exhausted. It had been a day full of surprises. What would tomorrow bring?

Chapter 3

Morning brought Bella back to the reason she'd come to Phoenix. She was here to carry out her grandmother's last wishes, and today she would find out what they were. The cable people were scheduled to arrive this morning, her appointment with the lawyer was this afternoon, and dinner at Linda's was this evening. It was going to be a full day. She grabbed an apple and yogurt. It was too hot to eat heavy here. Besides, she wanted to remain clear and alert to deal with everything on her plate today.

The cable guy came early, and that freed her up for the next couple of hours. She decided to start sorting through Granny's things. The logical place to start was the suite she was in. The bathroom vanity drawers contained a brush and mirror that appeared to be antiques. Bella set them aside. She would keep a few of Grandmothers things for herself, if given the choice. The rest could be donated or sold at an estate sale. Bella put the brush and mirror on the dresser in the bedroom as the first of a cache of keepsakes.

Next, she tackled the dresser. She figured this must've been the master bedroom, because there were clothes in the dresser and the chest of drawers. Bella pulled things out and combined a few drawers to make room for her own clothes.

Walking into the closet, she sighed. Granny's hanging clothes were well organized, as were the boxes stacked on the shelves. Sorting through those would take time. She wondered if her grand-mother had any close friends who might be interested in going through them for keepsakes. This was another item on her list of questions for Linda.

In need of boxes, trash bags, and a step ladder, Bella made her way downstairs and out into the garage. She found bags and ladder, but would have to stop by the market later and get some boxes. She also grabbed a lawn chair, so she could sit to sort through Gran's possessions.

The morning flew by while Bella sorted through jewelry, gloves, hats, purses, scarves and a host of other items neatly stored in the top of the closet. She'd made good progress, working through at least a third of the boxes. Piled on the bed were things Bella wanted to keep for herself, her daughters-in-law and her granddaughters. The thought of being so far from them made her lonely. She couldn't imagine not being part of their lives. If only Grandmother could've met them. But there was no use dwelling on that. It couldn't be changed.

Bella couldn't help but wonder what could've possibly happened between her mother and grandmother that drove them away from each other for good. How could they let all those years go by without being a part of each other's lives? It didn't make sense.

It was time to get cleaned up and get ready to meet with the lawyers. Bella took a quick shower, wanting to leave a little early to make sure she got there on time. She got the hair dryer out, and remembered she'd taken the brush out into the bedroom. Where was it? She was sure she put it on the dresser. With no time to waste, Bella rooted through her purse for hers.

While getting dressed, she heard the house phone ringing. When she picked it up, it was the law office. The meeting had been postponed for two hours due to a busy morning in court and a traffic accident. Bella found herself with a little extra time. She decided to go through the bathrooms in the guest rooms and look for toiletry items on her list. There was bound to be soap, shampoo, and toilet paper somewhere.

Bella went into each bedroom suite, looking a little more closely at what they contained. Surprisingly, there were clothes, shoes and boxes in every closet. Grandmother was just like Mom, or vice versa. She chuckled silently. Mom filled every closet in the house with clothes. She was a clothes horse. Her sister always remarked that, if she'd let her, Mom would put stuff in her closet, too. Bella sat down on the edge of the bed a minute, smiling, fondly remembering her mother. They were very close, and she still missed her.

Gathering up the armload of toiletries she'd collected, Bella walked back toward her room.

"Shoot!"

One of the toilet paper rolls dropped and rolled down the stairs while a bottle of shampoo fell and rolled to a closet door. Funny, she hadn't noticed the door before. When she opened it, she saw a very narrow stairway that led to the attic. Bella made a mental note to check it out later.

The toilet paper roll had unraveled as it bounced along. What was left of it was laying in front of the library. She rerolled it and set it on the bottom step to take up with her next time.

Remembering the conversation she had with Grandma last night, or…the one she had with herself, she wasn't sure which, she headed into the library. The room appeared the same as it had the night before, with one exception. There, sitting next to the photo of the lady she saw by the pool, was the brush. Bella very carefully retraced her movements, beginning the night before. She was certain she hadn't placed the brush there herself.

Checking the time, Bella hurried out of the library. She grabbed the brush and the toilet paper and headed up for her purse and keys. It was time to go.

"I hope we get to spend time together, Gran. I look forward to telling you all about your great grandchildren. I'd like to know all about you, and about my mother when she was young. I don't really know how we'll do that, but I'm sure we'll find a way."

With that, she was off.

Attabury & Murdock, Attorneys at Law, Complete Will & Trust Preparation. The office was easy to find and had free parking. Bella was fifteen minutes early. When she entered the office she was greeted pleasantly by Maura, the legal secretary.

"Hello! Can I help you?"

"I'm here about the estate of Anna Neusa."

"You must be Bella Sanders."

"Yes." Bella took a seat right across the room from Maura. The office was cozy. The coffee table had magazines stacked neatly on top. There was a water cooler on the wall by the window, and a coat rack on the opposite wall. The energy was good.

"I loved your grandmother," Maura began. "She did…still does…a lot of good for a lot of people."

"What do you mean by that?" Bella's curiosity was peaked. As of yet, she knew almost nothing about Anna Neusa.

"You're going to find out a lot about her today." Maura raised and lowered her eyebrows, indicating that Bella was in for some surprises.

"Did you know her well?"

"Yes. As much as you could know Anna, that is. She didn't have much time for any one person, as it were, because she spent time with so many different people. She helped…helps…a lot of people. May she rest in peace…*or not* would be more like her." Maura chuckled.

"You talk about her like she's both here and gone."

"You're exactly right. That would be the truth of it."

"What do you mean?" Bella wanted to know more, especially in light of what was happening at the house.

"There's no time for that now. They're ready for you." Maura got up from the chair and led Bella back to the attorney's office. She opened the door for Bella, winked at her, and then closed the door behind her. Bella had butterflies in her stomach.

The next hour was filled with providing proof of her identity and discussing the disposition of Grandma's assets. It was an hour of surprises. She owned the house and grounds outright. There were eleven acres in all. The furniture and vehicles were paid for. Those were pleasant surprises for Bella. But Grandma owned one property that was heavily mortgaged and barely scraping by. Bella would have to make some decisions about it. On her way out the door, Maura slipped her phone number into Bella's hand.

"Call me if you'd like to know more about your grandmother. I loved her dearly."

"I will. Count on it." But for now, Bella had another agenda.

As it turned out, Anna Neusa founded a wellness institute designed to help reintegrate military veterans and first responders back into the community after traumatic experiences. The clinic focus was on their spiritual and psychic health. It was something Bella had never thought about. But she believed that thoughts and attitudes affected recovery. That was something she had in common with Gran.

Driving along, Bella drifted back to a conversation with her mother. She'd called Grandma a fortune teller. Had Grandma been a psychic?

Since Bella had a couple hours before she had to be at Linda's, she decided to drive by and see the clinic for herself. Pulling into Star Bucks, she ordered a latte, found a table, and began to browse through the paperwork she'd been given. She might as well jump right in. There was a lot to do before she could go home. And tomorrow she would add regular publishing business meetings as well. It was going to get busier.

Bella made a note to call Maura. Getting in touch with some of her grandmother's friends might be useful. They might be interested in some of her things.

Inside the large manila envelope was a small plastic bag with two keys. The tag on one key ring read 'desk.' She supposed that Gran's bills and other important papers were locked there. The other was an old skeleton key with no tag on it. Bella's curiosity was peaked. This trip served up one surprise after another. It was a perpetual treasure hunt. Bella wasn't sure whether it was the latte or her peaked curiosity that made her feel so alive. But whatever it was, she was enjoying it. There was just enough time to go to the clinic for a brief walk-through before dinner with Linda.

The building was at the edge of town. The acreage was private, and offered anonymity to the heroes that entered here for care. The clinic itself was small, but modern. It had ample parking, which was nearly full. She chose a spot away from the door, an old habit aimed at getting more steps in. Walking through the parking lot, she encountered a young woman who appeared to be limping. Bella's attention was on details that normally escaped her. But things were changing.

Bella held the door for the young woman, whom the receptionist greeted by name. Those kinds of personal touches made businesses successful. Next she looked at Bella and smiled in a way that made Bella feel like an honored guest.

"Good afternoon! My name is Carol. How can I help you?"

"Hi! My name is Bella. Is it possible to get a tour of the clinic?" Bella thought it prudent to remain distant with folks here in case she had to make a hard or unpopular decision about its future.

"Are you in the military or are you a first responder?"

"Neither."

"Are you interested in care?"

"No. Actually, I'm Anna Neusa's granddaughter, Bella."

"You're the new owner!" Carol's eyes got big as she finger-combed her hair. She tucked her blouse back in and put her shoes back on under the desk. She was nervous about meeting Bella.

"Relax, Carol. I'll just be here for a few minutes. I'm on a tight schedule today. Can you give me a quick walk-through, please?"

"Certainly, Miss…"

"Sanders, Bella Sanders, but call me Bella, please."

"Right this way, Bella."

"I understand that you help heroes heal here."

"We try. Some cases are more challenging than others." As they walked the halls, Carol explained the basics of how the program worked.

"How do you attract clients?" Bella wondered about their marketing program.

"We don't. They seek us out. Most of them learn about us through word of mouth. There's no shortage of patients here. We're bursting at the seams."

"How are you funded?"

"I'm not the person to answer that. Let me introduce you to our director."

"I'd appreciate that." Bella was impressed with what she'd seen of the clinic. She wanted to set up an appointment with the director to go over the finances.

"Mr. Baker, this is Bella Sanders, our new owner." Carol turned to leave.

"No need to be so formal. Call me Rick. It's nice to meet you, Ms. Sanders."

"Thanks. Please, call me Bella."

"What can I do for you, Bella?"

"I'd like to make an appointment with you, when it's convenient, please."

"Okay. How much time do you need?"

"For starters, block out a morning for me. I want to know everything about how this facility is funded." Bella was all business.

"How soon would you like to meet?"

"The beginning of next week, if possible." Bella felt time passing quickly. There would be more to do than she originally anticipated. There were lots of things to consider.

"Can you make copies of financial statements, please? I'd like last years and the first two quarters of this year. I also need a copy of the budget and marketing plans. I need to review them prior to our meeting."

"Can you give me a few minutes?" He looked like he was put on the spot.

"Sure! Do we have a coffee mess for staff?"

"Make a right out the door, first door on the left."

"Thanks."

Bella walked down the hall with the oddest feeling. She'd never been here before, and didn't even know this place existed, but the people who worked here knew about her. That meant that either the lawyers or her grandmother told the staff about her. Linda did say that Gran made all her own arrangements.

The energy here was great, another pleasant surprise. So far, this visit opened the door to a life that Bella didn't even know existed, but was a part of, long before she knew of it. She couldn't wait to find out what would reveal itself next!

Bella had her back to the door drinking coffee when she heard someone enter the room. She turned around in her chair. Her jaw dropped. It couldn't be!

"Aren't you going to get up and insist that I sit in your chair?"

Bella laughed out loud. It was the soldier from her flight to Phoenix. What a coincidence! As if reading her thoughts, the soldier initiated a conversation.

"Bella, right?"

"Yes. Allen, right?"

"Right." He smiled broadly.

"You're Anna's granddaughter? I didn't put it together on the plane, but I should've."

Bella was curious. She wondered how he could have put it together on the plane.

"I don't understand that remark."

"I can explain. Come with me."

Allen led her down the hall. He unlocked the door with a key. The modestly furnished office was evidently her grandmother's. There were awards, diplomas, and licenses hanging on the wall. They'd done good work here, and were recognized in their community. When she walked behind the desk, she saw the wall with pictures of her at different ages. She was stunned. Nearly falling into the chair, she sat speechless.

"How did she get these?"

"What?" Allen didn't understand the question.

"I'm sorry, Allen. I've had a lot of surprises on this trip."

"I understand. Can I do anything for you?"

"No, thanks." Bella sat perfectly still. "Just shut the door on your way out, please."

"Will do."

How did Grandmother get all these photos of her? Some of these pictures were taken long before Facebook and Google. She must've been in touch with some of Mom's other relatives who kept her in the loop. It seemed she had more questions than answers, now. Every attempt to clarify something led to another question. She felt like the main character in a mystery novel.

"Oops," Bella looked at her watch. She got up, locked the knob, pulled the door shut, and practically ran all the way back down the hall. Luckily, Mr. Baker was walking in her direction with the reports.

"Thanks so much. I'll call you for an appointment after I've had a chance to review these."

"Great."

Although Rick replied that it was great, he didn't really feel that way. Right now he was pretty insecure. Anna Neusa was committed to this clinic and the work done here. Her granddaughter seemed more focused on the finances than the well-being of the patients. If she based her decisions, ones they all knew she had to make, solely on the profit and loss statements, they would probably close the doors. The need was greater than their profitability. But, she was Anna's blood, and out of respect for his friend, he'd give Bella whatever help she needed.

"Anna my friend, I believe you can hear me. If you're listening, open your granddaughter's eyes to the benefits of the work we do. And open her mind to the possibilities we both know exist for healing the scars of our heroes."

Bella had to make a concerted effort to stay present during rush hour traffic in Phoenix. Her mind kept jumping back and forth from her discoveries at home this morning, her news from the lawyers, and the clinic visit. Her emotions were reeling. She could really use a friend to bounce things off of right now. But 6 p.m. was a busy time for her kids and friends at home. Bella wondered if she could trust Linda with information. She would see what impression she got during dinner. If not, perhaps she would call Maura and see if she were free for lunch tomorrow. It would help to have a local support system.

Bella was right on time. Linda answered the door smiling, looking relaxed. It set Bella at ease instantly. When they walked into the living room, Linda introduced her family.

"You met my son, Jake, and this is my husband, Tim." They reached out in polite gestures. Everyone seemed comfortable.

"I recognize you from your grandmother's pictures," Tim began the conversation.

"I have questions about that, Tim. First, how do you know about the photos, and second, where did my grandmother get them?"

"Well, the way I know about them is that I worked a lot with your grandmother. You might say I was her private photo editor. I also photographed events and images for Anna. She had a brilliant mind, and very 'out-of-the-box' ideas about energy transmission and expression.

She was a talented woman and brilliant scientist. Some of her ideas could still be big, very big. You may wish to examine them for merit."

"How did Grandma get the pictures of me? She and my mother were estranged. I met her when I was three or four, and saw her only one other time, when I was around ten years old. Who took the pictures?"

"Your dad sent negatives to Anna on the holidays and special occasions. And may I say, I had to do a LOT of editing to bring the photos up to the quality your grandmother displays today. I worked very hard on them."

"Thank you for that. You never know what I'll find when I go through her things. I may have some other old photos. I might ask you to restore them for me when the time comes."

"I'd be happy to. I thought the world of your grandmother. She helped me through a very hard period in my life. If not for her, I wouldn't have my own business."

The doorbell rang. Linda jumped up to answer it. In came Maura. Bella was happily surprised to see her.

"Bella, this is Maura?"

"Yes. We met this afternoon. Nice to see you again, Maura!"

Just as Linda sat down, the bell rang again. This time it was Carol and Deidre. Bella was amazed at the synchronicities these past two days. She couldn't have conjured a story like this if she tried. Excitement stirred deep within her for the unfolding unknowns ahead. This was crazy!

Deidre had a resale shop in town. Her friends lovingly called it the Antique Road Show of Phoenix. She specialized in one of a kind items. Bella was excited about finding the perfect place for her grandmother's things, but had a lot to do before she got that far.

Dinner was fantastic, and they laughed all through the meal. Bella felt right at home. She sat quietly for a moment, thankful for forces unseen, God, spirits, perfect friendships, support circles… It was as if some 'fairy godmother' was watching over her and placing everything she needed in her path.

"Care to share those thoughts?" When she looked up, the others were staring.

"My thoughts?"

Carol spoke up. "I see guides and advisors huddled around you. Are you receiving a message?"

"Guides and advisors? Do you mean spiritual guides?"

"Yes!"

It was an odd thought. Guides and advisors? The closest thing to spiritual guides that she'd ever thought about was her guardian angel, whom she prayed to every night as a child. Was it possible? In light of what had happened at the house, perhaps it *was*. Bella looked around the room bewildered.

"Spiritual messages, guides and advisors…they're you guys?"

They all smiled. Once again, Bella felt like she was the last to know.

"Are you all psychics?"

"Everyone is psychic, Bella," Linda began, "but some of us work to develop our abilities. Maura, Carol and I all worked closely with your grandmother, who also demonstrated highly evolved ability."

"Mom called her a fortune teller."

"Call it what you will," Maura joined the conversation, "she had a powerful gift. And her gifts didn't end with her psychic abilities."

"What do you mean?" Bella's curiosity was once again peaked.

"Well, she was a teacher and a scientist…" Carol added.

"A life coach and healer." Tim looked at the ground with a smile that shined kindness and love. He was fond of her.

"She believed people could do anything they wanted, and she showed them how." Bella wondered how she helped Deidre, after her kind words.

"You guys know that I never knew her, right?"

They all nodded.

"But she knew you." Linda said, as they all nodded in agreement.

"That sounds mysterious, but I don't feel threatened."

"Anna had nothing but love for you. She gushed when she brought over more pictures for me to work on…a proud grandmother."

"I never knew any of that. And as far as I know, neither did my mother. Do you guys know what happened between them?"

"Anna never mentioned anything being wrong between them. She never talked about it."

"If only that were true," Bella was saddened by the thought, "but it's too late now. My mother died two years ago."

Bella looked up and saw that, once again, she was the last one to know. She was becoming very uncomfortable. Her time here was limited, and she best get home. Deciding to play along for the interest of expediency, she contemplated what to say next. She decided just to ask for what she needed.

"My grandmother's house is very big. I was wondering if you could help me gather her things and get them to the right people. Deidre, can you help me determine how much to ask for her furniture and larger belongings?"

Unanimously, they agreed to help.

"I wish you'd consider staying and continuing on with her work." Carol looked at Bella like she was planting a seed.

"I'm sorry, but I have a booming business of my own back in the St. Louis area. I can only be gone for a short time. I'm playing a game of beat the clock. Prior to coming to Phoenix, I had an idea of what Grandma's house and affairs would be like, and then I got here…" They were all laughing.

"She was a large woman…and I don't mean her size." Carol was obviously an admirer. She worked in the clinic with Grandmother. Bella looked forward to learning all about it. Suddenly, with no effort at all, Bella felt her whole body relax into the idea that there could be a surprise around every corner. That had been true so far.

As if her companions understood her discomfort, they changed the subject. Maura started the conversation.

"Bella, tell us about yourself."

"What would you like to know?"

"Whatever you're comfortable sharing." In the next hour, the conversation focused on getting to know each other.

Bella learned a little about Tim and Linda. They were both retired from primary professions, and each had a second career and businesses of their own. Linda was a retired teacher, running her property management business to save for the restaurant she always wanted to own. She was an extraordinary cook. Like Bella, she loved good food. Tim was a retired insurance adjuster and avid photographer. He was building his business while indulging his passion. Bella admired people with the courage to follow their dreams.

Deidre lived far from her family. She was great with new technology and believed there was history and art in every object created. Her knack was the ability to store information about people in her encyclopedic mind. She could perfectly match people to belongings. That combination of gifts made her shop a huge success. Deidre was the youngest in this group.

Maura's husband didn't believe in psychic ability, which both their children inherited. His discomfort was palpable. He preferred to live among the familiar and predictable. At times, it created distance between them. Maura embraced life, open to people and circumstances of all kinds, and lived fully. She belonged to a group that prayed daily for peace and healing in the world. To her, there were no bad people, only bad influences or spirits.

Carol was close to all her children and grandchildren. She knew the importance of remaining close, having spent a few years in an orphanage. All four of her kids inherited the gift. She was born an Alaskan Native, and longed to return to the land of her birth. She had a brother somewhere, whom she longed to reunite with. Reaching out into the otherworldly for guidance, she considered herself a Shaman, another new idea for Bella.

And then there was her.

"I don't seem to fit in this group," Bella finally confided. Her new friends were looking at each other with knowing glances. She was afraid it was happening again…being the last to know.

"Your grandmother said you had heightened abilities as a child. According to Anna, in her family line, each seer's oldest daughter (or granddaughter if she bore only sons) inherited the gift. What's your place in her birth order, Bella?"

"I'm Anna's oldest granddaughter, and Mom's oldest daughter." The realization hit Bella like a brick. "You don't mean…"

"That's exactly what we mean." The school teacher in Linda's voice spoke what sounded like truth. And as far as these folks were concerned, that was that!

Bella didn't know what to think about it. Yet another new idea for her to consider. Up to now, she'd never given a single thought to psychic ability. She'd seen the movie *Ghost,* but until she got to Gran's, had never seen one.

"I won't poo-poo the idea, but I find it very hard to believe. I don't really know what to say." Bella thought about the last 24 hours. In those hours she had seen a ghost and had even attempted to speak to it. So perhaps there was something more to learn about what happens in the afterlife.

"I think we've said enough for one night." Linda got up and went into the kitchen to put away food and start dishes. Bella joined in the clean-up, something she was intimately familiar with.

"You don't have to help, Bella."

"Nonsense. I have dinners for every occasion at home and get stuck with the clean up every time. Many hands make light work." Bella relaxed as she worked with the others. It was good to be doing something routine.

"Ladies, I'd like to share something that I probably couldn't share with anybody else I know." When she looked up, they were all smiling, knowingly. This was nuts!

"Do you know what I'm going to say already?"

"We know how it feels to enter into the discovery of psychic connection with those on another side." Maura spoke the words like they were the most natural thing in the world. It wasn't unusual at all. Another side…another new concept for Bella. How many sides were there?

"Well, yesterday by the pool I saw my grandmother twice, as clearly as I see you now. I didn't even know it was her until I saw her picture in the library. I'm not sure why, but I wasn't afraid. I asked her to give me a sign to let me know if she could hear me. I asked her to change something on the study desk if she were able to hear and see me. This morning, walking from the spare bathrooms to my bathroom, she knocked some stuff out of my hands and led me to two places. One was the door to the attic. The other was to the study, where she had moved a brush that I'd placed on my dresser yesterday. It was right next to the picture of her in the library. So I know she can hear and see me. I know how to talk to her, but can't seem to hear her."

"Clairaudience. We'll start there." Carol looked at the others, all nodding in agreement. "Can you come to the clinic tomorrow?"

"I'd rather not. I have some hard decisions to make about the clinic, and I don't want my feelings to influence my business decisions." Bella was firm. The others looked at each other with caution. It was an unpopular thing to say.

"Okay…" Maura regrouped, "we can meet you at Anna's tomorrow afternoon. We can make dinner together and figure this all out."

"Maybe you guys can see if there's a keepsake of Gran's that each of you would like to choose."

"What time? I don't get off until 3:30." Carol was full time at the clinic.

"I can rearrange my late afternoon appointments." Linda was concentrating on her schedule.

"I'm in. Rex is taking his mother to her doctor's appointment at 4. I'll have them drop me off on the way," Maura added, making a mental note.

"I'll leave early and be on call, if that's okay." Deidre thought it was too late to ask someone to trade, or to come in and cover for her.

"Great! I've got the meal," Bella announced.

"Drinks," Maura claimed.

"Dessert," Deidre jumped in.

"Appetizer," It was all that was left by the time it got to Linda.

"Bella, I'm gluten free and Linda is dairy free," Carol added.

"I'll just run into the market and get some fresh foods. How's that."

"Perfect," they said in unison, laughing. Bella was the first to go. She couldn't believe how late it was. Tomorrow was supposed to be her first Skype meeting with staff since her arrival. There was work to do to prepare for the meeting. She'd be burning midnight oil tonight. But she was free to take a nap after the meeting. The house was clean and her only errand was going to the market.

It was 1:30 a.m. when Bella finally finished preparing for this week's projects. She emailed everything to her staff. They could simply open the documents and print them before she connected up. The meeting was in a few hours. She only had time for a nap. Bella turned the lights out, set her phone alarm and went upstairs.

"Gran, I really want to talk to you, but right now I'm beat. I have a meeting in few hours. After that maybe we can attempt to connect up. I don't know how to work that out, but some of your friends are coming over tomorrow afternoon. Maybe they can help. Good night."

Chapter 4

Bella woke up just in time to get a cup of coffee, gather her notes, and boot up her laptop. She opened the meeting early in case anybody wanted to speak to her privately. They had a lot of ground to cover. The agency was working with eight new authors this week. Everyone was very busy. Bella regretted placing extra pressure on her staff. She asked her assistant to ship the boxes she had packed, and to forward a couple of the larger projects. She would do more.

Life had become crazy here, and there was much to do. Today, three months didn't seem like enough time to take care of all of Grandma's affairs. She could stay in Arizona longer, but she'd either have to take on more work, or hire a temp.

While online, she looked at a list of second hand and consignment shops in Phoenix, getting an idea of what her options were for disposal of grandmother's clothes and shoes. Some items in her closet still had the tags on them. They had never been worn. She wondered how Gran supported herself.

Bella grabbed the packet of papers she'd been given at the law office, poured herself a cup of coffee, and went into the library. Much to her surprise, Gran's desk was unlocked. Flipping through the folders, she was easily able to find her running bills. But now that Bella thought about it, she hadn't seen her purse. Where could that be? Wandering through the house, she found all types of things that peaked her interest, but no purse. It seemed strange that a woman didn't have a purse. Maybe she had a special place she put it, or maybe she left it where she died. Then it dawned on Bella...she didn't even ask when, where, or how Grandmother died. She was overcome with guilt.

Thinking logically, Bella narrowed her search to the kitchen, bedroom, study, and cars. But it was nowhere to be found. She then went through every room again, and came up empty handed. Frustrated, she went back to the study and began reading through the papers.

Toward the bottom of the stack, Bella found an envelope. It was unmarked and sealed. When she opened it, she found what she needed. It had bank, utility, and credit card accounts, usernames and passwords, and the information necessary to remotely access emails and confidential information about the clinic. Jackpot.

Bella got to work checking the status of everything. Gran had acted responsibly and taken good care of her finances. All of her bills were paid to date. There were very small balances on a couple little credit cards, which Bella paid in full with the money in Gran's checking account. Gran was smart. She paid everybody with bank checks. She was technologically adept. Not bad for a ninety-six year old! She was of sound mind right to the end. Bella hoped that was in the cards for her, too. Women in her bloodline were beautiful, smart, and successful. And, if Gran's friends were right, they were psychics as well.

Bella put a copy of the checklist the lawyer's had given her on the desk. Having paid all of Gran's bills, she began transferring utilities and closing credit card accounts. Next, Bella wrote down the address of the bank, so she could transfer estate monies into her own accounts. She would have to appear with the necessary paperwork to conduct the transfer. But not today. She had some loose ends to tie up with Gran's clothes and other personal belongings before the ladies arrived for dinner. She'd done enough paperwork for now.

Bella went back to her bedroom and sorted the rest of Gran's clothes, dividing them into stacks of tops, shorts, shirts, socks and intimates. Of course, the intimates would be discarded. Then she set out the boxes of hats, scarves, and jewelry that she'd already picked through. The girls could take what they wanted, and the rest would go to consignment. She felt good about her decisions and her progress. Finally, she was getting somewhere.

The doorbell rang and Bella bounced down the steps to see who it was. UPS had an overnight package for her. Inside were dozens of cards and gift donations to the center in her grandmother's name. There were substantial amounts of money contained in the cards. Bella looked at a note the clinic director included with the cards.

Mrs. Sanders, I thought you might need to deposit these before changing over any existing bank accounts. I wasn't sure what provisions were made for donations to the center over time. Let me know what to do about deposits like these in the future. — Rick Baker

Bella hadn't thought about that, but would ask Maura later today, since she worked at a law office.

Going back into the study, Bella admired all the beautifully bound books Gran had collected over the years. One bookcase was dedicated to the healing arts. There were manuals on ancient Chinese medicines, new thought philosophy, emotional and spiritual self helps and therapies, extrasensory perception (ESP), telepathy, Ayurveda and a host of other, less conventional, ways to heal. It was an impressive collection.

Bella paused a minute. She drifted into a memory of her mother, who'd set out to read every book in the library. Mom said that just because she didn't go to college didn't mean that she wasn't smart. And she was one of the smartest and most loving people Bella knew. If Grandma had only known…

Suddenly, Bella was snapped back into the present, when a book fell out onto the floor. Bella picked it up and put it on the desk.

"Is this your way of letting me know that you can hear my thoughts, Gran? I don't mind if you listen in."

Bella moved over to the next built in bookcase and began looking at how Gran had organized her collection. She had lots of great stuff here. Bella was definitely keeping the books. She would figure out where to put them later. Perhaps she could create a library at her office in St. Louis, where there was plenty of room. Gran had one bookcase dedicated to books, old journals and diaries of a man named Nikola Tesla.

"Wait a minute…" Bella spoke out loud. She walked back over to the desk and looked at the book that had fallen out of the other bookcase. Leafing through it, she realized that it wasn't actually a book, but a combination of formulas, drawings and notes that were professionally bound like a book. It contained notes on direct energy transfer. Was it Tesla's?

Spellbound, Bella leafed through the notes. A photo fell out. It was a picture of two small children, one boy and one girl. On the back someone wrote 'Niko & Anna.' Bella nearly fainted. She sat down right there. Bella rubbed her hand over the leather binding, then hugged the book to her chest like a child. She was learning about who her grandmother actually was.

Re-opening the book, she saw the writing on the inside cover. It read: *Anna, if women had a place in science this work would also have your name on it.* Signed, *Niko.*

"This was your work, Gran?" Bella didn't get an answer, but the most peaceful feeling possessed her. Her grandmother was a psychic, an entrepreneur, a patriot and an inventor! Fascinating!!

"Thought Transference… Was this out of place, Gran, or was… is this a viable alternative therapy? Why did you bring it to my attention?" Bella studied it for a little while, but wasn't able to make any sense of the formulas. The drawings seemed to evolve. They went from two circles, to a rectangle, to what appeared to mimic glasses. Was Gran working on some sort of thought transference glasses? Then Bella had an 'aha' moment. Was her grandmother able to make a living telling fortunes because of a scientific method she'd developed to read thoughts?

WOW!

Bella wasn't sure what to do with the information she'd discovered. Certainly, it was proprietary. Did she or Nikola Tesla patent it?

Was she a Tesla, were they relatives, classmates, neighbors or what? She was so excited she didn't know what to do. So, she did what she always did when she was mulling something over – engage herself in chores.

She did a load of laundry and went to the market.

It was 10 a.m. and she was finished with her publishing business, chores and marketing. The food would take only minutes to prep before grilling, so she went back to looking through her grandmother's things. Despite only having two hours sleep, she felt energized and fully alive.

Being a type-A personality, Bella went back to the closet in her room to finish going through the boxes on the top shelf. One contained bundles of letters. They were letters from Gran to Mom, all returned unopened. She placed them on the nightstand, which was nearly full. She wanted to read them later, perhaps by the pool.

Bella was lost in thought. She marveled at how much planning Anna Neusa put into her granddaughter's journey of discovery. The oldest letter was written before Bella was born. Anna had been saving these letters for 50 years. But…she couldn't have known that her granddaughter would be the heir when she wrote them. This journey was probably meant for her mother.

Bella had lots of questions. She had seen her grandmother when she was a very young child, and again when she was ten. These letters existed then. Why hadn't they been given to her mother at either of those times? Why were they all postmarked, returned, and in a box in the closet all these years later? What could've happened between them that was bad enough to separate them forever? If Gran was clairvoyant, did she know that her granddaughter would outlive her daughter? She had so many questions for the mastermind group, as she now called them.

Suddenly, Bella realized what time it was. The girls would be arriving in half an hour. She had a meal to prepare. Tidying up, she stored the items she was taking home. Everything else was neatly displayed so that the women could select what they wanted.

Bella looked for the grill in the garage, but didn't find it. Perhaps it was outside somewhere. She found it under a tree by the pool. It was in a nice shady spot. Bella put on some shorts, a bathing suit top and some flip flops. She generously applied sunscreen, grabbed her iPod, and headed out to barbeque.

After putting the meat on the grill, she jumped into the pool to cool off. It was 100 degrees. Even the pool water was a bit warm. But it was cooler than the air. She decided to swim a lap or two before her guests arrived. While heading toward the shallow end, Bella saw a rock on the bottom. She dove down and brought it to the surface. Taking a closer look, she saw that the smooth deep blue rock had an inscription on it. B E L L A. How could this be?

The rock couldn't have been there yesterday because Jake vacuumed and cleaned the pool. He would've seen it. Pausing for a moment, Bella remembered some language she glanced over in the packet from the lawyer. Gemstones, it read. She hadn't seen any precious or semi-precious stones in the house. Perhaps they were stored in the attic. She would make it a point to go up there to see what she could find. There was a lot more house to go through.

Bella sat the blue gem on the grill, grabbed the tongs and marinated the meat.

"Something smells fantastic!" It was Deidre. She was the first to arrive. As if she were home, she walked right over to the pool house and put her bacon wrapped jalapeno poppers on the shaded table. She went inside and made herself a cold drink, stripped off her cover-up and joined Bella on a lounger by the barbeque.

"Mind if I jump in?" Deidre asked.

"Be my guest. I'll join you."

"The summers are hot here. You'll have to put cool water in with a hose every afternoon before you swim. The days will soon be 120, and this pool will be like a Jacuzzi!"

"Thanks. I hadn't thought of that."

As they got out and walked back toward the loungers, Deidre eyed the blue gemstone.

"Oooo, Lapis Lazuli. Nice stone! Anna's?" Deidre picked up the shiny stone and fingered it admiringly.

"Lapis Lazuli?" Bella had never heard of it before.

"The truth stone. Some use this to boost the power of the spoken word. But Carol is the specialist with this stuff. She's, I mean she was, your granny's gemstone supplier."

"I didn't know she collected gemstones." Bella was casually turning the meat.

Deidre watched Bella. There was a lot she didn't know. There were powerful and complicated surprises in her future. Deidre hoped she wouldn't make any snap decisions about things when she became overwhelmed. A whole new world was about to unfold before her very eyes. But she had the same spirit of wonder, and appreciation for creative pursuits as Anna had. Deidre liked her. Even though Bella was a little older, she thought she'd enjoy her friendship. The question was, would it be a long distance friendship?

"A penny for your thoughts…" Bella coaxed Deidre.

"I was thinking that you didn't know that Anna made jewelry and stuff."

"Jewelry? I didn't see any evidence of that in the house."

"You mean you haven't been to her jewelry studio yet?"

"Where's that? In town someplace?"

"No. It's in that building over there." Deidre pointed to the two-story stucco behind the pool house.

"That's Gran's, too?" Bella was dumbfounded. "I don't know how I'm going to get everything done in three months. I can't get a single task completed without adding something else to my list."

They both laughed. Deidre didn't know a lot about Bella, but knew she had a publishing business in St. Louis. There was a lot on her plate right now.

"Maybe I can help. I would only be available some nights and on weekends, but I'd be happy to do whatever I can."

"That's fantastic, Deidre! Thanks! Maybe after dinner we can take a walk over to her studio and see what kinds of treasures we can find there."

"I'm in!"

"Where do you suppose she keeps the key?" Bella didn't recall seeing it anywhere.

"Not sure. Did you check her purse?"

"That's the funniest thing, Deidre…I never found it. I looked everywhere."

"Oh, it'd be visible from across the room!" Deidre made a large comical gesture by putting her hands in front of her eyes as if to deflect a bright light. They both laughed.

"Where do you suppose it might be?" Bella didn't really know where else to look.

"Did you check the safe?"

"What safe?"

"Come with me. Anna keeps notes on her pet projects there. I can take you to it, but I couldn't tell you the combination." Deidre got up.

"Wait…let me take this meat off the fire." She put the shrimp and chicken on the top rack of the grill individually wrapped in foil pouches.

"There's a surprise around every corner in this place. I'm constantly amazed by not only what I find, but what I find out!" They both laughed. Bella was comfortable with Deidre. She was pleasant and easy going.

The safe was behind a mirror in the library. The mirror opened out like the front of a medicine cabinet. Behind it was a recessed safe with an electronic combination lock.

"I feel like I'm in an action adventure movie," Bella chuckled. "What's next? Is Indiana Jones coming through the door?"

Practically before those words were spoken, the doorbell rang. They stared at each other before bursting out laughing.

"Lapis Lazuli…the power of the spoken word…you manifest fast," Deidre remarked.

Bella opened the door.

"It's only Maura."

"ONLY Maura? You take that back, Deidre!" The three of them wallowed in the good-natured teasing, enjoying each other's company.

"Any idea where my grandmother kept her purse?"

"Sure, under the bed. She wanted to be able to get it fast if something happened." The three of them went upstairs and there it was. It was more like a carpet bag than a purse. It contained everything from scoop to nuts. Deidre looked for the key to her studio. The doorbell rang again.

"Hey, Carol!"

Bella and Maura were discussing the possible locations of the studio key when Deidre and Carol entered the room.

"It's in the pantry, on the key caddy." Carol knew right where she kept it.

"I am so glad you guys are here! I'm sure Gran is, too."

"We all love Anna! Being here is nice. She's here with us." Carol looked at Maura, who was smiling and nodding in agreement.

"In life, we were inseparable. Now we get to have inter-dimensional love!" The three women laughed and made naughty gestures, cracking each other up. What a happy bunch! She understood why Gran kept company with them. They were very upbeat.

"Where's Linda?"

She's on her way, Carol spoke up. "She had to stop for some non-dairy cheese and gluten free chips for her taco dip.

"Oops!" Bella took off in a flat run toward the barbecue pit.

"If we're staying out until dinner, I'll go in and put my suit on." Carol walked toward the pool house.

"I'll go in with you and make a pitcher of virgin daiquiris, even though Maura's no virgin!" Deidre shouted in the door after Maura.

"Don't you wish you weren't?" Maura poked back.

"What's all the racket back here?" Linda came through the gate carrying her famous dairy free taco dip and gluten free chips. She walked over to the table in the pool house and emptied her arms. They dove for the food like a bunch of vultures.

"Did you know Anna was a foodie?" Everyone was laughing.

"Like attracts like," Bella piped in.

They ate and laughed and swam a little until dinner was ready. By the time they had dessert, they were all ready for a nap.

"I'd like you guys to look through Gran's clothes and shoes. If there's anything you'd like to have, please take it with you. The rest will go to consignment.

"How can you part with her things?" Maura genuinely wanted to know.

"I never knew her."

They were all quiet as they picked through their friends belongings. Fortunately for Bella, they took almost everything she had. But it ruined the party atmosphere. They said their good-byes and Bella agreed to call them all again for their help. She knew she would need it.

It was 7:30 and Bella still had two hours until dark. She got the studio key from the pantry door and walked over. She had no idea that this building was part of the estate. And everything was paid for. This house was big enough for a family of four to live in, and it was a jewelry studio. As she walked through she wondered how Gran got so much done. Between keeping up her house, fundraising for the clinic, helping people heal, telling fortunes, and making jewelry, she must've been busy every minute of every day. Bella was half her age and couldn't imagine keeping up with a schedule like hers.

Entering the studio, she felt something she couldn't explain. The closest she could come to making sense of it was to say that she felt peaceful, rooted, and clear. The foyer was furnished with glass display cases full of fine jewelry. Each piece was unique. It came with a certificate of originality and craftsmanship, and was guaranteed to be one of a kind. There was literature about the powers believed to be contained within the gemstones, and how they contributed to physical, emotional and spiritual balance. This was incredible!

Working her way through the displays, Bella found herself at the base of the stairs. As she climbed up, something seemed to be happening to her center of gravity. She got a strange feeling that instead of climbing up, the energy from above seemed to be lifting her toward it. She felt as if she was floating.

At the top of the stairs were boxes of gemstones in all stages. There were raw, tumbled, polished, chipped and cut stones. They were all sizes, shapes and colors. Bella examined the tools, precious metals, catalogs, drawings and calculations. Anna created some fine designs. Each piece was created to release the natural energy already inside the gemstone and combine it with the properties of the metals around it. Together, they became wearable works of art. It was fascinating.

Bella ran her fingers over the stones as she visited the different works in progress. It appeared that Anna (which she had just begun to call her) was working on several men's designs. Bella didn't know for sure, but she suspected it was for someone at the clinic. She wondered if these stones were part of the healing work being done to help veterans and first responders.

"Hmmm…did I just have an experience of psychic awareness?" Bella wasn't convinced, but she was open to the thought.

As she walked through the upper gallery shutting off lights, she contemplated Anna's ability to draw healing powers from nature. An image of her grandmother was forming in her mind. In the three days she'd been in Phoenix she'd learned a little about Grandma Neusa, the fortune teller. Those words didn't come close to describing her. Bella was forming a much broader impression of her as a naturopath, a person who used things found in nature to help heal. Yet, she was much, much more. Gran was an explorer, a scientist, an inventor, an artist, a jewelry designer, a benefactor, and a smart business woman. Anna Neusa was the total package.

Bella sat on the stairs a moment, thinking about her mother. *Mom was a chip off the old block*, she mused. She was just like Grandma. Mom was a healer, but in a different way. If anything was bothering you, or just plain hurt, she had a way of making it better. She used whatever was at her disposal and heaped on a ton of love. The love made everything else go away.

Bella remembered seeing her mother reading every chance she got. She spent lots of time at the library. Mom once said she'd like to read every book. Grandma spent lots of time in her library, too, and Bella suspected that she'd read every book in it. The two seemed very similar. And…true to her bloodline, Bella loved books, too. She not only read them, she wrote and published them.

Her mother loved jewelry, too, especially rings. She had lots of different metals, pearls and precious gemstones. On her dresser, she had standing racks with rows of earrings to match her rings. On the wall were countless necklaces, something for every outfit. Now, Bella knew she was a chip off the old block. And she was following suit. Seeing the similarities gave Bella a feeling of belonging, of being connected to this place. She felt at home. On an emotional level, it was mystical, a journey to self. Learning about her grandmother was teaching her something about her mother and herself.

Bella felt amazing. She was energized, clear, strong and balanced. Was it this place, the stones, the psychic energy, these people, or what she was discovering about her ancestry and herself? Bella got an impression…an intuitive nudge…that this was the work being done at the clinic.

"Are you trying to tell me something, Gran?"

Bella got up off the step, turned off the lights, and walked back to the house. She'd lost track of time. The same thing happened to her when she was writing books.

"Ouch." Bella stepped on something. She reached down to pick it up, since she loved walking barefoot in the grass. It appeared to be a small gemstone. Tucking it in her pocket, she continued on toward the house. It was a gorgeous night. The air was warm and the sky was clear. As Bella passed the pool, she dropped one foot in and swished it. No…she couldn't…yes…she could!

Bella stripped down and slowly entered the water. It was like a tepid bath. Her body felt silky smooth. Her thoughts drifted to warm springs and mineral waters, and the healing properties associated with them. Was everything about this place designed to heal? If so, what was Grandmother healing from?

Bella noticed her thought pattern. It was as if she were the observer in a lucid dream. She wondered if lucid dreams were throw-backs from inborn psychic abilities. Was she psychic? Or was it this place that held the power? Something was happening to Bella, something palpable. Oddly, she wasn't afraid. She knew it was good. It felt like a reunion, a journey back to a lost self.

Bella wasn't sure when she drifted off to sleep, but was awakened as she felt the water enter her airways. Snapping back to reality, she swam to the shallow end of the pool and got out. She walked over to the chair to get dressed and realized she didn't have a towel. She headed into the pool house to grab one. As she strolled leisurely back to the chair, she encountered a man crossing the yard in his trunks. Bella stood still wondering whether or not there was really a man in the yard. So much had happened that she wondered if she were in a trance, imagining him.

"Wow! Are you an angel?"

"I'm Bella." In her confusion she forgot she was standing stark naked in front of the man.

"I'm Bruce." Bruce took his trunks off and walked into the pool.

The action caused Bella to realize why Bruce stripped down in front of her. She was embarrassed.

"I like free spirits, Bella."

"I'm not normally this free, Bruce. I..." she wasn't sure where to begin.

"No matter...coming back in?" It was apparent that Bruce thought nothing of her nakedness or coming over uninvited and using the pool. Who was he?

Bella dried off, dressed, and headed back into the pool house for a cool drink.

"Can I get you something to drink?"

"The lemonades on the door are mine. Can you also grab me a plastic glass with a straw, please?"

"Ice?"

"That'd be great. Thanks." Bruce swam over to the poolside.

"Do you use the pool often?" Bella wasn't sure how to start the conversation without offending Bruce. This was her property now, and the liability of strangers around the pool when she wasn't there was huge.

"Only on nights when the sky seems dark."

That seemed odd. Why would somebody only come to swim on dark nights? Bella didn't notice any scars, birth defects, or other body flaws a person might want to hide. In fact, the opposite was true. He was very nice looking. His body was slim, but fit, and his upper body was very well developed. He had just the right amount of body hair. In fact, the white v-shaped patch nestled among the black on his upper chest was quite distinguished. Had she noticed that much about him?

"Am I doing something wrong?" He seemed genuinely interested in knowing the answer.

"What?" Bella must've been staring at him while daydreaming.

"Is something wrong?"

"No. I'm...well, it seems that since I got here, something has been happening to me that keeps my senses heightened and helps me read between the lines. I drift off and…"

"Ah…you're a psychic."

"No, I'm not. I mean…" she was stumbling. "I don't know if I am. I'm finding out that my grandmother and all her friends are, and being around them…"

"…it's rubbing off?"

"Yes! I mean, maybe."

"So you're the new owner?"

"I am." Bella sat down. "Bella Sanders."

"Bruce Sutton."

"How did you know Anna?" Bella spoke of her by name.

"Now that's a long story. The short version is, I make all her furniture."

"Do you live around here?"

"Yes, I do. Caddy corner from the jewelry studio. I saw you over there tonight. Awesome stuff, huh?"

"I can't believe how talented she was."

"You weren't close?"

"No. She and my mother were estranged. I met her when I was three or four, then once more when I was about ten, I think. But that's it. I never knew her. Funny…since I've been here, I'm finding out that my mother was a great deal like her, and so am I." Bella couldn't believe how much she just told this total stranger about herself.

"Did she leave that Lapis for ya?" He looked over at the blue stone, which was still lying on the barbecue pit.

"I was swimming and found it on the bottom of the pool. Funny thing is, it has my name on it."

"You'll get used to lots of 'funny things' happening if you stay around here for very long."

Bella relaxed into the circumstances and enjoyed her visit with Bruce. She told him about her idea of the little house with a white picket fence. He laughed with her. She admitted imagining her grand-mother before she saw the photo on the desk. Then, she confessed being in such a trance that she didn't remember moving the hair brush from the dresser to the desk. He smiled and nodded in a knowing way.

"So, how'd you meet her?" It was his turn to entertain her with his stories. They'd laughed at her long enough.

"Well…short story…I was stuck, on the verge of suicide, and wandered into her in the desert. She saved my life then brought me back to life. Now ask me what you want to know specifically."

"How long did all that take?"

"Not long. I suffered alone for a whole lot longer than it took her to bring me back. Well, not just her."

"What do you mean by that?" Bella really wanted to know. This was what Gran's clinic was all about.

"The story is too long for tonight. But I'll take a rain check. The flash forward ending is that she knew that I could look at a piece of wood and see what it wanted to become. She called me the Michelangelo of wood. She was the only person in the world who actually saw what I knew, but was afraid of. Anna coaxed me out and provided an op-portunity for a future. Without her, my furniture company wouldn't exist. In fact, I probably wouldn't either."

"Why wouldn't you be here?"

"Another time, Bella." He walked to the shallow end and up the stairs. Bella couldn't take her eyes off him. It wasn't every day she saw a great looking naked man in the moonlight.

"You can still use the pool any time, Bruce. At least, until I go." Bella felt herself blushing.

"Thanks. I look forward to meeting you here again sometime." Bruce picked up his trunks and walked home, gradually blending into the darkness.

Chapter 5

It seemed as if she was just getting to know her and now it was time to lay her grandmother to rest. Oddly, knowing that there was something beyond physical death made the idea of her funeral less final. It was as if there were scores of people and powers co-existing with Gran in a world Bella had no knowledge of. She felt as if she was among the company of unseen others who lived a whole life parallel to her. Bella knew that talking about this to certain people would be social suicide. But here, where countless others lived it every day, she was liberated. It was hard to put these concepts into words...life, death, end, and final. It was closer to transition/physical life, transition/spiritual life.

These new ideas allowed a whole new world of possibilities to reveal themselves. Could Gran have been a genuine psychic? Were her friends also psychics? Bella had more questions than answers. Yes, this was the prevailing feeling...with every answer came a host of new questions. It was exponential personal discovery, rapid evolution. She supposed the changes wouldn't be evident to others, but she felt like she was on a flying carpet taking a mystical journey.

Maura picked her up right on time. There was nothing pretentious about Anna's life celebration. The farewell ceremony was in the Heard Museum's private garden. As Maura and Bella came around the corner, the crowd was wrapped all the way around it. The garden and museum were packed to capacity. Mouth agape, Bella stared at the evidence of a life well lived. It was strange, this lump in her throat. The tears she shed weren't really for her grandmother, but for herself. Mom and Grandma were gone. She was the oldest remaining female member of her bloodline, the matriarch. It was as if she was cast into this unwanted right-of-passage without her permission. She felt lonely, vulnerable, and fragile.

Bella wanted to believe in the romantic notion that Mom and Grandma were now reunited. It was what she wished for them both. And if all that she was experiencing now was real, she might even be able to contact them both at some point.

After the celebration, there was bottomless food catered by the Courtyard Cafe. It was like the miracle of the fishes and the loaves. The people and food just kept coming. The countless stories of how Anna helped them rolled off the lips of those paying respects. By the time she'd spoken to the last person, she felt as if she'd been lifted six feet off the ground. It was exhilarating.

Resting on a wrought iron bench, Bella watched as her new found friends helped the museum staff clean up. These were Anna's closest friends, and it was easy to see why.

Bella decided to walk home. It was only a couple of blocks. Suddenly, she felt guilty for living a whole day without thoughts about work or life back home. It was as if she'd been transplanted into an entirely new existence. She was completely absorbed in the activity presented with each moment. Was this what it was like to die physically? Were you somehow magically transported into a kind of perpetual presence?

Chapter 6

The next morning Bella woke up feeling better than she had in a long time. There was work to do, so she brought her coffee upstairs. Rearranging the dresser, she made room for her clothes. Today UPS would be delivering boxes from home. She moved Gran's remaining items to one side of the closet, making room for her things. There was plenty of room for both.

It was a perfect day to shop, so she made a list. After looking over the packet of financials from the clinic, Bella called Jake to see if he could continue to clean and treat the pool. She enjoyed using it. Wandering down the hall, she refilled her coffee cup before heading to the study.

Bella felt right at home among her old friends, books. She had ten minutes before her daily staff meeting, so she previewed her material and highlighted a few areas of special interest.

Things were going well at the agency. Two of her editors were spending lots more time than usual at the office. Since they were salaried, she made a mental note to reward them with nice bonuses when the estate was finally settled. These good people exhibited dedication and loyalty to the agency when it was most needed. These were qualities that couldn't be bought, but could be recognized and rewarded.

It was time to make a working schedule of her own. She had lots to do, including the work she'd accepted for the agency. It would be necessary to set aside about three hours a day, or night, to give attention to her primary means of support. Budding authors and staff were counting on her.

Since the primary estate needed nothing immediate, extra effort could be put into making a decision about the clinic. High on her list were studying financials, staff, and the clinic itself. Uncertain of the best way to go about that, Bella would set up an appointment with Mr. Baker. Together they could make a schedule that would allow her access to the everyday work being done there.

Rick Baker wasn't thrilled about Bella's idea. The words he spoke were appropriate, but his tone of voice conveyed his true feelings. Nonetheless, she would appear at the clinic on Friday morning to work through her questions on the financials then set a schedule to observe in the clinic. As an observer, permission would have to be granted by patients. She would respect whatever decisions they made.

It was time for her third and final cup of morning coffee. Down she went. As she turned the corner the doorbell rang. It was UPS. The boxes from home had finally arrived. She showed the driver where to put them. Some went upstairs and others in the library. It felt great to have her own things here. Since she was already comfortable in the study, she began unpacking there first.

Bella opened all the desk drawers, leafing through to determine how best to organize them. There was plenty of room for her files. Her workload was prioritized with the most pressing in front, and that's the way everything went into the drawers. She left one empty for clinic business.

She leaned back. The high-backed leather chair fit like it was made for her. Strangely, she didn't feel like a visitor here. So, with everything organized and in place, she dug in.

Bella looked through the clinic Profit and Loss statements and the Balance Sheets. She had questions about income. Because the reports were generated by QuickBooks, Bella knew the detail was readily available. The first item on her list was to understand how the clinic was paid. How did they actually accrue revenue?

Everything looked good. The reports reflected favorably on Mr. Baker's ability to responsibly manage resources. They weren't making a profit, but they weren't losing money either. This would be okay in the short term, but for the long term health of the clinic, additional funding would be required. Bella had ideas about that, but first things first. Because she had only one real question, she sent an email requesting the detail she sought. She followed up with a phone call. Mr. Baker sent the income detail to her email while they were on the phone. They agreed that she would just appear in clinic on Monday, when she would be introduced to the work being done there. Again Bella got the feeling that Baker was uneasy. It caused her to wonder if he was hiding something. She would proceed with caution, but withhold judgment.

Bella had set aside more time than needed to study the financials. So she decided to Google the clinic and see what she could learn about it. Surprisingly, there was nothing at all about it online. That takes some doing. She interpreted the lack of web presence to mean that funding must come from some type of endowment. Bella looked through the paperwork she'd been given. Surely if there was an endowment, it would be named someplace in the legal documents she had in her possession. Since she was responsible for the clinic debts, she would certainly be an endowment trustee. But there was no mention of it. Bella made a call to Maura and asked her to provide details, if possible.

Feeling like she'd really made some progress with paperwork, she relaxed. Her eyes wandered to the pictures on her desk. Hmm…she'd just called it *her* desk. Earlier she'd called it *her* bedroom. She cautioned herself not to get too comfortable. After all, the people she loved most lived near St. Louis, her home.

Gosh, she missed Mom. They were best friends. There wasn't a day that went by that they didn't talk to each other. How sad it must've been for Mom to be separated from Grandmother. What could've gone so wrong? Grandmother seemed to have a rich and fulfilling life. How could she go on to do so many things with such a big hole in her life? As far as Bella knew, Mom was an only child.

Remembering the letters Grandma had stuffed in the box in her closet, Bella bounded up the stairs two at a time. She would postpone her editing projects. It was time to find out the truth.

The letters were sorted oldest to newest. It seemed logical that the oldest ones contained the fallout from whatever happened. In over an hour of reading letters, over half of them, no answers came. How could something that would separate them for life happen and never be mentioned again? Didn't either one of them ever want to make amends? It didn't make sense. This was going nowhere. She put the letters back in the box, and then back in the closet. It was time to move on to her own business commitments.

Engrossed in her work, the day passed unnoticed. There was time for a swim before supper. She got out her flip flops and headed out to the pool house. Her suit would be dry by now. Her thoughts drifted to Bruce stripping down right in front her while she was standing there naked. She had to giggle at the awkwardness of it all. It was quite a surprise!

Walking into the pool house through the sliding glass door, Bella glanced at the table. There was a note right in the middle. It read:

Anna, contact me. Carol

Thinking it was an old note, Bella threw it in the trash. After changing into her suit, she returned to find the trash dumped out. As she picked it up, she noticed that the note was missing. Bella sat down right there on the floor. There must be a logical explanation for what just happened. Maybe Gran had a cat that lived in the pool house and ate yellow post-it notes.

"Looking for something?" Bruce stood looking down at her.

"My sanity," she sarcastically retorted.

"Is it usually on the floor in the middle of a trash pile?" He extended his hand to help her up.

"I'd talk to you about it, but you'd probably call an ambulance and send me to a psych ward."

"Try me."

Bella felt bad joking about a psych ward the minute it was out of her mouth. After what he'd confided last night, she was ashamed.

"I might've imagined it..."

"Imagined what?" He was a persistent man.

"Well, I came out to change into my suit for a swim before supper. When I came through the patio door, I saw...I think I saw... a note on the table. I picked it up and read it. It was a hand written message on a yellow post-it note. Carol wanted Anna to contact her. Thinking it was an old note, I crumpled it up and threw it in the trash. When I returned, the trash was dumped out and the note was gone. Now...I'm questioning whether or not it was real. But if not, how could I conjure that?"

Bruce gestured understanding with a slight nod. His eyes looked down at the table. He wasn't looking at her. Bella interpreted that as reinforcement that she was going crazy.

"Maybe it's stress or something." Bella rubbed her eyes and cheeks, resting her chin in her hands.

"Or something..." Bruce finally uttered.

"Excuse me?"

"Or something, I said."

Bella got up and went outside. She walked to the shallow end of the pool and sat down on the second step. Half of her was under water. Bruce sat down beside her.

"Wait. You can't come in like that!!" Bella's remark was stern.

"They're just work clothes. It's okay."

"No it's not...take off the shoes. No shoes in the pool. New owner, new rule."

Bruce untied his work boot. Slowly, he unwrapped the lace from the eyelets, dunked the boot under and dumped the water right on Bella's head.

"No self-doubt, new owner. New rule!" He laughed heartedly and dove out into the pool. They splashed each other a couple of times and then Bella followed up on a comment he'd made inside.

"Two questions, Bruce. One, what are you doing here? And two, what did you mean 'or something'?"

"I came to see if you wanted to come over and see the woodshop. I'm working on a commission piece I think you'll like."

"I'd love that."

"There are things you don't know about the people around here. They will be revealed a little at a time, but there's nothing to fear."

"Oh…that answers all my questions." She rolled her eyes and splashed him again. Was she flirting? What if she was? They'd already seen each other naked!

"Come on. I want to show you my project before the sun goes down."

"Okay. Just let me dry off. Can I just throw some shorts on over my suit?"

"Sure."

"Will you tell me what you're trying to sidestep about the note, please?"

"Carol has a special gift. Some call her a shaman. Does that word scare you at all?"

"Not really. What's a shaman?"

"Carol can communicate with people in different places."

"Do you mean…like dead folks?"

"Among others. Under certain circumstances, she can see and hear messages."

"Does she know who they're from?"

"Sometimes. Often, she can see them, but doesn't necessarily know a name. But she can understand their purpose for being there."

"How would she know that?"

"She asks them. For example, if she were doing a shamanic reading with you, she might ask guides to show themselves and leave you a message. Then she would describe what she sees. It's not always a person. Some guides are animals. Or sometimes, the guide might leave the idea of something…like…maybe the picture of an auto accident pops into her mind. Do you understand?"

"I think so. How does she discern between a wandering mind and guidance."

"You'd have to ask her that."

"Does she have a message for Anna?"

"Perhaps, or perhaps someone else does."

"How does Gran communicate with her?"

"I'm not sure."

They walked quietly the rest of the way. Bella was deep in thought. She didn't have any more questions for Bruce right now. The conversation about Carol was over.

Bruce pushed the shop door open for Bella to enter. She was taken aback by the exquisite detail in his designs. His drafting table had blueprints drawn with the precision of an engineer. These weren't cookie cutter pieces of furniture, they were one of a kind original works of art!

"What are the numbers on those chunks of wood?"

"They match the corresponding blueprint. See…in the corner here is number 21, and that slab of oak over there has this inside."

"And you see that?" Bella was truly amazed.

"I do." When he responded, he had the dreamiest look in his eyes.

"You love the wood." She was almost embarrassed by the degree of intimacy she felt in this moment.

"That's an understatement. I wish I could tell you about it."

"You don't have to. I can see it in your work."

She walked around to the different projects, matching them to their wood counterparts. Then she saw it, the most breathtaking wood carving she had ever seen. Unable to voice her appreciation, she walked to the west window. The setting sun was shining through prism set inside the eye of the dolphin, creating a rainbow. It was magnificent!

"This has to be the most beautiful work of wood art in the world." She felt hypnotized by its detail and refracted light.

"I'm pleased that you like it."

"May I touch it?"

"You may. It's yours." He looked right into her and smiled.

"What?" She couldn't believe it. He was playing with her.

"When would you like me to deliver it?"

"What?" She was still in a trance.

"Close your mouth!" He pinched her.

"Ow!"

"See, it's not a dream."

"Oh, Bruce, I can't accept this from you."

"It's not from me. Your grandmother commissioned it for you."

"What?"

"Can't you think of anything more profound to say?" He was teasing her again.

"I can't think of *anything* to say." She was genuinely moved.

"When do you want it?"

"Now."

"I'll be over with it in half an hour. Which door will I come in with it?"

"Give me your phone number. I'll have to decide where to put it."

Bella grabbed Bruce's number and ran all the way back to the house. She hadn't been this excited since...she couldn't remember when.

Entering through the back, she went straight to the west side of the house. Sunset through the prism was the most beautiful light she'd ever seen.

"Thank you Grandma! How'd you know?" She wasn't afraid to speak the words out loud. It was strange, but Bella thought she heard a voice whisper in her ear.

"You've always been a water baby, my brilliant girl."

"Yes. Thank you, Gran." Bella stopped cold, understanding that she was communicating with someone who was considered by most to be dead. Well, her body *was* dead…but her essence, her spirit, was alive and well. Although it was an outrageous idea, Bella felt great. It changed everything. The implications of it set her beliefs on end.

"It's called clairaudience, my darling. It's your gift from me since birth."

"This is the first I've heard of it, Gran. What does this mean?" Bella was clearly having a conversation with Anna.

"It means that if you listen with your heart, you can hear me."

"I can. I have questions, Gran." She didn't know where to begin.

"I know, my girl, but not tonight."

"Goodnight, Gran." Bella sat with what just happened. Clairaudience, huh? Well, she would just Google that and find out what it meant.

The doorbell rang. Bella ran to the door and opened it.

"Please, come in. I was just deciding where to put it and something wonderful happened. I can't wait to tell you all about it. But first…I'm thinking right here. What do you think?

"That's perfect!" He was pleased that she selected a high traffic area. He was proud of it.

While Bruce went out and unloaded the crate from the truck, Bella moved the standing lamp, magazine rack and chair out of the way. She'd figure out where to go with them tomorrow. Tonight she would admire her gift…her gifts…both of them.

It took a few minutes for Bruce to remove the piece from the crate and set up the stand. But once placed, they both stood quietly admiring it. Bella had her hands in prayer position, with her thumbs under her chin and her fingers resting against her nose.

"You don't have to pray for it," he teased her again. But when she looked over at him, she could see that her admiration meant something. They stood there for a few minutes longer, and then Bella remembered the news of her other gift.

"Have you eaten? I don't know what I have left in the fridge, but I think we could scrounge something up."

"Sorry, but I promised a friend I would be there for her first band concert. I'm cutting it close. I've got to go."

"Come over for breakfast then. I have something I want to talk to you about."

"Want to go to the concert with me?"

"How long do I have to get ready?"

"Fifteen minutes. Dress casual. It's at a grade school. I'll be back shortly."

Bella ran upstairs, rinsed off the chlorine and got right back out of the shower. She grabbed a jean skirt, white cotton blouse, and Gran's turquoise earrings. She ran to the pool house and slipped into corn-flower blue flip flops with daisies on top. As Bella spritzed herself with cologne, the doorbell rang. She grabbed her purse and twisted a hand-ful of hair into a knot as she walked out the door.

"I like a girl who's on time." He opened the truck door and closed it behind her. They arrived at the school just in time.

They just got seated when the doors closed and the lights dimmed. Sitting through the concert magnified Bella's longing for her grand-kids. She hadn't seen or spoken to them in over three days now. That was a long time for her. Drifting off in thought, she made a mental note to call them tomorrow. Before long they were on their feet giving a standing ovation for the concert finale.

Bruce and Bella waited in the back after the concert. Within a few minutes a small redhead with long curls and lots of freckles ran up and jumped into Bruce's arms.

"There's my beautiful concert musician." He kissed her on the lips. She squeezed his neck hard.

"Thanks for coming, Uncle Bruce."

"I wouldn't miss it, pumpkin. I would like to introduce you to my new neighbor, Bella."

"Pleased to meet you, Bella."

"The pleasure's all mine, pumpkin." Bella didn't hear her name.

"You can call me pumpkin, or you can call me Elizabeth, my real name. When I become a member of the philharmonic I will prefer Elizabeth."

"I'll remember that." Bella liked pumpkin very much. She was glad she came.

"Can you remind Uncle Bruce, Bella? Mommy says he forgets things."

"I'll do my best," she promised.

"I've got to go now. The band gets a reception. Bye Uncle Bruce. Bye Bella."

"Bye pumpkin!"

On the way home Bruce stopped by a neighborhood diner for a bite to eat. Over dinner he told Bella a little about his sister and niece. Bella told him about hearing her grandmother's voice.

"At first, I wasn't sure it was her. It was like…like a whisper, or the thoughts of the monkey mind. I couldn't decide whether or not it was real." Bella appeared dreamy.

"How'd you finally decide it was her?" Bruce was curious.

"I guess it was when she defined clairaudience. I've never heard of or even seen the word. Yet it's a form of psychic ability. Who else would be feeding me that kind of information? I don't know anybody. Do you?" She looked at Bruce, questioning him genuinely.

"Oh, yes. I know many. In fact, I'm surrounded by them." Bruce felt like laughing. He couldn't have surprised her more.

"You actually believe me?" Bella just sat there.

"Remember when I told you that there was a lot happening around you? I told you that little by little, much more would be revealed. The unfolding has begun." She didn't seem nervous, shaken, or in disbelief. In fact, he'd never been so attracted to her. He thought it better to change his train of thought.

"Clairaudience, huh?" Bruce had never heard of it, either. He'd known people able to hear voices, but he'd never heard the term clairaudience. It didn't bother him that she was psychic, and he didn't think she was crazy. Lots of inexplicable things had occurred since meeting Anna and her friends. It didn't much matter what long names they called their gifts, they were healers. Bruce was proof of that.

The evening passed quickly. Bruce drove Bella home. He hopped out to get the door, but Bella was already on the sidewalk when he came around.

"I really enjoyed tonight, Bruce. Thanks for the concert, for dinner, and for the beautiful art. I'm overwhelmed."

"You're welcome!" He wanted to stand closer, linger there. Her eyes, her lips, her very presence awakened parts of him that had been resting quietly for some time. The feelings of freshness, anticipation, creativity and possibility filled him with an energy he couldn't hold back.

He watched her until she was out of sight, then turned and got in his truck.

Inside, Bella keyed in the alarm code, climbed the stairs and laid across her bed for a minute. Her tummy was full and she was very relaxed. The morning sun was shining in when she woke up fully dressed. She didn't remember covering up.

Chapter 7

Bella logged into Skype a few minutes early. Surprisingly, one of her editors was online waiting for some private face time with her. He'd been looking at the work of an author who'd written a manuscript about his military service in Afghanistan. Peter found the work poignant, moving, and marketable. In his opinion, this work showed promise. Bella asked him to email the file so she could take a look.

The staff meeting was fruitful but uneventful. Peter was the only one who had anything interesting to move forward with today. There were some proposals that might be promising, but the authors had no track record. Her staff was moving ahead, putting their book projects through the beginning phases. Twelve new books went to publication. Marketers were busy with promotions for those. Authors were honoring deadlines, editors were on target with their manuscripts, and the publishers were making new books available. Things were going smoothly.

Upon signing off the meeting, Bella downloaded the book Peter forwarded. She didn't feel like sitting behind a desk today, so she decided to work by the pool.

Swallowed up by the story, each page drew Bella to the next. She didn't want to put it down to answer the phone when it rang. It was Maura.

"Hey, Lady!"

"Hi, Bella. I have some information about the endowment for the clinic. How would you like me to get it to you?"

"Are you free for lunch?"

"Yes. Would you like to come this way or meet in the middle someplace?" Maura was very accommodating.

"Since I don't really know where to go, I'll leave that to you." Bella didn't know much about Phoenix yet, and had no idea where to meet.

"Okay…let's meet at the Courtyard Café. It's close to you, the energy's good and the food is great. Our office is closed from 11:30-1:00."

"11:45, Courtyard Café. See you then!" Bella had her first business lunch since arriving in Phoenix. She was happy about the fact that so many projects were coming together with efficiency and ease. Great people, great results!

There was time to dive back into the manuscript. An hour later she was forced to put it down and get ready for lunch. She thought about a fundraising idea for the clinic. Thinking about all that had occurred since her arrival, Bella wasn't sure the idea was hers exclusively. Being told that she had clairaudience, or the ability to hear promptings from other…other…what? Dead folks? Live folks? Aliens? She really didn't know. Either way, it was a good idea. But could she sell it?

Could they ask people helped by the clinic to write their stories and combine them into an anthology? Book sales would bring forth awareness and support for the clinic. But she had concerns about privacy, and wouldn't want it to become a circus. There was much to discover before putting any effort into the idea. She had more immediate concerns to address.

Bella got to the café right on time. Maura walked through the door just as Bella was being seated. They ordered food and drinks. A well-dressed man approached the table.

"Maura!" The man put the drinks down, hugged Maura and kissed her on both cheeks. "So good to see you!"

"Gordon this is Bella." Bella shook his hand and sat back down.

"Ah, Anna's granddaughter! Delightful!" His eyes radiated appreciation.

"Yes. She's here to make decisions about Anna's estate."

"Young lady, your grandmother was a most remarkable woman."

Bella loved his accent. She didn't know his country of origin, but listening to him talk reminded her of a café she'd eaten in during a visit to Rome.

"I'm discovering just how true that is, Gordon." Bella meant that.

"Ladies, enjoy your lunch."

"Thank you Gordon." Maura turned to Bella. "He's the nicest man, and is also a clinic success story."

"How many people have been helped by the clinic?"

"I couldn't say. MANY! The exact number would be a question for Carol or Rick Baker. I have other answers for you, though. Here's the information on the endowment." Maura passed her a manilla envelope.

"Thanks. Have you read it?"

"No. But then, I didn't have to. I already knew the answer."

"Why didn't you just say so?"

"You have to find your own answers, Bella. And you will. Have you discovered your gift yet?" Maura looked at her and smiled.

"Maybe…"

"How exciting! Tell me all about it." Maura looked as giddy as a child.

"Am I the last to know…again?" They both laughed.

"When I saw the Lapis, I knew you would be opening soon."

"The stone has significance?" Bella had so many questions she didn't know how to ask them. She just followed the conversation and marveled at the ease with which everything seemed to be unfolding. She couldn't have made a path to this place. Every question seemed to have an answer before she knew she had a question. It was the strangest feeling.

"The meaning in the stones can be discussed at lunch with Carol. I want to talk about the endowment. Open it."

Bella opened the envelope and began to read the documents. She couldn't believe her eyes.

"No way!" She was dazed, completely surprised. She didn't understand.

"I'm the benefactor?" Her stomach got butterflies and her thoughts began to race. She heard rushing in her ears. Was she going to faint?

Bella browsed through the remaining documents. There was a scandalous amount of money being managed by a group called The Arizona Community Foundation. The foundation managed the part of the endowment that funded the clinic.

"Only the amount necessary to make ends meet flows into the clinic. It's set up as a non-profit. There's another money manager that invests the rest." Maura seemed to know a lot.

"Who knows about this?" Bella was struggling to wrap her mind around things.

"Now…the money managers, the law firm I work in, and you."

"Not the clinic?"

"No. The check comes from the foundation, but the benefactor's name does not appear."

"Can this be our secret?"

"Of course. That goes without saying. Anna knew exactly what she was doing when she set things up. She was brilliant, Bella, and gifted."

"I'm getting a clearer picture of that every day." Bella stuffed the documents back into the envelope. She soothed with food, needing comfort. Even though this was good news, it was stressful.

"Anna kept this information in the safe. I take it you haven't figured out the combination or found the key yet?"

"No. I haven't given it a thought. Actually, I forgot all about it."

"There's a lot to wrap your mind around here." Maura looked at her empathetically.

Bella smiled and began eating. Turning the conversation to something she was more comfortable with, she told Maura about the manuscript she was reading and how excited she was about it. Next, she rambled on about Gran.

"I can hear her sometimes." To Bella, the words sounded crazy. If she were with anybody but one of Gran's close friends, she would have to keep this all to herself. But because it was Maura, she could speak freely.

The time passed quickly as she recounted yesterday's events. Maura wasn't surprised at all. She knew and loved Bruce, and knew all about Anna's commission.

"Did Gran ever say what happened between her and Mom that drove them apart?"

"No. She spoke of you both as if you were close. Her heart was filled with love and pride."

"I just don't understand it, Maura. You'd think that time would heal the wound, whatever it was." Bella felt regret for them both.

"May I make a suggestion?" Maura looked as if she were about to say something very controversial.

"Please." Bella didn't think she could be much more surprised than she'd been numerous times in the last three or four days.

"Linda has a very special gift. She's what I'd call a medium. If you like, you could ask her to set up a time to ask Anna these questions."

"She could do that?" The possibility was mind-boggling! How could she get to middle age and not know these types of encounters were possible? Or were they? If they were, wouldn't most people beat a path to the door of these mediums to make up for unresolved issues from the past? Bella was skeptical.

"Would you like me to open your mind's eye?" Maura looked at her expecting an answer.

"Will it help me or make me afraid?"

"I'm sensing that it's all good." For some reason, Bella believed her.

Maura reached up to a spot between her eyes and made the motion of grabbing something and tossing it out. She made the same motion three times.

"I opened your third eye. Now, when you want to get a good sense of something, quiet yourself, and read it clearly."

"My third eye?"

"OMG! My lunch hour is over and I still have to drive back to the office. Google it, my dear." Maura stood up, came around for a hug and kiss, then rushed out the door.

Bella sat at the table crinkling up her face and lip-syncing 'my third eye?' What just happened? Now she'd heard it all.

"Open your mind, Bella." The message was loud and clear. She wasn't sure who sent it, but she got the message. Bella ordered Crème Brule and sat a few more minutes, enjoying the atmosphere at the café. There was no reason to rush home. Her afternoon schedule included working through the rest of the bedroom dressers and closets. She made a note to ask Bruce if she could borrow the truck when she had a load to take to the consignment shop.

Bella stopped at the market to get groceries, boxes and trash bags. Gran's furnishings were well made and there were items that Bella would likely keep. They were much nicer than what she had at home. Getting them home could be tricky, but she'd figure something out.

Wow. Bella made it through all the bedroom dressers and closets. Again, she would offer Gran's friends first pick. Whatever was left would go into the boxes she'd just picked up. Gran wasn't really a pack-rat like some depression era people were. She was neat and organized, and her things were well made and in great condition. The only throwaways, so far, were her intimates.

Bella couldn't decide whether to tackle the dining room or the attic next. She could probably tackle the dining room in one day, while the attic might take a little longer. But, not knowing for sure, Bella went upstairs. She felt a breeze on her feet from the crack under the door. Walking in, she could see the problem. There was a hole in the attic vent. When she walked over, there was a dove sitting on a nest just underneath the vent.

"Hello, Dovey," she spoke gently to the mama bird. She didn't try to touch her, and the bird didn't move. "I'm afraid you'll have to share this space with me for a day or two. I have some work to do up here." Bella noticed how hot it was. She looked around to find the lights and plugs. It would be best if she worked up here when it was cool, either early morning or late at night. She'd need a chair and a fan.

To work comfortably in the attic, she put a folding chair and an oscillating fan near the door. Then she went down into the dining room, where she'd work the rest of today.

Bella ran her hand over the beautiful mahogany table. She pulled out one of the heavy chairs and sat down. Drifting away on thoughts about her own family gathered around the table, she got lost in the smiles and sounds of her little grandchildren. She missed them terribly. Back home, she checked in with her kids either driving to or coming home from work every day. She'd known every bruise, cut or scrape, how many teeth were coming in, or whatever problem any of them had. It made her feel important in their lives. Since she'd been here, almost five whole days, nobody called or texted her. They were all getting along quite nicely without her. She wasn't missed.

Bella looked through the china cabinet. This furniture, the linens and the dishes were all going home with her. She would keep Gran's china and give hers to the girls. Another thing she had in common with Mom and Gran was a love of beautiful dishes. What was it about a well set table that called her name? Bella took a china cup and saucer out into the kitchen. She loaded the Keurig and brewed a big cup of Chai Tea. The china cup was too small to hold all the tea, so she went back to the dining room for a teapot. She had a choice between two pots, a one or a four cup. What if she brewed another cup, iced it, and took the pot and cup out to the pool? Happy hour by the pool, what a refreshing idea.

Bella heard the tea ball inside bumping against the china pot. She thought about The Green Earth Store and their fragrant loose teas. Another note to self, select a few fresh teas from the market. With the Keurig, no tea ball was necessary, so she dumped it out. Inside it was a key. Was this the key to the safe? Bella took it to the study and tried it. It didn't fit. She thought about whether or not she'd seen anything else in the house that required a key. Nothing came to mind, but she began another, more thorough, search.

This time, as she wandered through the rooms, looking with a more careful eye. She opened every drawer, looked over and under everything, even moving the rugs. Nothing revealed itself. Believing it could fit an old jewelry box or cedar chest in the attic, Bella tucked it back inside the tea ball and put it in another small pot in the china cabinet. When she found something it might work with, she'd come back for it.

Bella went up and put on her suit, shorts, flip flops and sunscreen. She grabbed her sunglasses and draped a towel over her shoulder. By the time she got back downstairs, the ice in the Chai was melting. Bella put a few more cubes in it and headed to the pool. She grabbed her phone and put it in her pocket.

This time of day there was only one shady spot near the pool, and that's where she'd be. She walked over to the pool house to grab the book written by the young soldier. There was time to read another chapter before dinner. Settled in the lounger, Bella sipped the cool tea and wrapped herself up in the manuscript.

"You know this author, Bella." The thought snapped her out of the story. Was this a psychic moment? Was Gran whispering in her ear?

"Is that you, Gran? How do I know the author?" Bella sat quietly, listening, open to a conversation, but with who? Was Gran's voice the only one she could hear?

"Knock, knock…" Linda walked across the yard. "Enjoying the pool?"

"Yes! Come join me?"

"Linda went in and put on one of the swimsuits that had been hanging on the oar in the pool house. Ah, the floppy hat was hers. She had a scarf wrapped around her and tied like a cover up. It was really cute. She pulled her lounger over near Bella's and helped herself to tea.

"Nothing better than Chai from a Keurig." She leaned her head back and closed her eyes. Bella thought there must be a reason for her to drop by, but a restful moment was welcome.

"How are things coming over here?"

"As far as getting things in order, it's going great. Gran was neat and organized. She wasn't a collector. All of her belongings are nice and well cared for."

"Everything she kept had meaning for her. Most of her belongings were gifts, tokens of gratitude and friendship from those she helped along the way. She was greatly admired and dearly loved."

"How did she help you, Linda?"

"She helped me understand the difference between being crazy and having psychic ability."

"How'd she do that?"

"Long story. The answer to your question is that I thought I was going crazy because I could see things that others couldn't. I could talk to people on the other side, dead people. Needless to say, nobody believed me. My mother thought I was nuts. She wanted to send me away. So one night, lying in bed, I tried to talk to my dad. I'm not sure why I never thought of it before…but…I'm lying there and my dad comes in. He tells me about the clinic. So I went and talked to Anna. And the rest is history."

"I think I'd like the long version of that." Bella was opening to this whole psychic ability and healing with gemstones thing. It had merit.

"Well, I get upset when I drag it all up. How 'bout we just fast forward to the end."

"Okay. I didn't mean to upset you."

"It's okay. So Anna put me through a battery of tests, and showed me the results. Seems I wasn't crazy after all. I had psychic ability. After that she introduced me into the mastermind group, as she called it, where I was surrounded by others with similar abilities. In this group, I'm normal. It saved my life."

"Fascinating." Yet another story of how her grandmother made a difference in the world.

"Linda, do you think you could help me find out what happened between my mother and grandmother that separated them?"

"I'm not sure. Let's talk a little first."

"Okay…" Bella felt hesitant. She waited for Linda to lead the conversation. She wasn't sure what Linda wanted to talk about.

"First off, from Anna's viewpoint, they weren't separated."

"I noticed that." Every time Bella told people she didn't know her grandmother, they looked at her like they didn't believe her.

"Did you know your mother had psychic ability?"

"No." Bella was completely surprised and intrigued by the idea. "Mom never mentioned it, and she never demonstrated it."

"Your dad knew. She was shy and ashamed of her ability, and tried to deny it. Keeping close to home and away from big groups of people sheltered her. It made her feel safe."

"How do you know that?"

"Ask yourself. Was she shy? Or comfortable only in small groups of people she knew well?"

"Well yes, but that doesn't mean she was a psychic." Bella felt a little defensive now.

"True. I don't mean to make you uncomfortable. I'm just trying to give you enough information for you to make an educated decision about whether or not you want to know what happened between them."

"Go on."

"Anna and your mom communicated telepathically. Your mom was a transmitter and Anna was a receiver. Your mother could visualize an event, or send a message, and your grandmother could interpret it."

"You mean Mom could think something and grandma could read her thoughts?!?" Bella felt a rush of adrenaline. Her body was tingling.

"Exactly." Linda just continued to lay back on the lounger with her eyes closed. This wasn't anything unusual to her. But she knew she just rocked Bella's world.

"You can't prove that." Bella was wild with emotion, disoriented.

"Would you like me to leave?" Linda spoke the words but made no move to go.

"I don't know what I'd like right now. I'm sensing that you know I have a gift of my own." Bella didn't know what was going to come out of her mouth. It must be this place. It enabled things, drew them out...or something. That's what Bruce meant when he said, '...or something.'"

"It's called clairaudience. You can hear things."

"Yes!"

"Your mother and grandmother had different ideas about how to help you develop your abilities. Of course your mom didn't want to encourage development at all. She was afraid that people would think you were a freak. She forbid your grandmother to speak of it to you, even though, at age four, it was apparent to both your parents and your grandparents?"

"What did Dad think?"

"He thought that if your mother wanted to speak freely of her abilities and encourage you to develop yours, they'd have to move to a community where the gifts were normal... accepted."

That made sense. That was why her mother stayed home so much. That was why she was never allowed to spend the night at other people's houses, and why Dad never let them have overnight company. He must've been afraid that others would see something. It all seemed to make perfect sense.

"Your grandmother came west to find just that sort of community. She never actually found it, so she *founded* it instead. But as the years passed, formal education seemed to extinguish your power, and your family's need to move dissipated."

"Gran has lots of letters she wrote Mom over the years. They've all been returned unopened."

"Well, your Mom was a transmitter. She couldn't receive back. Anna had to reply with letters."

"But Mom never read them. She just sent thoughts, but she couldn't receive them, right?"

"Right."

"So I feel like I only have half the picture. I have another question. How come my abilities kicked back in now, after being dormant for fifty years?"

"The time you spent with stones in the studio, and the Lapis you handled."

"The stones?" This was more than Bella was willing to accept right now.

"I can't deny that I'm experiencing something, but believing that stones have the ability to activate some recessed trait is a bit much to accept." Bella was overwhelmed.

"There're lots of forces that can't be seen with your eyes that are real. Think about it."

"Believe me, at times it's hard to think of anything else. I'm getting wet." Bella got up and walked around to the pool steps. As she turned the corner she saw Bruce coming over in trunks and flip flops.

"There goes the neighborhood." Linda smiled at Bruce. He walked up to her and gave her a warm hug.

"How's Uncle Bruce and Miss Elizabeth?"

He walked down the steps and dunked in. When he came up, he put his elbows on the pool side, resting his head on them.

"Man, she's awesome. She's not a grown up, but she sure is grown up! We saw her in a band concert the other night!"

"What does she play?"

"She's learning the flute. Learning is the key word. She's driving her mother crazy!"

"As it should be!" Linda smiled at him teasingly.

"I take it you two have been here together before." Bella joined the conversation.

Bruce winked at Linda and she smiled and winked back.

"I don't need to know everything!" Now it was Bella's turn to tease. She was enjoying joking with friends. It was much more fun than trying to understand something that couldn't be explained.

"Do you guys want to order some pizza and wings and stay for supper by the pool?" It was too hot to work in the attic.

"Sure! I'll put a couple of beers in the frig to get cold, if it's okay."

"Be my guest." Bella reached for her phone.

"I can't stay. We're going to Maura's for dinner tonight. But, I'll take a rain check."

"Any time, you're always welcome." Bella meant that.

"So, you start in the clinic on Monday?"

Bella wondered how Linda knew that. Was it her psychic ability or did the word get out from the clinic already.

"I saw you on the schedule for next week. It looks like you'll spend a little time with us every day."

"I hope to be able to. I didn't realize you worked there."

"I'm a consultant. I go when they need me. But I will be there a couple hours next week, so I'll see you then."

"Sounds great!"

They all hugged and said their good-byes.

"I'll stay for supper and help you with stuff if you need me." Bruce was happy to help Anna's granddaughter. Anna was so good to him that it was the least he could do.

"It'd be hot and dirty work." Bella just wanted to be up front about it.

"You're not roofing, are you? I don't do heights."

"Actually, I was going to work in the attic. When I went up there early this morning, there was a mother dove sitting on her nest next to the roof vent. It has a hole in it. "

"Instead of ordering pizza delivered, why don't we order carry out, pick up a new attic vent, and then bring them both back."

"Perfect."

"I'll see you in about 15 minutes."

"Okay…I'll pick you up this time."

"Fine."

Bella stripped down at the pool house and ran back to the house in a towel. She quickly rinsed off, slathered on some lotion and got dressed. She grabbed her purse and sunglasses, and out the door she went. As she pulled up outside Bruce's, he was walking out the door.

They were home in under an hour. While Bella got the plates, Bruce ran out to the pool house to grab a couple of beers from the refrigerator. They had a casual dinner, the kind that Bruce really enjoyed. Bella was relaxed. She wasn't flirty, needy, or boring. She spoke of her love of exploring new ideas, something in abundance around here. Considering everything she had on her plate, she was pretty comfortable. Her energy was good. Bella was clear, decisive and driven. The combination was attractive. When she was around, she didn't require anything of you. She shared time with you, no ulterior motive at all. It was refreshing.

Bruce ran out to the truck and grabbed the attic vent and his tool belt. Heading up the attic stairs, he grabbed the fan and folding chair. Bella stowed the bottles of water under her arm and grabbed the boxes and trash bags. Luckily it was twilight. The only light they had right now filtered in through the broken vent. Either the light switch wasn't working or the bulb was burnt out. Bella went back downstairs for a flashlight and a bulb. In no time, they were ready to get started.

"What do we do about Mama Bird?" Bruce looked around, but didn't see her.

Bella walked over to where she'd been sitting earlier, but she wasn't on the nest. The eggs were still intact. She would be back. Bruce stared blankly at them, then tried to put his head as far out of the vent as possible to see what options they had. He pulled his head back in and stuck his arm out. Just below the vent was a small ledge. It would be close, but the nest would fit.

As he reached out to grab it, Bella squeezed his arm.

"You have to wear rubber gloves. If the Mama smells you, she'll abandon the nest." Getting up, she went downstairs in search of at least one glove. There were none to be found. Instead, she came up with a colorful gardening glove she found in the garage. Bruce's hand was too big, so Bella had to relocate the nest. With the dove family successfully moved, it was time to repair the vent.

Bruce got the broken vent out and the new one in within minutes. But by the time he was done the sweat was rolling down. He took off his t-shirt and wiped his skin.

"Can I use that?" Bella teased him. The fan created a breeze, but it was circulating hot air. Instead of complaining they dug in.

"Any place special you want me to start?" Bruce looked around at the years of accumulated stuff and got tired right away. Bella turned around and starting laughing hysterically. It was contagious.

"She *was* 96!"

"Do you want to work together or start at opposite ends and meet somewhere in the middle?" Bruce was used to planning before execution.

"Let's start where we are and go from here." Bella liked sitting close to him.

"OK." He was fine with that.

As they opened the first boxes, they looked at each other and cracked up. Christmas decorations! Actually, thinking about Christmas would probably keep their minds off the heat.

"Thanks, Gran," Bella thought to herself.

"You're welcome," Bella heard in her ear. Maybe Linda was right.

Maybe she did have psychic powers. If so, they seemed completely normal. They weren't scary at all. In fact, neither the abilities nor the psychics themselves were scary. It was all pretty passé.

"You're pretty quiet over there."

"Just thinking…this psychic thing…there's not much to it, really." Bruce didn't respond. "Linda told me what she knew about the relationship my mother had with Gran. She said my mom had a psychic ability, telepathy. Mom was a transmitter and Grandma was a receiver. They were able to communicate with thoughts. She also said that Mom and Gran knew about my abilities when I was a young child. My mother was afraid I'd be considered a freak, and forbid Gran from doing anything at all to encourage me or help me develop my gift."

Bruce remained silent. He didn't know what to say. His abilities were quite different from Bella's.

"Just so you know, I'm not a psychic. I have special site, but it's related to shapes and possibilities when creating with wood. I can't read your thoughts, see the past or the future, feel emotions, or send thoughts. I have different talents."

"That's comforting, actually. It seems like everyone else is always one step ahead of me."

"I know," he chuckled, "I feel it, too."

"It's almost like there's this whole subculture of people we rub elbows with every day that have the ability to tune in to frequencies that are unavailable to the rest of us. Now, that feels strange…which one am I, the ordinary…or the extraordinary."

"It doesn't take a PhD to figure that one out. There's nothing ordinary about you."

"I'll take that as a compliment."

"Good. That's how I meant it." Their eyes met and Bella knew it was true.

"Linda claims to have the ability to be able to communicate with the dead."

"Who can prove her wrong?" He raised one eyebrow and looked at her cautiously. "Are you thinking of talking to someone?"

"Maybe I don't believe Linda. I think something happened between them, and I'd like to know what." Bella felt comfortable talking to Bruce about it. He wasn't like the others. He was more like her.

"Why does it matter? What will it change?" He looked at her with genuine curiosity.

Bella thought about that for a while. Why did she care so much? She hadn't missed out on anything because of it, and her mother wasn't sad or bitter. In fact, it wasn't a factor at all. So why did she care?

"You've got a point. Perhaps some self-examination is in order. Maybe I should focus on my own motives instead of theirs...misplaced energy...interesting."

"Did Gran ever confide anything else about her past? Any other family, husbands or children?" Bella didn't think so, but she didn't want to assume.

"Nope. She stayed present. Her life was filled with interesting challenges. She was always helping people try to get to where they were going. That required constant expansion."

"You sound like one of those authors who write about higher consciousness or something."

"Or something."

Bella looked over at him again curiously.

"Will you mark all those boxes with their contents?"

"With what?"

"I'll go down and get a marker. Want a beer?"

"Yeah...and a cool cloth to put around my neck."

"I'll be right back." Bella went down the narrow staircase into a dark house. She didn't even know where the hall light switch was. Groping along the wall she felt the switch. Maybe she should spend a little more time practicing presence. If she did, she'd know where the light switches were." She chuckled and made light of herself.

She grabbed a couple of beers, and put a plastic glass upside down on her bottle. She opened and closed drawers trying to find the dish towels. Finally, she found two thin ones and soaked them. She put them in the freezer while she used the bathroom. Forgetting that she'd left the drawer open, Bella bounded around the corner at breakneck speed and bumped smack dab into the drawer.

She must've yelped, because before she could stop cussing Bruce was standing in the doorway. He reached inside the freezer for ice, but grabbed a cool towel. He knelt down on one knee, lifted her shirt and placed the cloth right on the welt.

"Look, Bella." Bruce pointed to a key that was dangling from the bottom of the drawer. It was stuck to a piece of masking tape.

"Pull it off."

Bruce ripped it off the drawer, then bent down to see if there was anything else taped to the bottom. There was a small plastic bag with a piece of paper in it. It had a set of numbers on it that appeared to be a combination.

"If that don't beat all…" Bruce was completely surprised. "Well, if I were a crook, I wouldn't think of looking there. Clever woman. What do you suppose these are for?"

"I'm not sure. Come with me." Bella left the kitchen and went down the hall into the study. She pulled the middle drawer open, revealing a combination lock box stored in the back corner. As Bruce read the combination, Bella typed it into the keypad. The spring latch released. Inside was a built in key box. Bella took the key from Bruce and put it in the lockbox. It opened, revealing what looked like a lens. Both of them looked at each other dumbfounded.

"What do you suppose it is?" Bella wasn't sure. She pulled the drawer out and looked underneath it. There was no false bottom.

"Do you think it's a fingerprint scanner?" Bruce's curiosity was peaked now, too.

"You mean like one of those biometric fingerprint sensors or something?"

"Try it."

"Well, if it is, and I'm not the print it expects, will it set off an alarm?" Bella wasn't sure. She had no experience with advanced technology like this.

"I don't know. Where's your alarm box?"

Bella knew this! She was pleased as punch because she finally knew where something was! Bruce followed her.

"I can't see very well. Do you have a flashlight?" Bruce handed her his phone. I need my glasses. She ran into the kitchen and grabbed the readers from her purse.

"I don't see a listing for scanner. This all looks pretty straightforward. It's not on this security system. Let's take a chance."

They raced back to the study and looked at each other like two kids on a treasure hunt. Bella put her thumb on it. Nothing happened.

"Turn your thumb," Gran whispered in her ear.

"Which way, Gran?" she asked out loud.

"Hand to the right, thumb out at a forty five degree angle."

"Here goes…"

"I heard a click. I also heard you speaking to Anna."

"Yes…to both."

"Follow me." Bella walked over to the wall and opened the mirror.

"That's funny…it's still locked." Bella looked at Bruce with a blank stare. "What now?

"Well, I heard a click. Anna was a clever woman. She never did anything the easy way. There's got to be another secret here that she wants to share with us. There's an explanation somewhere. Let's look."

The two walked carefully around the room. They looked at anything that might open, but without success. Then Bruce noticed a book that was tilted slightly toward him. He went over and pulled it out, but nothing. When he pushed it back in, the whole section of bookcase opened up about six inches. Bruce walked over and pulled it open about three feet.

"Shine your phone light in there, Bruce."

"I can't see anything." It was completely black.

"There must be something. She wouldn't go through all this trouble for nothing. We need more light." Bella unplugged the standing lamp near the high backed leather chair. She tipped it over and unscrewed the lampshade, exposing the bulb. Dragging it over near the opening, she realized she needed an extension cord to reach the space. Hurrying out to the garage, her heart raced. This was very exciting.

It occurred to Bella that there could be some hideous family skeleton behind the bookcase. Should she proceed with Bruce beside her to witness what she found? Then, as if she were reading her thoughts, Gran whispered in Bella's ear.

"You can trust him."

Bella was getting used to hearing the voice. She was learning to trust it, and had begun making decisions based on the whispers. This is a psychic ability, she finally admitted to herself. Now it was time to concentrate on non-verbal communication in the presence of others. It would take practice.

"I can't see anything at all, Bella. But I sense there's something here."

"Can you explain that?"

"No. But…it's like…I feel something, a hidden something, and it feels like I might bump into it. It's like the inner part of my brain that manages spatial relationships is telling me to stop. Does that sound crazy?"

Bella looked at him for a minute. He wasn't afraid, just bewildered.

"Let's shed a little more light on the subject." They stuck the lamp in what appeared to be the center of the space and turned it on. Even with the light, they couldn't see anything.

"There must be some kind of trick switch in here, too. Let's feel around for it. The walls are dusty." Bella continued feeling around for the light.

"Maybe there's a spring locked door in here too. Press on the wall a little and see if anything releases." Bruce was trying, but the walls were solid.

"Walk through the wall in front of you." Gran's voice gave Bella direction.

"You might be able to walk through walls, but I can't, Gran."

Bruce turned to look at Bella. Anna was guiding her, but she must be resisting her. She was motionless, expressionless, as if she were in a trance.

"What did she say, Bella?" Bruce's curiosity was killing him!

"Walk through the wall in front of you."

With that, Bruce grabbed Bella's hand and proceeded to the wall in front of him. He put his head down, as if to guard himself from a face plant, and moved forward, Bella in tow. Within seconds, they were inside. But inside where, and what just happened? Bruce couldn't wrap his mind around it. It was like something out of a Harry Potter movie.

"I'll get the lamp." Bruce turned around and headed back out, but out of what.

Bella stared at the shadows in front of her. What would she find when Bruce brought the lamp in here? Was Anna a mad scientist? An inventor? Did she have gold, silver, and diamonds hidden behind the wall? Was this some kind of escape route or safe room? Bella felt an adrenaline rush. She could feel life coursing through her at a rate that had every cell in her body singing! OMG!

"How did we get here? What just happened Gran?"

"Hologram! Clever, eh?" She was actually conversing with Gran. Had she spoken out loud? Bella wanted to practice speaking with thoughts. So, very carefully, she focused her thoughts and asked Gran if she could talk to her without speaking. She could.

"You are a clairaudient telepath."

"What does that mean, Gran?"

"Clairvoyance, in all its forms, is inherited. You have a rare combination of genetic traits. You already know you have the ability to hear, clairaudience. What you've been taught to squelch are your telepathic abilities. Most telepaths have only one ability. They're either a transmitter or a receiver. Your mother was a transmitter and I am a receiver. But somehow, you got both abilities."

"So, who can I communicate with? Anyone besides you?"

"I don't know the answer to that, Bella, but I'd like to."

"How?" This time she spoke out loud.

"Are you speaking to me?"

"No."

Bruce just stood there. He'd never witnessed a clairvoyant actually making a connection before. It wasn't scary, just weird. Bella didn't appear to be scared at all. She didn't appear different in any way. But she was paying close attention to the conversation that was happening in her head. This must be what it's like when people say they hear voices. But Bruce knew without a doubt that Bella wasn't crazy. Look where he was standing.

"Bruce?"

"Yes?"

"Can I ask a favor of you?"

"Sure." His voice was soft and filled with wonder.

"Can I ask you not to repeat anything about what we see, hear or observe here? I'm not sure what's happening to and around me right now, and in the hands of the wrong people, a whole lot of things could change for me."

Bruce looked directly at her. She could see his response, but he proclaimed it.

"You can trust me, Bella."

"Okay! Let's see what we've got here."

They looked everywhere but couldn't find a light switch.

"Ask her." It was an order.

"What?"

"Ask Anna where the light switch is."

"Just think 'light'" It was Gran's voice.

"Light..." she spoke out loud. The lights came on.

"Dark," Bruce commanded, but nothing happened. "Say it Bella."

"Dark," nothing.

"It responds to thoughts, not words. Think about the dark." Gran was instructing her.

Bella thought about the dark and the lights went out. Then she thought about the light and the space was illuminated. Fascinating.

"Whoa...how'd you do that?" Bruce was standing completely still, holding his breath.

"You can't disturb it. Breathe, Bruce."

"If this is a dream, I don't want to wake up! Can I do it?"

"I don't know. Try it. Don't speak words, think the thought." He did it!

"Gran...he did it!"

"I know. Everyone is born with psychic abilities. Most are taught, through the development of logic, to override their natural tendencies. Gifts can be nurtured and developed. It is actually possible to recapture those innate abilities side by side with other disciplines, like logical thinking. There is a place for both. Combined, they have the potential to become powerful forces for good."

"What's she saying, Bella? Can I hear?"

"Ask her with your thoughts, Bruce, like you did with light and dark." Bella could see him concentrating. Bella couldn't tell if he heard Gran or not. Even though she was a receiver, she supposed it worked only for thoughts meant for her.

"Not true, Bella." It was Gran. "You can hear more, if you want to. But it takes work, the kind of work they do in the clinic. You will be enlightened there."

"Gran, can you send your voice to both of us at the same time?" She spoke out loud so Bruce could hear the request.

"I am."

"I don't hear it, Anna."

"Yes, Bruce, you do." His face lit up. He spread his arms out wide, as if welcoming the world. It was as if he expected to receive a standing ovation. Mouth dropped down and eyes wide open, he stepped over to Bella, picked her up, spun her around and kissed her right on the lips.

"I'm one of you!"

Bella was delighted. When they settled down, both knew there was more to explore.

"What next, Anna?" Bruce spoke, then bowed his head as if he was praying.

"What're you doing, Bruce?"

"Concentrating on the words I just spoke." Bella raised and lowered her head in understanding.

"Touch the glass in front of you."

Both reached out and touched the glass. A screen illuminated. It was a computer screen.

They could see it booting up. A menu appeared.

"There are lots of files on energy transference here, Gran. Who's Nikola Tesla? I saw the photo of you two together as kids."

"Ah, Niko..."

"Can you hear her, Bruce?" He nodded that he could. He put his hand out, as if to stop Bella from speaking so he could hear Anna. Bella smiled at him. He was eager to be even more amazed, like her.

"Children, this is enough for tonight. There is work for you in the attic. Please leave me here with my memories in private now."

"Sure, Gran."

"Good night, Anna."

Bella headed toward the kitchen. She opened the frig. She wanted to graze. She opened the cabinet and got down a bag of blue corn tortilla chips.

"How about I make us some fresh guacamole to go with our beer and chips? I've got the munchies."

"Sounds great. I can't believe I can hear Anna. This blows my mind!" He was still very excited. He was thoughtful for a minute or two. Bella was curious.

"Penny for your thoughts..."

"I was thinking that whatever invention, or whatever, she was working on must have some merit if it pays enough to support the kind of technology she's got back there. What do you suppose it's about?"

"I'm not sure. Did you notice the inflection in her voice when she said the name Niko?" Bella thought it might mean past romance.

"Not just Niko, but *her* Niko."

"They look about the same age in the picture."

"What picture?"

Bella walked back into the library for the picture. While she was in there, she closed the secret door and the boxes that revealed the biosensor. Everything was buttoned up. She walked back to the kitchen to find the avocado pealed and mashed.

"Wow...you cook, too?" Bella set the photo down in front of the bowl.

"It'll be our secret." He smiled, picked up the photo, then set it back down and continued mashing. Bella prepared the rest and added it in as he blended it by hand. She sat at the breakfast bar, and he stood on the other side. They ate before they started processing what just happened.

"See what I mean when I say that there's a surprise around every corner here?"

"I thought I understood before, but I didn't...still don't. This is all so amazing that it borders on Batman!" They both laughed out loud.

"I'm looking forward to working in the attic. I wonder what delightful new secret we'll find up there."

"Secrets...plural. Mountains of treasures await. I feel like a pirate saying that!" He laughed again. Bruce was as giddy as a child.

"I think you've had enough beer, Bruce!" Bella teased him.

"Who needs beer around here?" They nodded their heads in agreement. It was Bella's turn for introspection.

"Anything you want to share?" Bruce didn't want to intrude.

"I feel like I've known Gran all my life. It's like we've always been close. But the truth is that we don't know each other at all. We're strangers. Weird, huh? Who leaves all this stuff, these high tech secrets, to a stranger? It blows my mind. I can't even tell my kids about it because I'm afraid they'll think I'm crazy."

"There's truth in that. You'll have to understand it before you can explain it to anyone else."

"Except you…" She looked at him quietly, admiring what she saw. Here was this man with amazing talent and special gifts sitting in the kitchen drinking beer and eating guacamole at midnight on a Friday night. Wow. This was like something one of her promising authors would write in a book. And this was her life right now.

"Are you going to kiss me?" He looked at her dreamily.

"You wish! I'm going to dunk you!" She sat her beer on the counter and headed out to the pool, shedding her clothes as she walked along. Looking back, she could see Bruce following right behind her adding his clothes to the ones already on the lawn.

The water was perfect. The moon was full, but the stars were partially hidden by the radiant city lights. Bella missed the stars that shined on a clear night back home. You could see a million of them. Her oldest grandson, who was 12 now, had a telescope. She missed home…that is, until a certain someone dunked her!

"You'll pay for that!"

Bruce and Bella enjoyed the water for quite a while before feeling refreshed and ready to lounge. Bella got out first, went into the pool house and brought out a couple of beach towels.

"This is all so far from life back home. Back there I'm Bella Sanders: publisher, writer, mother, grandmother…and here…well, here I'm just Bella: heir, psychic, new girl in town. It feels good to make new friends, get a change of pace, and see a different place. I feel like a completely different person. At home we know everything about each other. Here we know nothing at all, and it's all family. Talk about a contrast..." Bella felt dreamy.

Bruce didn't really have any response to Bella's reflections about her life and her family. He had been connected to and disconnected from family in his life, too. Same story, different people. That's what Anna always said.

Bella turned his phrase on him.

"Anything you'd like to share?"

"Not really...nothing you don't already know intimately. I was thinking about what a blessing and what a curse family can be. I've been both."

"I can't imagine you being a curse." Bella looked for the deeper meaning he was avoiding.

"Can you imagine me putting a voodoo curse on somebody, then?" He made a hideous face and did a cannonball right in front of her chair, soaking her. He was playful. Bella ran inside the pool house for dry towels, and grabbed a cup of ice. She started pelting him with cubes. It was like a game of dodge ball. They were having a great time together.

After the horseplay, Bella got serious.

"What do you know about Nikola Tesla?"

"Nothing." Bruce shrugged his shoulder and twisted his lip on one side.

"Same here."

"I'll run and get my phone and Google it. I'll be right back." Bella walked back to the house and grabbed her phone off the counter. As she reached for it, she noticed a text from one of her sons.

"Mom, call, important."

She immediately called and woke her son up.

"What's going on, honey?"

"Mom, it's 1:30 in the morning. Why are you calling me back now?"

"I just saw your message."

"What are you even doing up at this hour?"

"I was swimming."

"Where do you swim at 1:30 a.m.?"

"Out back, in the pool."

"She had a pool?"

"What's important, Derek?"

"Kyle's getting ear tubes tomorrow morning. He's had another double ear infection and he's been in so much pain. The doctor said he can't give him any more medicine for it. So they have to release the fluid from behind his ear drums. They have to put him under for that."

"I went through that with you."

"I know. I was calling to tell you how much I appreciate all that. Now, I can understand what it was like for you."

"Aw...it wasn't that bad."

"Liar." They both laughed.

"What time will they do the procedure?"

"That's the hard part – noon. He can't have anything to eat or drink beforehand."

"Wow. Where will he be?"

"SLU, Cardinal Glennon."

"Well, babe, thanks for letting me know. I'll let you get back to sleep."

"K. Love you."

"Love you, too."

Bella stood there for a moment. She thought about how she felt being so far from home the first time one of her grandchildren had to go under the knife. It didn't feel good at all.

"When you said you wanted to Google it, I thought you'd come back out with the results." He was teasing, but she wasn't in a playful mood any more.

"My grandson is having surgery tomorrow morning. I've got to get home."

"What kind of surgery?"

"Ear tubes. I know…it's not that serious, but I want to be there."

"Get ready. I'll take you to the airport. While you're doing that, I'll book your flight. Hey," he shouted at her as she climbed the stairs two at a time, "…to where?"

"St. Louis…Lambert."

Bella was quiet on the ride to the airport. If things went according to schedule, she could get home, pick up her car, and get to the hospital in time to kiss him before surgery.

"I can't tell you how much I appreciate this, Bruce. It means a lot."

"What're neighbors for? Let me know when your flight's coming in and I'll pick you up."

"It's not necessary."

"I know, but I'd like to. Put my number in your phone." They exchanged numbers. It was nice having someone here to contact, if necessary.

"This is fantastic. Don't get out, just wait a second and I'll grab my bag out of the bed of the truck."

"Nonsense." He put the truck in neutral, pushed the emergency break, hopped out and grabbed her bag. She opened her arms for a hug and kissed him on the mouth out of reflex. He smiled in a mischievous way.

"That was a kiss between friends." She looked over her shoulder and smiled at him, as she wheeled her bag through the glass doors.

"Yep. Friends with benefits!" He bobbed his head up and down exaggeratedly, flirting with her.

Chapter 8

Derek was surprised to see Bella walk into the waiting room. Kyle toddled over and put his arms up. Bella scooped him up and kissed every inch of his face. Even though he was smiling, she could see that he didn't feel good. He pulled at his ears and turned his smile upside down and the puppy dog tears rolled out.

Before long he was called back into the outpatient surgery area and taken out of his clothes and put in hospital pajamas. Derek and Andrea answered a battery of questions and signed paperwork while Bella held her precious grandson. She said a silent prayer for the surgeon, asking that his mind and sight be sharp and clear, and his hands be steady. The prayer for Kyle asked for pain relief and a speedy and perfect recovery. Bella thanked God for an on-time arrival, so she could be with her family. She'd never missed an important day, and didn't want to begin now.

Everything went as planned. The recovery nurse gave them the blow by blow of what their little buddy had been through. He would be sleeping for a while, so Bella decided to get a bite to eat. She had traveled all night and skipped breakfast to get to SLU in time for Kyle's procedure. She was hungry.

"Food anyone?" Bella looked at her son and daughter-in-law. They weren't going anywhere. She took their orders and headed down the hall.

Standing in the cafeteria check-out line, Bella heard her phone vibrating in her purse. She grabbed a quick look. It was the office. OMG…she'd forgotten the morning meeting. Bella paid for everything and sat down at a table for a moment. It was her assistant that answered the phone. After updating her on everything, she agreed to come in to the agency in the late afternoon, after Kyle was released, and meet with her staff in person.

When Bella got back to recovery, Kyle was vomiting.

"He's having a reaction to the anesthetic," Andrea told her. "If he wretches too much, the pressure could push the tubes out. They're getting him something to settle his stomach."

"Poor baby." Bella walked over and kissed him on the forehead. After eating breakfast, she settled into a chair in the waiting room. The three of them traded in and out of recovery. The day was long, but they were happy it would soon be over.

"You didn't have to come back for this, Mom."

"I couldn't be anywhere else."

"It's been different without you."

"For me, too. It's different being in a place without family, although the people I've met have been pretty great. There's much to do there, but most of the time it feels like a vacation, you know?"

"I could use a vacation." Bella looked at the dark circles under her son's eyes. He appeared to have aged five years in the week she'd been gone. He looked uncomfortable in his body and tired to the bone. Having a sick child was no fun.

"Why don't you guys come to Arizona for a getaway? Stay a while. There's lots of room, a nice pool, and plenty of stuff to do. I'd really enjoy the company." Bella didn't expect an immediate answer, but she planted the seed. She made a note to go by and see her other son and invite his family also. There was room for everyone.

The staff meeting was uneventful, but there was a great deal of excitement for the book written by the young veteran. Her staff had worked up the numbers, considered his marketing plan to be well thought through, and highly recommended that Bella finish reading the book. Nobody knew how many publishers had the opportunity to review the manuscript. She would finish upon her return.

Bella picked up the phone and called Bruce. He didn't answer. She left a message. Walking to her bedroom, she changed into sweat pants and a t-shirt, turned on the television and promptly fell asleep.

It was nearly dusk when Bella woke up. She called about Kyle, who had just gone back to sleep and was doing fine. The next few days would be filled with doctor's appointments and medicine schedules. Bella felt like an important member of the family being available to care for her precious grandson. She also spent time with her younger son, Nate, her daughter-in-law, Kate, and her granddaughter, Maddie, too. Her life was filled with love. Time seemed to pass in a vacuum. Where had it gone?

Bella appeared at the agency one last time. She was going back to Phoenix today. It seemed like such a long time since she'd thought of bio-scanners, holograms, psychic ability and the decisions she would have to make in the next few weeks. Life made many demands of her right now. She thanked God for good health, sound mind, and the love of her family. Bella prayed that her children and grandchildren remained healthy, safe and pain free. Although it seemed like a tall order, it was easy for God.

The airport was crowded with business travelers. Getting through security and to the gate was easy. Bella had only her backpack and one carry on. She had sent a few more things with UPS to free her up. It was about the same cost as paying for luggage, and she didn't have to keep track of it.

The flight was bumpy. Bella had taken some meclizine, but she still felt her head throbbing and her stomach churning. She couldn't wait to touch down. By the time she de-boarded, she was sick as a dog. It was all she could do to walk into the terminal and sit down. That's where Bruce found her. He got a wheelchair and pushed her out to the truck. It wasn't necessary to treat her like an invalid, but she was grateful he was there to help her get back to Gran's.

"I have to text the kids and let them know I landed safely."

"Here, let me." Bruce grabbed her phone and sent the message letting them know she'd arrived.

Bruce helped Bella to the couch in the living room. It was a room that she'd spent no time in. It wasn't a living room like the ones she was used to. There was no television. In fact, Bella didn't remember seeing any TVs at all here. She suspected that Gran grew up without them, and as life continued, she had less and less time for it. But either way, it was very quiet.

She'd forgotten Bruce was there when he appeared with a grilled cheese and some tomato soup. Bella wolfed them down like she hadn't eaten in a week. There was no conversation. She was remarkably quiet and clear.

"Can I do anything else for you before I go?"

"No, thank you, Bruce. You've been wonderful. I just want to rest."

"Call me later, if you feel like talking or want company."

"Will do. Thanks again."

"You bet." Bruce headed out the front door.

"Welcome home, darling." Bella had forgotten what it was like to hear Gran's voice. She got up off the couch and walked over to the dolphin Bruce made her. She was admiring it.

"Yes, he has a remarkable gift." Bella was having a conversation with Gran without thinking twice about it.

"Gran, I want to know about my gift. Can I turn my abilities on and off at will? Will I be able to hear everyone, just a certain few, or just you? Is this hereditary? Do my children and grandchildren have abilities, too? I have a million questions."

"I can't answer your questions, Bella. Only you can. Go to the clinic. There are more surprises there for you."

"I'd like some time to finish exploring the ones here at the house. And I have a book I have to finish in the next couple of days."

"Carol has news about that. Go see her."

"Okay."

The next morning, Bella called Rick Baker and set up an afternoon appointment. She had actually stumbled upon the financial answers she'd been seeking on her own, at least many of them. She inherited the endowment that kept the clinic going, but there were other investors. The meeting would be brief.

Since Bella was living in the house temporarily, she didn't see any reason to put the key back on the bottom of the towel drawer. She put it under the pencil holder. Combination in hand, Bella opened the lock box and scanned in. The bookcase opened and Bella went back into Gran's research room. This time she walked right through the holographic wall and into the lab. Thinking 'light', the room was illuminated. She touched the computer screen and looked through the files. Was there anything else in here that didn't appear to the naked eye? Bella was sure there was, but the technology she was using was so far above her head that she'd have to master it before she could go any further.

"Reveal yourself," she thought. When Bella opened her eyes there were computer screens in two other places. One screen appeared to contain a 3-D hologram of what looked like a pair of glasses. From what she understood, the glasses made it possible for the person wearing them to see the thoughts of the person(s) they were interacting with.

The third screen seemed to be an algorithm and diagrams creating technology that would allow communication with the past. What Bella didn't understand was whether or not it was your own past or someone else's. It was mind boggling either way. But her questions would have to wait. She had an appointment with Mr. Baker in just over an hour.

Bella was changing clothes when the phone rang. It was Derek, calling to tell her to prepare for house guests. Both of her boys and their families were planning a trip to Phoenix next weekend. She was overjoyed.

Her mind was buzzing with ideas for site seeing while driving to the clinic. Maybe they could rent a van and drive to the Grand Canyon.

Bella always dreamed of taking them there when they were growing up. The idea of taking them with their kids was even sweeter. She was going to try to make that happen.

Rick Baker was edgy in her presence, but he was professional and to task. She had her financial questions answered by midmorning, and was discussing operations by lunch. Bella was surprised to learn of the many volunteers that worked at the clinic. A large portion of those who were helped here came back to reach out to others having similar issues. Bella wondered what brought Allen, the young soldier she met on the plane, here. Then she remembered the book. She would finish it post haste.

"Hi, Bella! It's good to see you again," Carol spoke as she walked over. "Starting today?" She smiled so brightly that Bella felt her chest warm. She moved her hand to touch it.

"Good. Open heart chakra…that's perfect." Carol looked pleased.

"Heart chakra?"

"The body has different energy centers. When they're open, energy can move freely and we experience a feeling of well-being. When they're closed, or blocked, our bodies feel out of balance."

"So, you just opened my heart chakra?" Bella was curious.

"No, I just checked it. It was already open."

"How do you know?"

"I sent energy to it, and you felt and responded to it. You're clear."

"Wow. Is that what you do here, then?"

"That's part of it. Why don't you come into one of the healing rooms and I'll demonstrate a few things for you while everyone has lunch?"

"Don't you want to eat?"

"I'll eat after. Come on."

"Lead the way."

Bella followed Carol into a healing room. She was surprised at the

Native appearance there. Hanging on the wall were a dream catcher, a small animal skin and a drum. There was a massage table in the middle of the room. Beside it, there was a small table with oils, incense, small statues, herbs, candles and stones like those Bella had seen in Gran's jewelry studio. Across from the table, there was a small chair with a hanging bag of larger stones beside it. It all appeared very benign to Bella, but she was open.

"Have you ever had any energy or shamanic work before?"

"I've never even heard of it before."

"Great. You're in for a treat."

She got out what appeared to be bunched up herbs and lit them. She was walking around the room chanting silently and making motions, which Bella interpreted as shamanic magic or a spell. She told Bella that sage cleared the space to allow the spirits and guides to come through. Bella thought about a show she'd seen on the travel channel where the African shaman danced and chanted people back from all different kinds of illnesses and conditions of peril. She wasn't sure what to expect.

"Okay. Take your shoes off." While Bella untied her shoes, Carol rolled back the sheet on the massage table and placed a handful of very large stones on it.

"Now…pick four stones that you resonate with."

Bella did as she was instructed.

"Now…" Carol walked over to the hanging bag and brought it to the massage table. Pick three more."

Bella loved all the beautiful stones. There must've been fifty or sixty different types in the bag. She wondered about the role they played. Were they part of a ritual, or was the purpose for choosing them to bring her thoughts to the moment she was in? This was all so fascinating that it was hard to think of anything else.

"It's both," Carol answered. She gathered the stones chosen by Bella and put them in a bowl.

"Come on up." She patted the massage table. Carol placed a small pillow under her head and a roll pillow under her knees, then covered her with a sheet. Next, she turned native flute music. It was very relaxing. She dabbed essential oil on Bella's forehead. Words from an old prayer, 'He anointed my head with oil...' came to mind.

"Nice thought, Bella. Try to clear it. I want you to relax and try to empty your mind. I'm going to check all your chakras and clear them. Then we'll begin your journey."

"Okay. Should I do anything?"

"If I need you to do something, I'll tell you. I'll be talking to you and touching you as I clear you. If at any time you become uncomfortable with what I'm doing, you can tell me and I will stop. Okay?"

"Okay." Bella was both comfortable and uncomfortable. If she told anybody back home what she was doing, they'd think she was nuts. Maybe she was.

"Try to withhold your judgment until after our session, okay? Just relax. There's nobody here but us and nobody knows what we're doing but us. Enjoy it."

This psychic thought reading stuff was amazing. It seemed like she was always the last to know things. Is energy and thought that easy to send and receive?

"Yes." She heard Gran's voice in her ear. It was comforting knowing that Gran was present with her. It was sort of like having a scary medical test with a family member beside you to reassure you.

"It's not a test, darling, it's an unfolding. Relax. You're going to love it." Gran seemed amused.

Bella opened her eyes and saw Carol's hands, palms down, hovering a few inches from her body. She placed the stones that Bella selected on her body in different places.

"What are the stones for?"

"I'm placing them on your chakras to help draw energies into balance in your body. I'm detecting some blockages. I'm going to work with your body now. Let me know if you feel uncomfortable."

Carol put her hand on Bella's knee. She could find her sore knee with rocks and intuition? Fascinating! Oddly, Bella felt relief. Next, Carol began manipulating her feet. As she worked with trigger points, Bella felt her legs and feet relax. As she massaged the bottom of her foot, Bella felt her whole body relax. When she was finished there, Carol swished the energy away with her hands, and made motions to move the energy past herself.

Moving around her body, Carol was able to detect an old shoulder injury that had been giving Bella trouble. It didn't always bother her, but it had been noticeable lately. Bella checked her thoughts to see if Carol was somehow reading her mind. She wasn't. Carol had put her hand under Bella's shoulder before the thought entered Bella's mind. Remarkable.

Next, Carol removed her hands and the stones she'd placed on Bella. She put them in a bowl and made some motions. She informed Bella that she was clearing them before beginning her shamanic journey. Bella relaxed. Lying on the table, she realized that she felt wonderful! The free flow of energy in her body was palpable. It was exhilarating!

Carol selected a few new stones. She placed them on the table and on different parts of Bella's body.

"Why did you place the stone on my stomach?"

"I felt like I should. Does it bother you?"

"No… just curious."

"Now, relax and empty your mind."

"How do I empty my mind?"

"Just try to listen to the music and be present in the room. I am going to say a prayer and asked your spirit guides to appear. If they come, I will tell you. Then, if you see something, you tell me. We'll go back and forth. Okay?"

"Okay."

Carol got a chair and positioned it next to Bella's upper body. She put one hand under her neck and the other under the small of her back. Carol closed her eyes and she began the prayer and the chant. Bella was swept up in the native music, the smell of the incense and the chanting. She'd never experienced anything quite like it before. Then came silence. It wasn't awkward. Bella knew she was on a journey. In her mind, she was sitting near a lake in tall grass. She was looking out onto the water. It was very peaceful and relaxing. She felt wonderful.

"I see the Eiffel Tower and a tall, dark, handsome man holding your hand. It's the early 1800s. You're wearing wedding rings. You're married to each other...I see an owl and a hawk. These birds are two of your guides...I also see someone I don't recognize. It is a man dressed like an ancient Egyptian." Carol then spoke to the guide.

"Spirit guide, please reveal your name so we will know who you are."

Bella couldn't see the guide, but she could picture what an ancient Egyptian looked like.

"T...H...O...T...H. Thank you spirit. Bella have you heard that before?"

"No. When we're done we can Google it."

"What do you see, Bella?"

"I see myself sitting in tall grass by a small lake, or pond."

"What are you wearing?"

Bella's mind had jumped to Carol's words. She had to think back to the peaceful scene she'd glimpsed earlier. It was some kind of animal skin...and beads.

"Animal skins. I was dressed like a squaw. I was caressing a smooth bead on a necklace I was wearing."

"Did you see anything else?"

"Not that I remember."

"Okay." Carol removed her hands from behind Bella's neck and under her back, grabbed both of Bella's hands and closed with a prayer thanking the spirit guides for what they'd revealed today.

"You can open your eyes now."

"I don't want to." They both laughed.

"Put your shoes back on and meet me over there." She pointed to a table that had some books, cards, stones, and what Bella knew were other tools of the trade. Carol was busy clearing herself and the objects that carried Bella's energy.

At the table, they discussed each other's impressions and looked up the guide Thoth. The name was pronounced, Tee oh tee, and he was the Egyptian god of writers. Carol didn't know that Bella was a writer and publisher. Well, maybe she did, but Bella hadn't told her. Carol saw the man in Paris as her husband, and said that he continued to come back to marry her in other lifetimes. It was Wayne, who was the man of her dreams. She thought life was over when he died, and his love still lingered deep within Bella. But Carol couldn't know that. Bella couldn't explain why, even as a child, she was drawn to Paris. As a teen she knew that one day she would have lunch in the Eiffel Tower and dinner on the Champs Elysees. Just like she knew she would take her granddaughters there one day. Carol couldn't know any of that, and Bella hadn't thought about it during the journey. Bella wasn't sure if she believed in reincarnation, but she didn't disbelieve it either. What she knew was that something magical just happened. She also knew that it was her belief that would guide her journey from here. What fun!

"Carol, how do people pay you?" Bella still wasn't sure how that went.

"They don't pay me, the clinic does. Nothing is asked of people who come to us for help. They've already paid us with their service. We repay them here."

"Thanks." Bella thought about that. The clients here saw things most people don't even think about. She couldn't imagine being the first responder on the scene of an accident where they had to cut bodies out of mangled cars. It was equally unimaginable to think of herself killing people in a war zone. These folks had paid dearly so Bella could lead her life without regard for either condition. She admired the idea of pay-back.

"Baker would be glad to know that." Carol heard Bella's thoughts.

"What?"

"Baker thinks you're going to close us down because we're not profitable."

"He said that?" Bella wanted to know what he was saying about her.

"No," Carol laughed, "he's not one of us."

It took Bella a second to get that, but when she did, she laughed. It must be very difficult to work in a business full of clairvoyants and not be one. He'd be guarding his thoughts constantly, as not to reveal what he was entrusted to keep to himself.

"That's right." Carol winked at her.

"That explains why he feels so uncomfortable around me." Bella was getting a different impression of him now.

"He's a really good man, Bella."

"Thanks, Carol. I'll see you later. I'm going to go get lunch, want to come?"

"No thanks. But I don't think Rick's eaten yet. He stays out of the lunchroom if any of us are here." She laughed out loud again.

"Thanks for the tip." Bella walked back down the hall and knocked on Baker's door.

"Let's get lunch." Bella said it more like a command and got a reprimanding look from Baker.

"Since you're my boss, I guess you can order me around, but you might as well know that you get more bees with honey than vinegar."

"Not that old cliché...I'm sorry, Baker. Would you like to get lunch, on me?"

"Sounds great. I have a couple of ideas to run past you anyway...or did you already know that?" He wriggled a little when he asked.

"I can't read your thoughts, if that's what you're asking. At least not yet." Bella could see Baker relax instantly. He had a totally different demeanor.

"Yet?"

"Since I've been here, I've learned that I do have some psychic ability, but I think it's with a select few. Or maybe it's in a certain environment, I'm not sure."

"I don't have any, at all, and I always feel like I'm the last to know everything."

"Me, too!" She said it with such excitement that when she looked over at him, they connected instantly.

"So how do you function with all the psychics around you? How do you keep anything private?"

"Why can't you just ask me if I'm married or something?" They both laughed.

"I'm sorry. I've just skipped past pleasantries and formalities and become the bull in the china shop...another cliché."

"It's okay. Anna designed the glass that boxes in my office so that psychic energy cannot transfer through it."

Bella couldn't believe her ears. Gran had been as much scientist as psychic.

"The more I learn about her, the more amazed I am!"

"What does that mean?" Rick looked confused.

"I didn't know my grandmother."

"I can't believe that. The way she doted on you, the photos...How do you explain that?"

"I was completely surprised when I saw them. She and Mom were estranged. At least I thought they were."

"What does that mean?"

"It means I'm not sure of anything, and there's a surprise around every corner here. It's disorienting."

The ride to lunch was very comfortable. Bella explained what she'd learned about her mother's and grandmother's abilities. The story about her own abilities was beginning to unfold, but Bella really knew nothing about them. She was trying them on for size right now. Rick wasn't surprised when Bella told him of discovering that Anna was an inventor and a scientist. He even knew about 'Niko.'

"Was he an old boyfriend of hers or something?" Bella really wanted to know.

"No, nothing like that. Although, the romantic tone of voice she used when talking about him made me wonder. I think she was mostly just in love with his ideas about energy exchange. From what I've heard her say about him, they met when she was very young, maybe five years old."

That made sense.

"I found a photo in one of Gran's books that was of two small kids, and on the back it said 'Anna and Niko'. They looked young, but the picture wasn't dated. Where do you think they met?"

"I'm not really sure. She said that she met him on vacation one year. His father was a priest in a village they visited. Anna was a freak of sorts at home because her gift was well developed at a very young age. From what I remember Anna telling me, he found her abilities fascinating because he believed in energy transfer, even as a young child. He reasoned that thoughts were energies and could ride just as easily across the air as other energies. Anna said that was the beginning of her love of science. To Niko, she was just a girl with a gift and good ideas."

"How sweet." Bella thought about what it must've been like for her grandmother. Although the story Rick just told her was romantic, Gran's everyday life must've been challenging. She had abilities that separated her from most folks.

"I don't think so. Anna always made the best of things, but she kept most of who she was under lock and key. She went to great lengths to keep her theories and scientific achievements under wraps. Unlike Tesla, she wanted privacy."

"How do you know so much about my grandmother?"

"I spent a lot of time with her when this clinic was just a pipe-dream. I might have even been the seed for this whole shebang!"

"Explain that, please." Bella was mesmerized.

"Let's go in, get a table, and order first."

"Good idea."

Lunch went fast. Bella was beginning to realize that nothing was as it seemed here. There were undercurrents everywhere. Thoughts, motives, laboratories, inventions, and talents were veiled, hidden from the naked eye. That is, except for at Anna's house or the clinic. Bella was growing fonder of those destinations every day. On a side note, she wondered how she would explain all this to her kids. But, she'd figure that out later.

As it turned out, Gran met Rick Baker when he was the curator of the museum in her neighborhood. Anna, as he called her, would periodically visit new exhibits, and they exchanged greetings. One day, Gran sensed trouble for Rick. Chatting over coffee she was able to see beyond what Rick was telling her, and point to the root of the problem. Realizing that, Rick was able to transform his experience. They became friends. Later on, Rick asked Anna if she would be willing to use her gift to help a friend who was having trouble living normally with his family after two tours of duty in Iraq. Anna invited Rick, the troubled veteran, and his family over for a picnic by the pool.

While his family was playing volleyball with Rick in the pool, Anna asked the soldier to take a walk. He was proud of his service, and the medals he'd won, but admitted being plagued by survivor's guilt. While Anna believed his story, she sensed he was holding something back.

With a little convincing, the man agreed to let her look into his thoughts. When she saw a dead boy on the ground, a boy his own son's age, she understood. While he went back to the pool, Anna contacted Linda. Shortly after, she appeared at the party. With her help, he was able to contact the child on the other side, and learned that the child wanted to kill him. After that, he was able to forgive himself for living, while the child died.

Although Bella still had questions about the methods that cultivated the cure, the results spoke volumes. Rick was so impressed by the impact of Anna's work with thought transfer and, as she called it, undercurrents, that he suggested that she use her inventions and gifts on a broader scale. After a series of brainstorming meetings, the clinic was born.

Rick motioned for the check. Bella insisted on paying with a company card. They quickly walked to the car and were on their way back to the clinic.

"Did Gran fund the project" It was probably the last question Bella would get before they arrived back at the clinic.

"She got an endowment."

"She IS the endowment. Or, I guess I am now." It was the first time Bella had mentioned it aloud.

"What?"

"I just found out earlier today."

"Wow. That changes everything." A tsunami size wave of relief, washed over Rick. He put the car in park, tilted his head back against the head rest, and let a stream of tears run down his cheek. Bella didn't know what to do or say, so she sat motionless, letting him release his emotions. People were pretty open about that around here.

"I'm sorry, Bella." Rick pulled out his hanky, wiped his face and blew his nose. "I thought for sure we were done here. I believe that the clinic offers something that isn't available anywhere else in the world. We're one of a kind. If we closed our doors, who would help all those struggling heroes that are destined to walk through our doors? I've been seriously losing sleep over it since Anna died. But now..."

"Now what?" Bella wasn't so sure she'd done the right thing by revealing the information about the endowment.

"Now that I know it's you, I have a chance to show you what the money is buying. You are trying to determine the value in what we do here. I couldn't say as much for a management company that makes decisions based solely on the bottom line."

"True." Suddenly, she felt overwhelmed. "Look, Rick, I think I'm going to head home. I've absorbed a lot of information today and I feel like I need time to separate from it emotionally before taking on anything more."

"Fine. But come in about an hour before opening tomorrow. I want to show you Anna's latest invention."

Well, now her curiosity was peaked.

"Hey, wait up," She called out after him. They both laughed.

Rick took Bella into Anna's office. He closed the door behind them. Standing in the middle of the room, he put his hands in his pockets, closed his eyes, and they both heard a click.

"Thought transference," Rick began. "You transfer the command 'open' and the lock releases." Rick looked at Bella to see if she understood. She did. But Bella didn't tell him that most of what she had in the house operated the same way. Beginning to understand the magnitude of what her grandmother developed, she began to wonder about how safe she was with all this technology around her. Could others steal these ideas and duplicate her inventions? Were these commonplace already among members of this community? Were they patented? Were all of them inventors, or just Gran's trusted circle? She had more questions.

Rick walked over touched the wall. Suddenly, the hologram covering the case disappeared. Before them was a case containing what looked like a two jeweled headbands. Bella recognized some of the stones from Gran's jewelry studio. What were they for?

"I know these are probably for energy transfer, but explain, please."

"I wish I could. These are for you to explain, Bella."

"How could I do that?"

"I'm not sure. But when Anna finished these she said that they would be of no use to anyone other than her oldest granddaughter, then *her* oldest granddaughter, and down the line. She said the bands were activated by a specific feature in the genome. Ancestry is a key component in the activation of the magic."

"Magic?"

"I can't think of any other word like it. But I saw a demonstration of it once."

"Please don't keep me waiting. Just tell me."

"Well…Anna wore one headband and put the other headband on her client. After the patient saw the block and got clear, he didn't know what to do with the information. He couldn't pinpoint his gift. So Anna helped him probe his subconscious until he remembered.

In another session, when the young man couldn't figure out how to use the gift, he and Anna sat together again and examined his ideas. Together, they took the ideas apart and put them back together in his subconscious, so he could recognize the cues and work his way to what he wanted. The next thing you know, the man had one of the most innovative furniture and wood art workshops anywhere.

Bella knew the man, Bruce. When Bruce told her that Gran was the one who got him started, she thought he meant that she bought all his furniture. She had no idea he meant that she helped him activate his ability to see inside the wood. It was mind boggling.

"Until now, nobody has been able to activate the bands. So that part of our program is on hold."

"Are you asking me to step in and take her place?"

"Nobody can take Anna's place. I'm asking you to join us."

"Rick, I…"

"Don't say no. I know you have a publishing business in St. Louis."

"No, actually it's in Illinois, but near St. Louis."

Suddenly, Rick got very quiet. Bella wasn't planning to stay. He didn't know why he had jumped in so fast and revealed so much. He was blaming himself for blowing everything. But clients that needed this help from the program were lining up. Much good could be done if she could spend time with them.

As if reading his mind, Bella spoke up.

"Don't blame yourself, Rick. You didn't know."

"Didn't know what? I thought you couldn't read my thoughts." His tone was sharp and cutting.

"I don't deserve that."

"Sure you do. You walk in here and make demands, giving people the impression that you're open to the treatment that's going on here. You meet with them in their private lives, forge friendships, and then lead them on by letting them believe you actually care about what happens here, which just happens to be their hope for the future." Rick was on a rant.

"I am NOT my grandmother!" It was Bella's turn. "I didn't even know her because she never came around. I met her twice in my life. She didn't care enough to learn what my dreams were, and neither Anna Neusa nor you have a right to make your dreams trump mine. Make your place in the world based on what *you* can do. Don't hold me hostage for your happiness or well-being. The decision I make about this clinic, how it's run, and by whom, are mine Mr. Baker. Mine! And I'll thank you to address me with respect if you wish to keep your job."

Rick Baker stormed out of the office and slammed the door. He didn't utter the words 'I quit' but Bella understood he was right on the cusp of walking out for good. What seemed so good just an hour ago was now a disaster with fall-out. There was no going back.

"You're right, Bella. I had no right to choose for you. I'm sorry." Bella heard the genuine sorrow in Gran's voice.

"Gran, why does it have to be the oldest granddaughter? Isn't there anyone else in the bloodline who can do this?"

"No. At least, not that I know of. It's always been this way."

"Maybe there's another way."

"But how?" Gran was listening.

"I'm not sure. But there's so much genome development across the board right now, maybe we can find a way to develop whatever specific trait the technology binds to and replicate it. That way, perhaps we could affix the trait to the bands, and not to people. Does that make sense?"

"It makes sense, but is it possible?"

"I don't know, Gran. I don't know."

Bella put everything back into place. She locked the office and walked back to Baker's office to gather her things. When she got there, he was gone. The office was locked, but her things were laying on a chair outside the door. Sitting on top of her purse was a note that read: *Carol will lead you through the rest of this week.* Bella was fine with that.

"Had enough for one day?" Carol saw Bella reading the note.

"Why? Is there something else you'd like to go over with me?"

"Yes. There's a young naval officer who is having problems. I understand you were in the Navy."

"Yes. How did you know that? Did your psychic abilities see that?"

"No, silly, it was your background check."

"What would you like me to do?" Bella wasn't sure she was up to it. She didn't know what to do?

"Nothing. Just observe, be present. If she addresses you directly, answer honestly. If not, just hold the space."

"Hold the space?"

"Yeah. Use your energy to keep the undercurrent relaxed, peaceful, and safe."

"Safe from what?"

"Psychic attack."

"How will I know if there's a potential psychic attack?"

"You'll know."

"Okay. Lead the way."

Bella followed Carol into the room. Allen, the young soldier she met on the plane was in the room with the naval officer. Bella assessed her as being late twenties and about six months pregnant. During their time together, Allen was able to get enough information about Kendra to know that she wasn't aware of what was keeping her stuck. They would need Maura. Allen explained that there was a consultant who had a special gift for helping people discover what was keeping them stuck. Kendra was very happy to know that it was a woman.

Allen excused himself from the room, which left Bella and Kendra alone together.

"When's your baby due?"

"In about three months."

"You don't seem very excited. Is something's wrong? Is there something else you'd like to tell me?"

"No. I'd like to never speak of it again."

"I'm sorry. I'll walk you out then."

"Okay, thanks. Who is Maura?"

"She has a gift that allows her to see the deeply buried thoughts that keep us stuck, and bring them out into the open."

"Then what?"

"Well, that'll be completely up to you."

"Oh, right…like I know. My best work got me here."

"What could be so terrible that it caused you to doubt yourself?"

Bella received a message, psychically. She not only saw images, she felt pain. She leaned against the wall and slipped to the floor to keep from passing out. Kendra was flashing back to being beaten and raped.

"Bella?" Kendra tried to squat down, but was unable.

"I'm okay. Just give me a minute." How does someone deal with what she'd just seen? Kendra hadn't mentioned anything about the rape to Allen. How did she get here, to the clinic? She wasn't a veteran or a first responder. She was active duty military, and pregnant at that.

"Ask her why she's here." Gran was prompting her.

"Kendra, why are you here?"

"I don't love my baby and I can't kill it."

"What do you want from us?"

"What?" Kendra looked confused.

"Why, of all the places you could've gone, did you come here?"

"To find out why."

"You know why." Bella looked at her knowingly. "Are you a believer?"

"Yes."

"May I speak freely, then?"

"Please."

"I had a flash of your thoughts a minute ago and I saw what happened and felt some of your pain."

"None of that was my baby's fault."

"It wasn't your fault either." Bella didn't need to tell her that. She'd been to counseling, group support meetings, court and doctors.

"Are you reading my thoughts?"

"I'm not sure. But I understand that you've been to doctors, police, court, counseling and support meetings. Why did you come here, really?"

"I'm desperate." She broke down crying.

"For what?" Bella couldn't read it.

"Please...let me speak to Anna. She can help me."

"I'm afraid that won't be possible, Kendra."

"But..." Kendra began to sob. "I know I'm not a first responder or veteran, but I will be. Please...please let me speak to Anna."

"Why must it be Anna?" Bella didn't understand.

"I heard her voice. She told me to come here."

"I'm sorry, Kendra, but my grandmother's dead."

"No...no..." Kendra sat and wept for a few minutes.

"Ask her how she became a believer?"

"Kendra, my grandmother wants to know how you became a believer."

"What? Do you hear her?"

"Yes. She wants you to think of something that nobody else in the world knows. She will tell me the answer and you will know it's her."

After a few minutes, Bella asked Kendra if she was ready. Then Gran whispered in Bella's ear.

"You prescribed the psychotic drug that caused your patient to rape you."

Kendra sat back and nodded her head. Her body was relaxed and she wasn't crying. It was as if she were free.

"And now we're irreversibly linked for life."

"Because of the baby?"

"Yes. Because of the trial, a paternity test was done and he was determined to be the father. The military will ensure that all of the rights of a military member's child will be mine."

"I see."

Both women sat there contemplating the gravity of her situation. It wouldn't be easy to find the trigger that blocked her love. It was easy to understand the events leading up to it, but to find the exact thought, and help clear it, would be tricky.

"Will you give Maura a chance to help you?"

"Okay."

"Come on…I'll walk you out. Carol will get you all set up."

"Miss Carol, please get Miss Kendra set up with Maura."

"Okay." Carol smiled and nodded her approval.

Bella walked over, picked up her things and went out to her car. She was done for today. Driving home she pictured herself plunging into the pool and washing away all the negative energy she'd absorbed during her session at the clinic. It was exhausting.

There was really nobody that Bella could talk to about what she'd been part of that day. Because of patient privacy, she couldn't repeat what had transpired in session. Because of the anonymity of the clinic, she couldn't really talk about her fight with Rick. Because Gran's invention wasn't patent protected, she couldn't talk about that either. But she didn't want to carry it around with her either. Bella felt the double bind.

Walking through the house she threw down her purse and took off her shoes. She kept on walking through the kitchen and out the back toward the pool house. The walk was hot, so she stepped off into the grass. Walking across the concrete pool deck on the shady side, she found herself passing Bruce.

"Don't you ever work?" Bella nearly bit his head off as she put his flip flops on.

"Ouch! Bad day at the office?" Bruce kept his head low and his eyes on the magazine.

"I'm sorry, Bruce. Yes. I just kept getting into tight spots all day long. I did one thing wrong after another. I was a disaster on two feet." She was talking and walking, shedding clothes along the way. Donned in a high cut one piece, Bella dove in and swam to the shallow end and back. She wanted desperately to shake the bad energy off of her.

"Here." Bruce handed her a stone. "It was in the pool when I got here. I took it out while I was swimming, but it might be best if you put it back in now. Anna must think you'd benefit by it."

Bella threw the stone in the pool.

"What is this for, Gran?" Bella spoke out loud in front of Bruce.

"Calcite, dear. It's for purification and balance."

"Perfect. Thanks, Gran." Bella wasn't sure it was the stone or the thought that seemed to be releasing her from the bondage of her day, but she was feeling better. She swam back and forth a few times before joining Bruce on the deck.

"My sons are coming next weekend." Bella switched the conversation to something less stressful. "They're bringing their families with them for a vacation. I was thinking of taking them to the Grand Canyon. What do you think?"

"Oh, it's about 240 miles, about a four hour drive. That's the closest point, the Grand Canyon Village. You guys could easily get there in a half a day."

"I was thinking of renting a van. Any ideas where I might do that?"

"Why don't you ask if you can borrow the clinic's shuttle van?"

"I didn't know they had one."

"Yep, a nice one, too. Since you own it, you might be able to use it."

"That's great advice. Thanks."

Bruce stayed on the down-low for the remainder of the evening. He sensed that Bella preferred to be alone. So he gathered his towel and magazines and said his goodbyes. Bella appeared relieved.

She grabbed the novel she'd promised to finish and immersed herself in it. The hours passed quickly, and before she knew it, she had turned the last page. She stretched out as she watched the sun come up. What a compelling read. Bella decided to meet with the author and see where his head was right now, and if there were any more books in him. Bella would get his contact information during their morning meeting.

Bella was delighted at the pace her staff was keeping. Getting into the swing of things had taken a little time, but they were making excellent progress now. She patted herself on the back for hand picking every single one of them.

Today she wanted to talk about the book she just finished. Nancy, Bella's assistant, forwarded the contact information for the author. Surprisingly, he was living in Scottsdale, a suburb of Phoenix. Bella would contact him and set up a time to meet. Things were going beautifully. She was surprised at how good it felt to be at the top of her game. Being part of the publishing world for an hour recharged her batteries. It restored her confidence and feelings of competence and mastery. It was the flip side of what she'd experienced yesterday.

There was another project that the staff brought to Bella's attention. Nancy forwarded the manuscript to Bella, along with a list of other matters that required her attention. After the meeting ended, she prioritized them and got to work. Bella would put an hour of focused effort to good use. Time flew. She was having fun!

As Bella buttoned everything up she thought about how lucky she was to be able to do what she loved. She knew people who hated their jobs and fought themselves every day just to get up and get ready for work. Not her. She'd always loved reading and was destined to write. It took her a while to pursue it professionally, but once she'd made up her mind, there was no going back or staying stuck.

Chapter 9

Bella was up, showered and ready for clinic. She made some oats and fruit and sat down at the table. Her thoughts drifted to the healing powers she observed in the clinic yesterday. How could rocks and waving hands clear and balance someone's energy centers? These solutions were unbelievably simple. They could be practiced anywhere or by anyone.

The rocks, or gemstones, as they were referred to by Carol, carried properties endowed by mother earth. The power within them was the direct result of the elements that formed them. So the shaman or healer didn't do anything to make the gems magical, they just gathered them for tools. Yet, they needed to be cleared and re-energized. Bella was curious about that. It implied we could draw out the life force of the stone and use it ourselves, then, by simply placing them in the sun or moonlight, re-energize them. Could the solution really be that simple? Sleeping well and sitting in the sun by the pool reenergized her, so it wasn't such a big leap to think that something made of the same elements as her would experience the same renewal.

Bella thought back to her personal experiences in the clinic yesterday. When Carol was doing her energy work, she felt the healing as it was happening. The influences that contributed to her experience were sounds, gems, and energy movement. Combined, it created a restorative cocktail. She couldn't deny the results.

Then, considering what happened with Kendra, Bella isolated what she thought the healing components were. There were only people. At first, the combination didn't evoke the desired result. Bella wondered if Allen left the room because he sensed that Kendra was

uncomfortable with him, or if he was clairvoyant and intuited the necessary change. Why didn't he come back?

While the three of them were in the room, Bella's ability did nothing more than stabilize the environment, or, as Carol put it, held the
space. As she examined her memory of it, Bella realized that while
Allen was in the room with them, her telepathic abilities were dormant. At least she thought they were. But after Allen left, Bella was
able to receive the information from Kendra about the rape. Why was
that? Again, Bella had questions.

Rick Baker was outside pacing back and forth on the sidewalk near
the lobby entrance. Bella wondered if he was resigning today. If he
was, that would create extra work for her, but she would cross that
bridge when she came to it. She parked in the last row, as usual. Rick
walked out to meet her.

"Bella, I..."

"I have a new list of questions. Who will I be shadowing today?"

"Bella, stop. Please."

Bella stopped and faced him. She wasn't angry with Rick, but she
had no intension of staying. There was no use in pretending. She was
leaving in two months or less, depending on how quickly she could
make arrangements to liquidate the estate and its furnishings. By the
time that was done, she would have also made her decision about the
clinic. If she kept it, she would hire someone local to run it. Her decisions were business, not personal.

"I'm sorry about yesterday. I had no right to accuse you of anything.
My passion about the work we've done...do...here is so great...I
can't make any excuses, Bella, I'm just sorry, that's all."

"Fine. Apology accepted. But make no mistake, Mr. Baker, I'm not
interested in staying. This was my grandmother's dream, not mine. I
didn't even know this place existed until you met me that first day. I

have a successful business of my own, one that I feel as much passion for as you feel for this one. And my intention is to return to it. Are we clear?"

"Yes. But where does that leave the clinic?"

"I don't know yet. But when I do, you'll be the first to know."

"Okay, fair enough."

"Who will I shadow today?"

"Allen."

"Got it." Bella went in, put her purse in a locker and silenced her phone. She walked out into the hall and was greeted by Allen.

"Bella! Good morning."

"Good morning. What's going on today?"

"Well, for one thing, Kendra's in with Maura right now."

"This fast?"

"Things move quickly here. When people finally summon the courage to face whatever they're battling, we act fast. It's like taking your car to the garage. If the place you take it can fix it in the time you have, with the resources you have, they get the job. Otherwise, someone else gets the work."

"Do we have any competition here? I mean, aren't we one of a kind?"

"Yes, but…"

"But what?"

"Not everyone is open to psychic and spiritual healing. If they're on the fence about it…and they come here not sure if it's really the right thing or not…and we don't act fast…"

"They might not come back. I get it. So what if they don't come back, Allen?" Bella looked right at him. He was green.

"That's just not possible, Bella. We just can't let that happen."

"Why not? Isn't it the patient's right to decide when and where he or she goes to heal?"

"Of course, but…"

"But what, Allen?"

"But, a person isn't completely healed without a healthy psyche. It's requires just as much attention as healing any other part of the body."

"And we're the only ones who can do that?"

"Yes, presently." And Allen would know.

"So why is psychic healing so urgent?"

"Well, for one thing, our first responders keep going back out into similar situations repeatedly, and their decisions can mean the difference between life and death. They need to be clear and present each and every time."

"I see. And how many of them do we treat regularly?"

"Just about all of them."

"Quantify for me. How many?"

"80 - 100 per week, first responders. Plus our vets, add 20%. We average three patients per hour, forty hours per week. We help stabilize a lot of people. And think of the ripple effect on their families. It's made an impact. We've made a difference in the quality of a lot of lives. We help free those who've paid the ultimate price for our freedoms. That sounds really fantastic, doesn't it?"

Bella looked at Allen and smiled. He was great PR for the place. She would remember that when it came time for marketing.

"How do patient's get to us, Allen?"

"Word of mouth. Those who need us, find us."

"I see."

"Bella, this work isn't exactly mainstream, and these folks value privacy and anonymity. There's no other way."

"Thank you for the information, Allen. You've been most helpful."

"There's Maura and Kendra."

"Hey, girls!" Bella could see that Kendra had been crying. Maura's loving demeanor was cocooning Kendra. She had changed. Bella could sense that her guard had come down and she was open.

"How'd it go?" Allen was looking at both women awaiting an answer.

"You were right. She's awesome!" Kendra was praising Maura.

"Great! Let's debrief. Right this way." He led them all into a small conference room where they discussed what to do next. By the time the meeting was over, they were directed and connected. Kendra would come back one last time and see Carol. Carol would help her find direction for her future. The rest would be up to Kendra. She appeared empowered.

After Kendra left, Bella asked Maura if she could share what was keeping the young woman from loving her baby. Maura could not, but once she entered her notes into Kendra's record, Bella was free to review it. Bella would make a decision as to whether or not she would actually do that. Did she really need to know? It was enough that Kendra knew and was able to begin to foster the relationship she desired with her child. That was all Bella really needed to know.

"You're wise beyond your years, Bella," Gran whispered. "Now go have lunch with Rick."

Bella was past the point of resistance. She walked over to the office, knocked, and opened the door. Since the walls were glass she could see she wasn't interrupting a meeting, either in person or on the phone.

"Lunch?"

"Sure."

This time Bella drove and took Rick back to the café in her neighborhood. Gordon appeared after they were seated, and greeted them both by name. Again, Bella was pleasantly surprised.

"How do you know Gordon?"

"I met him at Anna's a few times."

"She was quite the entertainer."

Rick looked at her. She really didn't know her grandmother at all. Every time she voiced an observation about Anna, it was pretty far off. Rick now believed that she couldn't read his thoughts.

"Gordon and his wife went to Anna for readings. They were private clients that she saw at home."

"That must be the 'the fortune teller' my mother knew. What a small word for such a big gift."

"Gordon's daughter committed suicide as a teenager."

Bella pulled her hand to her chest. She lowered her eyes as she felt a sense of loss for Gordon and his wife. She would be devastated if something happened to her child.

"What did they expect from my grandmother's reading?"

"I don't understand your question, Bella."

"How would a psychic reading help a couple that just lost a child?"

Rick sat there for a moment. Bella was truly a novice when it came to psychic experiences.

"Anna put them in touch with Linda. Her gift is to be able to reunite loved ones who are separated by physical death. She can facilitate conversations between people on both sides. Through her, the couple was able to learn that they were in no way responsible for their daughter's death. Actually, she didn't mean to kill herself, just dull the pain of a break-up with her boyfriend. It was an accidental overdose."

"Tragic. But I see that it must've been a relief to know they hadn't somehow failed their daughter. It sounds so crazy, though…"

"Which part?"

"Having conversations with people who've died."

"That's why we can't advertise the clinical services we provide. There's no accrediting agency in the world who would license us for that. We don't have any doctors on staff, or certified therapists. We don't prescribe any medication, or formulate treatment plans. You either believe or you don't…or you're so desperate that anything is better than what you're going through."

Bella recognized the truth in everything Rick said. She wasn't sure what prompted her, but she asked what felt like a final question.

"Rick, is there anything else that I don't know about my

grandmother and her craft? Anything? Maybe it's insignificant to you, but would be key in my decision making?"

"Like what?"

"I wouldn't even know."

"The glasses would give you those answers, not me."

"Glasses? Do you mean eyeglasses or drinking glasses?"

Rick dropped his fork. It made a clank that drew the glances of those at surrounding tables. He couldn't believe it. She didn't even know about the glasses!

"Sorry," he flushed with embarrassment. "You really *don't* know anything about your grandmother do you?"

"I told you I only met her twice. The first time I was four years old and once more when I was ten. No I didn't know her." Bella was getting aggravated.

"Finish up. Let's go." Rick was getting anxious.

"I'll just get a box."

"That'd be good."

"Where are we going in such a hurry?" Bella didn't understand the big rush. She guessed that according to Rick, she didn't understand much at all.

"To get the glasses." Rick was in a hurry. "Where are they?"

"What? I just now found out about them. How would I know where they are?"

Rick sat in the car counting to ten. He could feel his face flush as he tried to suppress his emotion.

"Look, Rick…" Bella began, "I know you think I've done something wrong again. I don't know what that is, but I'm sorry to keep upsetting you."

"I'm not upset with you, Bella, I'm upset with Anna. How could she bring you here amidst all that we've spent years building and dreaming about and not fill you in on everything? How thoughtless of her to subject you to all this without the information and education to help you make an informed decision! And how irresponsible she was to leave the clinic in such a precarious position. I'm pissed!"

Bella sat in the car for a moment and let him calm down. She began eating her lunch with her fingers. Luckily it was the other half of her sandwich and some chips.

"Gosh, Bella...I just keep dragging you over the coals. Please forgive me for not even allowing you to finish your lunch before I exploded. I'm having trouble keeping my emotions in check since Anna died. I don't really know what's expected of me, or what my future holds."

"It's unanimous, then," she uttered with a mouth full of food. "But for the record, I'm not pissed. Where do you think we'll find the glasses?"

"Knowing Anna, they're probably in her purse."

"I know right where that is, at home."

"Funny, how you call it home..."

"For now, it's as close as I come."

Rick and Bella went back to the estate. Bella ran up the steps two at a time to get the purse. She found a tiny glass case and opened it. There were a pair of reading glasses inside.

"Well, where do we look next?"

"Nowhere. Put them on.'"

Bella put them on. Surprisingly, she could see clearly out of them. Rick then instructed her to touch the little metal piece near the left hinge. Suddenly, Bella could read his thoughts.

"Just think the instructions."

"Can you read my thoughts now?" Rick wasn't speaking, but Bella knew his question. She didn't hear his voice or anything, she just knew.

"Yes."

"This puts you on even playing ground with anybody in your presence. These glasses were designed by your grandmother as a result of her beliefs about frequencies and energy transfer. She believed, and these glasses prove, that thoughts also travel on frequencies. If we can tune in, we can hear them." Rick wasn't speaking this explanation, but she could hear his thoughts.

"Respond to me in words, Bella. I can't hear your thoughts. The glasses are one way. The bands, however, work both ways."

Bella took the glasses off and laid them on the counter. How do these work, exactly?"

"Only Anna knows that."

"Do you think she ever cheated anybody, or listened in without permission?"

"I couldn't say. But listen, Bella, I have to get back to work. I have a stack of stuff on my desk that I want to get through today."

"Okay. Let's go."

Bella grabbed the glasses and put them back in the case. She wasn't sure whether or not it was a good idea to carry them around, so she would put them inside the case with the bands when she got back to clinic. They would be well out of sight and out of reach for those who shouldn't be concerned about them.

Bella drifted into thoughts of Gran as a young woman. If she had the glasses then, it's no wonder she made a mint as a fortune teller. She did have a gift, but not a psychic one. Anna Neusa inherited a love of science. But that didn't account for her ability to communicate with Bella today, months after she left this life. Could leaving this life have a completely different meaning? Where did one go? Instead of feeling that she had a greater understanding, she just had more questions.

"Listen, Rick, I'm not going to stay at the clinic this afternoon. I have a meeting with a young novelist about his book. I'd like to get a key to Gran's office. I want' to put the glasses in the secure display case, if that's alright."

"Use my key today and make yourself one. I'll see you tomorrow then."

"Great, thanks."

Bella passed Allen in the hall as she came in. He was leaving. She waved. Bella thought about the strange string of events surrounding Allen. First they meet on the plane, where she makes a fool of herself. Then she comes to the clinic as the owner, and he works here. He actually knew more about her grandmother than Bella did. She couldn't have made a path to that. Fate had its twists, she thought!

"Sure does!" Carol smiled and waved to her as she was leaving. Bella smiled back. She was getting used to this psychic thought-reading thing.

Bella picked a last row parking spot at the Barnes and Noble in Scottsdale. She was right on time. The prospective client promised to wear a camouflage baseball cap and stand near the coffee counter with his manuscript in his hand. He would be easy to spot. *G.I. Issue*, his pen name, was clever, but a bit too clever for her liking.

"It can't be!" Bella said out loud as she walked toward the counter. "Allen?"

"Bella! What are you doing here?" He was just as surprised.

"I'm meeting you." They both stood stark still for a few moments before Bella pulled out her wallet. She could NOT have conjured this. It was almost too creepy for words.

"Close your mouth. What would you like?"

"Tall house blend, room for cream," he told the barista.

"Make it two, please."

Allen picked a table for four, even though they were alone. His manuscript was bulky and he was sure that Bella had stuff of her own. Talk about the surprise of his life! How many ways had fate conspired to bring them together? If ever he doubted that there was some organizing force in the universe, today he was certain of it.

After they got settled, there was an awkward moment. So Bella just started with talk of that.

"It's amazing how many times we've crossed paths under different circumstances, isn't it, Allen?"

"It's amazing! I was just thinking that myself. So you'll be going back to St. Louis when Anna's things are all sorted out?"

"Yes. I'm moving right along. This week my progress at the estate has slowed down as I began work at the clinic, but I have hopes to be back home within two months."

"I wish you well on that. If you need help, just ask."

"I will. Now…for the business at hand. G.I. Issue? Where did that come from, and how attached to it are you?" They both started laughing. "Tell me when and why you wrote this, and if you've written any other books like it."

Allen and Bella spent the whole afternoon talking about his experiences in Iraq. Although the book was written solely from Allen's perspective, it was based on truth. It was the only book he'd written, but he had an idea for a series he might call The Soldier Series or something like that, talking about conditions in Iraq. Unlike similar books Bella had read, Allen's examined issues GIs faced every day in the war zone, from every perspective. They looked at what the soldiers were sent there to do, how the people of the United States viewed that, how the Iraqi government viewed their presence, how much the terrorist factions hated them, and about how the people who lived there felt about the American presence in their home towns. It was compelling and very well done. It spoke from the hearts of all parties honestly.

Allen and Bella talked about who the audience would be for his book, and if he had ideas about how to market it. They talked about the potential for a synopsis for The Soldier Series, and then got down to the brass tacks of actually publishing the book. Bella didn't have an offer, but she did have interest, and thought he had a pretty good chance to bring this book to market. By the end of the meeting, Bella was Allen's favorite person in the world.

"Allen, how do you feel about keeping this completely private, just between us? I'm not offering anything at this point, but I am seriously considering it."

"Bella, you have my word on it, but…"

"Out with it."

"But you're in a house full of psychics there. One thought of it and…"

"I see. Well, I guess there's no harm in folks knowing you're a damn good writer, GI Issue!"

"You know…the more you say that name, the less I like it."

"Good." She winked at him. "I'd like to book another appointment with you in a week to talk over any questions that might come up. Why did you want to meet here in Scottsdale?"

"I live a few blocks from here."

"Would you consider meeting at Anna's estate? And would you object to some face time with my staff? They're very interested in your work. Actually, they not only brought it to my attention, they forced me to read it right away. They'd be tickled to talk to you about it."

"I'd love it. Anything that'll move the project ahead is okay with me."

"Great! Then we're done for today. I'll be in touch."

"Bella…"

"Yes?"

"Did you like it? Did *you* like my book?"

"I stayed up all night reading it. I couldn't put it down." She smiled and took possession of his manuscript. Allen was smiling ear to ear.

As Bella was leaving, she could see Allen pick up his phone. There was someone special he wanted to share his news with.

Chapter 10

Bella turned down her street, but at the last minute, drove into Bruce's driveway instead of hers. There was no answer at the door. She walked around back to the woodshop and looked in the window. The sound of the saw was very loud. He was wearing ear protection. Time seemed to disappear as she stood watching him work at his craft. His moves were smooth, calculated and repetitive. It took skill, patience and an artist's eye to bring the wood to life.

Finally, Bruce caught a glimpse of her through the window. He took off his respirator and ear protection, set them on the drafting table, brushed off the sawdust and headed for the door.

"You spying on me, lady?"

"How else will I get your trade secrets?"

He stepped outside. There was dust in the air in the shop. Bruce was surprised to see her. After his last visit, when she was so sharp with him, he'd been keeping his distance. He forgot how attractive she was.

"Dinner plans?" Bella felt like cooking.

"Nope. You cooking?"

"Yep. One hour enough time for you to finish?"

"Perfect. I'll bring the wine."

"Bathing suit optional!" Bella flirted as she walked away.

There was big news to discuss with Bruce. She was really excited about Allen's book. And Allen was right, it would be hard to keep their secret between them with all the clairvoyants in the clinic. Could she somehow prevent others from reading her thoughts? Bella knew she had telepathic abilities, but up to this point, she didn't know how to turn them on or off. The only time she had actually been able to read a thought was with Kendra. And it was probably more accurate to say she saw a horrible memory. Perhaps she could learn more from the people in clinic. As for Allen's book, in a week they'd probably be bringing forward an offer, and secrecy wouldn't be an issue.

That might be the perfect time to bring up her idea about the patients writing an anthology to help support the work. The only wrench in the works was the cloak of anonymity that surrounded the clinic. The idea would have to evolve. Bella laughed at herself for the thought that to get Rick Baker's true opinion, she'd have to wear Gran's glasses to the discussion.

Bella heard the doorbell. This evening Bruce came over in khaki shorts, a polo shirt and deck shoes. What a hunk! Bella felt under dressed, wearing her navy blue one piece, tea length white handkerchief skirt and navy flip flops. Why did she care if she were underdressed anyway? They'd be in the pool in an hour.

"I have things set up in the pool house tonight, Bruce. I just came up to get desert." Bella finished cleaning the strawberries. Since Bruce had a free hand, Bella handed him the berries. She got the whipped cream from the frig, stacked a baggie of pecan halves on top of it, then grabbed the French vanilla ice cream in the other hand. Out the back door they went.

Bruce followed Bella, admiring the view. The navy swimsuit was backless. Her skin was smooth and lightly tanned. The curves of her back met in a valley in the middle, which wandered all the way down to her tailbone. Even though he couldn't see it, he'd seen it before. Her hips swayed gently as she walked across the grass, causing her skirt to swing rhythmically, like a pendulum. He could match her rhythms easily. Lingering in that thought, Bruce noticed his khaki's getting tight. She was sexy, and he had the whole evening with her. Then it occurred to him that she might be able to read his thoughts. He got embarrassed and snapped out of his fantasy.

"You're awfully quiet tonight." She walked through the patio door and put the ice cream in the freezer. Bella grabbed the berries and the wine and put them away, too.

"We have a few minutes before dinner. Would you like to take a swim?"

"Sure." Bruce noticed that Bella had set a table inside. On it, was a white table cloth, linen napkins, chargers, fine china, and wine glasses. The centerpiece was a single candle. Beside it, rested the lighter. Had she planned a romantic evening? It had been so long since he's participated in one of those that he wondered if he remembered how. But, oh, his body remembered.

"It's too hot to eat outside today. The pool's probably like bathwater. Do you think I should put the hose in it and pump in some cold water? Maybe we could swim after dinner."

Bruce was trying real hard not to want her so much. He was so uncomfortable in his shorts that he had to adjust himself. He hoped she wasn't looking.

"Either way."

Bella went out and put the hose in. She dipped her foot in, and found the water tepid, but not warm.

"Actually, the water's perfect, Bruce. Join me."

"Do you need me to check the grill or anything?"

"Nope. Dinner's done. It's warming in the roaster. We can eat whenever we're ready."

"Great." Bruce couldn't remember where he left his trunks. There was no blood left in his head. He couldn't go commando like this. It would give things away too quickly.

"I hung your trunks on the paddle in the bathroom."

"Thanks."

Bella grabbed the net to make a quick sweep of the pool. On the stairs, just below the water, were two stones.

'What are these, Gran?' Bella thought the question.

"The bloodstone releases body blockages, and the Herkimer Diamond enhances natural energies."

'Do you think I need help?' She was being playful.

"Couldn't hurt! I'm leaving you now. Niko and I have a science date tonight."

'Thanks, Gran.'

Bruce was standing in the glass watching her, and noticed her making motions and focusing her thoughts.

"Is there anybody else here with us?" Bruce's excitement deflated at the thought of Anna watching them.

"Nope. She just left. But not before she explained the energy she put in the pool."

"And what might that be?" He lifted the stones out of the water.

"The bloodstone, to release body blockages, and the Herkimer Diamond, to enhance natural energies."

"Playing matchmaker, eh? Thanks, Anna!" He smiled widely, looking at Bella to see if she was open to it. He couldn't tell.

Bella walked over to the lounger and took off her flip flops. She put her thumbs into the waist band of her skirt and slowly came out of it. Bruce watched as the skirt slid down over her hips, hugging her thighs, and finally falling to the ground. When she bent over to pick them up, and he saw her breasts fall forward in the suit, he throbbed. His need transformed from a dull ache to a bursting with a desire to take her right there.

Bella walked over to the steps. The energy Gran put into the pool was working. The minute her feet touched the water, she had the urge to take off her suit. Starting with the shoulder straps, Bella slowly removed it, teasing Bruce.

"You gonna use that thing?" Bella could see Bruce's desire matching her own.

He literally reached up and pulled her down on top of him. When they came up from under water, he kissed her open mouth. In the hour that followed, the pool and their bodies worked a magic worth remembering. When they finally came up for air, Bella made a note to keep those stones nearby for next time. She didn't want to pull apart from him. They were wrapped around each other like a couple of high school kids. That was the nice thing about water, buoyancy!

Bruce's hands were all over her again, touching every inch of her. She could feel his softness inside her becoming tighter, and its rhythm beginning again, gently, longingly calling her back. There was no need to bother about dinner. Her hunger wasn't for food.

"Bruce…"

"Bella…"

The moon was high in the sky before they decided on dinner.

Bruce was star struck, admiring the beautiful brunette sitting across the table from him. Although he could hear every word she said, he was more focused on the light in her eyes, the smile on her face, the curve of her chin, and that neck, that long, luscious, kissable neck.

"And then the pope's gay lover burned down the Vatican" Bella said. Just as she thought, Bruce wasn't listening. He was looking at her with desiring eyes. Without talking, she got up, went over, and sat on his lap. She lifted his face and kissed him slowly. They could talk later.

"Bruce, you know I'm leaving in two months, right?"

"No strings attached."

"What would you call this then?" Bella really wanted to know. All of her ideas and thoughts about life were changing.

"Call it whatever you want." Bruce was casual. He didn't really care.

"What would *you* call it?"

"Friends?"

"No."

"Friends, with benefits?"

"Yes. I like that. Friends with benefits. No strings attached." Bella liked that very much.

"Ready for desert?"

"At your service, ma'am," Bruce offered playfully.

"I meant strawberry sundaes, goofy!"

"Oh, sure…" he played with her. It was fun.

As they ate their ice cream, Bella told Bruce about Allen. She talked on and on about every little detail of her meeting with him, and how he asked her if she liked his book.

"I liked it, too. It needs a little work, but I couldn't put it down."

"You read it?" Bella was caught off guard. How did he get it? Was there another magical crisscross in the universal fabric or something?

"You left it by the pool, so I picked it up. Couldn't put it down." He was talking with his mouth full.

"I also had an idea, even before Allen, about an anthology written by the people helped in the clinic. I thought it would be powerful,"

"And profitable?"

"What?" Bella was surprised at his condescending tone when he interrupted her.

"Profitable."

"What does that mean?"

"Nothing, go on."

"NO!" Bella was pissed. "You started it, now finish it."

"You want to profit from the misfortune of others?"

"You think I'd…Please leave."

"What?"

"Leave." Bella grabbed his half-full bowl right out from under his nose. She yanked the spoon out of his hand and went inside.

"A spade is a spade, Bella, even if it comes in a pretty package."

"Get out! NOW!" Bella was screaming at the top of her lungs. As he walked away, Bella was throwing his clothes in the grass behind him.

"Take your stuff with you. Oh…and get your own pool if you want to swim. This pool is now closed to the public!"

As Bruce walked home, he knew there wasn't a person within two miles who didn't hear her screaming. She had quite a temper!

Bella stormed around the pool house kitchen tidying up after their evening together. What kind of Neanderthal would think she wanted to make money off of sick people? He hadn't even let her finish her idea. But...she couldn't help but wonder what others would think after Bruce's reaction. Maybe it wasn't such a good idea after all. Well, she didn't have to settle it tonight.

Bella walked out to the pool and picked up the towels. She sat down in the lounger and cried. It had been one of the most romantic nights of her life. Why did she have to bring up business? Why couldn't she be like other women and just dote on the guy she was with, feeding his ego with how well he performed? That felt bitter. It wasn't a performance. They both had a great time. It was nice. No...more than nice.

"I can't let the night end like this." Bruce was standing at the end of the pool deck. "I'm here to let you throw something at me, or shout me down, or call me names, but...I won't go home without patching things up. That's my final answer."

Bella didn't know whether to laugh or cry.

"I shouldn't have talked business tonight. It's my fault. I'm sorry. But I can't believe you think I would actually exploit the tribulations of heroes and then accept money for it. I didn't know your opinion of me was so low."

"I have a very high opinion of you, Bella, the highest. But publishing a book written by clinic patients? Come on!"

Bella and Bruce went toe-to-toe in a heated discussion about the pros and cons of Bella's idea. They couldn't come to an agreement. They ended their quarrel when Bella discovered that Bruce was ultra-sensitive because he was once a patient there. And Bruce surrendered his fury when he realized that Bella had never been through anything like what the patients at the clinic had been through. She couldn't understand how important privacy and anonymity was. Nobody could, if they hadn't received benefit there. It was a draw.

"Well…I wish I could say I felt better…or that I agree with you…or that I've changed my mind…but the best I can do is…I'll think about it."

"Fair enough. I'll do the same. Good night, Bella, you sexy, bull-headed thing."

"Good night, Bruce."

Bella wanted to smile, but she didn't feel it. She felt inner turmoil, discord. Yet another decision she would have to make! If the anthology was out, was there another source of revenue for the clinic? With the managing company recommending that the endowment remain untouched for at least two consecutive years to recover from the market drop, how would she come up with the clinic's expense money? She couldn't. What would happen if she didn't accept their recommendation? It felt like she was back to square one. Speaking of square one, Bella had a house full of belongings to sort through.

It was 2 a.m. and she was wide awake. Well, it was Friday night and she could sleep whenever she wanted the next two days. It would be wise to do as much as possible this weekend. Next weekend the kids would be here. After she got through Gran's things, she could let the kids sort through them and ship them home. The rest would be liquidated before she left.

The attic wasn't as hot as Bella thought it might be. She decided to start with the boxes just at the top of the stairs. Her idea to use a fan to blow air conditioning from the hall downstairs into the attic was a good one. She could feel the cool air sitting at the top of the steps. It was a place to start.

Much to her surprise, there wasn't much junk. The things Gran took the time to pack away had value, either sentimental or material. Anna had an eye for fine things. Mom's brief dismissal of Gran, calling her 'a fortune teller' didn't even begin to describe her. She had so many talents, helped so many people, and invented so many things, that she'd amassed a collection of fine, rare, and beautiful belongings. And it couldn't even touch the friendships and collaborations she'd forged in the meantime. What was Mom so afraid of?

"Of power beyond measure, Bella." It was Gran.

"That's cryptic! What does it mean?" Bella was being sarcastic and mean spirited.

"Don't take your anger at yourself out on me. I don't deserve it. You're upset about what happened with Bruce."

"I thought you were leaving! Were you spying on us?"

"I did leave. But I am looking into your thoughts right now. Do you have feelings for him?"

"Just friends."

"I see. And do friends treat each other this way?"

"Friends have disagreements, yes."

"And then what?"

"And then they get over it."

"And what if one friend completely disregards the others opinion, and moves forward in a direction that causes ethical conflict in the other?"

"Then they part ways, Gran."

"I see. Is that what you want? To part ways?"

"I'm leaving soon, anyway, Gran. Best not to get too close."

"You know best." And with that, Gran was gone. It was funny how Bella was getting good at knowing when she was around. She could sense her presence somehow, once she heard from her. Was that how the gift worked, did one or the other allow or disallow the connection?

After unpacking the boxes on top, it was time for Bella to dig into the cedar chest. It was locked. Bella looked at the lock closely. She got up, went down to the teapot in the dining room, and brought back the small key. It fit. She removed the lock, leaving the key in it, so she could keep track of it. Bella opened the lid and removed the newspaper that was laid across the top of the contents.

The trunk was filled with memorabilia. At first glance, it appeared to be a treasure chest. There were items from as far back as the mid nineteenth century. She would never part with these. By the looks of some of them, her grandmother carried them across the ocean when she came.

Wrapped in a folded piece of white silk, were a set of six silver spoons. There was an antique photo of a beautiful woman in a locking photo case made of old leather. Bella wondered if it was her great grandmother. There was a crocheted doily, yellowed with age. Bella's mom had one something like it. She said her grandmother made it for her when she got married. Maybe Great Grandma had made this one, too. Bella worked her way through to the bottom of the chest, wiping her tears with her filthy hands. Some of these items were over 150 years old. They were her legacy. These were real life items used by the women of her bloodline, connections to her past.

Then Bella found a wooden box in the bottom. It looked like a small bible case. She opened it. There, displayed on red velvet was a pearl necklace. The clasp was unlike any that Bella had ever seen. It had a safety catch. There were three strands of pearls attached on it. They were gorgeous. Bella always loved pearls. The ring her mother left her when she died would look stunning with these. Bella touched every single pearl, knowing that the oils from her skin would add luster to them. How many of her ancestors had worn these?

Finally, she was interrupted by a text. She put the pearls back in the box, put everything carefully back in the trunk, and locked it. She took the key and put it back in the teapot. As she did, the doorbell rang.

"Bruce!" He'd caught her completely off guard.

"You look like you've just seen a ghost." Her face was black and smudged. She looked like she'd been crying. Her clothes were dirty and she had dust up to her elbows.

"Have you been cleaning the chimney or something?" He started to laugh.

Bella stepped back and looked at herself in the sitting room mirror. She burst out laughing.

"Coffee?" Bella stood aside, opening the door wide.

"I brought Asiago cheese bagels and pineapple cream cheese. Have you been up all night?"

"Yum! Yes." She was making coffee and getting out some saucers and knives.

"I hope you washed your hands first!" he teased. "Have you been crying all night?"

"Yes."

"I'm so sorry, Bella."

"No, Bruce. I wasn't crying over our difference of opinion, I was crying because I found a cedar chest full of treasures that must be every bit of 150 years old. I believe they belonged to my great grandmother, grandmother, and Mom. It's amazing how alike we all are. We like a lot of the same things. I wondered if my abilities would kick in when I handled the stuff, like when I touched Kendra, but nothing."

Bruce walked over to the sink, wet a couple of paper towels and began wiping her smudged face. It made the tears flow once again. He put his bent finger under her chin, tilted her head up, and kissed her full on the mouth.

She finally pulled away, cleared her throat and took the dishes to the table. Pouring two cups of coffee, she walked over and sat down.

"Bring some napkins, will ya?"

"Is that all you have to say?" Bruce was playing with her.

"Read my thoughts." That was all she had to say.

They ate quietly for a few minutes. Neither of them mentioned anything, good or bad, about the night before. Bella's mind was still on the treasures in the chest.

"You know, some of the keepsakes I looked at came from 'the old country,' as Mom called it. I can't imagine what that must've been like. My grandfather came over at age 18, in 1902. That took guts! He later sponsored my grandmother and great grandmother. Can you imagine leaving everyone you love and everything you know to come to a place you have no idea about? And think about the long, rough trip across the ocean. Can you imagine?"

"Nope. I get motion sickness."

"Me, too. Can you imagine sitting below deck in a storm on the high seas?"

"I'd be puking on everybody!" They both laughed, but realized it was no laughing matter.

"I'm afraid I didn't get very far in the sorting. It seems like I want to keep most of what I find. Even though I didn't know my grandmother, these things feel precious. They have meaning for me…a connection to my heritage. Silly…"

"Not at all. But I think you have to reach maturity before you can appreciate it."

"Agreed. Sounds old though…the age of maturity." They both laughed.

"Take my word for it…it doesn't look old. You look great. About last night…"

"Look, Bruce, I'm leaving soon, and…"

"No. Stop. I'm leaving now. I don't want to hear another thing you have to say." Bruce got up, picked up his bagel, and walked to the door waving.

What a strange bird. Bella wasn't sure why he would try to run from the truth, but it wouldn't change anything, whether she said it or not. She didn't want to lead him on because she wasn't staying. Fun is fun, and then it's done.

Bella went back up into the attic. She loved so many of the odds and ends stored up there. It felt like it used to when the kids were small. Every Christmas they would go through the kids' toys and put the ones they didn't play with much down in the basement. Then the toys in the basement made their way out to the garage. Then the toys on the garage floor would go up to the garage attic and the toys in the attic would go to Good Will. Bella felt that going on here. When she got home she would have to make room for this stuff. She smiled happily.

Remembering that she hadn't slept all night, she went down for another cup of coffee. It was Saturday, and a week from today the kids would be here. The thought filled her with joy. Sitting completely still, her mind drifted from Kyle's to Maddie's antics. They were so precious in their little kid worlds. Their parents wanted them to grow up fast, and Bella wished they'd stay this age a little longer.

Getting nowhere fast, Bella decided to pack it up and have some fun. She Googled some touristy spots, but decided that it was too warm for that. Suddenly, the thought of spending time in the jewelry studio seemed attractive. Bella was in the library before she even realized it. Looking through the section next to Tesla, she found what she was after. Because she knew so little about gemstones, she would use the reference manual. Who knew, she might design a powerful piece of her own!

Donned in shorts, swim top and flip flops, she practically ran to the studio. She was surprised at how hot it was in the closed up house. Before hunting for the thermostat, she opened the windows upstairs to let out the hot air. Bruce was working in the shop. Bella felt like a peeping Tom, looking in when he wasn't aware of it. Drifting, she could feel her body responding to him. He was an attentive playmate. After lingering a minute, she shrugged him off and walked over to the drafting board. What should she do first? Running her hands over the raw stones, Bella made her selections. After collecting a handful, she went back to the drafting table.

Laying the stones apart on the table, she began to study the shapes. Designing the mountings might be tricky the first time. She rearranged the stones in rows, columns, a circle…and deciding where each stone would rest, finally satisfied herself. Now she would need to figure out how to mount them.

Walking over to the metals, she noticed a book.

"I better make sure about the power of the stones I'm mounting." She giggled at the thought of creating a love-potient necklace and having every man she met follow her around.

Bruce was staring at her. Man, she was pretty. He couldn't remember ever meeting such a talented woman. This girl had skills. And now she would try her hand at jewelry design. Like Anna, she was good at everything she did. He'd like to get closer to her, but she wouldn't allow it. She kept him at a distance, but a fun distance. He'd like to get his hands on her grandmother's glasses and see what was behind the wall. But part of the thrill was the chase.

Bella walked through the studio hunting for mountings. Along the west wall was a large chifferobe. Behind the big doors were a set of small narrow drawers. Inside were mountings of every shape and size. Bella examined every one. There were two she really liked. One was shaped like a bunch of grapes and the other like leaves and a vine. She took them both over to the drafting table and arranged the stones in various ways in each. As she worked with them, names came to mind. As the names appeared, ideas for other pieces poured in. Before she knew it, the drafting table was covered with sketches of original designs for the girls.

Back at the drawing board, Bella began to intuit stones for the boys. After selecting a handful, she went to the reference and read about the powers within each one. Finding that her selections seemed to fit not only the idea for the piece, but the balance and benefit she wished for each of her family members, she felt excitement course through her veins. It was as if her blood was on fire. If there was music, she'd be dancing.

"Think it. Want it." She heard Gran's prompt.

"Stereo." The power of thought was remarkable. She walked around until she saw it. It was on the lower level behind the counter. Bella found a station she liked. The music was jazzy and upbeat. She turned it up just enough to create a mood, but not loud enough that she couldn't concentrate.

"Thanks, Gran." Bella bounced up the stairs and back to her designs.

For Maddie, her oldest granddaughter, wait a minute…oldest? She only had one. Or did she?

"That's right," Gran whispered in her ear. "Make two. There's a surprise."

Maddie's was a one year old sized iolite. The small polished stone was a translucent shade of violet. This stone enabled untapped powers to emerge. If it was true that 'the gift' passed to the oldest granddaughter, it would be awakening within her. Or maybe the gift was already awake and she just didn't know how to see it. Bella welcomed the possibility.

As the ideas poured in, Bella reconsidered the thought of a necklace for Maddie. Perhaps a bracelet would be more practical for a girl her size. If she made bracelets, she could design one for Kyle, too. She'd seen boys wearing braided hemp bracelets. Maybe she could find a way to weave a stone into hemp for her tiny toddling grandson. Labradorite popped into Bella's mind. Bella walked around the tables, picture in hand, until she found just the perfect size piece for a tiny bracelet. It was a beautiful blue that seemed brighter in the middle. It was as if the stone hugged the joy inside itself. Corny, Bella thought.

"So this is the wizard stone, huh, Gran?"

"Yes. Kyle is a wizard of the heart."

"Yes, Gran, he is. How did you know?"

"The way I knew you."

"The gift?"

"Yes."

"I'm thinking of the moonstone for Andrea, since it's the wish-granting stone."

"She has her wish already, although she doesn't know it yet. That one's for Kate."

"Okay. Then turquoise. With two kids she'll need balance and peace."

"Perfect choice."

"Why don't you make rings for Derek and Evan?"

"Great idea." Bella danced around a while longer selecting stones for their rings.

"I think azurite, the stone of infinite possibility for Evan, and snow-flake obsidian for Derek, to keep him calm, cool and collected." Azurite was blue, and Bella liked it better in the silver mount. The snowflake obsidian was beautiful in both gold and silver. The black was offset by either metal. But Bella liked the white snowflakes against the silver her-self. These were great choices."

"Maddie's gifts will be enhanced by the gemstones. The energies will converge and create a world of magic for all of us."

"Cryptic, Gran, but believable." Bella thought about how she felt walking around the tables, feeling limitless among the countless choices. She was free to design whatever she conceived. The thought made her feel like a capable and powerful creator. Her body was in tune, singing and dancing. Why not Maddie, too?

"Gran, what happened between you and Mom?"

"Nothing, as far as I know, but you can ask your mother."

"How, Gran?"

"Ask Linda for help. She's waiting for you."

"I will." The idea that she could actually communicate with her moth-er on the other side blew Bella's mind. But, since arriving in Phoenix, she found cause to rethink things daily. Perhaps she needed the azurite herself, to release her limiting ideas. She walked over to the table of cut stones and picked one up. It was small enough to carry and big enough to easily keep track of.

"Knock knock…" Oh, this was just too much. It was Linda. Psychic synchronicity blew her away!

"Hey, Linda!"

"Nice designs! You've got Anna's gift."

"You think so?"

"Well, Anna's *and* Ann's."

"Mom's?'

"Yep. She says to take another look at her ring collection. Although she didn't make her rings, she has stones of all kinds. She says to look at the meaning of pearls, your favorite."

"Okay. Hi, Mom! Love you!"

"She says 'hi, love you, too."

Bella took the book over to the stairs. She sat down, leaned against the wall, stretched out her legs and began to read. Pearls are the oldest known gems. They've been considered the most precious for centuries. Bella always thought gemstones were of the earth, unlike pearls, which come from living creatures. They are said to have the power to soothe, restore peacefulness, and lift spirits. Bella always felt great wearing them, and had heard they were symbols of beauty and dignity.

"Interesting, isn't it?"

"Yes. I've often imagined what it would be like to be snorkeling along, find an oyster, open it and find a pearl. That would be the discovery of a lifetime."

"Or…you can just hang out where people sell pearls." Bella laughed at Gran's humor.

"So it's the actual pearl, Gran, and not the adventure that calls your name."

"It all calls my name. But I like simple and easy now. It's the stage of life I'm in."

"That's interesting, Gran…stage of life. I think of it more like after life."

"It's all life, no matter what you call it. Death feels like the end for some and the beginning for others. You get to choose what you want to think and experience."

Bella didn't say anything. She was digesting Gran's ideas and insights. Bella liked what Anna had done with the choices she made. When things fell apart with her daughter she could've buried her head in the sand and lived a different life. But she chose to develop herself and help others do the same and ended up with a big life. Bella admired that. It took what her mom called 'gumption.' And to think it possible to start fresh at something new, or continue doing what you love from another side of life was rather appealing.

"Gran, are you and Mom all patched up?"

"Do you mean are we in relationship the way you'd always wished we would be?"

Bella thought about how peculiar that question sounded. It was exactly what she wanted to know, though. To her, mothers and daughters called each other on the phone, visited each other and were close. But thinking it over, that's what being close looked like to Bella, but it wasn't the only picture of closeness.

"What do you mean?"

"Well, you just *assumed* we weren't close because you didn't see the picture you were used to. Because you couldn't see evidence of closeness that you could recognize, you assumed it was missing. Our relationship didn't fit your picture. Right?"

"Right. Wait a minute…are you saying that you and Mom have been close through the years, but I didn't know it?"

"Yes."

"But, how? Oh, I get it, telepathically! WOW! Talk about a twisted thought…" Bella was almost in a coma trying to recreate the truth about her life. So Mom and Gran were close, communicating regularly with thoughts and images sent through invisible energetic means. Bella's beliefs about something horrible driving an irreconcilable wedge between them were false. She built a completely different relationship in her mind. But the truth was that it was all in *her* mind.

"So Mom knew…and you knew…everything."

"Yes, we were very close."

"How could I have missed that?"

"Did you ever ask about it?"

"No…I just assumed it was a sore subject, so I…"

"I see."

Bella slumped back against the wall feeling disconnected from her life, her beliefs, and her ability to understand things that weren't seen. She felt like an imposter living in a completely different story than the one Mom and Gran were in. Talk about a psychic adjustment!

"Your mom says she always wondered why you didn't ask about your grandmother. She assumed that since you didn't really know her, she was insignificant in your life." Linda was speaking for Bella's mom, who Bella was unable to hear.

"We've made a ton of bad assumptions between us, Mom."

"She's asking if the two of you could start fresh."

"Not necessary. I loved everything about you, Mom. This was just my misunderstanding. On that note, since I've been here, I've had questions…so… were you bothered by my psychic abilities? And… why did you hide yours?"

"She wasn't sure you had abilities, unable to send to or receive from you." Linda began explaining. "She did not hide her abilities. As far as she knew, she was only able to communicate with her mother, and grandmother, which she did."

"So you guys never discovered how to make the communication both ways?" Bella was fascinated.

"Anna did, with the help of the glasses." With Linda's help, Bella was beginning to understand things.

"In the meantime, I would send your mother letters, which she needed only to touch, to get my messages. Although she was clearly a transmitter, she could also receive information when she touched something I'd touched. So she sent the letters back unopened, and would respond to what she got from them with energy transfer. We were experimenting." Gran seemed to be able to hear Linda and Bella, and was joining in the conversation.

"What did you find out?"

"She sensed accurately. Now, knowing your gift, I'm rethinking things, considering some type of transformation. I could only receive in my earthly body. Your mom sent only, but was manifesting features of receiving. Then you were born with both. It's as if, during her lifetime, something began to activate both features, and with you it became fully enabled. Does that make sense?"

"Yes!" Bella got it! "But how? And, why did you keep it a secret?"

"She says nobody ever actually asked her!" Linda cracked up again.

"What did you do about others hearing your thoughts? Do you think others can hear me, too?" If Bella got the gift, she needed to know.

"Cloaking." Bella heard Gran's and Linda's voices respond at the same time.

"How does that work?"

"Simple intention," Linda answered her.

"So if I want everything to be private, I must have the presence of mind to check myself, and consciously choose to close myself off from transmitting?"

"You can send and receive?" Ann wanted to know.

"I think so. You and Gran can hear me, but I can only hear Gran. If I had both, and you are a transmitter, why can't I hear you without Linda being present? "

"She doesn't know, but she'd like to."

"Bella could feel the tears washing away her ideas that she would never talk to her mother again. They'd spoken every day for as long as she could remember. It was nice to know that with Linda's help she could talk to her again."

"So how often can I talk to you both?"

"Whenever we're not cloaked."

"Mom, does Linda have continuous access to you?"

"No, I don't. I don't know what has to happen for me to be able to channel her, but it's not all the time. I heard her today for the first time. She found me, not the other way around." Linda looked puzzled.

"How'd you find Linda, Mom?"

"Mom, she says."

Bella got frightened that this might be the only time she could talk to her.

"That's a false belief, Bella. We're connected...always." Bella felt the relief wash over her like spring rain.

"Your mom says to lay down your fear and live fully, that you'll always be together."

"Love you, Mom. Love you, Gran."

"Love you, too."

Bella knew she was loved. She wasn't sure how long she sat there, but by the time she decided to get up, it was hard to move. Exercise was in order. Walking through, she buttoned everything up for the night, turned out all the lights and locked the door. A couple of laps in the pool and she would begin to put the pieces back together again. Humpty Dumpty had a great fall today, but it was just that – great. All was right in her world, maybe for the first time ever.

Walking out she noticed Bruce deep in creative mode across the yard. It was nice to know a neighbor, especially one as open minded as he was. The kinds of stories she told couldn't be repeated to just anybody.

This time when Bella went inside, she looked around with different eyes. She looked with the eyes of a granddaughter who was cherished. When she looked at the photos that stood on tables and hung on the walls, she saw them differently. Suddenly, although nothing else changed, the people became family, loved ones and friends of family. All at once, she belonged here. Now, the fact that people knew her before she met them wasn't so weird. She had been a source of pride and a beloved grandchild. Gran *had* cared about her and checked on her and asked for pictures. Mom sent her images she could see without holding anything, and Dad sent her snaps she could hang on the wall.

The furnishings were no longer meaningless. All at once, everything there was a gift to her grandmother for her help with something. That gave all these things sentimental value. Now what? Now she had lots more to do before she left. How could she part with her precious family heirlooms?

Bruce was hot, sweaty and full of sawdust. When he ran his fingers through his hair it looked like snowfall. He was grateful for his respirator and safety glasses. He glanced over at the jewelry studio, which was dark and deserted. He needed a break. He pulled out his cell and called Bella.

"Dinner tonight?"

"What do you have in mind?"

"I don't know…something spicy with sangria… or margaritas?" Bruce was thirsty.

"That sounds fantastic. Count me in. But I need an hour to get ready."

"Authentic Mexican. Blue jeans are fine, sombrero is optional," he teased. "Just come over when you're ready to go. It won't take me too long."

"K…see you soon."

Bella sang through her shower. She felt as light as a feather. Shedding her old misperceptions left her floating on air. It was good to release her old emotional baggage.

She tucked her driver's license and credit card in her jean pocket and pulled down the sleeves of her peasant top to expose her shoulders. Gran's pendant and a pair of dangly earrings were the perfect accessories. She tied an orange chiffon scarf around her waist to add color, and fluffed out her blouse. It was a perfect outfit for an authentic Mexican fiesta.

"Ola, Senorita!" Bruce looked her up and down and smiled approvingly.

"Strawberry margaritas, here I come." Bella fanned herself, blushing.

The air was hot and the evening felt electric. Bella enjoyed chatting with Bruce about every little thing. The chips were light and crispy and the salsa wafted of fresh cilantro. Her margarita was frozen, and she sipped it slowly, savoring the tastes of sweet and salty. As the darkness fell, the patio lights cast a seductive glow over Bruce. The mariachi's strolled over to their table and began to play. Bella was enchanted by the sound of the guitars. Although she didn't speak Spanish, she understood. As the song ended and she began to clap, their dinner was served on sizzling platters. Everything was perfect. They ate off and on for two hours, sipping drinks, chatting, and dancing to a band that started some time during dinner.

Walking out to the car, Bruce reached for Bella's hand. She laced her fingers through his. When they got to the truck, he opened the door for her.

"I'd put the top down, but…"

"I wouldn't want to mess my hair up," she joked back. She was delighted.

They walked straight to the pool house. There was a half empty bottle of wine on the bottom shelf. She grabbed a couple of wine glasses and headed outside. Bruce was sitting in a lounger.

"Aren't you getting wet?"

"Don't you know you have to wait an hour after eating?" He was smiling mischievously.

"Does the time start at the beginning or end of the meal? I think I ate for two hours." Bella joked lightheartedly. She felt fabulous. Setting the glasses down on the little table, she poured them each a glass of wine.

The air was hot, the moon was full, and the wine was cool and fruity. What an intoxicating combination. Bella put down her glass, walked over to the pool stairs, looked Bruce right in the eye and started undressing. Undoing every button on her blouse very slowly, she teased him.

Bruce stayed reclined, sipping wine, as he watched Bella strip slowly in front of him. Why was she going so slowly? It seemed like every movement took twice as long as it should. He could feel the blood draining slowly from his head. As she shed her last garment and dipped into the tepid water, he walked to the steps to join her. He slowly teased her, too. By the time he got in the water, he felt as if he were on fire. The silky water washed away the last of the days cares. Suddenly it was a hot, very hot, summer night.

Bruce woke up beside Bella in the pool house. It was Sunday morning. He got up to scrounge some breakfast. There were only drinks in the frig, which meant he had to go up to the main house. It was closer than his place. Wrapping himself in a towel, he went outside. There were his clothes, piled right on top of Bella's in the stripping spot. He could feel himself reliving some of the moments, and had to adjust to put his boxers back on. He couldn't remember ever enjoying the water so much.

Bruce looked for a bag to put a few things in. Now, where would Anna hide a bag? He looked under the sink, in the pantry and in the mud room, but didn't find one. So he got a cookie sheet out from underneath the cabinet near the stove and began stacking it up. Eggs, veggies, cheese, yogurt, bagels and cream cheese. He made a couple of cups of coffee and was on his way.

Bella smelled the veggies sautéing. She got up and put on one of the cover-ups. Searching though the medicine cabinet, she found a couple of Tylenol for her hangover. While Bruce finished cooking, she set the table. The coffee was just what the doctor ordered. Everything was perfect. It was a quiet breakfast. Bella's head needed a minute to clear. Once the coffee kicked in, she'd be ship-shape.

After dishes, Bella went back into the bedroom, slipped out of the cover-up and went back to bed. Bruce kissed her on the forehead and said good-bye. He had to finish his commission. They were expecting him to deliver it tomorrow.

When Bella woke up she showered at the pool house and put the cover-up back on. Tidying up the pool deck, she picked up the clothes and grabbed the wine glasses. Her body was singing. She felt fully alive and lingered in the feeling. She was in tune with every inch of herself, and didn't need a magical gemstone in the pool to energize her. This was her current natural state. How was this possible for a woman her age? She felt like a woman in her twenties.

"Age doesn't really matter, Bella. It's just a number."

"Gran, how long have you been there?"

"Relax, I just got here. But I wish I'd come sooner."

"Can you tell me about cloaking again, please?" She heard Gran laughing with her.

"You have no idea how much yesterday meant to me, talking with you and Mom and clearing up a lifetime of misunderstandings. I can't describe how free I feel."

"You don't have to. Your energy radiates it. Everything feels it… people, objects, elements…"

"Is this what your work is about, Gran?"

"Yes. We are constantly emitting a field of energy. It surrounds us and mingles with outside energies. Every thought we think, every word we speak, every move we make creates."

"Creates what?"

"Experience…energy…a stepping off point…"

"For what?"

"Whatever you're in the process of creating."

"So…you're saying that the thoughts I think effect my energy."

"Exactly. They affect what you say and do. If you put your energy on something negative, it creates anger and dis-ease, which manifests illnesses like stress and headaches. Stress and headaches rob you of creative power. Most people who carry that energy are tired and crabby, and that energy travels with then, effecting everything in its path."

"That makes sense, because when a person feels really good and is creating something attractive, everyone wants to be part of it.

"Exactly. Everything has energy, Bella. People, plants, the air, water, foods, objects, elements… all energy. Since we've all originated from the same cosmic soup, we're connected, each to the other. My work focuses on how to tap into what we all share. With my gift, I'm interested in thoughts and transferring that energy consistently, or consciously."

"Is that what you have in common with Tesla?"

"Niko considers himself a master of hard science. Although his focus is different than mine, he agrees that everything is energy. In fact, it was Niko who introduced me to the endowment benefactor."

"Wow, Gran, just like that?"

"Oh, no, Bella. The man was imprisoned in an insane asylum. Everyone was convinced he was crazy. Niko asked me to visit and assess him. My findings were that he had telepathic abilities and was in communication with someone, a deceased twin. Expanding upon that, I demonstrated the connection of twins to his family. They finally brought him home after years of institutionalization. He'd never married or had any kids. Like me, he realized that there were people all over the world that were trapped in experiences they couldn't explain. When I described what my work was about and what I was trying to do, he found merit in it. He kept in touch with me over the years. And when he died, he left me money to develop my ideas. He also wanted to help others heal from their traumatic experiences."

"What a story!!!"

"Yes, but you can't publish it."

"So, Gran, are you ready to try to bring me up to snuff on your inventions?"

"Which ones?"

"How many are there?"

"Many."

"I'm interested in the glasses and the headbands."

"Okay. We can start there. Those are going to enhance the work at the clinic, which, by the way, you won't actually have to make any decisions about. The work will go on. There is enough money in the endowment to fund the work for the length of your life. In fact, the way that it's set up, it can only be used for the continuation of the work. So…"

"It's really out of my hands."

"Exactly. Unless you can find a better way of applying the same concepts and techniques without the campus itself, it's there to stay."

"That's a relief! Thanks for being so visionary, Gran. So I'm the owner in name only, and I just…"

"You examine the reports from the endowment managers, making decisions about their recommendations, and you examine clinic financials to make sure that resources are being managed properly."

"So really, there's no need to be involved there, right?"

"Wrong. The technology you're interested in only works with you in it."

"Gran…do you know about the genome?"

"Of course."

"Have you ever thought of piggybacking some of those discoveries with yours to allow someone outside our direct bloodline to use the glasses?"

"Of course. Have you thought about the possibility of someone irresponsible using the technology for some other purpose than healing?"

"No. Actually, until now, I've never thought about any of this before. I'll think about it. Gran…you know that my dream is the publishing company, right?"

"I know it's *part* of your dream, yes. But your dreams are much bigger than that now, Bella. We both know that. There's no going back. You're here to stay."

"And what if I don't want to stay?"

"From my point of view, I don't see a reason why you'd have to move. Just make some time available for the work being done here. You seem to be managing your St. Louis business very well right now. I see no conflict there. If your objection is getting back and forth, we could provide transportation to and from Phoenix...say, by private plane."

"What? My own private plane?"

"Well, I don't see you owning a private plane, but a contracted pilot and small plane for designated period of time could be arranged."

"How much time, and who would make the arrangements?"

"Should you choose it, you would be arranging it. The expense would be covered by the endowment. You'd have to develop a regular schedule. You'd have a residence here. In fact, you could even set up a small publishing office right here on the grounds. You could put an office in one of the bedrooms of the main residence, or set up shop in the pool house guest room, or in the studio somewhere. That would be up to you."

"I didn't know there were so many new thoughts to think, Gran. I'll consider it."

"I love you, Bella!"

"I love you, too, Gran."

Bella felt like she might rename this place The Land of Oz! Every inch had a curtain to look behind. Thinking about all the decisions she would have to make made her feel very tired. She needed a nap.

Chapter 11

Time flew by here. This was her fifth Monday in Phoenix. It was just about time for her usual morning meeting. She'd spent most of the night tossing and turning, thinking about what Gran was asking of her. Could she do it, or would she be spreading herself too thin?

Reality was setting in. Before she even knew whether or not she was interested, she needed to go to the clinic and actually do the work. She would give her publishing staff full attention during their meeting, sew up loose ends for the agency, and then turn her focus to work at the clinic.

Bella felt preoccupied during the meeting. Nobody called her on it, but she wondered if they noticed. The package containing Allen's offer was being prepared and sent UPS Overnight Air. She was scheduled to meet with him on Wednesday

Gran's idea about adding an arm of the publishing company in Phoenix was a good one. But before she mentioned any of this to anyone, she would have to give it serious thought. Since last night, she was actually considering it.

Bella needed some exercise. She had nervous energy to burn. Going to Google Maps, she discovered that the clinic was approximately five miles from the house. If the bike she saw in the garage was in good condition, she might just ride it to work today. Surely Gran had a helmet.

Turning the bike upside down on the back lawn, Bella examined and oiled the chain. She checked the brakes and the tires. Everything appeared to be in order.

"Is there anything wrong with this bike, Gran?"

"No. There's a basket for that thing somewhere in the garage, too. Have fun."

"Thanks."

Bella went back into the garage. It wasn't in plain sight, so she climbed up on a ladder and looked in a box on the shelf above her. There it was. It appeared that she could either put the basket on the back or on the handlebars. She thought putting it on the front would make her look like an old granny. But she was apprehensive about loosening the back wheel to rest it behind her seat.

Bruce saw her walking across the lawn, coming in his direction. He put down the wood chisel and opened the door to the shop.

"Hey!" He was glad to see her. "You look like a woman on a mission."

"Do you have a minute to help me put a basket on my bike?"

"Sure."

Bruce grabbed an adjustable wrench and followed her back to the bike. In two minutes he had her all fixed up.

"Where are you going on this thing?"

"Work. I've got a ton of nervous energy, and exercise will help."

"Well, be careful in traffic and make sure to pack a couple of water bottles. It's hot."

"Good advice."

"Okay then. Swim after supper?"

"Sounds great. See you tonight. And Bruce..." he turned around and looked at her. "There's something I want to talk to you about."

"Great. Me, too."

Bella traveled light. She tucked her ID, credit card, keys and iPod into her backpack. She loaded a small soft sided cooler with a couple of bottles of water in the basket. She memorized the first leg of her directions before putting her cell phone in her pocket. It would get her half the distance. By then she would be ready for a drink and directions for the other half of the journey. Bella hopped on and started peddling. She was delighted.

The bike rack was right out front. She didn't have a lock, but didn't feel she needed one. She walked in the clinic carrying her cooler.

"Nice hat." Carol was teasing her. She'd forgotten to take her helmet off. When she did, she had helmet hair. They both laughed.

She put her cooler on the table in the break room and laid her helmet on top. She wanted to talk to Rick about the endowment.

"Knock, knock…" She opened the door

"Come in." He was deep in thought and up to his elbows in paperwork, but he seemed relieved to take a break.

"Rick, I wanted to talk to you about the endowment."

"Wait. Before you make a decision about that, I wanted to show you something."

"Okay. What have you got?"

"Well, I've been crunching a few numbers here, and thinking about creative ways to supplement our income here."

"I'm open to that…maybe."

"Well, with the help of your agency and its contacts, maybe we could put together some CDs or DVDs of our techniques. I have NO idea how we'd market them, but…I know it sounds wacky…"

"Actually, Rick, it piggybacks on an idea I have. I want to talk to someone this evening about it, and after that, let's brainstorm.

"That sounds great."

"Right now, I need your help trying to figure out how to use Gran's technology."

"Give me about a half hour to finish these reports and I'm all yours."

"Fantastic. I'll be in Gran's office."

Bella walked down the hall and thought about what it would be like to have Gran's office as her own. Would she be able to fill her shoes? Anna was a seer in so many ways. Yes, she had the gift, but it's all the things she did with it that made her shoes so big. Would Bella be able to wrap her mind around Anna's science? Would she be able to use her inventions? If so, would she know how to interact with people? Were these patent protected? If not, could they be? As usual, she had more questions than answers.

Rick came through the door. His face registered a look of surprise when he saw Bella sitting behind Anna's desk. She felt right at home.

"Have a seat, Rick. I wanted to talk to you about something."

"What's up?"

"Well I got some news about the endowment, and I wanted to enlighten you as well. I know you're worried about the future of the clinic. I've learned that the endowment is structured so that the money can only be used to support the care we provide here at the clinic. The money cannot be used for anything else. So the decision about whether or not to keep this clinic open is off the table. The clinic will remain open indefinitely. My decisions will be as a figurehead. As long as you properly manage the clinic and its resources, your job is secure."

"That's great news!"

"There is something you must know, though. I've met with the investment brokers, and we've suffered from the downturn of the market. They are suggesting we put the interest back into the investment for a two year period to recoup the loss. Doing so would mean no cash flowing from the endowment into the clinic for 24 months."

"What would happen?"

"I don't know. You should know that I don't have the capital to invest personally."

"So where does that leave us?"

"I'm not sure. But I'm sure that because of this discussion, you now know that there's only one side, and we're both on it."

"Thanks for that."

"You're welcome."

Rick and Bella unlocked the cabinet and got out the glasses and the bands. Neither was sure how to operate them or what to expect from them. Rick knew what they were for, but didn't know how to turn them on or off.

"Let's try them."

"I don't like the mind reading thing. Let's get somebody else in here who can experiment with you."

"Okay."

Rick left the office. In two minutes Bella heard a knock and in walked Allen. Bella was delighted.

"What's going on in here," he joked lightly.

"Can I read your mind" she volleyed right back.

"I don't know, can you?" Andrew was skeptical.

"How about this? I'll put on these glasses and ask you a question with my mind. You write down my question, then answer it with your mind, and I'll write down your answer. We can trade and see if what we heard was what was said. Does that make sense?"

"Perfect sense. Got a paper and pen?" Allen was excited.

Bella put the glasses on.

"I don't know how to turn them on, Allen."

"Since it's Anna's invention, you probably either speak the word aloud, or think it with your mind and the device will activate."

Bella closed her eyes and thought the word activate. She couldn't hear anything turning on, but she thought she felt a slightly different pressure behind both ears.

"Do the glasses look any different or anything, Allen?"

"No. Ask me something without words."

Bella left her eyes open, looking through the glasses. She supposed that Anna left her eyes open and looked directly at clients when wearing the glasses. It seemed logical.

"Just ask a question, will ya?" Were those Allen's thoughts?

"What're you in some kind of hurry, sassy pants?"

"Sassy pants, how old are you?" Allen spoke the words allowed. They both cracked up. This was fun.

"Okay, Allen, now you put them on and see if you can sense my thoughts while wearing them."

"Okay." He reached out and took the glasses. He put them on, closed his eyes and tried to activate them. He opened his eyes and shook his head.

"Did you try the word activate?"

"Yep."

"Okay, so the genetic trait is truly a factor. Do you have time to try the bands with me?"

"As long as there's no hidden camera in here." They both laughed again.

"I wonder if it matters where you put the band. Will it only work on the head?"

"Let's find out." Allen put the headband on. He closed his eyes and said the word activate. Nothing.

Bella put the band on and thought the word activate. Her device emitted an almost undetectable energy where the ends of the band touched her head.

"Wow. Do you feel that, Bella?"

"Yeah!" she was super excited.

"So this band won't activate until that band is turned on. I wonder if I have to say activate first, or if it will activate automatically when yours comes on."

"I'm not sure. Let's start again." Bella closed her eyes and thought deactivate. She felt the surge of energy vanish. "Okay. Let me try to activate both." Bella closed her eyes and thought the word activate. She felt it, but Allen did not. "Let me try something else here." She thought the words 'activate both' and both came on. "Cool!"

"Can I try to hear your thoughts, Bella?"

"Sure. Let's start simple, though, easy questions, just a couple of words or a phrase."

"Okay." He closed his eyes and asked a simple question. 'Is your agency going to publish my book?'

'Yes, if we can work out a deal.'

Allen got up out of the chair and started dancing around.

"Nice moves! I guess we know how these work."

"Can I talk to you about the book?"

"Nope, proprietary information until a formal offer is made." She smiled. Allen sat back down. He tried to act nonchalant, but Bella could see his excitement.

"The meeting's tomorrow, Bella."

"I know! Okay, back to this…how do you suppose this thing sees into the deep psyche and discerns what's tripping a person up?"

"I don't know. Does it work both ways or is one a control band?"

"Good questions. Do you know where the information about these is stored?"

"Maybe." Allen walked around the room touching the walls. Suddenly, a screen appeared. When he touched it, it prompted him to scan in.

"Your move, Bella." Allen put his hand into the hand symbol on the screen, but the message read: *DNA mismatch.*

Bella walked over and put her hand on the symbol. The screen said: *Partial DNA Match: Stand in front of camera for photo recognition.* Bella looked around for the camera, then spotted a dot just above the hand symbol. Suddenly her photo appeared. The prompt below it read, *Place thumb in bio scanner.* Since Bella had been through a similar authentication sequence at home, she was familiar with this process. In a matter of seconds, there was a 3D image with calculations and instructions. There was a ton of sensitive information being projected onto the screen. Bella turned around and addressed Allen.

"Forgive me, Allen, but would you mind if I had some time alone with this stuff?"

"Not at all." He took the band off and laid it on Anna's desk. "See you tomorrow, Bella."

"See you then. Thanks, Allen!"

"Quite exciting, eh, young lady?" Gran's voice was filled with a mix of pride and joy.

"How did you do all this, Gran?"

"It took a lifetime of seeking, studying, research and development, and a lot of help from my friends."

"How do you ask questions that net answers like these?" Bella was spellbound.

"It came from a greater knowing."

"That's cryptic, Gran, explain please."

"I'm not sure I can." There was a long silence. Bella sat down at the desk and looked at the revolving 3D prototype in front of her. She was so enamored by it that she'd forgotten about Gran.

"Think about what the real you knows for sure. You don't have to tell yourself to breathe or blink your eyes. The real you knows how to manage that. You never have to give it conscious thought. Well... the idea of pinpointing that organizing intelligence has fascinated me since birth. I can read people's thoughts and communicate with them on levels known by few others. Why is that? And... why was I chosen, or was I? Is it a genetic trait? How many others carry the trait, or the aptitude toward it? I've just always been filled with curiosity."

"Gosh, Gran, you and me both. And it's exponentially greater in this place."

"I guess that's why I stayed."

"I'll probably stay, or, some form of that."

"I know. Carol told me."

"You guys blow me away." Bella said it and meant it fondly. Bella looked at her watch.

"OMG, Gran, I've got to go. I didn't realize what time it was. I have to get home before dark. I rode your bike today." She gathered things up and began to put them away. Holding the glasses, she experienced a change of heart, and decided to take them home with her. She placed them in their protective case and tucked it in the backpack.

She used her thoughts to shut everything down and tuck it away out of site. Bella locked Anna's office door and walked down the hall.

"Bruce, what are you doing here?"

"You can't get home before dark. I came to pick you up."

"Thanks. How long have you been here?"

"20 minutes or so, not long."

"Are we the last ones here?"

"Yes, except for Rick." She glanced over and saw him looking her way, so she waved and turned toward the door.

"I have so much to tell you that I don't really know where to start."

Bruce burst out into a song from The Sound of Music.

"Just start at the very beginning...a very fine place to start..." Bella burst out laughing and joined him in song. It was a very pleasant ride home.

"Let's stop and get a bite instead of cooking, want to?" Bella was starved.

"Fine with me. Any place special?"

"No. Anything's fine. What about right here?"

"Never been here before. We'll discover it together." Bruce was easy about it. Bella liked that. And she liked the idea that neither of them had ever been there before.

"So what was it that you wanted to talk to me about?" Bella was curious.

"I've been thinking about your idea of an anthology written by patients."

"What about it?"

"Well, I'm not sure exactly, my ideas are rough, but have you thought about starting a foundation of some sort to raise funds? There are ways to title the book to protect the anonymity of the patients. If they agreed to participate, that money could go to the foundation instead of the clinic. It's just an idea."

"And a good one. Since our little spat, I've discovered some things about the endowment. We have a two year slump to recover from. The managers advise putting the interest back into the fund for the next two years to help recover the loss from the downturn. I can accept or reject their recommendation. Either way, even using the interest now, the clinic will be set for life with the current endowment. But if we accept the recommendation, and find ways to operate without the interest, we would most likely be able to continue to fund Gran's science and inventions as well."

"Who would conduct the research?" Bruce hoped it was Bella.

"Well, I haven't actually thought that far ahead. It seems like every day some big surprise causes me to consider another factor. It's like living in Disney Land."

"Sounds like you have a lot on your plate."

"The thing is, almost as quickly as I ask a question, answers come. I've sort of relaxed into fate, if you will."

"That's great. I'm here if you need me for something."

"Thanks, I appreciate that."

Bella turned the conversation to this weekend's family visit.

"Do any of them play golf? We have around 300 golf courses in the area." Bruce's insider information was valuable.

"Both my boys play, but one really loves it. I actually thought he would make a career of designing and building golf courses. I'm not sure about the girls."

"Well, if you'd like me to, I can arrange tee times and stuff for them."

"I'd appreciate that. I'm sure you'll see us around the pool, and you guys can make plans. It's always nice to have a local to show you around."

They talked all through supper, planning the trip to the canyon, discussing Bella's first experience with Gran's new inventions, about biking in Phoenix, Bruce's nearly complete commission, ideas for his next piece, Bella's jewelry designs, and Gran's suggestions about expanding the publishing company.

Bella was glad to have Bruce to process things with. He was an attentive listener and open to new ideas. Bella wanted to look into his brain with Gran's invention. But not now, maybe later.

Time flew by and it was getting close to 10 p.m. Bella was yawning when Bruce finally asked for the check. The ride home was quiet.

"You falling asleep over there?"

"Yep. I was just thinking that I hope the UPS guy is on his toes and gets me the package for my meeting tomorrow. I want to review it first."

"Well, nothing you can do about UPS. Rest well. I'll talk to you tomorrow sometime."

"Thanks for dinner, Bruce. Good night." Bella kissed him on the cheek and got out. She walked in, set the alarm and went to bed.

The powers that be must've heard her cosmic cry because Bella got her UPS package at 9:15 a.m. She had just closed the staff meeting when it arrived. The timing was perfect. She opened the envelope and took out the contract, proposed marketing plan and a host of other documents she and Allen would talk about today. She reviewed the preliminary offer. Everything seemed to be in order. Bella felt really good about this one, and hoped it would be the first of many with Allen. After the meeting was over, she planned to read and sip latte at Barnes and Noble for the rest of the afternoon.

During her drive, she was consumed with thoughts about expanding the publishing company to include a branch in Phoenix. Like Gran said, she had office space already available at the estate. She would have the work of two properties, and at least two businesses. Three, if you counted the jewelry. If she used it only as a hobby, the investment already in it would eventually disappear. If she sold the pieces Gran already made, she could use the money to restore supplies.

"You probably won't need to sell the jewelry."

"Why not, Gran?"

"The people you will help will gift you many times over. You will pay it forward and the things you need to continue on your gifted path will be continuously provided for you. You will never need to worry about money, Bella. Your worries will be bigger now."

"How big?"

"That will be up to you, but I see that you will give voice to all those left without one. This work will heal families, communities, businesses, governments, and our planet. The transformation you initiate through this work will exponentially outlive you."

"Nice romantic notion, Gran, but how will I do that?"

"You can choose that, but you'll need everyone in both your lives, now, people here and folks back home. They believe in you."

"That's really big...but not scary. I think I can do this, Gran."

"You can. And in case you're wondering, Allen's in your life for good."

"Ah, a trump card...thanks, Gran."

The air was filled with excitement as Allen and Bella reviewed the paperwork. They discussed plans for marketing and advertising, consideration for other books, copyrights, book covers, editing and distribution. When all was said and done, the meeting had lasted almost three hours. But both felt lighter than air, and were excited about the prospects ahead. It was the beginning of a whole new business relationship for them both.

Allen was smiling and shaking his head. Bella was curious about what was so amusing.

"The first day we met, that day on the plane, I knew that I'd see you again. Call it instinct. But I never dreamed you owned my place of employment, or would own the rights to my books."

"Ah, books, pleural, I like that!" She winked at him. "As long as you deliver on your promises we will remain great friends."

"So, no unconditional love, huh?"

"Not on your life, Mister."

"Well, I hate to eat and run, but I can't wait to tell my family. My wife will be dying to know how things turned out."

"I'd like to know how that all goes. Fill me in at the office."

"You got it." And with that, he was gone.

"Bella opened her email on the iPad and texted her staff, announcing that Allen was onboard. Bella put the signed contracts back in the pouch. She would take them to the closest UPS store on her way home to cement the deal. What a great day!

Suddenly, instead of staying cooped up inside, she felt like hanging out by the pool and in the jewelry studio. She had three days left to finish her gifts. On automatic pilot, she went through her project checklist in her mind. The way she figured it, she would finish the pedants today and the rings tomorrow. Then she got an idea about her grandkids.

"Gran, would it upset you if I took the six silver spoons you brought with you from Germany and encrusted jewels on the handles to pass down to my grandchildren?"

"I'd be honored. Someday I'll tell you their history, but not today."

"Gran, when am I using my telepathic powers? Do I have any control over them? Can I reach others? If so, who else can hear my thoughts?"

"You're always using your powers, unless you make a conscious choice to turn them off. It's like the power of creation, Bella, you're always using it, but sometimes you create without thinking."

"Ah, you're referring to the law of attraction."

"That's one name, yes. But the creative process doesn't just create for you, it creates for everyone. The energy you summon or emit is distributed to the world around you. It radiates out from you, mingling with the energy fields of all life."

Bella thought about the impact of that. What she initiated in the microcosm (her world) created energy that fed the macrocosm (everybody else's world), too. Wow, talk about responsibility…

"So by focusing our efforts on creating goodness and love, it becomes the foundation for the world around us." Bella understood.

"Exactly. Live large, Bella. Because whether you know it or not, you do."

"That blows me away."

"Me, too."

"Can I change the subject, Gran?"

"Sure."

"What was your relationship with Nikola Tesla?"

"Acquaintances."

"Why do I get the feeling that it's more?"

"I was in love with his ideas. They were fantastic! And he was the only person I ever met that believed that psychic abilities had their roots in the ability to receive information on different frequencies. "

"The photo I saw of the two of you was when you were small kids. Did you get that from him then?"

"Heavens, no. His father was a priest at my aunt's church. We met when we were four, and saw each other only a few times in our lives. But we shared a fascination for invisible energies. As a teenager, I had a crush on him, but it was one sided. His first love was science. He had interest in little else."

"And now?" Bella knew she was pressing the envelope.

"And now my consciousness, or spirit, drifts in and out among the many, hoping to meet up with him again."

"So…what did you mean when you said you had a date with Niko the other night?"

"I had a date with his energy transfer theories, my darling, the science."

"Oh."

"Is anything really ever as it seems?"

"Hardly ever, Bella."

Bella got right in and out at the UPS store. She felt like dancing! Strolling down the walk, she saw all kinds of different boutiques she would like to visit. Perhaps when the kids got here she could bring the girls out for lunch and an afternoon of shopping boutiques.

"Hey, Bella!" Deidre walked right up to her. "What are you doing here?"

"I just dropped some stuff off at the UPS store and saw the shop. I decided to come by and browse. That okay?"

"It's great! If you need help or want information about a piece, just come get me."

"Thanks, Deidre!"

Bella was moving slowly through the aisles. At this pace, she would need pajamas if she wanted to see everything. These pieces were incredible! Then Bella saw it…a piece like no other she'd ever seen. She sat down on her heels and fingered it. Between the detail in the carving and the feeling she got from the wood, a tear rolled down her cheek."

"It's carved from a piece of mahogany."

"I'll take it."

Deidre got help to move the piece for Bella. She wrapped it in a soft cloth, then covered the cloth with newspaper and taped it securely. It was too big to carry. Deidre placed it on a rolling cart and walked Bella out to the car. Together they loaded it.

"You'll need help getting this out of the car and into the house."

"That won't be a problem. Thank you. Listen, I'm working through a few details, but I think I may have some pieces for you in the near future. Can we have lunch and talk about that?"

"Any time. The shop closes from 11:30-12:30 every day. Call me and we'll set something up." Deidre stood on the walk and watched Bella drive away. She wondered what would happen when Bella found out who the artist and wood sculptor was. Luckily, she hadn't asked.

When Bella got home there was a package on the porch. It was addressed to her son. She brought it inside, realizing how close their visit was. Instead of storing it by the door, she decided to take it right upstairs. It was time to get the rooms ready for their arrival.

The way the house was laid out, the suites were on one side of the hall and the single bedrooms were on the other side. So the parents would be right across the hall from their kids. There was plenty of privacy. She laid the box in one of the suites. If she got more, she'd know where to go with them. It was smart to send things ahead instead of carrying everything with them on the plane, especially with kids.

Bella went into the rooms and stripped the beds. Linens needed to be washed, furniture needed to be polished and bathrooms needed to be cleaned. She got her iPod from her purse, grabbed a cup of coffee, rounded up the cleaning supplies and got right to work. In two hours she was done. Oops, she'd forgotten to unload the car. If she skipped that, there was still time to work in the studio.

Bella figured she'd work until around 9 p.m., which was about two hours away. She could get the stones mounted and the clasps picked out for the necklaces. She would have to work on the spoons in a private moment while the kids were golfing or something. It wasn't practical to think she could get it all done. Then a stone dropped onto the floor. Bella turned around. She wasn't even near the table.

"Is this a message, Gran?"

She walked over and picked up the stone. The card on the table said azurite. Carrying the stone with her, Bella went to the reference book and found the meaning. *This stone was a reminder not to limit herself.* She tucked it into her pocket and went to work. The pendants were finished first, clasps and all. They needed to dry, but the pieces were complete. The ring stones were set. Bella was circling the tables, thinking about each of her grandchildren. OMG, she'd been consumed with creativity and worked well past the time she'd set aside. But much to her surprise, she felt fantastic. She wasn't tired at all.

Turning off the lights, she glimpsed Bruce still out working in the shop. She could see him clearly through the darkness. The piece he was

working on was captivating. The attention to detail had him hypnotized. She knew exactly what that was like. Thoughts flowed through
Bella, telling Bruce goodnight. Suddenly, to her surprise, he turned
toward the dark studio and said good night. Bella couldn't hear his
words, but could read his lips. Did he hear her thoughts?

Bella was getting wet. Stripping down as she walked along the
grass, she made a bee line for the pool. As always, the water made
her skin feel silky. Everything was wonderful here, all of it. Without
censorship, Bella found herself tangled up in Bruce, who must've followed right behind her. She wouldn't be sleeping much tonight.

As the darkness surrendered to the light, a host of endless possibilities for the day lay before them. If Bella could describe the way
she felt, she'd say 'whole.' Everything about her was active and she was
living fully. Her family was happy and growing, her publishing company was thriving, her love life was very satisfying, and now she got
to understand what had been misunderstood for most of her lifetime.
She now had the opportunity to expand in ways that, one month ago,
were unimaginable. This was the promise of fairy tales, and Bella was
living it. Life was simply fantastic.

"Bruce?"

"Huh?"

"Tonight, can I read your mind with Gran's glasses?"

"Sure. But you don't need an invention for that."

Chapter 12

Bella announced the possibility of expanding into the Phoenix market at the morning meeting. There was a buzz of excitement from her staff. There were questions about how things would all work out. Bella asked them to think about their immediate and long term career goals, and whether or not they'd be interested in moving to Phoenix, offering them first crack at the new positions. She also asked them to consider what else they would be able to take on during the transition.

The decision was made. She considered hiring a private pilot for the commute, but would need a regular schedule. There was much to do.

First, she would need a business plan for expansion. Even though the basics were in place, there would be an investment. How would she support it? Until she had the actual numbers, it would be mainly educated projection. Perhaps at the beginning, she would consider running it herself part time. It seemed like a more practical and manageable way to get started. But it meant more time in Phoenix.

The pilot interviews would be next. She Googled small airports and private pilots in Phoenix. The list was small. Reaching out to three, she set up interviews for the week after next. Bella didn't want anything to interfere with her family vacation. She wondered if she could eventually earn enough to get a private pilot on retainer, so her kids could fly back and forth. Or maybe she could simply pay for the costs on a card that offered frequent flyer miles, and be reimbursed by the foundation. Traveling to Phoenix regularly would certainly rack up enough points to get plane tickets. The thought of it all made her blood dance through her veins like fine wine. Bella stopped, remembering Gran's advice to 'live large'. She was doing it! Bella was actually making plans to expand her large-ness. Was that even a word? She laughed out loud at herself. This was wonderful!

Euphoria was interrupted by the doorbell. UPS was delivering another package, this one from her agency. It was her share of the workload. There was another promising young author they were interested in. Bella grabbed the package and put it on the desk in her library. It seemed strange, calling it her library. She would be making some changes in there, making room for her things. Perhaps Bruce could build a bookshelf under the window behind the desk for her references, printer, fax machine and photos. She had lots and lots of photos of her beloved children and grandchildren. Suddenly, Bella was reminded about the wood art in her trunk. When Bruce came over to bid the job, she would ask him to help her bring in her first local purchase.

Driving to the clinic, Bella was practically unconscious. She'd been deep in thought, thinking without thinking, just the habit she wanted to train herself to avoid. In order to be able to cloak, she'd have to consciously turn off her transmitter when she wanted privacy. At this point, only Gran could hear them. But sometimes she wondered if Bruce could, too. Bella wanted to bring the glasses home with her tonight. If Bruce wasn't busy, she hoped he would play guinea pig so she could figure out how they worked and what she could see looking with them. Maybe he would also be able to see her thoughts. It might be fun.

After getting settled, Bella learned that Allen was with a patient. She went down to her office and activated her computer. If there was instructional information, maybe she could figure things out on her own. Bella was stronger in the arts than the sciences, but she was smart.

She was getting the hang of the technology, and it recognized her now. Things were progressing nicely. Walking down the hall today, she knew where she was going and what she needed to do. Touching in, she searched the files and found what she was looking for.

Everything was activated by thought. There was a list of simple commands for initiating the technology, but there were no other guidelines.

"Gran, how will I go deeper into thought with someone?"

"You don't need to go anywhere. The band will give you automatic access."

"What if I don't see anything?"

"That can't happen. Brain's aren't empty."

"Gran, what am I supposed to do when I see something?"

"Tell the person what you see."

"Won't I be expected to *do* something? Isn't that why people come here?"

"They come here to gain insight into what's holding them back."

"From what?"

"From whatever they perceive as impossible. The key here is that what's holding the person back is a thought, and a thought can be changed. Changing is up to the person asking for the answer. It's not your work."

"And I tell them that?"

"You don't have to. Soldiers and first responders are already fixers. When they know what the problem is, they go immediately to work."

"I see...I think."

"Don't over think things, Bella. These people have already seen all the thinkers without successful resolve. See and feel. Give awareness. That's what we do."

"I can do that."

"Absolutely!"

Bella felt lighter than air. In the back of her mind she was harboring a fear that she would not be able to do the work, but that was off the table. The only thing she had to do was be present and open the door for the other person to walk through. She could do that. Not being able to see deep enough was also a doubt she'd been afraid to voice. Actually, all she had to bring was her DNA, and repeat out loud what the bands revealed. The technology was fabulous! She laid her fears to rest.

Allen knocked and entered. He stood looking over at her computer screen.

"Find anything?"

"Everything I needed, actually. Allen, have you ever witnessed this technology in action?"

"Yes. It's policy. There has to be a witness to every session with these. The patient may also have a witness, if they so desire. If it's a female patient, there has to be a female witness, either their own, or a staff member here. But, the female witness cannot be you."

"Smart."

"Do you need me then?"

"Not unless you'd like to be my guinea pig."

"What's in it for me?"

"Brownie points, Allen, lots of them." She smiled.

"Sign me up."

"Before we begin, can I speak to you confidentially about something?"

"Well, I guess it depends. Will you be asking me for personal advice?"

"No."

"Will you be asking me out on a date?" He was joking with her.

"Not yet." She poked him back.

"Okay then."

"Do you think that people who come here for help would be interested in sharing their stories?"

"With other potential patients?"

"No. Well, maybe…" Bella was treading very carefully.

"With who, then?"

"The public."

"No. No way. They only come here because there's no link back to them. Do you see any paperwork? No, you don't. We don't even write down their last names here. Anonymity is the thread that sews up the wounds treated here. Everything is private.

"I see."

"Is there anything else, Bella?" He was annoyed.

"No. Thank you, Allen."

Bella felt bad about angering Allen. He'd had the same reaction to her as Bruce did when she brought it up. She would table it for now, but she still thought the idea had merit. The experiences that changed these lives were worth sharing. They didn't have to say they had treatment for anything. Well, for now she'd concentrate on what was right before her.

She dug into the schematics of the bands, wondering if, like the stones in the study at home, they needed recharging. If so, how did that occur? There appeared to be no information about that in the schematics.

"Knock, knock…" The door opened and it was Bruce.

"Hi!" Bella was surprised to see him.

"Did you bring your lunch?"

"No."

"Good! Let's go."

"Okay. Let me get my purse."

When Bella went into the break room to get her purse, Allen was in there eating his lunch. Bella blew by, but thought better of it and came back.

"Allen, I'm sorry if I've upset you. I didn't mean to."

"It's okay, Bella, but the way I'm feeling right now, I'm not thinking of giving you access to my thoughts."

"Fair enough. I'll see you tomorrow." Bella went back into her office, grabbed the glasses, put them in her purse and went outside.

"Hey, Bruce, I've decided not to come back to the clinic this afternoon so I'll follow you."

"Okay. Where are you parked?"

"Last row."

"Let me guess, exercise."

She smiled and walked to her car. Bella followed Bruce to a pavilion in a park very near their homes. He had actually made a great lunch. He had barbeque pork, potato salad and watermelon. It was perfect! She enjoyed it tremendously.

"You seem preoccupied today."

"I made Allen angry."

"That can't be. Nothing shakes him up." Bruce looked at her amusingly.

"Afraid so...I mentioned the idea of people from the clinic sharing their experiences."

Bruce sat perfectly still. He didn't want to start a fight like he had last time, but this had gone far enough. Looking down he counted to ten and then thought about Bella. She was sweet, kind and determined. She'd come a long way, put her life on hold, and tried to embrace everything that had fallen into her lap. He decided she had earned his ear.

Bella explained what the investment managers told her about the endowment. She explained her financial position, what she was able and willing to do. Her predicament was immediate. Actually, her idea about the anthology was a good one. It could sell. Perhaps with some provision made for privacy, it might be worth entertaining. Maybe together they could think through privacy and anonymity. And with nobody profiting from the sale of the book, she might be able to convince patients. It would merely be a way to continue the work being provided at the clinic. After hearing her out, he had a totally different opinion than he had that first night.

"Bella, I'm sorry."

"About what?"

"About assuming bad motives the first time you brought this up. You've done nothing but try to keep everything going, and people have done nothing but present you with demands. I'm so sorry."

"Apology accepted. Now let's move on Bruce. My kids are arriving in the morning. Shoot...I forgot to see about borrowing the clinic van for our trip to the canyon. Excuse me while I make a quick call."

Bella had it all set up in a manner of moments. There was no immediate need for the van. The whole week was free. They were all set.

"I can't wait to kiss Maddie and Kyle's little cheekies a hundred times."

"Cheekies?" He burst out laughing.

"Laugh now..." she gave him a warning glance, "you'll see!"

"I look forward to it." It was true. He hadn't been part of a real family in a long time. There were things about him that Bella didn't know. She would probably think less of him when everything came to light. But the truth about a person at one point in life was not always so later on. People learned by their mistakes. The thing he loved most about his relationship with Bella was that there was no past and no future. They were just friends with benefits.

"Thank you so much for lunch, Bruce. I enjoyed it immensely. I'm going to run by the market and pick up a few things for the weekend. When the kids get here we can figure out what we're going to do for our trip."

"Did you contact my friends with the rental house?"

"Sure did. I appreciate the lead. I'm sure we'll be quite comfortable there."

"I'm sure you will."

When Bella got home from the market, she saw Jake's car out front. She wanted the pool to be ship shape when the kids got in it. He was also scheduled to come the morning they got back. After a long travel they'd probably all be ready for some exercise. She had purchased a pool volleyball and net, along with a host of floaties for the kids. Tomorrow they would likely be using them.

It was 10 p.m. and Bella was wide awake. The excitement was energizing. She wasn't sure how she got there, but she was standing in the open woodshop door with nothing on but a swimsuit cover up. Bruce was covered in dust.

As if he could read her thoughts, he took off his gloves, tool belt, goggles and apron. He lifted her up, walked her over to the outside shower, and pulled the chain. The water washed over them. They used the picnic table in the yard to spend all the nervous energy Bella had stored up. Sated, they headed for the pool.

"I'm going to miss this when the kids are here."

"Naw...you'll have your mind on those cheekies."

She splashed him right in the face. He dunked under and came right up in front of her, slithering against her as he pulled. He kissed her, lifted her up, and dunked her. It was fun playing around on a beautiful night like tonight.

"Every night is fantastic with you, Bella!"

"Thanks. Hey..." she stood still a moment thinking about the glasses.

"Sure, go get 'em!"

"You heard my thoughts!"

""Yeah."

"How long have you been able to hear?"

"...since the other day when you were in the jewelry studio."

"How much do you hear?"

"Well, I don't know..."

Bella wondered what turned it on and off.

"I'd like to know that, too." Bruce answered without her saying a word.

Try to answer me without words so I can see if I can hear you. Well, answer me! Bella was impatient.

Bruce thought, 'what's the question.' Bella started laughing. He was right, she hadn't asked him anything. But she heard his thought. This could be fun.

'Or not…' Bruce wasn't so sure.

"Hey…while I have you here," Bella was talking out loud again, "Can you help me get something out of the car and bring it inside?"

"Sure."

Bella pulled the wet cover up over her while Bruce got into his boxers. She led him to the garage. The package was bulky and heavy. Together they got it into the house. Bella was wondering where to put it. Bruce started looking around. He walked up the stairs and shouted for Bella to come up. He needn't have, because they were reading each other's thoughts now.

There was a mahogany sofa table against the wall in the hall. It was the perfect place. It took them a little while to get the package up the stairs. It was pretty heavy for Bella. She had to set it down about half way up. But they finally put it on its perch. Bella moved everything else off the table and began to unwrap it.

"Close your eyes, Bruce, no peaking." When she finished unwrapping it she went over to stand beside Bruce.

"Okay, open."

Bella was as excited as a kid in a candy shop. But when she looked over at Bruce, he looked as pale as a ghost. His eyes filled with tears and he sat down on the floor, leaned against the wall and cried. Bella was so moved she couldn't speak, so she read his thoughts. Sitting down Indian style beside him, she put her elbows on her knees, rested her head on her hands and sobbed. Without even a word, Bruce got up and walked downstairs. Bella heard the back door close. She looked out the window, overlooking the pool, and saw him picking up his wet clothes. He was despondent. So was Bella.

"Cloak." She said the word out loud, just to make sure her thoughts could not be read by anyone today. Looking at the clock, Bella had just enough time to get showered and get some food ready before her family arrived. She turned on Pandora and placed her phone in the cradle. She sliced fruit, made oatmeal, put her egg casserole in the oven, got out some yogurt and put a whole pot of coffee on in a regular pot. French vanilla creamer was her favorite, but she had hazelnut, too. Apple juice would be perfect for the toddlers. Bella was so happy she could hardly contain it.

Running to the door, she flung it open and kissed a bunch of cheekies!

"We rang the bell because we didn't think this was the place! Some little cottage out west!" They all chuckled together.

"Let me move the car out of the garage. You guys back in and we'll bring your luggage in at the base of the stairs. It'll be easier."

"I'm for easy."

"Food!" They all laughed at Kyle's simple word. Everyone was hungry.

"Let's eat first. We can unload the car in a minute." Everyone followed Bella into the kitchen. There were fingers in everything. The timer went off and the casserole was ready. They made their plates and sat down for their first meal together in a month and a half. Bella looked around at the faces of her loved ones. She'd missed the chatter and commotion. Her heart felt as if it would burst from joy.

After breakfast came a tour of the estate. She then showed them to their rooms. Everyone was comfortable. Anxious to get out to the pool, the girls got themselves and the little ones ready. Bella got out all her little toys and carried them down to the pool house. She turned on the compressor and began to blow up the floats. Opening the shed door, Bella pulled out a couple of rafts. She fixed a blender of Pina Coladas, got out some brightly colored plastic cups and sliced some fresh pineapple. The kids could have that. Bella had fresh fruit juice in sippy cups for them, too.

Maddie came across the lawn in her little bonnet, with her nose bright white with sunscreen. She toddled over looking like a gorgeous china doll. Bella's heart leapt! Right behind her, barreling out at full steam was Kyle.

"Roar" he was chasing Maddie, who was giggling with glee.

"Kyle, Maddie…" her daughters-in-law were shouting as the babes ran toward the pool.

"Got 'em!" Bella stepped out and shouted "Boo!" which started a game of tag and a giggle fest. The morning turned into afternoon, and soon it was naptime. With the young ones lying on a pallet in the shade, the guys hit the volleyball around in the pool, while the girls lounged in the Arizona sun. It was a typical day out west.

"I rented a house for our trip. We should be comfortable and have plenty of room. It's about five miles from the canyon, so we can easily travel back and forth when the kids need to rest." The boys were teasing her about driving slow and getting lost. They were having tons of fun at her expense, but the key word was fun. They soon retreated to the pool house for a beer and a deck of cards. They got a game of poker going in the shade. The time passed quickly.

"What's for supper?"

"Picnic food. You guys fire up the grill and I'll go get stuff." Bella went back up to the house for the pork steaks and chicken. She grabbed potatoes to bake in the microwave and cob corn they could cook at the pool house. She'd taken everything else down already. They cooked and ate and swam until after dark. It was an easy day. Everybody grabbed something on the way back up to the house. Many hands made light work. Soon the kids were in bed and their parents were settled into their bedroom suites for the night.

Bella was restless. She walked back outside. Passing the pool house, she strolled over toward Bruce's. The lights were off in the shop. The truck was gone. It seemed odd, but she missed him. Settling into the dark on the pool lounger, Bella thought hard about invading other people's privacy, both their thoughts and their anonymity. She now understood why Bruce had been so defensive about the anthology. She wondered if Allen also had something so private he never wanted to share it with anyone. There must be other ways to support the clinic, without rubbing salt in old wounds or dredging up the past. After all, the past was gone. What we have is the moment we're in. We can't re-live or pre-live.

"Can you see my grandkids, Gran?"

"Yes. They're even more wonderful than you told me."

"I can't describe their wonder, Gran. There are no words."

"I get it. I have you. Say nothing more."

Bella was tired now. She made her way back across the yard. As she climbed the stairs she heard Kyle through the cracked door. He was chattering away. She walked in and kissed him on the forehead. He reached his arms up. Bella picked him up and went over to the rocker. Sucking on his binky, he laid his head down on her shoulder. She rocked him long past the time he fell asleep. In the not-too-distant future, he would be too big to rock on nights like these.

When she finally put him down, her daughter-in-law met her outside the door.

"Everything okay?"

"Fine. I just heard him chattering and went in for a hug. Was that okay?"

"It's fine. He's growing up really fast, isn't he?"

"Yes. Want to come in?" She opened the door to her room.

"Sure. Derek's asleep and I'm wide awake."

Bella brought Andrea up to date about what she had sorted through, and actually showed her the box of things she'd set aside for them. She encouraged her to look through the things in the attic, and take whatever she wanted.

Maddie began to cry. Bella opened her door and saw Kate walking into her room. She and Andrea peeked in the door and waved. After getting Maddie back to sleep, Kate joined them in Bella's room. They were wide awake now. They decided have drinks on the veranda.

Bella told the girls about Bruce. Well, not everything, but she told them that she was seeing him, and wasn't sure if they were just friends or more than that. It had been fifteen years since her husband died, and she'd seen a few people casually, so the girls weren't particularly interested in this one either. They were happy she was having fun.

Bella took them down into the office, showing them the technology. She explained that until this trip she never knew her mother was a telepath and communicated with her grandmother that way. The girls were fascinated by the story, and Bella's new found ability. The girls were familiar with Tesla and his theories, and fascinated by Gran's spin-off from his energy theories. Bella got her purse and showed them the glasses.

"I haven't actually tried them yet."

"Let's do it!" Andrea wanted to be first.

"Wait." Kate had objections. "I think that before we do that, we should agree to keep whatever we see in this room. Agreed?"

They all agreed. Bella put the glasses on, closed her eyes, and activated it.

"Who's first?"

"Me."

"Okay, Andrea, you first."

"So what do I do?"

"Nothing, I think…I don't really know. Just think about something and I'll see if I can pick up on your thought." Bella got quiet and listened to what her mind was telling her.

"There's excitement, new life, a baby…you're pregnant!" The three shrieked quietly and jumped up and down hugging.

"Derek doesn't know yet, so keep this between us. I'm planning to tell him in a private moment sometime this week. I'm SO excited!" Andrea stepped out of the way and Bella focused on Kate.

"There's a big office, a door plate, Nurse Manager, Pediatric Critical Care…wait…Las Vegas?" Kate wasn't as excited about sharing her news. She had a lot of reservations about uprooting her family and being so far away from her support system. But Bella could see that it was the job of her dreams.

"Well, maybe you could do like I'll be doing, and commute back and forth." The girls both looked at her. There, the cat was out of the bag.

Bella went on to explain the short version of Anna's state of affairs. Since it was now light, they continued their discussion in the kitchen over coffee. There were a lot of details to work out, but the change in availability for family was minimal. She would come to Phoenix as needed, maybe every week for 24 hours, unless there was some unexpected psychic emergency. Bella was amazed that neither one of her daughters-in-law were shaken by the idea of psychic abilities. Their minds were open and they seemed accepting.

"So what can you see when you're not wearing the glasses?" Kate was curious.

"Not much, really. I seem to be able to communicate freely with Gran. I can hear her and talk to her with either my thoughts or my voice. I'm not sure my voice is really heard, but if I'm speaking something, I guess my thoughts are there and she responds. And there was one time that Bruce heard my thoughts. So, I'm not sure. I can't really turn it on or off, and I don't hear anything at all, usually. I don't really know much about it yet."

"Do you think you'll be able to develop it?" Andrea was curious, too.

"Your guess is as good as mine. But this is the first time in my life I've used it. I know that I can always see the end of a movie from the very start, though, so maybe I've had the seeds of full blown ability for a while. I really don't know."

"It'd be good if you could sort for only the things you *wanted* to hear." Kate was smiling.

"If I could do that, I'd be rich beyond measure. But now I'm beginning to understand how my grandmother used her abilities to make a good enough living to get to the United States. Who knew there were so many believers?"

"By the looks of the estate, she did well." Andrea was right.

"She did, and still does a lot of good for people." Bella discussed the work being done in the clinic. The need was great. They met with an average of three people per hour. Since both the girls were in the medical field, they understood exactly how important it was to debrief, as they called it in clinical circles. There were whole teams who worked with caregivers after the loss of patients. And the clinic was a place to heal your spirit.

Bella was so happy to be able to share the important details of her life with her family. This meant the world to her. Just having their support made a huge difference. Not once did either express doubt that she was capable of handling it. Her confidence was boosted by their belief in her, and their curiosity about her abilities. Neither was frightened by it. Bella decided not to tell Kate about the possibility that Maddie was a telepath since she was the oldest granddaughter. It could wait.

It wasn't very long when they began to hear the pitter patter of big and little feet upstairs. It was time for Bella to get dressed. Afterward, she would come back down and get breakfast started. Today she would make pancakes with strawberries and bananas on top. The toddlers would easily be able to eat that. Anything else the adult children wanted they could fix for themselves.

"What are the plans for today?" Derek was the first to wonder.

"No plans yet," Bella began. "What would you like to do?"

"Not sure, golf maybe, if you girls want to take the kids with you today."

"I don't mind watching them if the four of you want to play a round together." She was quite comfortable extending the offer.

"What would we do if we didn't play golf?" Kate didn't look too interested in it.

"Well, there's a section downtown that has lots of quaint boutiques, and I've made friends with a woman who has a really great little shop full of odd art and collectibles. We could stroll the shops and do lunch until nap time, if you like."

"That sounds like fun." Kate liked that idea better.

"I think I'd rather do that, too," Andrea agreed. It was settled.

"My neighbor, Bruce, said he'd be happy to take you guys to a good course if you'd like a local guide."

"That sounds good." Nate was for it.

"After we get things done here, I'll walk over and talk to him. Better yet, I'll give him a call and invite him for pancakes."

Bruce didn't pick up. Bella thought he was probably working with wood, so she put her flip-flops on and walked over. Little Kyle reached his arms up for her, so she picked him up and announced they'd be right back.

As she suspected, Bruce was hard at work with the loud equipment. Kyle put his hands over his ears. Bella walked over to the window next to where he was working, and she and Kyle waved. He smiled, turned off his equipment, and motioned them in. Bruce had already eaten, but said he could be available for golf in about 30 minutes, before it got hot, or close to sunset. He didn't want to be out in the heat of the day. Bella promised to call him within five minutes to let him know. The guys opted for an early 18. The girls liked early also. They wanted time by the pool this afternoon while the kids napped. They had a plan.

It was close to lunch when they arrived at Deidre's shop. She was delighted to meet them. While the girls were browsing, Deidre pulled Bella off to the side and asked her how she liked her purchase. It was perfect! Then, Deidre asked her who helped her get it in the house. When Bella told her what happened, she wasn't surprised at all.

"I should've had that delivered and set up for you. I'm sorry."

"Deidre, what is it that you're sorry about, actually?"

"Didn't Bruce tell you?"

"Tell me what?"

"I'm sorry again, Bella, but you'll have to ask Bruce."

"I don't want to ask him."

"Well then, just enjoy it. It's beautiful."

"Yes...exquisite!"

"All of his work is top of the line. What a gift! Well, let me know if the girls have any questions."

"I will. Thanks." With that, Deidre turned and walked back over to the counter.

Andrea selected an antique doll that came with a box full of clothes. It would be part of her plan to reveal her surprise. Kate selected a wooden golf club for Nate that was inscribed 'passion pays.' They were all very excited. Before stopping for lunch, they decided to put their purchases in the car. It was less to keep track of.

The heat was sweltering on the golf course. Derek and Nate were sweating through their shirts. Bruce was used to the Arizona sun, but it quickly became a 9-hole game. They'd decided! It was back to the club house, time for a cold one.

"Your mom is a remarkable woman." Bruce started the conversation with a familiar subject.

"Busy...as usual." Derek looked at Nate before turning to Bruce.

"It takes a lot to keep what she's managed to pull together operating without a glitch. She says you both have businesses of your own and know all about that." They both shook their heads in agreement.

"We don't work as many hours as her, though. "

"She's set now. Anna took care of that. But she'll be busy."

"What does that mean?"

"I'll let her tell you that. But you won't need to worry about her."

"Worry about her? Never. She's a tough old broad. She can take care of herself, always could." Nate was sure of his statement.

"And us..." Derek added. "...even when we didn't want her too."

"Sounds like you're lucky men." They agreed.

"Yep…but if we want to stay lucky, we better get back. The girls will be wanting some free time."

"Yep." They put money on the bar and headed home.

"How'd you guys meet?"

"Skinny dipping!" Bruce had them all laughing, even though it was true. "Naw, Anna always let me use the pool, and one night, just after Bella arrived, I showed up when she was there. We became fast friends. She still lets me use the pool. The woodshop's hot. It's nice to take a dip after working in the heat all day."

"I'd like to see your shop."

"Done." Just about that time they pulled up in front of it. They got out and Bruce gave them the tour. It was hot in there, alright. They were all ready for the pool. When they walked out through the back door, there were the girls, poolside already.

"Come on over, Bruce." Nate invited him to join in.

"See you later on."

They got a volleyball game going while the kids were asleep. Bella stayed inside with the air on today. She worked on her share of tasks for the publishing company on the computer while she had a block of uninterrupted time. It might be necessary for her to stay awake late to finish the manuscript. She promised to wrap it up before her trip to the canyon. Bella did need some rest, though, and thought that after the kids woke up, she would nap for a couple of hours.

The time passed quickly, and her grandchildren slept for two and a half hours. Bella got done with the busy work she promised to complete, and forwarded it on to her assistant. Yahoo! She looked outside at the four of them playing volleyball in the pool. It was everything she'd imagined. All were having fun. Seeing her stare out the door, the girls waved. About that time, Kyle woke up. Bella changed him, screened him up to block the sun, put a little hat on him, which he immediately took off, and walked him outside.

No sooner had she walked him to the edge of the pool when she heard Maddie calling from the open door. Bella scooped her up, changed her, greased her down and brought her out. She liked her little hat. What a cute bunch. Bella ran back inside for her camera. It was a wonderful photo. She would keep this one on her desk.

"The first photo at the new house," Bella announced.

"You're keeping it?"

"Yeah, I am. I was telling the girls I'm probably going to be living here one or two days a week. Let me change and I'll join you guys out here."

The afternoon filled itself up with questions and conversation about the new responsibilities that Bella would be shouldering, about how she would travel, and about all the technology Gran had invented. Finally, Bella told them about her telepathy. Surprisingly, they didn't mind at all. They were more interested in what was happening with Bruce. Bella made sure they understood that Bruce was just a friend.

"Skinny dipping with a friend?" Nate was yanking her chain.

"Is that what he told you?" Bella acted surprised.

"Co-ed naked skinny dipping!" Derek was cracking up.

"Sounds like I got here just in time," Bruce said as he walking down the steps into the shallow end. Everybody laughed. If only they knew.

The afternoon quickly became evening. Instead of going out, they decided to make some pizzas out of the ingredients they had on hand. Bruce had some stone ground tortillas and pizza sauce. Bella had bacon, sausage, veggies and cheese. Bella made up a blender of margaritas, and sliced some melon to eat by the pool. It felt just like a grand vacation. Suddenly, out of the blue, Bella realized that since she'd made her decision to stay, it *was* a vacation. She didn't have to clean anything else out if she didn't want to. Although she wanted to get rid of some of the clothes and decorations and stuff, she needn't be in a hurry. This was now her second residence.

Shortly after dark, Maddie and Kyle began to get cranky. They were tired. It was bed time. Bruce agreed to run Bella to the clinic to pick up the van, since they were leaving sometime tomorrow. It would be about a four hour drive one way, and Bella wanted to reach their lodging by dark. That gave them plenty time to eat and pack in the morning. She borrowed Bruce's outside shower and rinsed off the chlorine. Using a fresh beach towel, she dried off and headed to the beach house to dress. It was less than five minutes before she appeared at Bruce's.

The minute she hit the door he planted a serious kiss right on her mouth. He'd been dreaming of taking her slowly and deliciously right there. She welcomed his advances, getting carried away on the kiss. Then, snapping back to reality, she backed up and adjusted herself. There were children awaiting her return. After a slight adjustment, Bruce grabbed her hand and led her out to the garage. He couldn't help it, he wanted her more than anything, ever.

The ride to the clinic was silent. Both Bella and Bruce were turned on to the point of distraction. Immediately upon opening the van door, Bruce lifted her onto the seat, and kissed her passionately and publicly. Luckily, the night was cloud covered and there wasn't another soul in sight. Bruce was so turned on he felt like a man of twenty. A full thirty minutes passed before they came to their senses. Without a word Bella pulled herself together and put the key in the ignition.

"Have a great trip," Bruce cleared his throat and spoke huskily. "If you want, call."

"Will do," Bella's body was aflame. 'Bruce…" she was nearly shouting. He came back to the open driver's door and stood beside her seat. She turned and kissed him again. OMG, he couldn't get enough of her!

Upon arrival home, the house was quiet. The kids had retired to their suites upstairs and the babies were in bed. Bella sat down at the breakfast bar with a bowl of butter pecan ice cream. She was sitting alone eating, when she got a text.

'Dreaming of eating ice cream with you…' Bella looked at the window and there he was. She put her finger over her lips to keep him from speaking, and went to the pool house and sat down.

"I don't want any physical contact around my kids, please, Bruce."

"Got it."

They sat there for quite a while before any words were uttered.

"Bruce…"

"Hmmm?"

"The woodcarving on my table upstairs…who is that?"

"My daughter."

"Where is she?"

"In heaven."

Bella didn't ask another question. She just relaxed beside him, awaiting the details. Bruce finally woke her to go into the house. She had no idea how long she'd been asleep there.

Chapter 13

At breakfast everyone agreed that the best time to travel was an hour before nap time, so the kids would sleep. Breakfast clean up and packing went quickly. There was time for a swim before they had to go.

Bruce was asleep on the chase lounge. Derek did a cannon ball and splashed him. He nearly left the chair without touching the ground. Everybody roared. Little Kyle went up to him and said 'boo.' Bruce made a funny face and sound, and Kyle ran off giggling. It was a great time.

Bella felt the heat on her shoulders and decided to cover up. She'd forgotten her sunscreen. Sitting on the pool steps, she drifted off into thought. Since she was keeping the estate, should she go home early? It was something to consider.

"Please don't leave early, Bella," she heard from Bruce's thoughts. She looked him right in the eye. "Spend some time with me. Please."

"You know how much I love spending time with you Bruce."

"But..." he interrupted.

"Well, I haven't made my decision yet. I'll think it over. Cloak." Bella closed off her private thoughts. This was a decision she wanted to make herself. Bruce moved back physically at the moment she cloaked her thoughts. He looked offended. She didn't mean to hurt his feelings, but Bella needed to check herself at every turn now. She would have a lot to manage with two properties, two businesses, her children and grandchildren. As for Bruce, remaining 'just friends' would make things easier. When she was in town she could see him, and when she was home she could do whatever came up. It was uncomplicated. And...how could he read her thoughts?

"Bruce," Nate shook his hand, "…it's been fun. Thanks, man." Everyone else followed suit. They gathered everything up and headed for the main house. It was time to get on the road.

"Grand Canyon here we come!"

By the time everyone got their luggage in the van, it was packed from top to bottom. Even with rear air, Bella hoped the babies wouldn't be too warm in their car seats. Andrea wanted to be the first to drive. Since Bella got car sick, she sat in the front with her.

Their trip started on I-17. Montezuma's Castle was their first stop. The Indian ruins were a short but welcome walk from the car. They stayed only long enough for Maddie and Kyle to begin to fuss, then back on the road. They traveled steadily toward Sedona. Although they really wanted to stop, the kids had just gotten to sleep, so they decided to visit on the way back. They drove through beautiful Oak Creek Canyon for what seemed like twenty miles, and then got back on highway 17 for the drive into the park.

Two restless toddlers drove the decision to get something to eat and find the house before going to the canyon. Bella plugged the address into the GPS and off they went. When they pulled up, they couldn't believe their eyes.

This was a beautiful, single story, mission style home with a large in-ground pool. They walked up and punched the combination into the lock. Bella took both keys from the lock box. They stepped into a tile foyer that connected to a large living room with vaulted ceilings and a stone fireplace. There were three bedrooms and two baths. Near the pool was a covered patio. The place was landscaped beautifully.

"How'd you find this place?" Kate was a practical girl. She was a great money manager.

"Bruce's friend owns it."

"This is the life. First we get to the estate, then this. Nothing but the best."

"I'm glad you like it. Let's unload. Which bedrooms do you want?"

"Mom, why don't you take the smallest one? It's got a bathroom of its own."

"That makes sense."

They got unpacked and settled in. Walking into the kitchen, Derek found a note on the counter.

Bella, thanks for letting me use the pool. I believe you will find everything you need. Enjoy yourself. — Bruce

She browsed the cabinets and refrigerator. Everything was fully stocked. As she walked to the patio door, she saw a cooler they could use for picnics in the canyon. When she opened it up, it was stocked with cold beer, soda and bottled water. Bruce had gone to enormous trouble to make sure they had everything. He'd even ordered in Gerber juices and foods for toddlers. How very thoughtful.

"I'll call and thank him later."

"Maybe we'll find a nice chunk of wood to bring back for him or something." Nate was in souvenir mode.

"And maybe you can sit on it for the ride home," Kate teased.

"True."

"This was really nice of him. I'm for a beer and a dip in the pool. Kyle, do you want to go swimming with Mommy?" Little Kyle reached his arms up to her. They were off to get changed.

"Sounds great, I'll join you." Bella went to her room, the smallest room, which had to be twenty feet square. Small is relative," she chuckled inwardly.

Bella was pulling up her swimsuit when Maddie toddled in. She reached her arms up for Grandma to hold her. Scooping her up, Bella kissed her. She had the most kissable cheeks ever. Then she got the idea to try to communicate with her telepathically. Bella knew she had a gift, but she didn't know which one. Since Bella, her mom, and her grandmother were all telepaths, it was logical that Maddie was, too.

Bella put her down and thought 'come give me a hug.' Maddie

turned around and gave her a hug. And much to her surprise, Nate came through the door and hugged her also.

"This is great, Mom. Thanks."

"Nate, what prompted you to come in and give me a hug?"

"What?" He looked at her like she had a third eye in the middle of her forehead.

"Nothing. Just thinking about something."

Nate laughed and shook his head, making light of it.

"I'll be out in a minute, Nate."

"Take your time."

Bella sat on the edge of the bed for a minute. Could it be that since she didn't have a daughter of her own that the genetic tendency passed to her son? And was it limited to Nate, or did Derek have it, too? But Derek didn't respond to her thought. Nate and Maddie did. This was crazy. Bella made up her mind not to make an issue of it. She would downplay it, but would silently test everyone's abilities as the trip progressed.

"How does this work, Gran? Can there be more than one person who can receive messages from transmitting telepaths? Can a receiver hear the thoughts of more than one transmitter?"

"Well, I think you know the answers to those questions, Bella. Think about it. You can transmit to me, your mother, Bruce, and Maddie. And you receive from me. Most telepaths are one or the other, either a sender or a receiver. You have the very rare combination of both abilities. Your mother was only a sender, and as far as I know, when I was in my body, I was the only a receiver. But we can be contacted by Linda. So..."

"And you transmit to and receive from me, Gran." Bella just put it together. Gran's gift had morphed.

"You're right, dear! I do. My ability has expanded, I've changed. I wonder if I will eventually be able to communicate with everyone who's telepathic."

"Gran, every day I find myself experiencing something beyond my wildest dreams. There's so much more to us than what we know. It's mind boggling!"

"Have fun unfolding, Darling."

"Grandma, let's play ball!" Maddie telepathically called her.

"Talk to you later, Gran."

"Have fun."

Bella went out to the pool and Maddie was trying to throw the beach ball. Bella found it odd that Maddie could communicate with her telepathically in full sentences, when she was physically capable of only a few spoken words. She assumed that understanding language came before the ability to express words. It was interesting. Bella would have to be very careful what she thought about around her children, and she must remember to cloak her thoughts of Bruce.

"Cloak." Bella wanted to keep her observations and analysis private.

Over the next few days they beheld some of the most breathtaking panoramas they'd ever seen. They went hiking. Stroller rentals were abundant, and made the excursions family friendly. Because of Bruce's kind gesture, they enjoyed plenty cool drinks and snacks playing in and around the canyon. They were comfortable and having fun.

Bella observed Nate and Maddie over the days they shared together. But something interesting revealed itself. Derek and Kyle displayed the same type of interaction as Nate and Maddie. She wasn't sure if it was simply that they'd spent so much time together that they'd learned each other's unspoken cues, or if they also had telepathic abilities. Bella wanted to check it out.

While eating lunch, Bella looked at Kyle and, with her thoughts, asked him to wipe his face. He did not respond, but his daddy did. Nate, Derek and Maddie wiped their mouths. Was that a coincidence, an unconscious cue that they all had messy faces, or telepathic communication? Bella wasn't sure. She tried another experiment.

With her thoughts, Bella communicated, "I hear somebody's phone." Neither responded.

She decided to come out in the open about what she'd discovered since she'd been in Phoenix. She spent the rest of the afternoon by the pool with her family, confessing everything she knew about her abilities. Bella brought them up to date about their lineage, her mother and grandmother, their telepathic ways of communicating, and how she'd lived to age fifty without ever knowing her relatives had the gift. She wasn't aware of her own abilities until she came out west.

Having more questions than answers, she led an open discussion about what she knew, what was happening in the clinic, and the inventions and theories developed by her grandmother. Looking into the faces of the people she loved most, she could see the same fear, skepticism and intrigue she felt at first discovery.

"This blows my mind." Derek was the first to speak.

"I hear ya." Nate appeared more comfortable than Derek, but still skeptical.

"Well, my family has believed in psychic ability for years. It's a fact that we can communicate with thoughts. For me, it's old news. I believe in it."

"Maddie is a telepath, Kate." Bella expected Kate to react in an exaggerated way, but she was calm.

"I saw a psychic when I was pregnant with her, and was told that my daughter was going to be a very spiritual person, and that I should read everything I could get my hands on to keep up with her. But…I was thinking religion, not spirituality like this. How does it work?"

"I have been thinking simple thoughts and sending them to Maddie. She has been responding in action and thought. Her speaking abilities have not evolved as quickly as her ability to communicate with thoughts." Kate was thinking it through.

"Let's test it," Kate suggested. Being a nurse practitioner, Bella expected her to want some scientific proof. "How would we do that?"

"This is how I started. Write down something that Maddie can do and I will communicate it to her with my thoughts. Don't show the others until after she has completed the task."

"Okay." Kate wrote her instruction on the paper and handed it to Bella. Bella looked at Maddie and communicated the thought. She toddled over to the lounger, pulled out a diaper and some wipes, and handed them to her dad.

"You need Daddy to change you?" Nate asked her with words. Maddie shook her head, but then nodded. She was confused. Maddie wasn't wet, but she obeyed Bella's instruction to get a diaper and wipes from the bag. Bella turned over the paper, and everyone was still.

"You two knew the instruction before you saw the paper, didn't you?" She looked directly at her boys.

"Maddie's a psychic?" Derek was floored.

"Try Kyle," Andrea was intrigued, "If it's in the bloodline…"

"Okay, write your instruction."

Andrea handed the paper to Bella. Kyle did not respond. Andrea looked disappointed.

"So…" thinking out loud, "Gran's theory that the gift only runs in the females of the bloodline seems correct, judging by what we discovered today. But the questions I have are…1) why didn't my gift appear before I arrived in Arizona? 2) Why didn't I know about Maddie's gift? 3) Could it have something to do with geographical location or elements in the stones or rocks?) And 4) will the devices in the clinic work for Maddie, too?"

Suddenly, Maddie let out a scream. Kate went over and saw Kyle with her bottle. He promptly walked over to Andrea and handed her the bottle. Andrea was thrilled. Bella showed the others that Kai followed the instruction she gave him telepathically.

"Toss that theory out the window!" They started laughing. It was a great tension releaser. What Bella had feared was now out in the open. What happened from here on was completely unpredictable.

"One at a time, I'd like to take each of you to the clinic to test the bands that Gran designed to see if any of you can activate them. This might give us some idea of whether the bands will also work with any others in the bloodline than the first born granddaughter of each generation. We know it works for me. Since you boys are my direct descendants, perhaps it will work for you. That could open up other possibilities down the line."

"Like what?" Nate wanted to know.

"Well, I'm not sure. Right now there are only two people known of in the world who could activate the bands, Gran and I. With Gran on another side of life, that's limiting. If it worked out that the scope was broader, we might be able to do more work than is possible with only one facilitator."

"Is the need that great?" Derek had a point.

"Who knows? Right now, you know as much as I do."

"Let's go to the canyon." Everyone liked Andrea's idea.

On the way to the park Bella thought about the results of their preliminary tests today. So far, the tests indicated that some of Bella's direct descendants exhibited telepathic gifts. And so far, they are only able to communicate with those in the direct blood line known to be telepathic. At least that was true in Bella's family. But that didn't explain Bruce. It also didn't explain why the gifts revealed themselves now. Was it possible that they'd all possessed their abilities all along, but they just now became activated? If so, what activated them?

"We'll have some work to do."

"Yeah, if only we knew how to do it." They all laughed.

"How about we agree that when we're all together we just talk to each other?"

They unanimously agreed.

Four days in the park was plenty with two babies, but it was a trip of a lifetime. It was hard to imagine how many years it took to form the canyon. Bella couldn't wrap her mind around the number eighty million years! How could they determine that? Yes, the evidence was compelling, but to be able to say the number with any certainty was hard for her to imagine. She felt the same way about being able to calculate the exact distance to the moon and back. It was mind-boggling! The enormity of the canyon made her feel small. She occupied a miniscule part of this large planet, which was small in this big universe.

Trips like these expanded Bella. They created space for new thoughts, new experiences, new questions and unanticipated pleasures. Bella sat on the canyon rim and thanked God for her life, her family and this trip.

"One last thing before we go, kids…"

"A photo, no doubt!" They all burst out laughing. But as they stood along the canyon rim for one last photo, Bella's heart swelled to overflowing. The trip she'd hoped to take with her children, she got to spend with her grandchildren, too. It was a blessing and a bonus. And she would always remember it.

They piled in and didn't stop until they got to Sedona. After a quick lunch and a brief look around, they headed toward home. By supper they would be back in the pool. After tonight, only two more nights out west, and it was homeward bound for the kids.

"Maybe tonight at supper we can discuss what we'd each like to find out about Gran's inventions and Maddie's abilities before your trip ends. That way we can use our time efficiently." No words were spoken, but everyone was nodding in agreement. Bella closed her eyes and slipped into a deep sleep. She didn't awaken until she heard the van door open. They were home.

It was past dinner time, but nobody seemed as hungry as they did tired of sitting. The babies had energy to burn. Bella put some beach balls on the grass in the back yard for the kids to play around with. Eventually, they just decided to order pizza. They played in, out and around the pool for the rest of the night. At some point Bruce came over and the guys got into a game of poker. The cards were hot and the beer was cold. They were having fun. Bella, the babes, and the girls were floating around and chatting. Soon it was dark.

"It's time to get this little boy in the tub and to bed." Andrea picked him up.

"Maddie, do you want to take a tubby with Kyle?" Kate was coaxing her along, too.

The girls took the kids up to the house. The guys were still playing cards, but decided to call it a night before their wives reminded them that it was their vacation, too. They'd been watching them most of the evening. Bruce understood. He helped clean up before the Nate and Derek went inside. Finally, Bruce and Bella were alone.

"I have nothing else to do. How about you?"

"Not a thing."

They lounged by the pool, chatting under a rising moon. Bella thanked Bruce for the generous provisions that sustained them while they were on vacation. She told him about the telepathic testing they'd done, and all the questions they had. Bruce talked of the progress he's made on his current project, and about some ideas he had for a line of new woodcarvings. Bella loved listening to artists creating. It was fantastic to be privy to the process. She was learning.

"Bruce…"

"Hmm?"

"Can you hear my thoughts?"

"Sometimes. Can you hear mine?" Bruce sure hoped not.

"Maybe. The other night, when I was leaving the jewelry studio, I saw you answer my thoughts with words."

"I read your lips, not your thoughts. Sometimes I think I hear your voice. But if I answer with thoughts, you don't respond to me, so I know you can't hear me. It's confusing. When we're in certain places, I can hear a whole conversation we're having with Anna. Why is that?"

"I don't understand it either. You're not in my blood line. Are you a telepath?"

"Maybe. But I know people who have been together and can practically read each other's thoughts, and they're not telepathic." Bruce was trying to make sense of it all.

"Well, that's what I thought, too, but I'm not sure. Do you think there's something magical about this place? I mean, could it be this location?" Bella kept noticing that common denominator.

"What about it?"

"I don't have a clue…the stones, maybe? Could there be something, some kind of thought conductor in the elements of the canyons, the earth or certain rocks here? I don't know what to think."

"I'm too tired to think about anything right now, Bella. I'm going to head home." With that he picked up his belongings and walked across the yard.

Bella picked up what was left around the pool and put it away. She hung the towels on the paddle on the porch and turned off the lights. It was time for her to get some sleep, too. The next two days would be busy.

Bella woke up before the others, made coffee, and went into her study to get ready for the staff meeting. She closed the door. Reviewing the notes she'd been sent and today's meeting agenda got her in the publisher's frame of mind. Allen's work was coming along nicely. He was paying attention to his email, responding in a timely manner, and meeting deadlines. That would serve them all well.

Bella was disappointed to learn that one of her staff members was diagnosed with cancer. She would be taking a leave of absence shortly. After undergoing a course of radiation, she would have surgery. From just before surgery until after chemotherapy, she wasn't sure she'd be able to work. Bella understood. But it meant they would need another body. The most logical person was her. Pandora had a legal right to return to her job after completing treatment. But Bella wouldn't replace her because she got sick. Her dedication and loyalty had earned her a permanent place at the agency. But it meant Bella would be leaving Phoenix sooner than she thought.

At breakfast she shared the news with her family. There were final decisions she would have to make in the next two weeks. Her trip would be cut short by one month. She would have to work with Rick Baker to set a clinic schedule. Private pilot interviews were scheduled this week, and she would have to have some idea of what day(s) she needed the pilot(s). Getting the paperwork started for the retainer would also be a high priority. There was lots to do.

Talking through it with the kids, Bella decided that she would take Nate's family to the clinic in the morning, and Derek's in the afternoon. It would create less commotion.

Bella was proud to introduce her family to the clinic staff. Each person made it a point to welcome them. After getting into her office, Bella began the process of opening computers, explaining 3D holograms, reviewing instructions, and bringing them up to date on what she knew about the technology so far. Finally they began a battery of tests. Bella started with Kate. Before beginning the exercises, Bella looked at Maddie and, with her thoughts, asked Maddie to sit on Daddy's lap and be very quiet while she worked with Mommy. The child climbed up and remained still for a long time. Then she tested Nate. There was no telepathic connection between them here, yet there had been in the canyon. So far, only Maddie and Bella were connected here, in Phoenix.

Bella picked Maddie up and spoke to her out loud. Because Kate couldn't read thought energy, she agreed to conduct the whole test with words first. Maddie could send and receive from Bella.

"So…with what we know right now, we must all be careful to direct our thought. We have a mini telepath in our midst. I think she's too young to know who else she might be able to communicate with. Now…I want to see if she can initiate the band." Bella put the band on her head.

"Maddie, can you think the word 'on'?" Bella spoke the words out loud. The band initiated, but in almost that very instant, Maddie reached up and took it off and threw it down. Luckily, Bella caught it before it hit the ground.

"Okay, Maddie, Grandma's done. Thank you, big girl."

"So far, only Maddie and I can initiate the invention."

"Mom, if you can read thoughts anyway, why do you need this thing?"

"Great question! I can't read everybody, Nate. So far, it's just Gran, Maddie, and sometimes, Bruce. I can't turn it off or on at will yet. So, if somebody needs help and my gift isn't active, I can use this."

"Well, if you have people who can read what's tripping people up, people who can connect other people with their dead relatives, and people who can tell the future, why do you need this thing?"

"I don't have that answer. Perhaps Gran was working toward a patent or something."

"Or maybe there could be an emergency when a person can't make it. This might be Plan B." Kate offered an idea.

"That's a valid point. I need to look into it further. Well, we best get home for lunch. I'll come back this afternoon with Derek, Andrea and Kyle."

Lunch went quickly, and it was back to the clinic for Bella. This afternoon Bella wanted to start with Kyle so he could sleep when he got tired. He didn't respond to Bella's thoughts immediately. The same thing happened at the canyon. There was a delay. Did that mean he just didn't feel like responding? Bella suspected that he lived in an imaginary world, and kept his mind focused on other things. When she gave him instructions, he simply waited until he finished whatever thoughts he was having, and took his sweet time. So…maybe he had a gift and an attitude. They all laughed about it. The test was inconclusive.

Next Derek went through the testing. He was not telepathically connected to her, and he could not activate the band. Bella could, however, see into his thoughts briefly with the band. Since he didn't ask what she saw, Bella kept it to herself.

Andrea's results mirrored Derek's. No psychic ability was indicated. Bella could also read her thoughts while she wore the band but since she didn't ask… They walked out of the clinic the same way Bella did every time, with more questions than answers. None of them would have ever dreamed they'd be doing this today. It was another family first.

"When I was a teenager, I used to hear my mom's voice when I was thinking of doing something wrong. I just called it my conscience, but now I'm not so sure." They all chuckled.

"This stuff causes you to rethink everything, doesn't it?

"Yeah!"

At home that night, everyone was quieter than usual. Something in Bella kept surfacing. It was a feeling that her abilities came to life in this place. If not, why couldn't she ever use it before? She mentioned it to her family. It wouldn't be long before she could test her theory. Soon, she'd be home. Tomorrow was their last day together in Phoenix. She would miss everyone, but only for two weeks.

"Are you guys up for a great Mexican fiesta tonight? Bruce took me to a really neat place. It's noisy, has music and dancing, and the food and margaritas are fantastic." Everybody liked the idea. Bella called Bruce and got the number. She made a reservation, which included Bruce.

While the babies napped, Bella did a load of laundry and colored her hair. She figured out what she wanted to wear. Then she remembered her gifts.

"Girls, come with me. You boys listen for the kids, please."

"Where are we going?" Andrea was curious.

"To the jewelry studio. Follow me."

"There's a jewelry studio, too? This place is like Disneyland." They all started laughing. Kate couldn't believe it.

The girls spent a great deal of time looking at everything. They brushed against every stone and looked at every table.

Bella was thinking about the special energies contained within the stones.

"Tell me about that," Andrea spoke aloud.

"That stone you're holding enhances psychic ability. You're reading my thoughts, Andrea."

She looked up at Bella in amazement.

"I'm not trying to."

"I know."

"Kyle is pitching a fit. Let me call Derek." They all realized that she was hearing Kyle. After she was reassured that it was a temper tantrum and nothing urgent, they continued looking at the jewelry. When they came upon Bella's drafting table, and the layout with her designs, they marveled at how accurate Bella's selections were.

"I didn't choose these, they chose me. While thinking thoughts about you both, the stones activated. That sounds wacky, but on yours, Andrea, as I walked by the table the stone jumped off. I didn't touch anything. The stone chose you. And for Kate's...I was caught between two that I liked for the center when suddenly the sunlight shown right down on this one like a laser beam. I kid you not!" Both girls believed her.

Bella showed them the rings for their husbands, and the spoons. They all stood around ogling them until Bruce came walking in.

"What's up Bruce?" Bella was curious.

"I thought we were going to dinner now." He looked puzzled.

"Have we been out here that long?" They started laughing and rushed out and up to change.

"Sorry, Bruce...ten minutes." Bella felt awful.

"Fifteen, Bruce..." Andrea called over her shoulder.

He followed them across the yard and entered through the kitchen door. He pulled a beer out of the frig and sat down at the breakfast bar. Two minutes later Derek and Nate took a couple out and sat with him.

"We'll have time," Nate laughed.

When the women appeared ready to go the guys knew they were worth the wait. They all looked so beautiful that the men couldn't take their eyes off of them.

"Wow," was all Bruce could say.

"Puh," Kyle reached his arms out to Grandma.

"Up…can you say up?"

"Puh." They all giggled.

They stayed at the fiesta for three hours. The food and marguerites were fantastic. Bella felt lighter than air. She danced with her grandchildren, the girls and Bruce. It was great fun. Maddie and Kyle partied until they were falling down. They were smiling, but rubbing their eyes. It was late, and time to go.

Bruce insisted on paying the bill. He wouldn't accept any help, not even for a tip. Everyone was thankful and truly appreciated his generosity toward them during this trip. He seemed genuinely delighted to treat them to the evening.

"This is the best time I've had in ten years," he told them.

"You've got to get out more, Bruce," Derek teased.

"Don't I know it?"

"The kids got in the rental, and Bella hopped in with Bruce."

"Tomorrow's their last day, Bruce." Bella was a bit melancholy.

"I'm so glad I got to meet them. You have a great family, Bella."

"Don't I?"

"I almost had a family, once myself." Now Bruce looked melancholy.

"Pull over," Bella made a motion with her hand. "I'll drive."

Bruce pulled over and got out. They traded places and he poured his heart out. When he was twenty years old and in college, his girlfriend got pregnant. Neither Bruce nor his girlfriend wanted the baby, but she didn't want an abortion. They made a plan to give the baby up for adoption at birth, so they didn't tell their parents. When their daughter was born, he refused to sign on the birth certificate, not wanting his mistake to come back to haunt him. He later found out that she was placed with a loving family, but since she was born with a hole in her heart, she died before her first birthday. Bruce felt like he had a hole in his heart, and never got over it. He carved the angel baby that Bella had on display at the top of the steps in her honor. He just couldn't keep it himself. It was a constant reminder of the most serious mistake he'd ever made. Deidre convinced him to put it in her shop for the perfect owner. He made that symbolic gesture because it was similar to the choice he made all those years ago, when he gave his baby up to the perfect home. It seemed meaningful to Bruce that Bella got the little angel. It felt good to finally release the shame and guilt he had secretly carried with him for 30 years.

"Thank you. Bella."

"You're welcome." Gran was right. Nothing was asked of her, she didn't need to know anything special, and she didn't have to fix anything. She simply held the space with love, so Bruce could close the hole in his heart. Bella really liked this work.

"Now, come on in and say good-bye to the kids. They're leaving in the morning."

"If you don't mind, I'll just head home. It's been fun, though."

"I'll tell them good-by for you."

"Thanks."

"Are you going to be alright?"

"I am now."

Bella walked into a mad house. Kyle and Maddie were running in circles chasing each other and giggling. They had energy to burn. The short nap on the way home recharged their batteries and they were a couple of wild Indians! The atmosphere lifted Bella's spirits. She chased them around threatening to catch them, causing them to giggle and scream. It was utter pandemonium!

"Mom, do you have a TV here?" Andrea asked her a question she didn't have an answer to. It occurred to her that she hadn't turned on a TV in six weeks. They spread out and looked in all the rooms. They couldn't find one.

"Wait," Bella uttered, "let me use my thoughts to conjure one up, if I can." Suddenly, the lights dimmed and a television appeared. 'Remote', Bella thought, and nothing.

"It's touch screen TV, Bella." It was Gran.

"Gran says it's a touch screen." Andrea got up and began touching the screen. She picked a program and slid the volume up a bit with her finger.

"Is that creepy to have someone talk to you that you don't know is listening?" Kate was curious.

"Not at all." Bella felt very comfortable.

"Can she see you?"

"I don't know, can you, Gran?"

"No. I can sense you, though, and I can see the pictures in your mind." Bella explained it to Kate.

"What about during sex?" They all started laughing.

"I never thought about that, but I guess with Gran and Maddie being able to read me, I better become a lot more conscientious about cloaking my thoughts!"

"Yuck, Mom!" And that ended it.

They picked a Disney movie and settled in. The kids settled down some. Although they were not still, they continued to look at the screen every few minutes.

The smell of popcorn brought the guys down to the family room. Bella got a blanket and a couple of throw pillows and put them on the floor. It wasn't long before Maddie laid down on the pallet and put her head on the pillow. She was asleep in minutes. About twenty minutes later, Kyle followed suit.

"I'm so glad you guys took the time to come out and see the canyon with me. I've been wanting to do that for a long time."

"It was great." Derek enjoyed himself.

"This place is great, too…better than a hotel!" They all nodded in agreement.

"Well, it's ours now. This is now my second home. You can come any time you like. And if you come during one of my trips, you can fly free. You'd just need to pay for your ticket home."

"That'd be the way to go." Andrea was excited.

Bella filled them in on her idea about setting up a branch of her publishing company here. They were all enthusiastic about the expansion. They talked business for another hour, speculating on how to build a presence in this area. It was a little harder for independent publishers than the traditional houses, but the market was swinging around. Nationwide, 49% of books currently on bookstore shelves are from independent publishers. That's about half. Whatever she decided, she would have to do a market analysis first, and draft a business plan. That would take time. Time was the greatest factor for her right now. She was getting in the groove of juggling the old and new. But she had good help, and that was worth its weight in gold.

Everyone said good night and went up to their rooms. Bella wasn't tired. She got that let down feeling that comes at the end of every vacation. She was unsettled, but headed up to her room. Opening the balcony doors, she saw Bruce swimming laps in the pool. Bella changed into her suit and joined him.

Taking off his goggles, he greeted her poolside. She sat down and dangled her feet in the water. Neither of them spoke, but they were together. Bruce pulled his goggles back down and continued his laps. Bella leaned back on her hands and thought about what a well-oiled machine his body was. He was gliding through the water rhythmically, breathing steadily and barely breaking a splash.

Bella got up and went inside the pool house. She'd never really taken a good look at what was out here. This was a two bedroom house. It was fully furnished and completely ready for someone to move into.

She took a serious look at the spare room, thinking about it as an office. When Bella moved the branch to Phoenix, she could easily offer the pool house as temporary lodging until permanent housing could be obtained. That is, if it was a member of her current staff, someone she knew well. There was a lot to think about.

"What are you planning for in there?"

"Well, I was thinking about starting a new branch of my publishing company in town, and was considering this as temporary housing, if someone needed time to find a place and get moved in."

"That would certainly be a nice perk!"

"Yes, I think so. Listen, Bruce, there's an internal emergency in my company, and I'll be leaving a month earlier than I thought."

"I hope everything will be okay."

Bella explained her predicament, and what she needed to do for now. Bruce understood. He was disappointed, but was a good friend and supported her feelings and her need to be there.

"How often will you be in town during that time?"

"I wish I knew. Everything is still up in the air. I'll know more by the end of the week."

"Well, no more thinking business tonight. Relax and enjoy the moonlight."

"I think I'll go up to bed. I'm getting tired. I'll see you some time tomorrow."

"Sleep well, Bella."

"You, too, Bruce"

Bella was up early preparing a meal before her staff meeting. Derek got up early and helped. Nate was loading their checked baggage into the back of the rental. The girls were getting ready and getting the kids dressed. The house was abuzz.

While everyone ate, she met with her staff, announcing that she would be coming home before Pandora went on medical leave. Everyone was pleased to hear it. Bella cut the meeting short, explaining that she had to see her family off. Returning to the chaos, she noticed Bruce had stopped over to say good-bye.

The hugs and kisses were accompanied by tears. Bella didn't know why she was crying, but it didn't matter. Helping put the last of the luggage in the car, she stood back and away they went. As quickly as they arrived, they were gone. It had been fun.

"Now that they're gone can we go back to skinny dipping in the pool?" Bruce put his arm around her shoulder.

"I knew you liked me for my pool! Well, I'm off to work. I'll call you later."

"Sounds good." As Bruce walked home, Bella realized it was the first time she'd ever seen him walk down the sidewalk. He always came and went through the back yard.

Chapter 14

Even though it was the weekend, Bella wanted to get to the clinic and dig in. Upon arrival she realized that she needed a key. Her telepathy was useless for entry. She called Rick Baker, but he didn't answer. Then she tried Allen, who picked up the phone. Bella explained her predicament, and Allen invited her to come by for his key.

When Bella got to Scottsdale, she drove through Starbuck's for a cappuccino. She put Allen's address in the GPS. She drove through neighborhoods where lots of kids were playing together, and thought about her grandkids. Although it was a few years away, the thought made her smile. When her GPS announced her arrival, she looked up and there was Allen sitting on the porch waiting for her. He walked up to the car and handed her the key.

"Look, Allen…"

"Stop, Bella. There are things that you don't know about me, things nobody knows. And I like my privacy. I was wrong to storm out on you, and I apologize."

"Apology accepted." About that time a little girl with one real leg and one prosthetic leg came out onto the porch. She made her way over to the car.

"Who are you?"

"I'm Bella. Who are you?"

"I'm Dani."

"Say good-bye to Ms. Bella, she has to go to work," Allen instructed the girl as he picked her up.

"Bye, Ms. Bella."

"Bye, Dani!"

Driving down the street, Bella wondered if Dani was Allen's child.

She appeared of Middle Eastern descent. Perhaps Allen's wife was an immigrant. She hadn't gotten to know much about him. Perhaps while she was at work she would take a look at his personnel file.

Bella was surprised to see Maura's car at the clinic when she got back. Inside, she saw a treatment door open, and Maura preparing the room.

"Good morning, Bella. What are you doing here?"

"I might ask you the same."

"I'm meeting someone today. She's stuck in an extremely painful place and can't see clearly. I agreed to meet her here."

Bella walked into the treatment room and looked closely at stones and other objects that Maura placed around the room. She ran her flat hand over, then gently touched each one, but she sensed nothing insightful. Nothing here activated her gift.

"Do these help you see?"

"They're for protection and guidance. They're like conductors of good energy and a force field against the bad ones."

"So you believe in duality, good and evil?" Bella was trying to understand all the new ideas and techniques employed here in the clinic.

"I'm not sure why, but most of the people who are drawn to me for help are addicted. They're trying to medicate with some sort of drug or alcohol. They're trapped in a bad cycle. They need a way to break the pattern, to open up that bad energy and move it along. When it jumps, I don't want to be its host."

"So what is it you do?"

"I open myself up enough to see the problem. I don't' try to judge it or correct it, just see it. Then I repeat it to the person."

"Do they ever react poorly?" Bella felt frightened for Maura. If she hadn't come in, the woman would be all alone.

"That's why I call in my spiritual guides and the ascended masters, to shield myself from harm."

"Physical harm?"

"No, spiritual harm."

"Has it ever happened?"

"Not for a long time, but if it does, there are people I can call for help."

"Actual people?"

"Yes. I'm part of a very devoted prayer group of psychic and spiritual healers. Together we help healers who need it."

"If you can do that with your ability, why was Anna working on her inventions? It seems like she spent most of her life trying to duplicate with a machine, abilities that individuals already possess."

"Anna believed we could create a peaceful world...one that worked for everyone."

"That's a tall order."

"She believed it, though. Anna thought that if people could lay down their fear of self and others, they could open up and work together to create solutions for just about anything."

"Haven't others been chasing that dream for ages?"

"Yes, but until now we don't know of anyone else who's developed this type of healing center. Think about the impact of having people cured of their psychic pain on a global basis."

"Sounds big."

"You don't believe it?" Maura looked at Bella with skepticism.

"To be honest, Maura, I've had to reevaluate everything I've ever believed since I got here. I'm not sure what to believe. It seems like everybody here has a unique healing niche, yet the gifts bring about the same result."

"There are lots of headache remedies, and they all work."

"Why so many, then?"

"People learn in different ways. Even at a very young age teachers employ different methods of teaching children. Some learn by hearing, some by seeing..."

"Auditory, kinesthetic, etc....I follow you. So this is just another way to try to achieve what modern medicine cannot."

"Exactly. Most conventional treatments are aimed at physical and mental illness. They work toward a physically measurable level of something, like a range of motion, a medicine level or a blood count. Here, we help people discover thoughts or experiences that keep them stuck. Sometimes the psyche hides things from us to keep us from staring pain in the face. Taking medicine can help you live with feelings you have, but will not help you identify a problem thought and release it. It simply teaches you to effectively coexist with it. We try to detect and liberate it."

Bella didn't know what to say to that.

"So how do *you* get there?"

"Would you like to try it?"

"Bella hesitated."

"Will it help or hurt me?"

"What I see is good, Bella," Maura began as she gently put her hand on the back of Bella's left shoulder. She was looking, but not at anythng in the room. It was as if she was seeing behind a hidden curtain. Bella couldn't feel anything happening, but as Maura spoke about what she saw, doors opened for Bella. She was reunited with her past, and vividly remembered what Maura was looking at. It was an amazing process. And then it was over.

"I feel fantastic!" Bella felt lighter than air. It was as if she was weightless, no psychic baggage. "Can it be that simple, Maura?"

"Yes. Figuring out what's holding you back can be that simple. Designing a lifelong solution…not so much. So…where will you go from here?"

"Everywhere, Maura, everywhere." Maura shook her head as if she already knew the answer. Why did Bella feel like she was always the last to know? Remembering what she came for, Bella thanked Maura and went down to Rick Baker's office.

Surprisingly, it was unlocked. Bella looked through the standing files for the information about the endowment managers. There was no information about them in the files. Perhaps he was unaware of the specifics of the funding, but received the information he required from someone else.

There was nothing about Allen's family in his personnel file. But his military service was exemplary. He was a decorated patriot, wounded in the line of duty. Allen was willing to lay down his life for what he held dear. It was all she needed to know about him.

Walking back down the hall, she encountered someone coming through the front door. When she saw her, she turned around and went back out the door.

"Wait. Wait!" Bella went after her, but couldn't keep up. She went back inside and locked the door. Bella went to Maura's treatment room, but the door was shut. She was in session. Bella wondered if the person who walked in the front door had good or bad intentions. It was very unsettling.

"Who was that, Gran?"

"I don't know."

"Gran, why do my abilities seem to work sometimes, but not others?"

"I'm not sure. From what I've seen, your abilities only seem to work with Maddie and me. If I'm cloaking, you can't reach me. If Maddie doesn't understand it's you, she can't communicate with you. And...well...she may not understand how to use language well yet."

"That makes sense. So...I have the gift, but a very specific gift, telepathy, and it's only active around my grandmother and granddaughter."

"It seems that way, yes."

"Why do you say it 'seems' that way?"

"Usually, nothing is the way it seems. It's always somewhere in between. We see only a part of it, the part we're tuned in to."

"That's cryptic. Explain, please."

"Well, in simple terms, we don't see electricity, but it's there. We don't see radio frequencies, but they exist. We don't see sonar pulses, but they're real."

"And..."

"And, you can't rule out the possibility that there is another receiver or sender somewhere on this huge planet, or in your dimension, or on this side of life, that you can communicate with telepathically."

"How would I find them?"

"You wouldn't. They'd have to find you. If you were transmitting to them, and they didn't know they had the gift, they would be receiving your thoughts, but would interpret them as mere mind chatter, or as their own inner voice talking to them."

"So...when I work with your data or your inventions, or with other people's thoughts, I should cloak...no...that wouldn't be right. What should I do in those circumstances?"

"When you're using the invention, you needn't worry. The stones on the bands and glasses prevent other energies or frequencies from interfering. They are powerful tools, the gemstones. Make yourself aware of their properties, Bella. They can magnify or diffuse energy. Use them to your advantage."

"Gran, can anyone else use the stones to catch my thoughts?"

"Are you asking me about Bruce?"

"Yes. The other night I was walking out of the jewelry workshop and I believe I saw him responding to my thoughts. Then, one other time, we had a very brief conversation with thoughts."

"Has it ever happened again?"

"No. But I've tried to do it again."

"I can't explain that, Bella. There's always more to learn."

"One last thing, Gran... Is there anything I should be focusing on here that will be important to the plans I'm making? Is there anything else you'd like me to discover, or work with, or move towards?

Instead of me milling around and fumbling through, should we be working together on anything?"

"We should be working on psychic protection for Maddie. We don't know the full extent of her abilities yet. Perhaps we could design a pair of earrings for her, or a headband, with stones that keep her protected."

"Maybe. One of those elastic lace headbands with a jeweled decoration, something simple that she can wear every day might be good. What stone?"

"Snowflake obsidian protects with no toxicities. You only need a tiny stone."

"Is there an appropriate mount in the studio already?"

"Yes, and Deidre has just the type of headband you need on a doll in her shop. Ask her about it. Then, just replace the center stones in it, and you'd have what you need."

"I like the way you think!" Bella buttoned up her office at the clinic. She was getting hungry. Enjoying the memory of the lunch she had with her girls, Bella decided to eat there again, before running over to Deidre's shop.

Deidre greeted her as she walked in.

"So nice to see you again, Bella!"

"You, too, Deidre!"

"What specific item do you have on your mind?" Bella looked at her quizzically. "I read energy and body language, but not thoughts." She smiled. Bella met her gaze knowingly.

"I'm looking for something to make a headband for my granddaughter. I'd like something lacy, elastic and with an existing mount on it, one that I can add gemstones to, if you have it."

"I have just the thing you're looking for. Follow me." Deidre led her to a life size doll that had a necklace made of old fashion elastic lace. It had what appeared to be a daisy on it. The daisy would be perfect for the stones.

"The daisy is 100% sterling silver. The dolls were known for that."

"It's perfect. I'll take it." Bella was pleased. Once again, she carefully wrapped the purchase. This time, though, it went into a small gift bag with handles.

"So how do you like the little angel you bought?"

"It's perfect. Bruce helped me move it to a table at the top of the stairs. It's the perfect place for it. How did you know about it?"

"I don't exactly know about it, I just sense energy and read expressions, and I knew it was very dear to him. I could tell it was an important piece, and that he placed it here because he couldn't face whatever it was that it symbolized. What was that?"

"You'll have to ask Bruce about that, Deidre."

"I understand. Thanks for coming in. Come back."

"Count on it." With that, Bella was on her way. It was only a matter of minutes before she got home. Headband and phone in hand, she walked over to the studio. As she went up the stairs, she saw Bruce working away in the woodshop. She put some music on her phone and laid it on the drafting table. Walking over to the snowflake obsidian, she began sorting for just the right size stones. She didn't have enough small ones, so she got the chisel and carefully sized the last two. Bella matched them up with the pendant. She liked the stones better polished, so she put them inside the tumbler.

In the meantime, she removed the existing stones from the sterling mount. She got the Windex and gently cleaned the silver. She polished it with a soft cloth. It looked like new. Rinsing the tumbled stones, she laid them out to dry. Sitting on the window sill in the sun, it would be a matter of minutes before they were perfect for mounting.

Bella grabbed the Loctite. Since she'd never tried to squeeze out such a small amount, she wanted to practice first. So she squeezed the tube gently and a dot larger than what she needed came out. She tried again, and got the same result. Her plan became to squeeze gently, then use a paper clip to dab a tiny amount into each little petal before setting the stones. Then she could close the setting. That should secure the stones for a curious little one year old.

The headband was perfect. She couldn't wait to get it home to Maddie.

"Nice work!" Bruce was genuinely admiring it.

"It's for Maddie. I can't wait to see it on her."

"Is she a psychic, too?"

"Yes. She's a telepath, like me." For some reason, Bella took great pride in stating that.

"I was heading out to the pool. Would you like to go for a swim?"

"Sure. I'm finished here."

Bruce and Bella spent the rest of the daylight hours milling around the pool. At one time Bella was a water aerobics instructor, so they exercised a little, swam some, played with the volleyball, and finally sat in the loungers with a cool drink. Bella figured it was about time to tell him.

"Bruce, I wanted to tell you that I'm leaving."

"I hope everything is okay."

"Yes, it's fine. I mean, it's not really fine, but, as I told you, one of the editors on my staff has cancer and needs treatment. She's an amazing and talented person, is loyal to the company, and I want to keep her. Unfortunately, the business can't support hiring somebody else and paying her, so...I'm going to go back to help cover the workload."

"You're a great boss, Bella, and a wonderful person."

"Thanks, Bruce. Coming from you that means a lot."

"So what about us?"

"What about us?"

"How often will I see you?"

"I'm not sure. I don't have a clinic schedule set up, or a pilot for that matter. I'm not sure how it will go at the publishing company, either. Everything is just up in the air right now."

"So...I'm not even on your list?"

"Careful, or you could make the list…but not the one you want!" Bella was becoming annoyed.

"So, what we have isn't important to you?"

"What we have? We just met. We're friends!" Bella was getting aggravated. She just wanted to swim and relax.

"Just friends, huh?" Bruce was pissed!

"Friends with benefits, no strings," she poked with fun.

"Fine." Bruce picked up his stuff and stormed off. Bella was glad he was gone. The last thing she wanted right now was more pressure. She had enough to manage.

Bella gathered her things and headed into the pool house. It was getting late. She decided to rinse the chlorine off right there in the shower. Suddenly, Bella was down on the tiled shower floor. Her knee was bent completely back, and she couldn't move. There was blood everywhere. She must've hit her head. Then everything went black.

Jake arrived early the next day, wanting to get the pool cleaned before the extreme heat. When he got around back he saw water mixed with blood coming from the patio door of the pool house. He called 9-1-1 and then his mother, Linda. She told him to run over to Bruce's and get him.

Frantic, he ran across the yard and barged into the woodshop.

"Emergency. Help." Jake was out of breath and pale as a ghost. Bruce turned off his equipment and took off his gloves and apron. They ran back to Bella's.

Bruce yanked open the patio door and went inside.

"Stay here, Jake. Wait for the ambulance." Jake stood still beside the door.

When Bruce got inside, he saw Bella motionless in the shower. He turned off the water and assessed her. He covered her naked torso with a towel. She wouldn't want to be gawked at like that. Her leg had been completely broken, and her head was laying on the shower door runner, cut and bleeding. He knelt down and grabbed her wrist, try-ing to determine a pulse. He couldn't tell. Putting his ear next to her nose, he could hear a faint breath, but her chest barely moved up and down. She appeared dead, but was still alive.

The paramedics finally arrived. Slowly, they got Bella on a back-board, then onto the gurney for transport.

"Are you her husband?"

"No, but I'm the closest to family she has here." When he said that, his heart sank. To her, he was just a friend. "She doesn't have any rela-tives in Arizona. I'll get her purse and bring her information to the hospital. I'll contact her family in Illinois."

Bruce went in and grabbed Bella's purse and phone. He looked through her contacts and found Derek's information. He made the call. He got the name of Bella's primary care physician, that she was allergic to sulfa, and that she was on no medication at all. She had no illnesses or other health concerns. Derek and Kate agreed to take the first flight out of St. Louis. Nate and Andrea would stay home with the kids. Bruce would pick them up at the airport. While they traveled, Nate would be the contact for the hospital, and would provide Bella's information. Nate's wife Kate, who was a nurse practitioner, would be Bella's advocate while she was unconscious. Since she was qualified to decipher the risks and benefits of any suggested treatment plans.

When Bruce arrived at the hospital, he was once again asked his relationship to the patient. It just kept gnawing at him. From his per-spective, he was more to her than just a friend, but not from hers. Despite their disparity in the nature of their relationship, Bruce was being a very good friend right now. He provided as much information as he could to the hospital registrar. He dug into her purse and got her insurance information. He looked in her cell phone contacts and provided her sons' names and addresses as emergency contacts, and told her they would be at the hospital as soon as the first flight from St. Louis arrived.

Because Bella had no local family, Bruce was allowed to go back and answer a few questions about her status when he first found her. He gave the information to the emergency staff and doctor. He got Nate on the phone for the nurse to enter her basic health history. Since she was not able to answer for herself, and no immediate family was available to give permission for treatment, the medical staff was only able to stabilize her. They could save her life, but nothing more. Now it was a waiting game.

A few hours later, a woman from the front desk came back to let Bruce know that Derek called. He and Kate were at the airport. He informed the ER nurse that he was leaving to pick up family, and would return shortly.

Driving to the airport, Bruce realized that his clothes were soiled with blood stains. He wouldn't be able to get out of the truck without raising suspicion. He called Derek and explained his predicament and told him exactly where to meet. Things went off without a hitch and they were back at the hospital within two hours.

After being identified, Derek and Kate went over everything with the hospital staff. Luckily, she was breathing on her own. She needed blood, and had been crossed and typed. Derek was a match for her and insisted that she receive his blood, if possible. It was possible, but she would need more than that. Kate reviewed her record. The staff proposed testing to determine the extent of her head injury, the condition of her leg, which was swollen beyond belief and to determine if she had any other spinal injuries. Once they determined that her spine was intact, they could remove her from the backboard. Bella had been unconscious for quite a while.

The police then began to extensively question Bruce, who informed them of what happened. After being asked not to leave the area, Bruce understood that he might be a suspect in the case. Since Bella was the only person who knew he wasn't there, he didn't expect his status to change. The police saw him as a person of interest, at least. Next, they would be paying a visit to Jake.

Derek took Bella's purse and phone with him when he went back to the estate that evening. Kate would stay for the first half of the night and he would return in four or five hours. They would tag team. While driving home, Bruce called Derek on Bella's phone to remind him to contact her publishing office and the clinic. Derek was glad to get the reminder. He didn't expect to be doing this tonight.

Derek was able to reach Nancy, Bella's assistant. He had her number. But he had no idea who to contact in the clinic. He called Bruce, who came on over to sort through things with him. Bruce knew she'd been planning to interview private pilots in the days ahead, but didn't know the details. He suggested Derek check her iPad to see if she had contact information in her calendar. Everything they needed was right there. Bruce offered to cancel the pilot interviews, and gave him Rick Baker's contact information, in case Bella wasn't able to do it herself by morning.

When Derek mentioned the hospital shifts, Bruce wanted to help. They exchanged phone numbers so they could keep in touch. Together, they were a good support system.

"What happened, Bruce?" Derek really wanted to know.

"I'm not sure. We spent the evening together in the pool and then I went home, about 10:30 or 11:00. She was fine, still relaxing in the lounger. Then, this morning, Jake ran over in a panic stating that blood and water were running out of the pool house. He was afraid to go inside. He'd already called 9-1-1 and thought it was taking them too long to get there. I couldn't feel her pulse, so I put my ear by her mouth and could hear faint breath. I grabbed a towel and covered her, then turned off the shower. The water must've been running all night, because it was overflowing the patio door and running out onto the porch when Jake got here."

"Wow. I'm so glad Jake came over."

"Me, too. She must've laid there unconscious all night, even after the water turned ice cold. Her leg was mangled behind her. It has to be broken clean in half." He was so distraught he could barely express himself.

"Thanks for doing that, covering her up, I mean."

"I'd do anything for her."

Derek turned his head and looked right at Bruce. Why hadn't he seen it before? He was in love with her! Although he didn't know much about him, he seemed like a good guy, and he definitely cared for Mom.

"The base of her skull, right at the brain stem was on the shower door track. I hope her spinal cord wasn't severed."

"How do you think she fell?"

"I couldn't tell ya. But I didn't see soap or anything on the floor. But…I wasn't looking for it either."

"Let's walk out there, want to?" Derek got up off the chair. They walked outside, but were barely out the kitchen door when they saw the yellow crime scene tape.

"Could someone have attacked her, Bruce?"

"I guess it's possible, but I've been here for years and there's never been a problem. Folks in this neighborhood don't even lock their doors."

"But the house has an alarm."

"True. But your great grandmother was an inventor and had lots of proprietary information here."

"Do you think someone could be after something?"

"Anything's possible, I guess."

"Should we go under the tape?" Derek was bending down.

"Our prints are all over this place, so why not?"

They went inside and looked around. Nothing appeared to be disturbed. The floors were a mess, though. The place needed to have the water mopped up before it did any damage. They would have to alert police that they would be sopping up the water. There was nothing on the bathroom floor. The soap was in the nook. The shampoo and cream rinse were unopened. She never got that far. Could she have simply fallen? It appeared that way.

"Is there a reason why anyone would want to hurt her, Bruce?"

"I don't think so. She's never mentioned any trouble."

"Who would know she's even here? Could it be that someone knew her grandmother died and was out to rob the place?"

"Why now? The place sat empty before Bella got here. And it doesn't appear that anything's missing." Bruce found it hard to believe that a stranger came to rob the place. There were lots of valuables sitting out untouched.

"Well, not that we know of, anyway." Derek was concerned about the floor. He picked up his phone and looked for the local number for the police. He talked to a detective who said he would check it out for him and call back.

"Let's get out of here in case he shows up." They were walking up toward the house when the detective pulled up. He heard them out, went and took a look for himself, and then called to see if anybody had any objections to them mopping up the water. After a few minutes wait, they were given the go-ahead to clean up. The detective removed the tape.

"Thanks for coming out'" Derek shook his hand and Bruce followed suit.

"I'm sorry to hear about your mom, and her grandmother. Many of us have been to that clinic and have benefited from it. If there's anything I can do...."

"We appreciate your help and concern." Bruce meant it. Derek nodded his agreement.

They got to work on the floor right away. Unfortunately, the blood in the water created a stain on the white tile floor. Bruce got some bleach water and laid some rags soaked with the solution on some trouble spots. They hoped for the best.

Kate called while they were cleaning up. She agreed to stay a little longer so that they could work through the clean-up. Bella was still un-conscious. Test results had not come back yet. They were playing the waiting game. Kate downloaded Bella's first book onto her phone, and was reading it. The print was smaller than she was used to, but it took the edge off the wait. It helped her pass the time.

"Kate getting tired?" Bruce was concerned for them both.

"Just bored, mainly," Derek began. "She said she downloaded Mom's first book to help pass the time."

"Her first book?" Bruce didn't know she was a writer.

"Yep. I don't think any of us read it. We knew all about it because it was about an experience we all went through together. But Kate decided to read it. She's got nothing better to do."

"I've heard that writers write from their perspective and experiences."

"For Mom that'd be large. She's done a ton in her life. More than any five people I know put together, actually." He was smiling.

"She's amazing!"

"Man, Bruce, you've got it bad. Does she know how you feel?"

"Not really. She thinks we're just friends."

"Sorry, man…bummer."

Bruce didn't answer. Derek noticed he had suddenly become rather sullen.

"Just last night we had a fight about it, right before I went home. Well, not a fight, words. She said there wasn't an 'us'. It pissed me off."

"What did you do about it?"

"Nothing. I grabbed my stuff and went home."

"What'd she do?"

"Nothing. She just laid there like nothing happened. She wasn't bothered at all. She didn't care one bit. Her only concern was all the stuff she had on her plate."

"She's always been a workaholic. Sorry, man."

"I'm sorry, too. I wish she would come to."

"Me, too. She will."

A week came and went, and Derek and Kate had to return to their normal lives. There was no change in Bella's condition. Nate and Andrea made arrangements to come, but at different times. Bruce offered to trade shifts, so only one of them would have to be away from home at a time. They all appreciated his help. Nate was the next to arrive.

Nate got to know Bruce pretty well. Just about every subject under the sun came up during their time together. Bruce tried to get Nate access to the secrets behind the library book cases, but without success. At least they were able to use Bella's iPad for internet access. Nate managed his business and kept up with important issues from Arizona. But all too soon it was time to get home. He missed Kate and Maddie, and was anxious to be reunited with them.

Andrea was surprised at how many friends her mother-in-law had made in the short time she'd been there. She'd spent time visiting with every one of them, as they came to sit with Bella. Finally, Carol suggested that Andrea ask Linda to contact Bella's grandmother psychically to see if she could communicate with thoughts. Andrea was open to just about anything at this point. Traditional medicine had done nothing to bring her back from her sleep, which they were now calling a coma.

Carol set up the session with Linda. It was odd to think of a clairvoyant having to attempt to contact Bella's dead grandmother to ask her if her living granddaughter, who was diagnosed comatose, could actually be reached and communicated with. In a million years, Andrea never saw this coming. But just about everything in Arizona was like something from a science fiction movie. Although, having been there a while, Andrea was beginning to believe it was more science than fiction.

She suggested that Bruce be present. He was her closest friend. Carol agreed. They hoped that Anna wasn't cloaked and would respond. They would take their chances.

The next evening after work they all gathered at the hospital. Nate was skeptical. It was such a bizarre concept that he couldn't wrap his mind around it. But he was there for the others. He didn't believe that his mom's dead grandma could communicate with his mom in thoughts while she was in a coma. Then there was the idea that the dead grandmother could communicate with a medium who claimed to be able to talk to the dead. Then the medium would give the message, sent by Mom, to Grandma, then through Linda to them. Wow!

"Anna's here. What would you like to know?"

Bruce began the conversation.

"Bella, can you hear my voice?"

"She can."

"How do we know it's her answering and not you, Linda?" Nate wanted to know.

"She says that as a child you once had five warts in a cluster on your left knee." Nate fell back into the chair.

"Did someone attack you?" Andrea was next.

"She's not sure. Maybe *something*, not someone. She says she slipped when she tried to turn around quickly. She fell hard. She couldn't straighten out her leg. Her head hurt. When she looked around, she saw blood and passed out."

"How long were you on the floor, Bella?"

"Since right after you left, she says."

"Are you in pain, Mom?"

"No. She says her body may be in pain, but she cannot feel it."

"Are you in your body?" Andrea wanted to know.

"She doesn't know."

"Bella, if you're not in your body, will you please come back to it? Please come back to us."

"She says she doesn't know if she'll be the same. She wants to know if the doctors say she's paralyzed."

"No. They have not said any of that, Mom." Nate was firm and confident in that.

"She says she will try to come back, but is not sure how to do it. She doesn't want you to give up or pull the plug."

"There's no mention of that, Mom," Andrea reassured her.

"They all sat there. There didn't seem to be anything further to say."

"Anna is leaving the conversation now."

"Thanks, Grandma," Nate voiced.

"Thanks, Anna," Bruce was truly grateful to know Bella was still there.

"And thank you, Linda. I thought it went well." Andrea stood up and gave her a hug.

"Me, too," Linda responded. "I hope her body's restored to normal very soon."

Bruce decided he would sit with Bella for a while, so Nate and Andrea went back to the estate. They were leaving in two days. Upon arriving home, they called a conference to decide what they would do next. Mom had been in a coma for over two weeks. They all had jobs to do and families and homes to take care of. They figured out a tentative rotation, one at a time, for the next month, if needed. After that, when her leg and head wounds healed, they would have to make arrangements to bring her home to St. Louis for care. All hoped she would awaken soon, so it wouldn't come to that.

Bruce pulled the chair over to the hospital bed so that he could prop his feet up on it. For the first time in two weeks, he grabbed the remote and turned the TV on. There wasn't much on, so he switched to the create channel and watched a program about Swedish cooking. It took the edge off sitting in silence and listening to Bella breathe. He knew she was in there now. It was just a matter of time before she came back.

"Bruce, can you hear me?"

Bruce thought he heard Bella's voice. He turned and looked at her, but she was asleep.

"Bruce, can you hear my thoughts?"

"Bella?"

"Yes."

"How bad is my body?"

"You broke your knee and tore some of the muscles and ligaments that attach there. You've had surgery to correct it, but you'll need rehab. You've had eighteen stiches to the back of your head, but no broken bones there, luckily. The extent of the nerve damage you suffered is yet to be determined."

"Will it be very painful when I come back to my body?"

"Yes, at least for a while."

"What will happen to me?"

"Well, I don't think anybody knows yet. But I think that you will be taken home as soon as you can travel. You'll have physical therapy to get your leg back in shape. Then…well, I guess that's up to you."

Bella had lots of questions about who was doing what in her absence. Bruce filled her in on everything. He couldn't believe how easy it was to communicate with directed thought.

"Bruce?"

"Yes…"

"Is there any possibility that we could be related?"

"What?" Bruce was caught totally off guard. "Why would you ask me something like that?"

"Because of the telepathy. I thought it was inherited by the first born in my bloodline. Is there any possibility of that?"

"Absolutely not. No possibility."

"From what little I've read, the gift has been studied and documented in twins. We're not twins, are we?"

"Is that a joke? There you are, my Bella!" His smile was ear to ear.

"Here I am, Bruce. Bruce…"

"Yes Bella?"

"Get your feet off my bed!" She was sassy. And there she was, awake. Bruce got up and walked over to her and kissed her on the forehead. He went into the bathroom and got a warm cloth. He gently washed the sleep out of her beautiful eyes. Grabbing her brush from the bedside table, he gently brushed her hair. The tears rolled down his cheeks the entire time. Then he realized, he had to notify the nurse.

The nurse came in and there was a buzz in her room. While the staff contacted her doctors for orders, Bruce called Bella's kids. Andrea and Nate came right up to the hospital. Derek and Kate talked to her on the phone. She was back. Then police arrived.

The officers walked into Bella's room. They looked around at the people in her presence.

"Mrs. Sanders, can you answer some questions for us?"

"I'll try."

"Now wait a minute," Nate was on his feet. "She just woke up from a two week coma. She's tired and hurting. Can't this wait?"

"Of course, as long as there was no foul play."

"I thought I saw something. I can't explain it. But I turned around too quickly, slipped, fell and hit my head. Nobody attacked me or anything."

"What did you see?"

"I don't know...a shadow? An animal? Maybe nothing."

"But you were startled?"

"Yes."

"Ma'am, do you mind if we take another look around your pool house?"

"I don't mind. Nate will take you through tomorrow. Maybe a cat came through the door with me or something."

The officer turned and asked if anybody noticed anything missing, but nobody had. Bella explained that they weren't familiar with all the belongings in the estate, but that nothing of value appeared to be missing. All the electronics were still there. With that the police were gone. They would be in touch.

"Bruce…where are Gran's glasses?"

"I'm not sure, why?"

"I brought them home to try out with you."

"When did you last see them?"

"I'm not sure. I think I put them in my purse. I was carrying them back and forth to try with everyone."

"They're not in your purse. I was through that when I registered you here."

"Can you look again, please?"

Bruce looked, but couldn't find them.

"They might still be on your desk in the study. You tried them with me and Kate, Mom," Andrea reminded her.

"True. If you find them, will you let me know right away?"

"And if we don't?" They all held their breath.

"Well, we can't mention anything about the glasses to the police. And first, we have to see if we can find them."

"Agreed. Now it's time for you to get some rest. The doctors and nurses will likely be coming in and out all night evaluating you. Rest while you can and we'll see you in the morning."

"We'll come by on our way to the airport," Andrea said as she hugged her.

"Kate's going to come out next. She has a big job interview in Vegas this week, so she's going to fly out and stay with you, leaving only long enough for the interview."

"Fantastic! What kind of interview?"

"If she got the job she would be the director of nursing at a hospital in Vegas. It's a pretty big deal."

"And how do you feel about that?" Nate shrugged his shoulders and downplayed it.

"She has to want the job and get hired. First things first." He hugged Bella and walked out the door.

Bruce took both of Bella's hands in his and squeezed them tightly.

"If it'll make you feel better, Bella, we could have a DNA test to make sure we're not related."

"Let's do it, Bruce. Once we know we're not, we can dig into this telepathy thing and try to figure it out. And Bruce, please remember to look around for the glasses."

"I will. Tomorrow I'll bring your cell phone back up with me so you can make calls whenever you like."

"Can you bring my iPad and clean clothes, too?"

"You bet." And with that, they were gone.

Bella looked at her leg and felt around on it a little. She couldn't really feel anything yet. It was suspended in a machine that automatically exercised it. There was a tube that she supposed they put some sort of nutrition in. That would probably be coming out soon, now that she was awake.

It had been nice in the place where she was, wherever that was. She could communicate with Mom and Gran freely. But they were the only ones. At least until Linda brought her together with her kids and Bruce. It was good to be back.

Bella now knew beyond a shadow of a doubt that we live on infinitely. There's a place we go to when our body dies, but she couldn't name it. It wasn't like the ideas she had of heaven or hell, but there was definitely another existence.

Back at home Andrea and Nate scoured the house looking for the glasses. They couldn't find them anywhere. They went out to the pool house on the off chance that she took them out there, but nothing turned up.

Andrea walked over to the jewelry studio to search. The minute she went through the door she felt fabulous. She browsed the glass cases. There were some breathtaking pieces displayed there. As she climbed the steps she dusted the stones with her fingertips, admiring all of them. When she approached the drafting table, she saw Maddie's headband. She picked it up and put it in her pocket. Andrea was intrigued. There were lots of gorgeous pieces of jewelry in progress. After looking closely at everything, she began trying them on. Finally, she saw the glasses, and tried them, too. Nothing happened. But she tucked them in her pocket. Suddenly, the studio went dark.

Andrea crouched down and slipped under the drafting table. She heard footsteps on the stairs. As the sound got closer Andrea reached out and pulled both legs together, causing the intruder to fall.

"I have a knife and I'll stab you. Get up."

"Andrea, it's me, Nate. Don't stab me." He started laughing. "What's wrong with you?"

"What'd'ya mean what's wrong with me? What's wrong with you sneaking up on me like that?"

"I wasn't sneaking up on you, the lights went out. I came to see if you needed help."

"What are you going to do?"

"Look." With that, he turned his cell phone flash light on and led her down the stairs. They got outside and both started laughing. Then they saw it. Someone was crawling across the lawn near the pool house.

"Hey you! Stop!" Nate shouted as he ran across the grass. "You... stop!" Andrea caught up with him. They were both out of breath.

"Wow, Nate. Call the cops."

"And tell them what?"

"Just call, or give me your phone and I'll call."

The officer that showed up was one of the cops that had come the morning that Bella was found in the pool house. Things were beginning to take a turn here. Perhaps she did see something that night she fell. But what? Whatever they were looking for must be near the pool or in the pool house. That's where Bella thought she saw something and that's exactly where they saw it. There was something going on here.

Just as they were about to walk the officer to the car, the lights came back on.

"Where's the main breaker for the property?" The officer asked a good question. Neither of them knew. Andrea called Bella, but she didn't know either. They supposed it didn't matter much anyway, now that the power was back on. The officer told them he would make a report and asked them to call if there was anything further. They thanked him and went inside.

Both Nate and Andrea had the creeps after what just happened. They decided to walk back outside and double check the windows and doors on the studio and pool house. Satisfied, they went back into the main house and locked the door. Andrea called Bella, explaining what happened. She walked her through setting the alarm. After all was safe and secure, they made a bite to eat and each retired to their own suites. It was time to pack up. Tomorrow they would fly home.

Andrea took the headband and the glasses out of her pocket. She wanted to text Bella to let her know where they were, then remembered that her phone was in her purse at Bruce's. She could text her when she got her phone back.

Taking the glasses down to Bella's desk in the study, she began thinking about the new world that opened up for all of them as a result of Anna dying. It felt like her dying created a much larger way of living for them all. They had been given a glimpse into an invisible world that none of them knew existed until now. Each of them had expanded their minds and ways of living to include things unseen.

Before arriving, Andrea didn't know that there were natural powers in stones that enhanced certain aspects of a person. But it made sense. We're all created out of the same elements, we're just put together with different amounts of them. It wasn't a very scientific explanation, but it was life changing. She'd never given any thought to people being able to reach each other with thought, although there were times she'd had Mom on her mind and, out of the blue, she called. There were enough of those incidences that Andrea could accept the possibility.

As for clairvoyance, what she'd experienced here was pretty convincing. Linda's ability to glean information about what happened to Bella was pretty amazing. It was hard for Andrea to understand how, in a vegetative state, Bella could communicate with her dead grandmother with thoughts and then Anna could repeat them to Linda, who then told her. It was bizarre. But she believed it happened. So, now what? How would their lives unfold because of the events they'd witnessed? Or would everything remain the same?

Nate heard Andrea roaming around downstairs and decided to join her. Although he wasn't afraid, the idea that his daughter communicated telepathically with his mother was something he'd never dreamed was possible. Kate's family believed in mediums and clairvoyance, but in his family, nobody ever talked about it before, and he had clairvoyant relatives. How could his mother be clairvoyant and not know it? And how could she have missed the fact that both her mother and grandmother lived their lives communicating telepathically? Would there be a secret dialogue going on between Mom and Maddie that he would have no knowledge of? Was it something to be frightened of? Would he be able to parent her properly with her advanced psyche? He had lots of questions.

Yet, up to now, life was normal in their household, and so far, there was really no reason to be afraid. He wondered if there were things he could learn to raise her better. Now that he was aware of her gift, what should he do differently? He didn't want her to be a freak, but he didn't want her to hide her talent under a bushel basket either. Where was the line? And if he had more children, would they possess the gift? Endless questions.

"Hey…" Andrea walked over and opened the refrigerator.

"Hey…not tired either?

"Just a lot on my mind."

"I hear ya. Now what?" Nate really wanted to know.

"I was just wondering that myself. I wonder if our lives will change or not. I mean, nothing has really changed for us, except Mom will be busier…I mean, after she recovers." Andrea chatted casually.

"How do you raise a clairvoyant child?" Nate was genuinely concerned.

"I don't know. I guess just like you've done up to now."

"I have serious questions about her abilities. The idea that she can hear things blows my mind."

"Well, we all hear things others can't every day, and we go on with our lives knowing it."

"True. But knowing she's a telepath feels different."

"Well, as far as we know, she can only communicate with your mom. I don't see much harm in that."

"True. I wonder how much she can understand, though."

"Why is that a problem?"

"Well, will she want to be with other kids like her? If so, where will she find them? Will she get frustrated when Grandma can understand her clearly because they communicate full thoughts, but I can't because I only see her gestures and baby expressions?"

"Yeah…I get the question. Well, right now we can ask your mom to do her cloaking thing and allow Maddie to grow up normally, to develop the same way as others her age. Mom didn't even know she had abilities until she came here. So I think that should work."

"What's up with that? How could she get this far with no idea she was a telepath?"

"I'm not sure, but I guess that since she was only able to communicate with her grandmother, and she wasn't around her at all, she didn't know. That's really bizarre to think about."

"It blows my mind."

"Mine, too. Ice cream?"

"Sure. Let's watch a movie."

"Okay. That's crazy, too isn't it? Voice and thought activated holograms and electronics…"

They both laughed and relaxed. They settled into a movie and then turned in with thoughts of home. Life was changing, but then again, it always was.

Chapter 15

Bella spent a lot of time weighing the pros and cons of where she would convalesce. At home, she would be near family, but they would be consumed with their everyday lives. She would not be able to babysit or help them in any way until her injuries were healed. Since it was her right leg, she couldn't drive. As for the publishing agency, she would be receiving work at the convalescent center or at home, the same as here. So, from a practical standpoint, it was more cost effective to stay put. It would mean a two month or more delay in her return to St. Louis. Her daughters-in-law agreed to take her plants home until she could return, and that was the extent of special arrangements. It was pretty easy, actually.

For the time being, her participation at the clinic would be on hold. If there was an emergency that only she could address, special arrangements could be made. They would cross that bridge when they came to it.

Bella was concerned about the estate after what the kids had seen that night, and had asked Bruce to keep an eye out. He'd readily agreed to help. Since then, nothing had happened. Bella called Linda at the management agency to get information about the power at the estate. She wasn't in, so she left a message for a call back. It seemed odd to Bella that the power would go off only there, but not in the surrounding homes. Perhaps there was construction or something nearby, or maybe an animal chewed through a wire to the main power box. Either way, it would require attention.

Bella thought further about the young woman she chased down the sidewalk at the clinic that Saturday. She was wearing a black hoody. Nate and Andrea saw something black crawling across the lawn. Could it have been a person? Is it possible that someone would follow Bella home and be lurking around the estate? Is that what she saw the night she fell? Try as she might, she could not remember.

In the meantime, Bella had to get a pilot on retainer, or at least she had to see how much something like that would cost. It wasn't that you could put a price on the well-being of first responders, but there were practicalities to consider. There may not actually be a great need. This couple of months would be the tell-all.

Then Bella got an idea. If she wore a band from wherever she was, could a person wear one at the clinic and still be connected? She called Allen. He loved the idea, and agreed to try it with her. Since she was the only person who could open the case with the technology in it, it would have to wait until she could leave the convalescent center and personally appear at clinic. That wouldn't be much longer.

The week went quickly and it was time for Bella to go back to the estate. On the way back, Bruce dropped her off to pick up the bands. She removed both from the case and limped over to Allen's office on crutches. He wasn't there. She left him a note to come by at his convenience.

On the way home, Allen called and said he was leaving the clinic and would stop by. Bruce dropped her off, got her settled, then headed back to the woodshop to work. She was grateful to have him as a friend. Bella waited in the front room for Allen to arrive. The shortest distance was the best for her right now. The crutches greatly cramped her style. And with her cast, she wouldn't be in the pool for a while. It would take some effort to do simple things now. She'd have to take her time.

Bella greeted Allen when he got there, and asked where to put the band. Only her thumb print would activate and open the safe. That put them in a pickle.

"Are you in a hurry to go?"

"I have a little time, why?"

"Would you like to play around with them right now?"

"Sure. Where should I go?"

"Why don't you go out to the pool house and I'll stay in here."

"Okay. Where's the pool house?"

Bella showed Allen the way from the kitchen, and handed him the key. He looked around on his way down to the pool. It was obvious that he'd never been there before. Bella crossed him off the list of suspects crawling across the yard.

She hobbled back into the front room and awaited Allen's text, letting her know he was ready. It took a minute. Bella called him, put her phone on speaker, and laid it on the coffee table. She placed the band on her head. Allen followed suit.

"It isn't my money, Allen, my grandmother was the one who created this place." Bella was reading his thoughts. "She was a self-made woman. She worked her way across Europe and to the United States by telling fortunes. But she was so much more than that, as you know."

"I have nothing but the utmost respect for her, Bella." He was sending thoughts right back.

"And what about me, Allen, how do you feel about me?"

"I'm on the fence about you. You have your grandmother's intellect and drive, but not the passion for the work she had. She was driven to develop technology that would bring world peace. She believed that if each person were able to identify what was causing them pain, they could free themselves and live peacefully in the world."

"She was idealistic!" Bella summed it up.

"...altruistic and honorable," Allen corrected her.

"I'm going to change the topic of our conversation now, Allen, okay?"

"Sure."

"What happened to Dani's leg?"

There was no response from Allen, but Bella could see the answer to her question. She could see his reluctance to reveal himself. He felt responsible for it. When he was wounded in battle, they stabilized him and then sent him back to the U.S. He suffered a great deal of pain, and was heavily medicated. During his recovery, he felt frail and vulnerable. Loving his wife was the one way he could feel normal, like a whole man. She got pregnant with their daughter, but the medicines caused some birth defects. His wife would have no part of aborting their child, even after it was discovered that she was missing most of one leg.

Allen could feel her probing his thoughts. Somehow she was able to maneuver in past his internal armor and see the truth about him. It was interesting that Allen didn't feel any judgment from her. Bella didn't agree that Dani's disability was his fault. She wasn't trying to make him feel better, but was sifting through data, of sorts, to discern the truth. Suddenly it made Allen question his guilt. Could it be that something else caused her deformity? Although it didn't change the condition of Dani's body, he felt a hundred pounds lighter. It was as if the weight of the world was lifted off his shoulders. It was life changing.

"Thanks, Bella."

"For what? I didn't do anything."

"You brought things out into the light."

"It wasn't me. It was the technology. This is the power of transformation you were talking about. I wish I could take credit for it, but I'm just the vessel."

"I never dreamt it was this powerful."

"I'll tell you, Allen, I've opened my mind to many wonders since I've been here, and it's busted my life wide open. I'm amazed every day."

"Do you want me to come back up to the house now?"

"Sure."

Allen came back to the house and they talked for a while. Bella suggested that he take the band home so that they could try it from a distance. He agreed. Then he asked Bella if she would mind doing the same experiment with his wife. Bella didn't mind at all, but another day. They both agreed. Bella gave Allen a velvet bag to place the band in so that the stones wouldn't be scratched in transport, and he was off.

She made her way to the kitchen to grab a bite to eat. Before long, Bruce was at the door.

"Knock, knock…I brought dessert!" He walked right in. It was great not to have to get up.

"You're a dream. I've got a sweet tooth. What's that?"

"Cherry pie…ala mode."

"Yum…serve it up."

They ate dessert and chatted for over an hour. Finally, Bruce talked Bella into sitting with him while he took a swim. When she walked over to the door, she saw a golf cart parked right outside.

"I didn't hear you ride up on that. It must be quiet."

"It is. But, I drove it over earlier, before I picked you up from the hospital. I wanted you to have a way to get around. Are you ready for your lesson?"

"Sure."

Bruce helped her get in on the passenger side and turn enough to put her leg across the cart. He showed her how to go forward and reverse. She caught on right away, and was grateful for the cart.

"Can I ride this to the market?"

"Maybe on the sidewalk…" They both laughed. "I think we should hire someone to run errands, or take you to run errands, while you convalesce."

"Not a bad idea. But I'm kind of jumpy these days. Do you know someone? I'm not comfortable interviewing strangers or anything."

"How about Jake?"

"What do you think I should pay him?"

"You should probably ask him."

"Great idea." Bella felt better about it. She would call him first thing in the morning. Gosh, it was great to be home.

The cart would fit perfectly next to her lounger, but for now, she parked it a little farther back to make sure she didn't accidently drive it into the pool. She chuckled at the thought.

"It's nice to see you smile." Bruce was really glad she was back.

"It feels good, too. I've been meaning to ask you if you think there's someone prowling around the property."

"Well, I've never seen anybody here before, but I don't know for sure. What would someone be after, if not the electronics or valuables? It doesn't make sense."

"I thought about that, too. Who knows about my grandmother's inventions?"

"That's a good question. I'm not sure. But the people I know of realize that only you can use them. So it wouldn't do them any good."

"Good point."

"There must be some other explanation. Let's start with the lights. Where's the breaker panel for this place?"

"Each unit, the house, the pool house, and the studio have their own power panels. But they tie into a breaker box by the fence. Linda said it's somewhere behind the pool house."

Bella was struggling to get up with a whole leg cast. It was much easier getting down. Bruce got out of the pool and helped her.

"What are you doing?"

"I think I'll take a look behind there on my handy-dandy golf cart, and see if I can spot any obvious problems. Want to ride along?"

"Sure."

There was nothing obvious to the naked eye. But as they drove closer to the fence they noticed a big hole under the fence. They could see what looked like a power line exposed in the hole, but it appeared to be intact. Bella got her phone out to call the power company and see if they wanted to check it. Then she called the detective listed on the report and told him of their findings. At this point, it seemed that a large animal dug a hole under the fence as a shortcut out of the yard. Bella felt better.

They headed back to the pool. Bella dropped Bruce off and headed up to the house. It was too hot to stay outside without getting wet. She was ready for some air conditioning. There was just one problem, her crutches were still at the pool. By the time she got back, Bruce was already gone. Bella drove as close to the chair as she could, but it wasn't quite close enough. She tried to get off the golf cart on the side nearest the house, but with the cast, there was only one way off. So she backed the cart out and pulled in the other way. It was tight, but she did it. She hopped and hobbled, trying not to put any weight on her leg, but was unsuccessful. The next thing she knew she was on the ground, tailbone throbbing.

Bella attempted to use the lounger to help her get up, but it was no use. She was stuck. Her phone was in the house, she couldn't reach the cart horn, and there was nobody in sight. Making the best of her situation, she pulled the cushion from the lounger to the ground and sat on it. It would be dark soon. Every minute seemed like two as she pondered what to do.

If she pushed herself off into the pool, she could probably swim over to the steps and hop up. But then what? Then her cast would be wet, and she would risk the potential for infection. It was not the answer. She could scoot on her bottom to the glass door, but she had locked it, and her keys were in the main house.

"Excuse me, do you need help?" There was a woman standing in front of her looking nervous.

"Yes, actually. Do you think you could hand me my crutches over there?" The woman walked over and brought them back to her. "Now, if you could sit on this lounger to hold it down so I can use it to get up..." She sat right down. Looking at the woman, Bella could tell she was embarrassed for her.

"Thank you! I don't know what I would've done if you hadn't come by. By the way, can I help you with something? I'm Bella."

"You're Anna's granddaughter. I'm so pleased to meet you! I'm Donna, your neighbor."

"Hi, Donna. What brings you by?"

"My daughter, Olivia…well, her dog…a black lab. It's missing. It's expecting a litter of pups any time now, and it's been running off. Livvy said she chased her through the yard and under the fence a couple of weeks ago. I doubt the dog could fit right now, though. Have you seen either one?

It all fell into place for Bella. Rushing in like a riptide, she realized she'd seen the dog the night she fell. Nate and Andrea had seen Livvy crawling around after the dog. It was all so simple!

"Are you okay, Bella?" Bella explained everything that happened to Donna. They both had a good laugh. Donna offered Livvy as an assistant to Bella after school and on weekends until she got her cast off to make up for the upset she'd caused. Bella accepted the offer and welcomed her help.

"Hi, Donna." Bruce wandered back up to see why the cart was so close to the edge of the pool.

"Hi. Have you seen Moondoggy?"

"Nope. She have those pups yet?"

"I don't know. We can't find her. Right now I can't find Livvy, either."

"She's down at the end of the cul de sac near my place. I saw her just a few minutes ago."

"Fantastic." Donna got up and walked to the other side of the pool. "Nice meeting you Bella. Livvy and I will be over after school tomorrow afternoon."

"Great. See you both then." Bella hobbled over to the cart, put her crutches on, and got in while Bruce was still there. Driving back to the main house, she explained what had just happened. Bruce thought it was hilarious, at least once he knew it turned out okay. He waited long enough for her to get inside and then said good night and went home.

"You're full of surprises Bella," Gran whispered in her ear.

"How so?"

"I can't explain it any better than this. You seem to have a swarm of guardian angels around you. Every time you get in a pickle or need something, one shows up. It's like you have your very own private miracle network."

Bella thought about that for a minute.

"It does, doesn't it, Gran? Thank you for bringing that to my attention. These days I seem to be feeling sorry for myself a lot. It's good to turn it around in my mind."

"How's it going with your research on the bands?"

"Gran, I think I may have a really economical solution to flying back and forth so much."

"I wondered when you would figure it out."

"You knew?" Bella was really surprised.

"Well, I had an idea. But I don't know if there's any substance or invisible energy that can block the signal. You were in pretty close proximity to Allen during the test."

"I guess. What kind of invisible energy?"

"I don't know…lightening, maybe…or radar…magnetics…"

"Gotcha. We'll have to try to figure that out."

"If the right circumstances present themselves…"

"True enough." Bella suddenly felt very tired. She leaned back on the couch and closed her eyes.

She was walking in a park pushing the baby in the stroller. It was getting hot, so they decided to follow the others into the large domed building to see what was going on, and to change the baby. They got inside, but there were no seats. The baby wanted to get out of the stroller, so Bella unbuckled him. He stepped down from the little umbrella stroller and stood while she undressed him and got out the diaper and wipes.

Suddenly, the lights went out.

"Turn the lights on please," Bella shouted.

"Ma'am, the lights will not be turned on for one hour."

"Turn them on for just a second please, so we can get out."

"Ma'am, everyone knows the lights will not come on for another hour."

"I'll ask once more nicely. Please turn on the lights so I can get my mother and my baby outside." It remained dark. Bella grabbed the diaper bag, the baby and the stroller and let out the most blood curdling scream imaginable. It was still dark. She kept screaming until a tall thin woman actually turned on the light. In the light, Bella ran for the door, everything bundled in her arms.

"Hurry, Mom," she was yelling as they pushed through the doors. They'd made it.

Bella awakened startled. It wasn't her baby. Her mom had been gone for some time. What was the meaning behind the dream? In all the dream interpretation books she'd ever read, every character in the dream was the dreamer. So…she was the grandmother, mother, child, the three men sitting behind her and the woman controlling the lights. What significance did they have? What time was it?

Bella decided it didn't really matter what time it was. She had no pressing schedule. Grabbing her crutches, she limped into the kitchen and put a k-cup in the Keurig. She was awake. It was 3 a.m. There was a stack of work in the library that needed to be done. This was the perfect time to dig in.

Bella's quandary was how to either get the coffee into the library, or everything else in here. She looked through the cabinets for a cup with a lid. All of those were in the pool house. So, she would sit at the breakfast bar for coffee and then get to work.

Her mind drifted back to the dream. Why did the mother scream when the lights went out? Why did she want to leave? Was it because her son was naked on the floor without a diaper? Why was her mother suddenly in the room with them, when just she and the baby walked into the building? Was she already there? Why was the woman who controlled the lights so reluctant to bend the rules to allow them to exit the building?

Suddenly, Bella heard some commotion outside. She hobbled over to the door. Switching on the outside lights, Bella saw the black lab having puppies on the lawn. She appeared to be having trouble. Bella quickly limped over to her phone and dialed Bruce.

"Hello?" He'd been sound asleep.

"Bruce, it's Bella. I need your help. Please come quickly."

"Okay. What's wrong?"

"Moondoggy's having her pups in the back yard and she's in trouble. Please hurry."

"I'll be right there."

Bella gathered some towels and hand sanitizer and put them in a plastic grocery bag. She scooted down the back steps and into the golf cart. Driving over to Moondoggy, she saw a pup arriving tail first. Ouch. She struggled getting off the cart, all the while trying to soothe the dog with words of encouragement. The lab looked at her with kind eyes that let Bella know she appreciated her help.

Bruce was running down the yard. He wasn't sure who needed more help, Bella or Moondoggy. He grabbed some surgical gloves and his straight razor, some thread and a needle. He didn't know what he'd have to do. He was running and putting on the gloves as he went. As soon as he saw the dog, he knelt down beside her and began to talk to her.

"Bella, come to her head and straddle her." Bella was confused, but followed his lead. Standing behind her, Bruce lowered her to the ground. She was sitting just at the dog's head.

"I want you to pet her head and speak softly to her while I attempt to deliver the pup. I will have to push it back up inside a little to try to turn it. I don't want to cut her if I don't have to."

"Gotcha." Bella began to pet her and reassure her that everything was going to be alright. Bella felt deep down that it would. Moondoggy yelped and the pup was born.

"It's a girl!" Bruce beamed as if he were the father. Bella felt her heart on fire. It was love at first sight. As they stayed and soothed Moondoggy, the other four pups were born. Bruce came up and sat by Bella on the lawn. They both had tears in their eyes at the miracle of new life. It was incredibly moving. They watched as Mommy cleaned her babies and they nuzzled up for their first drink of mother's milk.

"It's a miracle, isn't it?"

"What's that?"

"That the cells in the body can create a whole new life and nurture it until it can sustain itself. It's brilliant. The intelligence it takes to manage that whole process is always working without a person or an animal having to actually manage it. It's automatic genius."

"And so much more."

Bella reached out and grabbed Bruce's hand. They just sat there for the longest time. It would soon be daylight.

"I've never seen puppies being born." Bella wanted to linger in the feeling of pure love that she felt sitting there with Bruce and watching Moondoggy with her litter.

"Me neither." Bruce looked over at Bella and smiled.

"You looked just like a vet running across the yard putting on your surgical gloves." They both started laughing. Moondoggy looked at them and began to wag her tail.

"That's our girl," Bella crooned as she petted her, "you rest and we'll get you home soon."

The sky began to light over Phoenix, and their experience had a happy ending, or a happy beginning. It was time to call Donna and invite her and Livvy to meet the pups. Overjoyed, they ran right over, still in their jammies!

Livvy threw herself to the ground and hugged Moondoggy. Then she jumped up and chased the pups around giggling until she had them all laughing. Bella noticed the transformation as it was taking place. The mystery of the missing black lab had been solved, and the ending was ideal. Could every moment be transformed into bliss?

"Penny for your thoughts..." Donna was looking at Bella.

"This is bliss." Bella looked right at her. "I was wondering what my life would be like if I could sustain this feeling."

"That's an awful big request, but it would be awesome, wouldn't it?"

"Yeah..." they agreed.

"You know, I had this dream that woke me up. If I hadn't I don't know what would've happened to Moondoggy."

"Some say everything happens for a reason."

"Now, if you and Livvy don't mind, I think I'll call Tim and see if he has time to come over and photograph Mom and pups. These are the first animals I've ever helped deliver."

"Be my guest."

"Would you like to get Livvy in the pics?"

"That's fine, if she wants to."

"Great. I'll try to arrange it after school."

Rushing to get to the library for her staff meeting, Bella thought about the connectedness of all things. Could she call it *thought energy* like Anna had? It was that invisible place where people's dreams intersect, propelling all of them in the direction they long for. Like today...Bella had a dream that awakened her and allowed her to solve the mystery of the night creeper. Bruce got to save a life, and they both got to witness new life. Livvy found her beloved Moondoggy. Donna got her giggly daughter back. Moondoggy got help to deliver her family. And they all made new friends, and helped each other through something. There was just too much synchronicity for it to be simply chance. There was some intelligent convergence of wishes...prayers...dreams...whatever you wanted to call it. It was a miracle.

During her staff meeting, Bella entertained her staff by recounting her adventure. They all marveled at how Bella, in her condition, turned her unfortunate situation into a funny story with a happy ending. It was a gift. Bella felt great. She was living fully. Contemplating that, she detected the direct cause. She was living every moment with no thoughts of the past, and no look to the future. There was contentment and peace in this place. And it wasn't the physical space she occupied, it was a place in her mind. Her thoughts were creating her experiences. By being willing to let go of preconceived notions, she freed herself from the turmoil of her monkey mind. When she did only what the moment demanded of her, she was free. No strings, past or future. It seemed as if the universe was conjuring, or out-picturing, what Bella had been asking for.

All of life is an asking, isn't it? Bella had many worries, commitments and responsibilities. Yet here she was, in what some called an unfortunate situation, having new experiences and witnessing everyday miracles. She could see that life had already given her the answers she needed. It was her job to merely show up and receive her blessings, or destiny, or lessons, however she wanted to look at it. And a new gift, the gift of telepathy, was introduced here. Again, she'd always had it and never knew.

Do we heap and pile a lifetime of training on top of our natural talents? Are we afraid to let the beautiful gift we each are unfold? Do we give more attention to what's wrong than what's right? Do we prefer the ugly to the beautiful, or are we just more comfortable there? Bella realized she could live her life in the bondage of her monkey mind, or pay attention to what was right in front of her and choose bliss. Today, it was a no-brainer.

Picking up her phone, Bella called Tim. He agreed to come by that afternoon and photograph the puppies. He said he would drop by a little early to get a feel for how to best get the pictures. Bella had time for a nap.

Just as she was about to doze off, she got a strange feeling. Try as she might, she couldn't shake it. What seemed unsettling wasn't about her, she could sense that. Then a picture of Bruce sobbing came to mind. Feeling like there was some sort of magnet pulling her, she got up and hobbled to the kitchen door. She got into the cart and rode down the back yard to Bruce's.

He was sitting in a pile of sawdust, head buried in his hands. He wasn't physically hurt, but releasing years of grief pushed down to hide his unspeakable secret past. Bella sensed forgiveness. Giving life to the pups had opened an emotional door. These tears were washing away old brokenness.

When he saw her, he rushed to wipe his face and pull himself together. Bella shook her head and put her hand up, letting him know she was leaving him to his healing. He made no move to get up. Bella thought about how we hold ourselves hostage with guilt and shame. We are programmed to accept what others, those we trust, choose for us. When we feel that we've disappointed them, there's collateral damage, guilt and shame. It takes time and maturity to process, to heal ourselves. We go from life designing us, to us designing our own lives. Although it sounded simple, it was anything but.

Even though Bruce saw her there, he couldn't cap the volcano of sadness that erupted with the first tear. Thirty years of grief poured forth like a monsoon. There was no stopping it. For all the times he'd wished for a do-over, for all the lies he'd told, for all the carelessness on his part, for the sadness of the family who adopted the baby girl with a hole in her heart, he cried. Then…for the years he'd clubbed himself with shame and guilt over one mistake he made at age twenty, he cried.

For hiding from life to avoid making more mistakes, for being less than he was capable of, for letting life pass quietly by, he cried some more. Finally, when the last tear fell, he was done. Something inside seemed to right itself. The process emptied out his separation and filled him with connection to life. He couldn't remember ever feeling anything quite like it. Is this what it was like to have what people called 'a healing?' Whatever you called it, it was time, and it was good. He was a better man because of it. Now eager to start fresh, he did the best thing he could – he reached out to the moment for a fresh start. And he got it.

Bella got back to the house and bathed as best she could. She wasn't allowed to get her cast wet. Hopefully, this week the doctor would free her from it and put on a removable brace. She couldn't wait. While she was drying her hair, the phone rang.

"Hey, Allen, what's up?"

"Bella, can I talk to you?"

"You're talking to me Allen."

"Can I come over?"

"Sure. Come on by."

Allen had concerns about his daughter, Dani. She was exhibiting behavioral changes. Her sleeping and eating habits were changing. She wasn't happy with any of her clothes, and wasn't talking about her friends any more. Something was up and Allen and his wife were unable to reach her. They wondered if Bella could help. She wasn't sure, but was willing to try. The problem would be getting Dani to agree to cooperate. It was important to be honest about what they would be doing, and why. Allen agreed. They set up an appointment for the next day. Allen would bring his band. Bella suggested they bring their bathing suits, so if it didn't go as planned, she could play with the pups and swim. They would make a day of it.

Shortly after Allen hung up, Bruce appeared. Bella could see that there was no napping today. She resigned herself to it and slowly made her way to the kitchen to make some coffee. Bruce was waiting patiently for his opportunity to have her undivided attention. She motioned him to take the coffee over by the window to the breakfast nook. She could prop her cast on a chair and they could visit comfortably.

"What's on your mind, Bruce?"

"Well, I think you know…"

"Without telepathy?" She laughed a little. He didn't find it funny. "I'm sorry, go on."

"Bella, I hate to ask, but…well…the little angel you bought from Deidre…can I have it back?"

"Sure. Why?"

"Well, when I made it, I wanted it as like…like…a headstone."

"I see. Do you want to place it on her grave?"

"I'd like to, but I don't know where she is. I thought I could create a space in my own yard to remember her. If I could use the piece to have a cast made of it, perhaps someone could design a copper or concrete…some kind of sculpture of it, and I could create a garden in her memory. I'd like to take all those years of trying to forget and turn them into a remembering place. Does that make sense?"

"I think it's a wonderful idea."

"I have to find someone to help, but I'll let you know."

"That'll be fine."

About that time the doorbell rang. Bruce hopped up.

"Are you expecting company?"

"Yes, Tim. Let him in, will you?"

"Tim!"

"Bruce."

"Come on into the kitchen." Bella was already up and moving. "Coffee?"

"No thanks, I'm not a coffee drinker. I'll take some tea, though, if you have it."

"Coming right up."

"Why don't you just point me in the right direction and I'll make it myself." They all laughed.

Bruce and Bella told Tim the stories behind the puppy birth. They explained Bella's accident, her children seeing someone crawling across the yard, the missing dog and finally the puppy birth.

"That's quite a story," Tim commented. "It's delightful."

"It is now," Bruce threw in. They all laughed.

"Where's Moondoggy?"

"Come on, we'll show you."

Moondoggy was nursing her pups when they came around the corner. She looked up to see who was coming, then laid her head back down. Tim got his camera and began taking photos. As he walked around the yard, the puppies got active. Since they were only a day old, they couldn't get very far, but they were as cute as could be. Moondoggy watched Tim carefully, but didn't growl or get up. He was keeping a respectable distance. The energy was high and they all felt as light as a feather.

It wasn't long before they heard Donna and Livvy coming around the corner. Livvy ran over to Moondoggy and threw her arms around her. The dog licked her like she was a new puppy who needed to be cleaned. Livvy giggled with glee. It was a joyful moment for them all. Tim continued to take photos for over an hour.

"Mommy says Moondoggy scared you and you had an accident."

"I broke my leg."

"Mommy says it'll get better."

"She's right."

"She says I have to help you after school. What will I need to do?"

"Well…let's see…" Bella was thinking about what she needed help with. "Moondoggy and her pups need fresh food and water every day. Bruce, will you show Livvy where things are?" As they headed off toward the pool house, Donna and Bella got a moment to talk.

"I hope she'll be a help and not a hindrance. If she gets to be too much, just call and I'll come and get her."

"Thanks. I will."

"This is great fun." Tim was smiling ear to ear.

"It's funny how a dog or puppies can make you feel so good."
Donna was smiling. "I wouldn't have believed it if I hadn't come over
and felt it for myself. There's something special about this place."

"It does make you feel good, doesn't it?" Bella agreed.

"Yeah. For some reason, it seems like…well, a place to take a
break from everyday life." Tim was enjoying himself.

"Yes…like a retreat or a vacation."

"Yes. I feel it, too."

"Well, I best be getting home. Linda and Jake will be home and
dinner will be ready. Linda's making her famous gumbo tonight. If I'm
late I won't get any.'"

"Thanks, Tim, and I want that recipe," Bella shouted out to him.

"Not gonna happen," he laughed. "Top secret recipe." He waved
as he rounded the fence and left through the side gate. Bella waved
good-bye.

Bruce and Livvy were coming around the corner carrying fresh
water and food for the doggie family. It dawned on Bella that it was
another universal illustration of how things work out. Bruce wanted
to heal a hole in his heart. In the last few hours, he saved a life. By saving the black lab and her litter of pups, he became a hero to the little
girl next door. What a beautiful beginning set up by God. The pieces of
Bruce's heart were allowed to begin to fuse back together because everything that was creating separation was being released and replaced
with love. We can't make a path to that by ourselves. It's yet another
healing intersection. There was healing power in every moment.

She thought about how much goes on in the undercurrent of life.
We can't predict how what we've asked for will appear. The package
arrives differently every time. Today was the convergence of five wishes. None of them could've predicted the packaging. It was amazing to
witness and wonderful to live.

The freedom of doing what's in front of you is powerful. Making
the most of the only moment you have, this one, fills life with newness.

It's not ruled by the past, or driven by the future. It's just this. It's simple. When I'm concentrating on what's here now, I'm enough. Directed thought creates. What was Bella creating right now? Right this moment she was living in a place filled with light and love. She felt warm and fuzzy. She knew this energy was radiating out and creating more love, more light and more happiness for whoever wanted to receive them. Just as Bella felt the sad energy Bruce was radiating earlier today from down the street, her neighbors were receiving this energy now. It was what they were creating together. What would the world be like if every person lived every moment this way? Taking that feeling out into the world with her, Bella felt as if anything were possible. As sure as she was sitting here, things would work out for them all.

Bruce stayed all afternoon with Livvy and Bella. They played around the outside most of the day and got a place ready inside the pool house storage shed for Moondoggy and the pups. Bruce cut a small doggie door in the bottom and put a piece of soft rubber for a door flap. The dogs would be out of the hot sun and weather, except for when they needed to be outside. It would be Livvy's duty to clean up the puppy presents they left in the yard each day. She would feed, water, and play with them, too. They were her responsibility until they were ready to go home.

Bella wanted to make an agreement with Livvy. She would set up paying chores that Livvy could also do to help her. Livvy liked her idea, but wouldn't accept money for now. She said Mommy insisted she give of herself freely to pay Bella back for helping Moondoggy. Bella liked the idea of helping each other - good for goodness sake.

Donna came over to get Livvy about supper time. She invited Bruce and Bella over for dinner. She said they had a huge amount of food and looked forward to 'breaking bread' with them. They accepted her invitation. Now Bella had met both her neighbors. It was a mini block party! She was surrounded by good people, just like back home. Bella thought about that. She now had two homes. It felt nice.

The day that began around 3 a.m. was finally coming to a close. Bruce walked beside the golf cart while Bella drove. There was no room for him. Her cast stretched across the whole cart. They chatted a little about how sweet Livvy was, and how much they enjoyed the meal.

"Bruce, do you happen to know of a cab company nearby? I have to go to the doctor's office tomorrow morning to get this hard cast replaced with a removable one."

"I'll take you."

"You don't have to do that. I can take a cab."

"I insist. We'll go to breakfast first, then to the doctor."

"My appointment is at 9:30."

"I'll pick you up about 8:15 and we'll get a bite to eat."

"That sounds great, thanks. I'll see you in the morning."

Bruce wanted to kiss her, but she didn't seem receptive. Since her accident, she hadn't been the same. Well, she was the same, but their relationship had cooled off a bunch. Bruce figured it was probably because everything was topsy-turvy right now. It probably didn't feel sexy to gimp around in a full leg cast. But it didn't detract from her sex appeal at all. Bruce found her more attractive than ever. She needed him now. It made him feel strong and useful.

The weeks she'd laid in a coma were tough on him. He sat there with her, holding on to what life with her was like before the accident. Even though he hadn't known her very long, they were a unit. He looked forward to seeing her, even if he wasn't with her. Just looking at her making jewelry or lying by the pool filled his life with something. He had someone to care about, who cared about him. She saw him, witnessed his life. And he thought the world of her. She thought he was talented, an artist. He thought she was intelligent, capable and creative. They went together, like a pair of comfortable shoes.

Some moments, those fearful moments in the middle of the night, he wondered if she would ever come back. What would life be like if her body returned but her mind was gone, or vice versa? Or what if she didn't remember him? What then? In those moments he'd prayed… hard, not just that she'd come back, but that she'd be completely restored. Those prayers were being answered. He was happy to do his part. Life was just better with her than without her.

Morning came quickly. Bella had slept like a baby. She looked forward to getting her cast off today, and to spending time with Allen and Dani. Maybe if Maura came over, she could get a feel for what was happening with the little girl without having to use the bands. It would be worth a shot. About that time she heard Bruce knocking at the door. When she saw him standing there in his khaki's, navy polo shirt and brown loafers, she couldn't take her eyes off of him. WOW!

Breakfast at the café was exactly what the doctor ordered. Bruce talked of ideas for his garden, and the spot for the statue. He wanted to have a tiny plaque made. Bella suggested they make it of wood and encrust it with some of her beautiful stones. They could build a display case or something. It was their first joint project. They were both excited about it.

Bella talked of spending time with Allen and Dani, and her desire to contact Maura. Bruce offered to take her by the law firm on the way back from the doctor to see if she was available. It would be on the way home if they chose to come through town. Everything was coming together nicely.

Bella asked Bruce to join them at the pool a little later. She intended to invite everyone for supper. They agreed to stop by the market for a few things on the way home. It was turning out to be a very busy day, a way of life for Bella. She was a social creature, and enjoyed being with everyone.

The doctor's office was busy, but the doctor was right on time. Bella was in the back getting her cast off right away. She'd allowed Bruce to come into the room with her, as if they were a couple. When the plaster finally fell away, Bella was floored at what she saw. Her beautiful smooth skin was all scarred up and the hair on her leg was quite long. Her muscles appeared atrophied. The disappointment she felt must've shown in her expression.

"I'm so grateful you will be up and walking around on your own very soon." Bruce was trying to change the direction of her thought.

"I made it to fifty without any scars other than one skinned knee from a biking accident as a child."

"You're beautiful, head to toe. Allow your body a chance to heal."

Bella looked up at Bruce. She looked past what he was saying and behind his eyes. In that moment, she wished she could read his thoughts. Bella wanted to believe him, believe that the scar wouldn't make a difference in her appearance. His gaze was unwavering, and he seemed to genuinely believe what he was saying. She was probably just sensitive today, and once she could take care of her leg and rebuild its strength, she would feel better.

"You're a good friend, Bruce. You're always honest with me and it means a lot."

Bruce's heart skipped a beat. He was crushed. Good friend? He was a lot more than that. At least he wanted to be. Was she blind? Did she see how he felt about her? Didn't she feel it, too? All that time he'd spent praying for her to be healed, and praying for things to be the way they were before her accident, and now this? He had questions for God. He wanted their old relationship back!

"Penny for your thoughts…"

"I was just thinking about…" But was interrupted by the doctor walking in with Bella's new x-rays.

"Everything is healing nicely. With some physical therapy you'll be back on that leg in no time."

"What about the scars, Doctor?" Bella wanted to know.

"Wear them with pride, Mrs. Sanders. Your leg was nearly broken in half. You're lucky to be able to walk at all. The scars are the least of your worries."

"Explain that, please," Bruce interjected.

"Well, with not only bone, but muscle and tendon tears, her come-back will be slow and painful. She will need extensive therapy, and she will have to be faithful to the home rehab strengthening exercises as well. There will be some joint movement restriction, and she'll have scar tissue and metal in her leg."

"Do you mean I'll have a limp?"

"Quite possibly, yes. And you'll have to re-learn some movements, as you won't have the flexibility in this knee that you do in the other."

"I see."

"What's her chance of a complete recovery?" Bruce was pressing it.

"Five to ten percent chance she could fully recover."

"So there IS a chance of complete recovery."

"I suppose it's not impossible, with total dedication."

"When will her rehab begin?"

"Today. I'll have my nurse come in and talk to you about it. Then the girls in the office will set it up. They'll measure you for a leg brace. Any more questions?"

"Doctor, can I swim?"

"As long as you have no open skin, yes. That would be very good."

Both Bruce and Bella were silent. This was enough to absorb. As promised, there was a flurry of activity as they got Bella fitted for her brace and went through some minor observations of her walking in it. They got her physical therapy arranged and set up a follow-up appointment. It was finally time to go.

"That doctor obviously doesn't believe in miracles," Bella finally broke the silence. "I've been snatched from the jaws of a bad prognosis before. I'll be fine. Period, the end."

"You're awfully feisty, lady!"

"You ain't seen nothin' yet." They both laughed.

Bruce dropped Bella off at the door of the law office. She went in to talk to Maura, who agreed to come over that afternoon. She was off at three, so that would work out perfectly. School got out around the same time. The universe was working its magic! Bella got done so quickly that they had time for lunch out.

Bruce had a taste for Thai food, so he took her to a quaint little restaurant in an ethnic neighborhood. There were only six tables in the place, but the carry out lines were unending. The food was sweet and spicy, and the rice was fluffy. Bella loved curry. The meal was great. They chatted about what to make for supper, and decided their menu. Because it was too early to tell if they'd be staying, she got enough for everyone. She would invite Livvy and Donna, too.

Bruce dropped Bella at the front door, and went home to change. He would be back to help her prepare for later, and would take on the task of the barbeque. By the time he got back she had changed and began preparing the ingredients for dinner. They peeled the corn, made the salad and sliced half of the watermelon. They cut and skewered the meats and put everything in the pool house frig. Everything was set.

Maura was the first to arrive. She went straight to the pool house and put on her suit and cover-up. She was done working, and it was the heat of the day. She wanted to be comfortable. By the time she got back, Allen and Dani were arriving. It wasn't long and Livvy arrived. Dani was glad to see her.

After the introductions, Bella took charge of the crowd.

"Bruce, could you take Livvy out to start her chores?"

"Okay, Miss Livvy, let's get started!" She stood up and took Bruce's hand.

"After you help me, can I go out and play with Livvy?" Dani knew more than Bella anticipated.

"Of course! What do you need my help with today, Dani?"

"My Dad says I need your help."

"Why did you bring her here, Allen?"

"Because I believe that she feels bad and that she doesn't want to tell me why."

"Is that true, Dani?"

"No, but Daddy doesn't believe me."

"Well…Miss Maura has a special gift. Sometimes she can see things that trouble us, even if we don't know about it."

"How does she do that?"

"Do you mean how does her gift work?"

Dani nodded her head.

"Will it hurt?"

"No, darling, you won't feel a thing." Bella reassured her.

"Can I put my hand on your back?" Maura asked permission before touching the child.

"Okay. Then what do I do?"

"Nothing. Just sit still a minute and I'll see if there's something troubling you deep down. Will that be okay?"

"Uh-huh." She sat still and stopped talking.

Maura put her hand on Dani's back and closed her eyes. Dani didn't take her eyes off of her. Maura began to speak a prayer out loud.

"Is that a prayer?"

"Yes, Dani, it is. It was a prayer thanking God for letting me see what's troubling your heart."

"You saw it already?"

"Yes, I did. Would you like to know what I found out?"

"No, not really, it's Daddy who wants to know. Can I go play with the puppies now?" All of the adults looked at each other in amazement. She wasn't interested at all.

"Sure, honey," Allen said. "Stay with Bruce and Livvy until I'm done talking okay?"

"Dani, is it okay with you if I tell your dad what I saw?" Maura would never betray a trust.

"No. I don't want you to." Dani seemed mildly alarmed.

"Why not?"

"Because he'll feel bad."

"So you do know what's been bothering you?"

"Yes ma'am."

"Dani, your daddy is feeling bad right now because he doesn't know what's bothering you. Won't you make him feel better by telling him?"

"This won't make him feel better."

"Why not?" Maura knew the answer, but Bella and Allen were hanging on every word.

"Because he thinks it's his fault."

"What's his fault?

"That I only have one leg."

"I'm so sorry, Dani," Allen got down on one knee and hugged her. "Why did you think that telling me this would hurt my feelings?"

"Because I overheard you telling Mommy that if you hadn't been hurt in Iraq that none of this would've happened."

"Oh, Dani, I'm so sorry." His eyes began to tear up. Dani looked at Maura.

"See, I've hurt his feelings," she hugged his neck. "But it's not your fault, Daddy, it's those ugly girls in gym class. It's their fault I feel bad, not yours."

"What did they do?" Allen wiped his eyes and put his hands on both of her arms. He looked right into her eyes.

"They called me a one-legged freakazoid!"

Allen started laughing very hard. It completely disarmed them all.

"Shows what they know! You're not a one legged freakazoid, you're a one legged wonder!" He kissed her cheeks at least four times each and sent her on the way to the puppies. Then he walked back into the living room.

"I can't believe how well you handled that, Allen!" Maura's face registered amazement.

"Two tours of duty in Iraq and a little girl takes me apart with a word..." He laughed with relief.

"She's pretty amazing." They all nodded in agreement.

"Let's go swimming!" Bella struggled a little, but got herself up. "Did you guys bring your suits?"

"I've got them in the car. I'll be right back."

"Thanks, Maura." Bella put her arm around her friend. "Let's get wet!"

"Sounds good."

It wasn't long and the girls were running around the yard chasing the puppies and giggling. Bruce called Donna and invited her over for swimming and dinner. She brought both their suits with her. All of the girls were inside changing, while Bruce waited outside. Livvy looked at Dani's prosthesis.

"What's that?" She pointed at her artificial leg.

"It's my leg. I only have one, so I get to use this one. It works great."

"How long have you had one leg?" Livvy wasn't mean, just curious.

"Since birth." She pulled her suit up over her arm.

"Do you swim with it?"

"Sure."

"Good. Let's go. Race ya…" The girls ran out the door and headed toward the pool. Bella, Maura and Donna looked at each other with love. Teachers came in all sizes.

"Just one moment young ladies…nobody gets in the pool without an adult." Bruce was stern. Allen was laughing.

"Get in, Daddy," Dani begged.

"I have to change first."

"Okay."

The afternoon was a smashing success. They ended up eating around the pool and staying out until nearly dark.

"Okay, girls, it's time to put things away and get ready to go. It's a school night." Donna began to put noodles and beach balls in the bin. The girls dried off and picked up the goggles and diving toys. They were fast friends.

"Daddy, can we come back here again?" Allen looked at Bella, who was nodding her approval.

"Sure, honey."

Everyone said their good-byes and, just like that, the quiet returned. Bella smiled at the thought.

"Penny for your thoughts…"

"The quiet returns," she smiled up at him.

"Ahhh…quiet. Personally, I think it's over rated." They both laughed out loud.

Bella filled Bruce in on what had been bothering Dani. He shook his head in disapproval of the mean remarks the girls made about Dani in the locker room.

"What if we put all the energy we spent in hurtful ways into building each other up? What would we be creating then?" He didn't require an answer. They both sat quietly a while contemplating the ripple effects of kindness, love and inspiration. If people would take time each day to spread that kind of energy around the planet, the world would be a much different place.

"Allen is the young author whose book you read."

"He's seen a lot for one so young."

"Far too much, if you ask me. And the clinic is full of people just like him."

"It's important work, Bella. Anna always understood that no price could be put upon the good done there. She dreamed of global rescue for the rescuers. It was her life's work."

"She was brilliant. I can't believe that all those years passed without getting to know her. I lived my whole childhood and most of my mid-life believing that Mom didn't know her either. I had no idea that they were in relationship all along."

"It's funny how many of our beliefs are founded upon false assumptions, isn't it?" Bruce was contemplative.

"Most of them, I'd imagine." Bella was too tired for the conversation. She was fading fast.

"Well, pretty lady, it's getting late. This ole boy needs to get cracking early after playing all day today." He got up and started tidying up.

"Let's let it go. I'll get it tomorrow morning after the staff meeting."

"Sounds good to me. Good night." With that, he turned down the lawn and walked toward home.

Bella was stunned. Two nights in a row and he didn't even try to kiss her good night. She couldn't figure it out. Maybe while she was sick he had second thoughts. Maybe he wanted to make sure he didn't have to take care of her. And seeing her leg this morning probably grossed him out. Or, maybe while she was in a coma, he realized that he only wanted to be friends. But, friend he was, and a good one at that.

That night Bella took her crutches and slowly climbed the stairs. She felt energetic at the bottom, but was completely exhausted by the time she reached the top. Full leg braces were anything but glamorous, but she needed a good night sleep in her bed. She took off her brace and was surprised to find that Bruce put a plastic lawn chair in the shower so she could sit. He did many kind things for her. She would miss him when she left.

That night she tossed and turned for over an hour trying to get to sleep. Finally, she got up and hobbled out to the balcony. When she looked out into the starlight, she knew why Gran had picked this room for her own. The view was breathtaking. She could see the stars, the treetops, the city lights, and imagined Bruce swimming laps in the pool. Bella wasn't sure how long she stood there before her leg got tired. She laid back down and drifted off.

Her dreams were filled with romance. She and Bruce were dancing the hours away, swimming, taking walks, and everything she hoped to be able to do again in the future. In the dream, she was whole. It felt so real that when she awakened, she forgot to pick up her crutches and actually stood on her leg. She was not supposed to bear weight until the bones healed. She instantly sat back down.

"I will be dancing in no time," she spoke out loud. "I will take long walks with Bruce. We will swim laps together, and take great vacations. I will walk without a limp." There...she had said her affirmations. Nothing less was possible for Bella. Well...except that Bruce may not want the same things. Time would tell.

Chapter 16

This was Bella's first day back in clinic. It had been a month since her accident, and she was ready to pick up the pace right where she left off. This was her final week before returning home to the St. Louis area. At this juncture, she wasn't sure how things would all work out, but if her internal gauges were back on track, everything was going to be fine.

"Knock, knock…" Allen tapped before entering.

"Hi, Allen. How's Dani?"

"She's back to her beautiful and amazing self. Thanks. Say, are we going to continue on in our experiments with the bands?"

"Yes. But I'm afraid we won't have much time. I'm leaving the first part of next week. So we may have to cram."

"Bella, I was thinking…if we think the bands will work long distance, and you take one back to Illinois, do you think the scanners at the airlines will effect it any?"

"I haven't the foggiest. What do you think Gran?" There was no reply. "She isn't listening. I'll ask her later."

"Sounds good. When do you want to start?"

"Well, I'm drafting a proposal for the endowment managers to introduce some ideas about ways to schedule regular time here. Since I'm leaving in eight days, I've got to finish it today. I'll call you after that."

"Great. I'll talk to you then."

"And Allen, I have some proposals for additional books to talk to you about, too."

"*Additional* books?" He was smiling from ear to ear.

"Yes. I'll forward some stuff my staff sent me today. Don't look for it until after dinner, though. The day is full. I have to review it myself first."

"I'll be checking my email every ten minutes starting at 5 p.m.!" He was obviously very excited.

Bella worked the remainder of the afternoon polishing her proposals. She didn't care if they accepted these or proposed one of their own, she just needed to settle on a way to travel back and forth regularly with some provision for the unexpected. As long as those needs were met, she'd be good.

"Ah, Rick, come in."

"Bella, there's a case we may need your help with."

"Tell me about it."

"Well, this one is a first responder, a fireman. Maura has pinpointed the thought that's tripping him up, but doesn't seem to be able to detect why he won't let go of it. Could you give it a try?"

"Sure. I don't have the other band here, but I can get it for tomorrow. Would that be soon enough?"

"I'll ask him."

"Have Maura come in when she's done. I want to talk to her about what she saw."

"I'll let her know."

Bella put together an email and attached her proposals. She just got things sent off when Maura arrived.

"Hey, Bella!"

"Maura, so nice to see you. Listen, I want to thank you again for helping with Dani."

"She's a lovely child. It was a joy to be able to help."

"I think she and Livvy will remain friends. Funny how things work out."

"I'm always amazed. I never get tired of marveling at God's handiwork."

"So what's going on with the fireman?"

"Ike? I'm not sure. I can guess at it all day, but why, we have you?" She giggled. "Ike responded to an accident, and it turned out to be his daughter. He had been on the back line of the call when the Jaws of Life arrived. As they began to extract the victim from the car, she was mangled almost beyond recognition. They immediately removed him from the scene, but he had already seen her, his daughter, there in the wreckage, and the thought is buried deep. I can see that there's more, but ...."

"I'm so grateful that I've never experienced that. It must be misery."

"Well, yes, but his daughter is alive and well. She's had many surgeries, but she's living a normal healthy life, while Ike is living in agony. I hope we can help."

"How's his wife?"

"She's doing well. For a while they spoke to people everywhere, formally and informally about the dangers of texting and driving, and created a whole movement to spread the word. Mother and daughter are moving on and thriving, but dad is stuck."

"Okay. Well I'll see if the bands can help us."

"Okay. Let me know how it turns out, will you?"

"You bet. Hey, you know I leave for St. Louis in a week. I wanted to get together with everyone again before I go. If you're not busy Saturday night, how about coming over with your family for a bon voyage party?"

"Sounds great. I wouldn't miss it. I'll talk to Carol, Deidre, and Linda, if you like."

"That'd be fabulous. If they can text me a head count, that would be splendid."

"What can we bring?"

"I think I'll have the food catered by this Mexican restaurant I love, so just bring your favorite cocktail and a dessert. How's that sound?"

"Sounds great."

Bella drafted and sent an invitation to the employees at the clinic.

She would mention it to Bruce, Donna and Livvy when she saw them later today. Bella picked up the phone to call Allen. He agreed to bring his band to the clinic the next morning, when Bella would arrive with hers. They made an early appointment to review the proposals her staff had mentioned for the possibility of more books. Things were all set. All the loose ends were tied up. She was ready to go.

Bella drove home wondering how to best supervise the care of the estate. Upon arrival, she went into the study and made a list of all the utilities and care takers, the Alarm Company and local police. She had to contact them all. Everything had to be forwarded to her Illinois home.

She gave police and the alarm monitors all of her contact information. She retained Jake for pool care, and Linda's company to maintain the property.

That night Bella looked around the house for stuff she wanted to take home with her. She might as well leave some of her clothes and shoes. But the place already had everything else she needed, Gran had seen to that. She called Carol and made an appointment for later in the week. She wanted to make herself a necklace, bracelet and earrings with special stones to enhance her abilities when she left. This place had magic. Maybe she could take some home with her. Carol would help her decide which stones to put together.

Bella was looking through the cabinets and frig when Bruce knocked on the door. She waved him in. It took a whole two minutes for him to talk her out of cooking. He was in the mood for some ribs and baked beans. The restaurant was just a few miles away. Bella was ready to go.

During dinner Bella talked about getting ready to go. Bruce listened patiently, trying to push down his disappointment and sadness over her leaving.

"Well, it's not like you'll be gone for good." Bruce was trying to sound nonchalant.

"True…but this won't be my primary residence any more. I'll just be here part time."

"Define part time." He was struggling to hide his displeasure.

"I'm not sure yet."

"Have you heard which proposal the endowment managers chose?"

"No, I actually just got them submitted earlier today." Bella sensed a shift in energy. Her defenses were going up.

"So what does that mean for us?"

"Us?"

"Yeah, you and me!" Bruce was getting angry. Hadn't she even thought about what it would be like not seeing each other every day? Did she care about him at all?

"Bruce, lower your voice." Bella looked around her. Patrons at nearby tables had turned their attention to them.

Just about that time Bella's phone rang. It was Allen. Ike had attempted suicide and had been admitted to a local hospital.

"What now, Allen?"

"I'm not sure. His wife is a nurse at the hospital. She said she would keep me informed, but thought that if he'd agree to it, we could have our session at his bedside tomorrow."

"Please keep me informed."

Bella told Bruce what she'd just learned. Although Bella had never met Ike, she felt for him. It was as if they were in this together. She thought about the connectedness of all things, and engaged Bruce in the conversation. The universe had diverted their heated exchange and instead of thinking about how they would be separated, they began discussing how we are never really alone. Bella talked about how she thought her mother was alone all those years, and yet she was in a continuous conversation with her own mother telepathically. She talked of feeling alone and being the oldest living member in her bloodline, and then she came here and was reunited with her mother and grandmother. It was mindboggling to know that people didn't really die, they moved on to another way of being.

Engaging in the conversation cooled Bruce down. The largeness of the universe, and the multitude of what it contained gave Bruce hope. Even if he couldn't work this out himself, he believed that prayer changed things. It was good to release his hopes for the future and just live this moment. After all, he was with her right now. He would pay attention and make it count.

"Bruce, I've been meaning to talk to you. Since I'm leaving in a week, I wanted to ask your help with something."

"Anything."

"I want to consolidate the jewelry studio all onto one floor. I think if we make some wooden cases that could contain separate areas for the different stones, we could stack them nicely against one wall. I want to open up the bottom floor for the publishing company office. I've decided to head this branch myself. I think that would be the best spot to start. This branch needs to be profitable before I invest in another location. For now, I'll have to share my time equally between here and the St. Louis office."

"So, what did you have in mind for the stones?" Bruce was elated. God *had* heard his prayer. Although she was talking of leaving for good, she meant that she would not be here full time any more. But she would be here, and that was enough for now.

"Well, let's brainstorm and come up with some ideas to get us started."

"When would you like to start?"

"I'm not sure what tomorrow will bring, so why not right now?"

The waiter brought out the slabs of ribs and the crocks of beans. The ribs filled a platter, which the waiter reminded them was very hot. They ate casually, talking about the stones. Neither of them knew if they could be stored so close together without affecting their natural properties. Bella told him about calling in Carol as a consultant. She was familiar with everything, being Gran's supplier. She was scheduled to come over before Livvy the next day, but with the news of Ike, Bella wasn't sure how the timing of the day would go. They'd have to fly by the seat of their pants. And Bella was getting good at it.

The evening turned out to be delightful. Each had turned their attention to the projects and work at hand, and had put aside all feelings about the unknown future. For now they were together, functioning as a solid unit. That would have to be enough. The future would take care of itself.

The next morning Bella got a call about Ike. Allen and Bella took the bands and went up to his hospital room. His wife and daughter introduced themselves and brought them up to date on Ike's condition.

"It's as if the weight of the whole world came crashing down... all the sadness and tragedy he's ever seen pressed down and flattened him like a pancake."

"Did he show you any sign that he intended suicide?"

"No. His doctor told us that when a person is serious about suicide, they don't give any clues. They don't want to be interrupted."

"How'd you find him?"

"Laying on the floor. We'd just gotten back from shopping...I guess he'd planned to go somewhere, but the pills kicked in before he could leave the house. He didn't intend for us to find him." The two were crying their eyes out. "Can you help us?"

"I don't know, but I'll try." Bella and Allen went into his room. He was sitting on the bed staring into space. They introduced themselves and explained why they were there.

"I miss the days when I could just talk to my mother and straighten everything out. She always loved me, no matter what I did. And believe you, me, I pulled some doosies." He smiled.

"We can help you with that."

"You can help me have a conversation with my dead mother? Right!" He was a non-believer.

"Well, we can't personally, but we know someone who can, a psychic named Linda."

"Psychics can't help me. I tried that yesterday."

"But we're not done trying."

"You guys are psychics, too?"

"No." Allen had no psychic powers.

"I'm not a psychic, but I have a gift called telepathy. I can communicate with a select few people who also have the gift."

"So how will that help me?

Bella and Allen explained Anna's invention and how it worked. Ike had questions, and the two were very patient, listening to Ike's objections.

"Ike, do you want to get better?" Bella decided to be direct.

"What kind of question is that? I've been everywhere and nobody can help me."

"Do you want help?" Bella wanted him to answer the question.

"Do you want to live, man?" Allen asked sternly.

"I want to live, yes, not just exist for the next gruesome emergency."

They looked at each other knowingly. It was life-altering to move from one bloody event to the next, day in and day out. It was a steady diet of gore.

"Have you ever thought of a career change?" It was out before Bella could sensor it.

"Only every day for two years. Since Sam had her wreck I've thought about nothing else. But I'm a fireman. That's what I do. The men in my family have always been heroes."

"You can be a hero without being a first responder, you know." Allen said it matter-of-factly.

"Okay, I'm ready." He was dismissive. Allen thought he was ready to get rid of them, and this was the only way.

Bella nodded her head. Allen handed the band to Ike and told him how to put it on. Bella donned hers and activated it. Allen told Ike how to initiate his. And just that quick, it was done. She asked Ike if it was okay to speak freely, or if he'd like to clear the room.

"I'd like privacy." Everyone but Bella left.

"Did you see what was at the root of it?"

"Yes."

"Would you like to discuss it?"

"Guilt and shame? Not really."

"Have you given in to the thought?"

"Until I saw her mangled in the car, I hadn't."

"And since then?"

He couldn't answer. Ike and Bella discussed his feelings. He'd modeled the dangerous behavior that ultimately caused his daughter to have her accident. There were occasions when he'd had too much to drink and drove anyway. He was sure that on more than a few occasions his family had been with him. He was sorry, so sorry. Over the years she had learned the behavior. If she hadn't been behind the wheel drunk that night, texting or not, all of what she suffered would not have happened. It was his fault, or at least partly his fault.

"What will you do differently as a result of what you now know?"

"I'm already doing that. I just want to make it up to her."

"How?"

"I don't know how!" He was getting despondent over it.

"Perhaps talking to her about what you feel were mistakes that you both made, can break the cycle for your son. Together, you can model responsible driving behaviors and move forward teaching others what you've learned."

"We're already doing that."

"So is there anything else you can do?"

"Not really."

"What about forgiving yourself?"

There was a pregnant pause. Bella could see him thinking it over.

"Has your daughter forgiven you?"

"She never blamed me. I'm her knight in shining armor! Some knight I turned out to be."

"So she loves you more than ever, and is glad to be around. What about your wife?"

"She never blamed me either. Never said a cross word."

"So it's self-punishment?"

"You're not tap dancing around me, are you, lady?"

"Do you want me to? This is life and death here. You're putting your wife and daughter through hell. Is that what you want to do?"

He didn't answer.

"I want to offer you something. I'd like to introduce you to my friends Linda and Carol. Linda has a gift for conversations with people on another side of life. She might be able to facilitate a conversation between you and your mother. Carol can help guide you in your journey of self-forgiveness. Would you allow that?"

"After what happened here today, I would say that I'm open to it. I'm not sure I believe that I could talk to my mother, but it'd be worth a shot. Nobody ever loved me more."

"I'll be in touch." Bella took the band from Ike and put it in a case in her purse and left the room.

"You can go in now," she told the others as she passed by.

"Bella, what'd he say?"

"I'm afraid you'll have to ask him, but don't worry. Everything's going to be alright." She knew it would because he'd chosen life and love over darkness and death. Only good would come of that.

Allen followed Bella out to the car. They decided to talk about the publishing projects proposed by her company over lunch.

Gordon greeted them with fanfare as they entered the café. He seated them near the window, in a round booth with privacy. It was as if he knew they were on important business. Bella noticed the synchronicity. You couldn't conjure this stuff. There simply is no other explanation than an organizing energy that manages the hopes and dreams of everyone, and brings them to strategic points in time where dreams collide. Bella liked that belief and the feeling it brought to her every time she reinforced it with another example.

It was a two and a half hour lunch which included dessert and coffee. Gordon was delighted that they spent their time in his diner. He knew both faces, and that they were doing very good things in this community. It pleased him that they chose to patronize his and other neighborhood businesses. Together, they could keep their community healthy and strong.

Allen was interested in the projects that Bella's group proposed. One looked lots like the idea that Bella had initially. He confronted her about it.

"It's still a good idea." She didn't try to defend it.

"What's good about it?"

"It lets regular folks know the price that others pay for the freedoms they enjoy every day. There are costs, costs that can't be paid for by governments or with dollars. There are effects from eating a daily diet of trauma and death. Nobody is immune to it. Regular citizens are in therapy for years to overcome traumatic events that occur once. These people are continuously inundated with it. If there's hope for folks who need help, why not share it?"

"Bella, your heart is in the right place, but..."

"But what, Allen?"

"But I don't want to be inundated with it over and over every day either."

"I see. Well...maybe I'll do this one myself. I'll take this proposal back to my staff and see what they want to do. I'd like to do it all as a package. I have other ideas for it. Either way, we'll stick with the offer for the book you have already completed."

"That doesn't sound so good." Allen was having second thoughts.

"Well, honestly, we have another young veteran who writes much like you. We wanted to do a series of books, not just a single. He may be interested in the project. With my guidance and my access to the stories, I think he could make it fit the bill."

"So you're going ahead either way?"

"Absolutely."

"There's no changing your mind?"

"Not on this, Allen. People need this. They need to know that nothing is impossible to overcome. Heroes need healing, too. If they don't have access to the clinic, understanding what helped others like them could be monumental."

"Okay then, I'll do it."

"Fantastic! Sign right here."

"I'll expect full anonymity, both for the clinic and its participants.

"Done, and by the way, where would you like me to deliver the advance?"

"Advance?"

"Yes. Our company has approved an advance on the project."

"How much of an advance?" Bella showed him the figure. He jumped up off of the chair and shouted out. The folks in the diner smiled, celebrating with him. It was very good.

"Miss Bella, you have made my day!" He kissed her on the cheek and bounded toward the door. As if he suddenly remembered something, he hurried back.

"Are we finished?"

"Yep."

"I got lunch!" He smiled and raised his eyebrows a couple of times, signaling his entry into the high life. He was on cloud nine. He snatched the lunch check off the table like it was the winning lottery ticket, and he was out the door with a flash.

Bella loved these types of meetings. Things were looking up for her agency. If these patriotic projects panned out, they would be well worth the time and effort to bring them forward. The books could be of help to many, and the proceeds would provide support for the clinic. Things were going well today.

Bella couldn't wait to get home and tell Bruce. So much had happened in one day that she wasn't sure she could stop talking. But then she remembered that he didn't like the idea of the book, either. That could be a bump in the road. Maybe he would feel differently after hearing the slant that Allen insisted on putting in. She supposed that every book had controversy. If others felt like Bruce and Allen, the press could skyrocket book sales and the clinic would be right on track for short-term support. Either way, God had her back.

Bruce wasn't home when Bella went by. His truck was gone. She went home and took some hamburger out of the freezer. She was in the mood for a grilled burger with juicy bread and butter pickles and a fat slab of fresh tomato! Hoping Bruce would be home by then, she made enough for two people. She wrapped some potatoes in foil and put them on the grill, too.

"Hi, Ms. Bella," Livvy came running through the yard. "Can I take my puppies home today?"

"I suppose you can, if it's okay with your Mommy, that is." She smiled at the child.

"I'll go check." Livvy ran down the yard at a full sprint. She was overjoyed.

About that time Bruce pulled up. Bella saw him unloading some wooden boards. She hoped they were for the cabinets or cubbies that they would design for the studio. Bella texted him to see if he needed help, but he didn't reply. A little while later he came over.

"That was nice wood you unloaded," Bella started, "Do you have something special in mind?"

"Yes."

"Well, that's quite cryptic."

"It's a surprise."

"Oh, okay!"

Just about that time Livvy came darting back down the yard.

"Can I stay for supper, Ms. Bella?"

Bella and Bruce burst out laughing. She was always welcome.

"Yes you may, if it's okay with Mommy, of course." Once again, she took off flying down the yard to ask permission.

"Mommy said no. But I can stay until supper."

"Great!" She ran around the yard chasing the puppies and giggling with glee once again. The air was filled with laughter, a barking dog and her clumsy newborn pups. It was a Hallmark moment. This was bliss. She looked forward to spending countless moments just like these with her grandchildren.

Bella began to talk to Bruce about her grandkids. She talked on for so long she almost forgot to tell him about Allen. But it could wait for another day.

The potatoes were poke-able and the burgers were done. It was time to eat. Livvy ran home. Bella didn't think she'd ever seen the girl walk.

They took everything inside the pool house for supper. Afterwards, Bella remembered to call Carol and Linda. Linda would go by on her lunch hour and talk to Ike. Carol wasn't sure when she'd get there, but it would be after Linda left. Bella asked each of them to let her know when they were on the way. She wanted to be there, too. Since she was still unable to drive, Linda agreed to take and Bruce would pick up. Bella had just hung up the phone when she heard a ruckus outside.

Bruce opened the patio door. Bella stepped out behind him.

"Oh no!" Bella was mortified!

Right there, in the middle of the lawn, a skunk was in a stand-off with Moondoggy. She was standing nose-to-nose with it, protecting her pups. The skunk was hissing. Suddenly, a puppy thrust forward and startled the skunk and the spray could be smelled for a city block. Bruce and Bella looked at each other with frowns, then burst out laughing.

"Now what?" Bella got in the golf cart and rode over to the main house for her iPad. She Googled what to do to clean skunk smell off of the dogs. She made a list of ingredients, and began to round them up. Baking soda, liquid soap, peroxide and water. She had them all. She didn't know if it would be enough for 5 baths, but they could at least get started. Bella grabbed the rubber gloves and bucket, and out she went.

"Bella," Bruce shouted across the yard, "go back in and dress in clothes and shoes you can throw away. Cover yourself up so this stuff doesn't get on your skin." That was good advice, and Bella followed it. "I'm going home to do the same thing."

"Okay, I'll wait for you. I don't know what I'm doing."

"Me neither. Call it up on u-tube and see if they have any tips."

"Will do, hurry!"

The next two hours went like something from an old episode of Lucille Ball. Donna and Livvy watched from Bruce's picnic table for a while. When all was said and done, Bruce and Bella went their separate ways to shower and change. Bella decided to take her shower at the pool house, keeping the stench out of the main house. She undressed outside and left her clothes on the concrete. When she was done, she took the towel outside with her. She put her rubber gloves back on and put everything in a trash bag and took it to the can. What a mess! Bruce texted to say goodnight. Bella was glad to get to bed. It had been another day full of surprises.

The week that followed was relatively benign. Bella was engrossed in getting all of the last minute arrangements made for going home. If all went well, she would be off crutches. She still notified the airlines that she would need assistance getting to the plane, using her injury to her advantage.

Her party was tomorrow night. It would be the last time she would see some of her new friends for a while. At least it looked that way right now.

Bella got acceptance from the endowment managers to take out a clinic credit card for airline and other travel expenses. They would not approve a private pilot. Her expenses would go directly to Rick Baker, who would submit them for payment.

Bella made arrangements with Allen to store his band at the clinic. He was given his own bio scan identity, allowing him access to the case. If it worked the way they hoped it would, they could help each other from remote locations.

With the wood he'd recently purchased, Bruce built the fanciest dog house that Livvy had ever seen. Moondoggy and the pups went home.

Linda and Bruce were given keys to the estate. Bruce and Bella would Skype about the design for the stone room. Deidre would be looking for the perfect office furnishings for the new branch of Sanders Publishing.

Back home, her family and publishing staff prepared for her return. Kate had her housekeeper come over and clean the house, so she wouldn't need to worry about it after being gone for almost five months. Andrea organized the family and got her yard in order for her. Everyone pitched in and stocked her cabinets and refrigerator. Bella would be all set to walk right back into her Illinois life. It was funny to think that she had two separate lives, and she wondered how it would all work out. Right now, it felt really good.

"Well, Gran, it's been good."

"For me, too."

"How'd you know, Gran?"

"Know what, Bella?"

"...that I'd be the one."

"I've always known. My grandmother had the gift. They called her a gypsy. I got the gift. They called me a fortune teller. Your mom got the gift, and they called her an introvert. Now you have it. What will they call you, Bella?"

"That's easy, Gran...fortunate!" "

"Aren't we? We pigeon-hole, stereotype, and box each other in with names and occupations and religions and classes, but...we're all made of the same stuff. We operate in the same energy fields and are subject to the same universal principles. We have the potential to achieve beyond our wildest dreams. Whatever we focus on, we attract."

"It's seems so simple."

"It is simple. What you put your attention on grows. So pay attention. Think about, act on and talk about what you want. Let the rest go."

"What if I can't?"

"You can. Your mind responds to your beliefs."

"So Gran, why can't I hear you all the time when I know I'm connected to you telepathically?"

"Why would you want to hear me all the time when there are so many other wonderful sounds and conversations to have?"

"Point made. Then...can I hear you when I want to?"

"Yes, as long as I'm not cloaked."

"Will you be listening, Gran?"

"Not only will I be listening, I'll hear you, Bella."

"And Mom?"

"She can't hear you. You'll need Linda for that."

"Can she hear you?"

"No, but I can hear her."

"I understand. It's all so mysterious, isn't it, Gran?"

"I call it miraculous."

Bella shook her head and knew it was true. They all had gifts they didn't even know about yet, but continued to discover. What promise that offered. Bella went up to her room. It was late, and she was tired.

The next morning she did a load of laundry and packed her bags. Her load would be light going back now, since she was leaving so much behind. UPS came by early to pick up the files and few things of Gran's she decided to take home. Even though it wasn't, it felt final. Bella did what she came here to do. But this wasn't the end. It was the beginning.

Right now it was time to get showered and changed. Linda and Carol were visiting Ike today. Bella promised to be there.

When they arrived at Ike's room, he looked better. The drugs were probably washing out of his system. His wife and daughter were on the way, but it was just the three of them right now.

Bella explained what happened when she fell in the shower and was in a coma. If it hadn't been for Linda, people wouldn't have known she was still alive inside. Her brain was fully functioning. She went on to explain her experience 'out of body' before she woke up. Ike related to that. He reported being alive in 'his other place' or inside, or wherever he was. He didn't feel dead either. So it wasn't so difficult for him to believe there was another place our energy and intelligence went. He wasn't a ghost, because he was living, just like Bella was. It was a meaningful conversation. Bella was enjoying it.

She told Ike about her dad's experience during open heart surgery to replace a valve. He said that his spirit was suspended in the room. He was conscious, he could see and hear everything, and watched them performing CPR on him from his perch above them. He didn't hurt or feel anything associated with a pain body. He was free. He was alive, yet clinically, his body was dead.

Being a first responder, Ike had been trained about the cycles of grief, and had read books written by those considered authorities on death and dying. He had read many accounts from those who had reported out of body experiences. It didn't seem like such a far-fetched idea.

Linda was ready. Ike had opened his mind, but was skeptical about being able to talk to his mother. Linda introduced herself and asked Ike a few questions. Then they were ready to begin.

It started with a prayer asking for help finding Ike's mom, Emma. There was an awkward silence. Ike asked if she was there, but she wasn't. Linda engaged Ike by asking him what questions he had for her, not asking him to tell her anything in advance, but to think of his questions. He was relaxing and thinking.

"She's here Ike. Where would you like to begin?"

"Mom?"

"Ike-a-rumba?"

Immediately Ike's eyes filled with tears. Linda couldn't possibly know that Mom called him Ike-a-rumba.

"Mom, what's it like where you are?"

"She says it's like where you are, but a little bit different."

"How so?"

"She says, the thinking, feeling, knowing her is there, but the body burden is gone. She wants to know what you're doing in a hospital bed when your body's in perfect shape."

"Mom, I...I let everybody down."

"She says that's nonsense, you're a hero."

"Mom, do you know what happened with Abby?"

"She knows."

There was a silence. Ike asked Linda if she was still there.

"She says she's always here. She wants me to tell you something."

"Okay."

"She's asking if you remember the time at the dinner table, when your dad grabbed your overalls in a fit of rage and yanked them so hard it ripped the bib?"

Ike cried hard at the memory.

"She says she was going to leave him that day, and take you kids from him. He was so sorry about letting his alcoholism get the better of him that he went into treatment. She says that the vacation she told you he took was his journey to sobriety. Hurting you in a moment of weakness was more than he could bear. He believed you would always think him a bully, and felt afraid he'd let you down."

"It wasn't that way at all. I thought I was the one who let him down! He was my hero. After that I decided to straighten up and be-have. I thought that he changed because I did. I tied the two together. I tried really hard to be like him. I loved the guy."

"She says that now you understand how your daughter feels."

"Mom, how do I straighten this all out?"

"She says you don't. You don't look back, and stop worrying about the future. What you need is right here right now – today. She says to let love show you the way."

"I'm not sure where to go from here, Mom. I'm not sure I want to do this work anymore."

"She says it's not the work you do that defines you, it's what you put into whatever you do that counts."

"But the men in our family have always been firemen."

"She says the women in her family were always housewives, but she wasn't."

"How did you break the tradition?"

"I decided that my life was my own to live, and I took a chance on my dream."

"Did you ever regret it?"

"No. She says going to work took pressure off your dad, and he was able to maintain his sobriety. The money she made helped with vacations, a second car and college tuition for you guys. It wasn't an easy decision, or a popular one with some people in the family, but it was worth it."

"So...you started your own traditions, then?"

"Exactly."

"Mom, I miss you."

"She says she misses being able to talk to you every day, too. She says she's got to go now."

"Can I talk to you again, Mom?"

"She says yes and that she loves you as much as she ever did."

"Love you, too, Mom."

They sat teary eyed for a while, absorbing the energy that emanated from Ike as he forgave himself. It was as if the room was filled with raw potential awaiting collapse, as if anything were possible. It was.

"Thank you, Linda." Ike's energy warmed the room. His gratitude changed everything.

"I'll see you later, Ike."

"Wait, Linda, can I have your card so I can do this again sometime?" Linda got into her purse and pulled out her card.

"So you're a property manager?"

"It's my day job. I'm saving for my restaurant. That's my dream."

"Do you need any handyman help?"

"Call me when you get your head on straight."

"Thanks again, Linda."

"You bet."

Bella walked over to the bed and put her hand on Ike's wrist. She told him she'd be back after lunch, when Carol arrived. As she left the room she motioned for Ike's wife and daughter to go in. Walking out of the hospital, Bella got an idea. She wanted to stop by Deidre's shop and get some sort of talisman for Ike, something he could touch to remind him that he was never alone. She would get lunch right up the street.

Walking to the boutique, Bella thought about the countless misunderstandings that people cling to and build on in life. She'd done it herself. Ike and his dad took ideas they had about one another and built their whole belief systems around them. All either of them ever wanted *from* each other was love. All they wanted *for* the other was happiness. It was all so simple and got so muddled up in a package of expectation that neither was ever able to fulfill. How is it that at this day and age people can't figure out that the only thing we have to do to be happy is to accept love and give love? She guessed that we interpret expressions of love differently. Could we simply ask each other what love looks like to them?

Bella walked two blocks to get to the shop. As usual, Deidre greeted her at the door. She explained why she was there and Deidre had a couple of suggestions for Bella. Two pieces came to mind, but she encouraged Bella to look for herself. Of course, in looking around, Bella found a host of items for herself, but she finally asked Deidre what she thought might be appropriate.

Deidre led her to the counter. She pulled out a small Goldstone.

"This is called the happy stone because it generates positive energy around you."

The second piece was a St. Christopher medal.

"St. Christopher is known for a couple of things. He is the patron saint of travelers, and the protector of those who carry the weight of the world on their shoulders."

Bella liked them, and asked Deidre to wrap them both and tuck her card in the bag. She didn't say why, but Bella wanted Ike to know this place. She also thought his wife and daughter would appreciate the meaningful gifts here.

"Have you had lunch yet?"

"No." Deidre grabbed her purse and let the others know that she would be gone for a little while.

"So, you're getting ready to go, how's that feel?"

"Strange. I wouldn't have believed that I could feel at home in two places."

"What a wonderful feeling."

"Yes. It's been amazing, really, this whole journey. It's like both places hold my destiny. In each place I feel empowered to make my dreams real while helping others achieve theirs. Does that sound crazy?"

"It sounds wonderful!" Deidre loved hearing success stories. It encouraged her to be more. "I've decided that I'm going to open a branch of my publishing company here in Phoenix and work it myself. I'm going to try to time-share my business."

"Oooo. Then you can see Brucey…" Deidre teased with that impish look that flirted naughtily.

"Then there's Brucey…Bruce was an unexpected…delight! He's…"

"Awe, Bella's got it bad for Brucey," she poked on.

"Yes, but it's not mutual."

"I don't believe that."

"Why not?" Bella was curious. She didn't know them together, just separately. But then again, everybody around here had fingers in the unexplainable. These people were seers. If she saw something, maybe it was there.

"It's hard to explain, but I'll try. When a person enters my shop I feel their energy. Something inside knows how to relate to that. Everything has an energy, even inanimate objects. They have a point of attraction. I may not recognize it right away, but when its energetic match comes through the door, I remember it. I'm like a Geiger counter. It's like a game of 'go fish.' I know all the cards are there, and I remember where the matching card is. Does that make sense?"

"Perfect sense. So you think Bruce and I are a match?"

"I do. I can't say anything more than that, like…it'll last forever or anything, but for now…"

"Now's the only moment we have, isn't it?"

"So true."

Deidre and Bella talked for nearly an hour before Bella realized that she had to meet Carol in a few minutes at the hospital.

"I'm sorry, Deidre, but I'm late for an appointment. I'll see you tonight. Bring your suit."

"Okay, I'll see you later." Bella picked up her check and headed out.

Carol was in with Ike before Bella got there. They were preparing to begin. Bella took a seat in the chair by the window and closed her eyes. She relaxed her mind and body, and prepared for a little nap after lunch. Neither of the others would care if she slept, as long as she didn't snore. She smiled inwardly at that.

Ike relaxed and opened his mind while Carol looked. She could see the guides who would lead Ike forward in the days ahead. She saw the strengths he brought with him on his journey, and gifts that were yet to appear. She showed him direction and togetherness, and left him with hope. It was a new beginning, a road thus far untraveled, a fresh start. It was just what he needed. At the end of the session, Ike appeared relaxed and resolute. It had gone remarkably well.

When Carol left, Bella gave Ike the gifts of the Goldstone and the St. Christopher medal. Although they were strangers, Bella felt connected to Ike. She felt it from him, too.

"I look forward to seeing you again sometime soon."

"Thank you. Bella."

"Be well, I've got to go, Ike." She turned and left his room. When she saw his wife and daughter this time, she stopped to talk to them a bit. Bella conveyed her wish to keep in touch, and her feelings that Ike was going to return home better than ever. She liked this family. You could see by looking at them that they'd walked over hot coals to stay together.

Chapter 17

Bella put on her earrings, a personal keepsake of Gran's. They were perfect for tonight. When the doorbell rang, it was the caterers. She led them out back and showed them where to set up the Mexican Fiesta. Earlier that day, Jake and Bruce set things up around the pool in preparation for the party. Linda's housekeeper cleaned the pool house. Bella brought out the table cloths and candles the day before, when she and Bruce strung the white twinkle lights.

Bruce came walking across the yard with the first sign of activity. He helped Bella arrange everything perfectly. Then Mariachi's arrived.

"I don't remember hiring them."

"You didn't." He smiled at her.

"Bruce..." Bella had stuff to tell him, things of the heart, but this probably wasn't the time. "Thanks." It was all she could utter right now.

Bruce turned to the first guests arriving through the back gate. As he greeted them, he looked at Bella. The way she looked at him a minute ago gave him hope. She was beautiful in the long red skirt. You couldn't see her leg brace. Standing still, without crutches, he didn't see her injury, and knew beyond a shadow of a doubt that she would recover fully. Life seemed to embrace her, support her, love her...and she felt the same about life. He wanted her to feel that way about him.

"Bruce...Bruce! You're staring!"

"Gordon, hello," he reached out and shook hands. "I'm..."

"I see it and understand it. She's amazing."

"She is, Gordon." He nodded his agreement.

"Her presence adds something to our community, Bruce. She's not Anna, but she adds something fresh and new. She brings promise. That woman took her grandmother's dreams and improved upon them. Expanding her dreams as well brings nothing but potential to us all."

"I couldn't have said it better myself, Gordon." He tipped his head and walked into the party.

Bruce stood by the gate greeting everyone as they walked in. Everyone from the clinic came with their families. Deidre brought a date. Linda, Carol, and Maura came with their families, too. Donna and Livvy brought the puppies, and they were received with joy and laughter. The night was a huge success.

The music, soft light, great company, fabulous food and Bruce's arm around her propelled Bella into a state of bliss. She was happy, and felt connected and committed to these people and this place. It had become a second home, and she loved it here.

Together with God, gifts, talents, and the help of family, colleagues and friends, Bella had it all. She was fulfilled, becoming everything she was capable of.

Feeling the miracle of life fully lived, she glanced up at Bruce. His eyes were deep, dark and sparkling. As she met his gaze their lips touched, and Bella felt the attraction drawing them together for a moment of truth. And love was the very last word.

Endnote

Anna Neusa was not in relationship with Nikola Tesla. The antics were all works of my imagination. His name was used without permission.

CPSIA information can be obtained
at www.ICGtesting.com
Printed in the USA
BVHW071923260619
552031BV00001B/18/P